MEADOWLARK

Author's Note: I found this journal, spanning 1911-1930, hidden in my great-grandmother Grace's ranch house nearly twenty years after her death. A faded blue hair ribbon was tied around it. A scrap of pink paper held between the cover and first page of the journal fluttered to the floor the first time I opened the book. On it was written in Grace's handwriting

There was but one way to heaven for me, and the path went straight through hell.

Two dried prairie roses fell, intertwined, from the last page.

MEADOWLARK

"I'll walk."

Open, empty prairie unrolled to the horizon in every direction beyond the narrow creek. Wind, edged with the heat of the coming summer, lifted the wisps of hair around Grace's face, loosened bits of grass from the tendrils and sent them floating to settle on her shoulders and twirl down to her feet.

Blood pounded in her temples, blurred her vision and smudged the horizon into a filmy seam connecting earth and sky. Wind rustled the leaves of the cottonwoods along the narrow creek just below where she stood. The scent of earth warmed by the sun mixed with the salty, metallic taste in her mouth.

"Suit yourself, then. Hope you can find it." Tom smacked the reins against the team's rumps and the wagon jostled forward and down the incline, down the creek bank, crossed the shallow water, then eased up the other side.

Grace watched until his silhouette crested the rise and slid from view, leaving only the wagon's tracks to mark his passing.

Grace heard nothing but the wind. She looked behind her toward town and thought of turning back. As a sudden pain brought her hand to her nose, the new gold band circling her finger caught the light of the sun. Ignoring the blood, and determined to follow the path she'd set for herself, she turned her back on the town and stumbled forward, the sound of her ragged breathing loud in her ears.

Grace walked.

She followed the wagon tracks until it was too dark to see. The stiff leather of her new boots bit sharply into her feet, but the numbness in her mind could not open to that pain or the competing aches in her body. Physical pain could not overcome the greater ache in her heart or the confusion she felt over what had happened.

Finally, she sank to the ground in a heap and quickly fell into an exhausted sleep.

She woke with the light and, once again, Grace walked. She thought of nothing, though her feet hurt and each step sent shooting pains up the muscles of her legs. Her face was sunburned. The hem of her dress hung heavy with mud and dust. Her tongue stuck thickly to the roof of her mouth.

With each new incline, Grace wondered if the summit would reveal the homestead. She felt a mixture of both trepidation and relief when it did not.

At midday, Grace topped another of the infinite knolls and froze at the sight of a sod house, a sod barn, a windmill and round corral below. Grace could see her mare, Mame, and she recognized Tom's geldings in the corral with her. The buckboard that had carried her the first few miles from town was drawn up alongside the barn.

Her gaze shifted back to the soddy. Chunks of roughhewn prairie, cut and stacked, formed the walls, with more covering the roof. The mound of earth with a wooden door beside the house must be the root cellar.

A creek curled down and around the barn and house. Grace could hear birdsong floating across the hollow. Open prairie rolled relentlessly to the horizon in every direction like the surface of a great golden sea. Only the green tops of a few cottonwoods along the water spoiled the illusion.

Beads of sweat ran down her chin and dripped onto the front of her dress already spotted with dried blood. Grace didn't notice. She was watching for any movement that might indicate Tom's presence.

Home.

Grace remained staring until Mame noticed the figure on the ridge, raised her head, and walked to the fence, ears pricked forward. Grace took one step toward the mare she'd inherited from her mother and walked down the slope and into her new life.

MEADOWLARK

1

Grace went down the hill and straight to the corral, through the gate to Mame and put her arms around the mare's neck, pressing her cheek against the warm gold of her buckskin coat.

Bright green algae floated on top of the water in the stock tank, thin strands hanging down into the depths. She skimmed her hand across the surface, moving the algae aside and bent to drink. The water's earthy warmth soothed her dry mouth and Grace cupped some in her hand and drew it across her face, feeling the grit of dust, sweat, and dried blood soften beneath her fingers. She lifted her eyes to the sod house just beyond the fence and saw a shift of movement behind the window.

She drew in her breath quickly and closed her eyes, and then slowly exhaled. Images of yesterday flashed through her mind: the wedding—no one but her and Tom, the preacher and his wife, her excitement and expectation as he helped her up into his wagon, his strange silence as she shared her thoughts about their new life together, the things they could do... And then he'd stopped the wagon.

He set the brake, taking great care to straighten the reins and coil them carefully around its handle before he jumped down, his boots sending up small puffs of dirt. His reached up for Grace.

Grace stood and looked around expectantly. "Why are we stopping?" She smiled.

As she took his hand and leaned down, Tom reached up with his free hand and twined his fingers through her hair. Suddenly, he jerked her down off the wagon, his other fist smashing into her face as she landed, knocking her to the ground.

An explosion of pain filled her senses as confusion swept through her. *What? Tom, what are you doing?* A thin trickle of blood edged down toward the corner of her eye. She blinked and saw the scarlet drops on her hand. More dripped from her nose and onto the dry grass. Grace tried to stand.

"Tom, why...?"

Tom's fist smashed into her ear and spun her to the ground again. Blood, dirt, and dry spikes of prairie grass filled her mouth. Stunned, she lay still.

Her left eye pressed closed against the ground, her right eye saw tips of grass framing nothing but the pale blue wash of sky. Even that disappeared when Tom kicked her, driving the toe of his boot into her back. Instinctively, she rolled over and curled into the fetal position.

"I've got a ranch to run," she heard above her. "Now, you expect me to take you on a picnic? What else do you expect? I got no time for picnics. Who's the boss here?"

Grace lay still, terrified that any movement would bring more pain.

"I can't hear you," Tom whispered in a voice that made Grace's blood run cold. "WHO'S THE BOSS HERE?"

Blood and dirt clogged her mouth. She stared at Tom. A weak croak escaped her lips against the dry, cracked ground. He grabbed her hair and yanked her head up.

"You are," she whispered through swelling lips.

Tom nodded, "That's right, Mrs. Robertson. Make damn sure you never forget that." He dropped her head, turned, and climbed back up into the buckboard, eyes forward.

MEADOWLARK

"Let's get on out to the ranch, then," he said in a reasonable voice, as though they had merely been passing the time of day.

Grace rolled over onto her knees and retched. She gazed with disbelief at the pool of vomit and blood on the ground. Her body throbbed. A piercing pain in her palm brought her hand up to her face. The straight pin that had held the ribbon tied around her crumpled posy of wildflowers, her wedding bouquet, was embedded in her skin. She pried it loose and looked up. Undulating grassland ran seamlessly to the horizon. *If I scream no one will hear.*

The world blurred and shifted. Grace gulped air, blinked her eyes. She tried to bring things into focus. Despite the pain in her hand, she grabbed for the earth. Dry grass poked between her fingers, rubbing against the shiny new gold wedding band, as she crawled on her hands and knees.

"Get on up, Grace." His voice was coaxing but firm.

The world around her resolved itself. Grace slowly sat up, then with painful effort, stood. She cleared her throat, her eyes swollen and hot with unshed tears. She lifted her chin and looked into his eyes. "I'll walk."

She continued to stare at the house from the corral, wondering what she would be walking into. There was no other way. She had to go to the soddy. She shook the slight tremble out of her hands and headed for the house.

When she opened the door, Grace found Tom sitting at the table, staring at his hands. He never looked up.

"I want to wash," she said.

Tom got up, taking his hat from the table, and left without a word.

Grace stood in the center of the room, looking at her new home. Light coming in from the open door highlighted the blocks of sod in the walls, threaded with dry roots and grasses. A table, with two chairs made from hand-hewn wood, was set with precision in the corner. Dented storage tins filled a shelf on the wall. Her trunk sat at the foot of the four chipped enamel posts that supported a plank bed with a stuffed tick for a mattress and a faded, threadbare blue and white quilt thrown over the top. Buffalo chips and twisted hay cats spilled over the top of the small barrel beside a blackened cookstove. There was a bucket of water. The dirt floor was uneven and deeply grooved with the marks of boot heels. For years this had been the home of a bachelor rancher whose mind was focused on the outdoors. Dirt and neglect filled every space.

Burlap bags leaned against the far wall. She took these to be the food Tom told her he'd bought on a trip to town the previous week. Grace walked over and untied the top of each bag, peering inside to discover their contents: flour, oatmeal, potatoes and carrots. The smaller bag on the end held coffee beans.

Grace took her hairbrush, a towel and clean clothes from her trunk, but paused to look out the window and make sure Tom wasn't near the house. He was saddling one of his horses at the corral.

She stripped off her dirty clothes and shoes, and dipped the towel into the bucket of water in the corner of the room. She washed the sweat from her body, but there was no time for a proper bath. She flipped her hair over her head and gave it a quick brushing to remove most of the grass and dirt before coiling it again at the base of her neck.

Grace looked out the dirty window. Wind blew against the panes. The wind flowed through Grace's veins.

Get busy, she thought.

"I keep most everything in the root cellar," she remembered Tom telling her. She opened the door and glanced toward the corral. There was no sign of Tom. She walked to the mound next to the house and tugged open the door. The musty scent of earth wafted up out of the depths. Earthen steps led down into darkness illuminated only by the light from the doorway. As she descended, she trailed her fingertips along the dirt walls, a few pebbles falling to the steps below.

"Snakes?" she called. "Any snakes in here?" She waited for a rattle in the darkness, before continuing down.

It was a small room, enclosed on all sides by dirt walls. Wooden planks ran the length of the roof, with several feet of dirt piled on top to create the mound. While the air outside crackled with heat, the air in the cellar was cool. Shelves lined two of the walls, each holding rows of glass jars filled with canned meat and vegetables. A thin film of dust covered the jars on the back of the shelves, those at the front gleamed in the band of light from above. Grace guessed it was enough food for the next six months, at least.

MEADOWLARK

A narrow frame bed sat against one wall, a roll of bedding at one end. Safe refuge, no doubt, from the tornados that tore across the prairie every summer, leaving a swath of destruction and often death in their wake.

She lifted a few jars to inspect their contents.

Supper was ready when Tom returned that evening.
They ate in silence.

Grace woke before the sun rose the next morning. Tom had gone to check cows. She blinked at the stars glinting through the single small window. The prairie glowed in the waning moonlight.

She lay in the darkness and peered at the rough plank ceiling above her and the thin pale roots that trailed down between the boards. Her body was raw inside and out. She closed her eyes to shut out memories of hot breath, heavy on her face. But she could still smell the stench of his sweat and she leapt out of bed naked, the dirt floor, gritty beneath her bare feet. She tore the blankets off the bed, and threw the heap out the door. Ripping dry grass from the ground beside the house, she rubbed her body, scraping her flesh until it was chafed and red.

Her sobs eased as a sliver of rising sun shimmered on the horizon, bleeding shades of scarlet and pale pink over the creases of the land, edging the swells in gilt.

Grace washed her face and dressed in the coarse brown skirt and white cotton shirtwaist she'd worn the day before. She pulled on sturdy stockings, and laced up her old pair of worn leather boots. She fired the stove, put water on to boil, and opened her trunk. Nestled between layers of her things she found two small bundles enclosed in dishtowels she'd spent hours embroidering with colorful flowers and birds.

She unwrapped the largest to reveal her mother's coffee grinder. Her hands caressed the smooth dovetailed wood along the sides as she placed it gently on the table. Grace lifted the other feather-light bundle, rubbing the tips of her fingers over the faded pattern of printed flower sprigs. She lifted the cloth to her face and inhaled deeply.

"Oh, Mama," she sighed.

She remembered that fabric from her mother's favorite dress blowing around her mother's legs as she hung clothes out to dry. Her mother was always moving, always doing, her skirts whirling about her as she bustled through life.

Now, all that remained was a trailing end of a ribbon and a diminutive satchel containing seeds from her mother's flowers—zinnias—and memories of the great mounds of color. Vibrant yellows, oranges, reds, and the richest pinks had graced her mother's garden and their family table in bright bouquets. She poured a few of the seeds into her palm and stared at the wrinkled disks. *Only a handful.*

The fall after her mother died, Grace had patiently collected the seeds, and sewn a pouch from the fabric of that dress, the one her mother had been wearing the last time Grace saw her alive.

Water boiled over and spit out of the spout of the coffee pot, drawing her back to the present. Grace jumped to remove the pot from the sizzling surface of the stove, and then poured the seeds back into their pouch, tightened the ribbons, tied them into a delicate bow, and tucked the small bundle back in the trunk, beneath her undergarments.

She dug into the burlap sack of coffee beans and poured a handful into the tureen of the grinder. As she turned the handle clockwise, she watched them dance down into the revolving blades. When the last bean dropped, she opened the drawer of fresh grounds at the bottom, inhaled the familiar fragrance, and dished them into the pot to steep.

Grace poured coffee into a tin cup and listened to the wind blow. She had once seen a woman from an isolated homestead throw herself from a wagon and drag herself over to a tree, sobbing. She wrapped her arms around its trunk, wailing, "A tree! A tree!" Her husband pried her off, shushing her as he forced her back onto the wagon. The woman glanced back, her face open and intense for just a moment before a shadow of eerie remoteness once again settled her features. Grace had heard that the asylum in Yankton included women who'd lost their minds to the wind.

MEADOWLARK

Tom returned when the sun floated at midpoint, high above the horizon. Grace heard the soft thud of hooves approach the soddy as she set the table. He pushed the wooden door open and stood still, a dark form outlined by bright light. He took off his hat. Grace froze, not knowing what to expect or what to do.

"Grace." His eyes darted back and forth between her and his feet. "I'm sorry." He shook his head. "Sometimes things come over me." His eyes begged forgiveness.

Grace's stomach tightened as she caught the tiniest glimpse of some sort of deep hidden wounds. Gone was Tom's arrogant glare. Gone were the eyes of a man. The eyes that looked back at her now were those of a hurt child.

"It won't happen again. I promise," Tom said. He pulled a chair out and sank down into it.

In a flash, Grace once again could feel him jerking her from the wagon, and knocking her to the ground. Kicking her. She forced it aside.

"What do you mean?" Grace asked, struggling to keep her voice even. What Tom had done to her—out on the prairie and last night in their bed—was not going to be forgiven with a simple "I'm sorry," yet she dared not do anything to shift his mood.

A thin patina of fear overlaid his features. *What had put that fear there?*

"What do you mean 'sometimes things come over me?' You haven't told me much about your life before the ranch. I only know that five years ago you left everything east of the Missouri River and came here."

"That's right. I did. Left it all. I was supposed to take over my father's mercantile. Instead, I saved enough money to buy a horse and saddle and headed west. I came with two other fellows interested in making a new life. At the sight of the mighty Missouri, they both turned back to the safety of towns. When I reached the river, I left off introducing myself with my given name, Barnabas."

Grace raised her eyebrows in surprise.

"That's too weak a name for any western man," he said with determination. "I loaded my horse onto the ferry on the eastern bank of the river as Barnabas and got off on the western side as Tom.

"My first cowboying job, I worked for Daniel Waters. He ran horses down along the Cheyenne River. He was married to a pretty

Sioux girl. He said I'd collect my pay when I'd worked six months, and until then I had room and board. Sounded fair to me. I hired on."

"But then you came here to the ranch, right? With your first herd of cows? Twenty head, wasn't it?" Grace desperately wanted him to keep talking, to help her understand.

"Yup, driving them home, I got caught in that blizzard of 1906 that killed half the livestock in the state. I drove the herd into the cover of the cedar trees down along the breaks, those ravines leading down to the Cheyenne River. Every last one of them made it. Figured it was God's way of telling me I was meant to be a cattle man."

"I believe you." Grace said. And she did.

After noon dinner, Grace explored the homestead. Tom had returned to the cows and wasn't due back until supper. She walked west, beyond the horse corral and barn, following the creek out of the hollow of the homestead. Wind curled along the creek bed, ruffling the tops of the grasses as she walked. The dull green of the stalks near the water faded slowly into the tawny shades of the surrounding prairie, not yet turned to green with the spring. Grace climbed up from the creek and stood, shading her eyes from the sun. The vastness of the prairie drew the eyes. *Something must be out there in that emptiness.* From the top of the rise, her eyes swept the open sea of land, gentle swells rolling away as far as she could see.

Grace took refuge in the hypnotic movement of the grass in the wind as it rippled like the surface of the sea. The prairie breathed and pulsed. Time ceased. The meter of her heartbeat, steady and profound, connected her to the earth. Her own boundaries blurred and softened as she imagined roots growing from the soles of her feet, strong and deep into the land. She became another blade of grass, one among the infinite number, swaying and supple.

Then the feeling ebbed, dissipated until she stood alone in the ocean of grass once again.

A cluster of prairie dog mounds pocked one of the swells. Grace saw the creatures dive into their burrows when she walked up over the rise. Their high-pitched chirps floated on the breeze as they began to cautiously poke their heads up. Sensing no motion, several emerged to stand sentry on their hind legs, only to pop back down when Grace moved.

MEADOWLARK

She turned back toward the homestead, the sod barn, differing from the house only by its taller walls, and the hitching posts. Her eyes trailed the winding creek she'd just followed and its deep cut through the hard shell of land, trimmed by a few scattered cottonwoods. Amidst the yellow and green grasses, tiny splashes of soft pink on the slope caught her eye. *Pink?* She walked over to investigate.

The colored sprays slowly acquired definition and resolved themselves into small prairie roses atop low-lying, scrubby vines. Pale pink opened around a cluster of bright yellow seeds on thread-thin stems. The outside edges of the petals blushed deeper pink. They appeared fragile under the harsh glare of the sun, and yet those flowers had survived year after year, through drought, blizzards, tornados, and the relentless wind.

If these flowers can make it in this harsh life, then so can I. She pulled up some of the long yellowed grass and scattered it over the blossoms, camouflaging them. *Something here will be mine, and mine alone.*

2

Through the window she'd just cleaned, Grace saw a small buggy appear on the horizon. The driver waved a bright yellow bonnet above her head. Grace's thoughts flitted with relief to her reflection in the glass that assured her the marks Tom had left there on their wedding day had healed over the past two weeks.

"Halloo? Halloo! Yooohooooo!" A robust young woman bounced on the buggy seat, her great breasts threatening to connect with her chin with every jostle. She was smiling broadly as she waved.

Grace laughed out loud, much to her own surprise, as she opened the door wide to meet the woman as she pulled up in front of the soddy.

"Hello there!" the woman called out in a clear voice. "Oh, dear, covered with dust the very first time I meet you! Not at all what I intended." She looped the lines around the dash rail and turned to climb down. One of her feet slipped and threw off her balance.

MEADOWLARK

"Oh!"

Grace raced forward just as the stranger tumbled backward, caught Grace in the chest, and landed on her, flattening Grace to the ground and pressing the air from her lungs.

"Oofta!" the woman said in surprise as she quickly rolled her amply proportioned self onto her knees then stood and bent over, offering Grace a hand up. "I'm Mae Thingvold, the local doctor. I am very pleased to meet you."

Grace gasped, caught between shock and a desire to breathe as she found herself eye level with Mae's tightly bound and overflowing corset. She stared, mouth agape.

"Quite an eyeful, aren't they?" Mae said without a hint of embarrassment. "I'd give anything to be built like you, thin and small-breasted. Heaven knows it would make riding in a wagon or on horseback far more pleasurable."

Mae cupped the mounds with her hands. "They're rogues, I tell you, rogues! They have a mind of their own. They're never going in the direction I want them to, and rarely going in the same direction at all. But what's there to do about it? The good Lord giveth and the good Lord taketh away. I've prayed and begged he would taketh some away, but apparently He feels I am in my rightful mortal body."

Grace burst out laughing and reached to take the extended hand. Mae popped her up with ease.

"Up ya go! Light as a feather."

Grace stammered through her chuckles. "Oh, I've completely forgotten my manners. I'm Grace Madi...I mean, Robertson."

"Yes, I heard Tom was going to marry." She eyed Grace, and appeared to swallow some further sentiment itching to be released. "I came over to introduce myself."

Grace took in the riot of thick, curly dark brown hair drawn back into a loose bun. Tendrils had escaped the pins and fell in disarray about Mae's shoulders. Grace found her nonchalant appearance, combined with her direct manner and irreverent sense of humor, irresistible.

"Will you have a bite to eat, Dr. Thingvold?"

"Oh, for heaven's sakes, call me Mae and I'll call you Grace."

They sat on a quilt in the shade of the soddy to eat bread that Grace had baked that morning. They spread the slices thinly with the plum jam Mae brought as a welcome gift. The shade cut the heat and blocked them from the wind. The trills of birdsong floated across the waving grass.

"I attended college in Boston," Mae started.

"I knew you couldn't be from around here."

"Did you? Well, I understand why and I'm not offended." Mae grinned and licked her lips. "I live on the claim south of here. Do you see that cottonwood way off peeking up over the top of the far hill there? That's me." Mae sipped her dark coffee and nibbled the crumbling bread crust.

"So close?" Grace shooed away a trio of investigating flies. "I had no idea. Tom never said we had neighbors. How in the world did you end up here?"

"Where else can a woman own her own land, I ask you? 'Pure foolishness!' my father warned, but I was determined and headed west. I bought passage on an immigrant car and…"

"A what?" Grace interrupted.

"Oh, honey, an immigrant car is a train car rented by families for their possessions. I knew several others coming west, so we pitched in and secured a whole car. I made it as far as Fort Pierre by train."

Grace's mind whirled with thoughts of people bustling and streaming onto trains.

"I purchased a horse and buggy and hired a locator to drive me around the various claims. As soon as I saw that cottonwood, I knew that was to be my home. I purchased an abandoned tarpaper shack from its owner, and had it dragged on a sledge to my claim. It's only eight by ten feet, smaller than the pantry of my parent's home. It only has a door and one narrow window, but it'll do. When I first saw the shanty settled into place on the claim, it looked so lonely. I stood and stared, thinking of the winter ahead. Then one day I came back and some nice soul had dumped a load of coal right at my door."

"When was that?"

"In the fall of last year," Mae paused. "I had a small barn and corral built for my horse and buggy. It was a long, cold winter. Just when I thought spring had finally arrived, another blizzard blew in. I wore my best dress last Easter Sunday, even though it was just me in my shanty. A girl has to do that sometimes," Mae looked at Grace, "even out here on the prairie. Maybe *especially* out here on the prairie. It can be hard to feel pretty out here."

Grace didn't know what to say. It was so good to have a

woman to talk to, and she had a feeling they would be friends.

Mae took up the slack in the conversation "So tell me, how have you come to this place? Where did you and Tom meet?"

"I met Tom at a dance in Faith. He literally swept me off my feet." Grace rose to pour them another cup of coffee, thinking of that night, remembering Tom's soft proposal: "Marry me, Grace. Your hair drifted like angel wings around your face the night we met." When he'd kissed her, a shock of dark hair fell forward across a face so handsome it seemed chiseled in stone. Something odd had flitted through his eyes as he said, "Be mine," but the warmth of his kiss made her think it had been a trick of the light.

She realized Mae was waiting for her to say something. "We got married in Faith and now here I am."

"I'm sure you were a beautiful bride," Mae said as she glanced out the window. "This has been a pleasure, Grace. I'd better be getting on home. I look forward to your friendship. And what a delight to speak with somebody who doesn't talk so loud all the time." Mae laughed, as both women stood.

"Loud?" Grace shook the loose grass from the quilt.

"Yes, *loud*!" she shouted. "When I first arrived here, I couldn't understand why everyone felt the need to shout all the time. After a couple of months I realized they were used to speaking over the wind. Now, I'm as loud as everyone else." She giggled, the curves of her body dancing.

Grace mimed shouting, her hands cupped around her mouth. "Well, goodbye then, Mae Thingvold. It's been a real delight to meet you!"

"You're a sassy thing, Grace Robertson." Mae climbed into her buggy. "That's good. You'll need that." Mae clucked her horse into a trot and yodeled, "Take care!"

The buggy crested the horizon and dropped out of sight. Grace stood with her arms folded around the quilt, feeling the empty space left by Mae's departure as the day lengthened, and scalloped clouds crusted with shades of orange and yellow haloed the sinking sun. The evening wind keened, sounding lonely, but Grace turned her back on it. She had a friend, a wonderful new friend. She dared not dawdle. Tom would soon be riding in expecting his supper.

The next day, Grace opened her trunk. On top was the journal her mother had given her, shortly before her death last year. It was bound in chocolate-brown leather and inside, in her exquisitely neat handwriting, her mother had written *To Grace, A place to commit to paper the many exciting and happy times you're sure to have. I wish you a lifetime of love and joy. Your loving mother. July 30, 1910.*

The journal had remained untouched until that morning when Grace had written simply, *Today, I marry.* She had written nothing since.

Beneath the journal was her treasured collection of her mother's books. "You'll never be alone, Grace. Take my books. I've written my thoughts in the margins. I won't be here to walk with you through your womanhood. Maybe my books will help."

Grace had spent many a night with those books, reading about the medicinal properties of herbs, firsthand accounts of women's westward treks, the complete works of Charles Dickens and Henry James, with *Portrait of a Lady* especially worn. Over time, she started to add her own notes, agreeing and arguing with a mother who now lived only in spirit. Exclamation marks, exasperated scrawls of *Why?* sprinkled the dog-eared pages.

Two of the books—*The 19th Wife* by Ann Eliza Young and *The Awakening* by Kate Chopin—raised uncomfortable questions that left Grace feeling uneasy. She understood why her mother had kept those two hidden behind the other volumes.

The little pouch of seeds was there, too. It was time to make a decision about where to plant her mother's flower seeds, Grace chose a spot right outside the front door. She spent the next two days driving a shovel into the hard-as-stone ground, turning the soil. At first she only managed to chisel off tiny pieces of the top crust of earth.

Tom shook his head as he jammed on his hat. "You're a danged fool if you think anything will grow there besides thistles."

Ignoring him, she continued to chip away, though the sun rose high, pouring down heat and bringing the wind. She wiped away the sweat, rolled up her sleeves and dried her sweaty palms across her apron to prevent them from slipping off the shovel handle.

Bit by bit, she chewed through the layers of earth. She spent hours turning and breaking the soil into ever-smaller pieces. She hauled rich muddy sand in a bucket from the creek and added manure from the corral to mix in with the dirt. Without those additions she knew the gumbo would revert to a rock hard slab when the rains came and went.

In the warm glow of the early morning light on the third day, Grace poured the zinnia seeds into her palm. Her knees stiff and sore, she knelt and pressed her finger into the softened earth in a random pattern, then placed a single seed into each hole before gently covering it.

"Oh, I hope you'll grow." She spoke out loud, her voice odd and strange after the near-silent days with Tom. That morning in her journal, kept in the bottom of her trunk under her clothes, she'd written:

> *I'll scatter the seeds. Like the prairie roses.*
> *You never see straight lines of plants in nature.*
> *Something about neat rows is unsettling. It feels too*
> *much like trying to control beauty instead of simply*
> *savoring it.*

She kept back ten seeds in case something went wrong. With the dipper she scooped precious liquid from the bucket and poured a tiny bit of water on each seed-marked spot.

Tom's shadow fell across the flower bed. Grace turned and looked up at his face, taking the pulse of his mood by the expression in his eyes.

"My mother likes flowers, too," Tom offered, his voice steady.

"Really?" Grace leaned back on her heels. She held her hand up to shade the sun from her eyes.

"Has them all around the house."

Grace waited for Tom to say more about whatever seemed to weigh so heavy on his mind.

"What did that woman want?"

It took Grace a moment to register the abrupt shift of subject in the conversation.

"What woman?" Grace hesitated, noticing the change in his voice. "Oh, Mae Thingvold? The doctor. She came by to introduce herself. That's all." Grace reached out to break up a dirt clod at her feet.

"People talk about her. She's caused quite a stir out here." Tom kicked off a bug crawling over his boot. "A female doctor. Hah!" he snorted. "I had the grades in school to be a doctor. Schoolwork came easy to me. Father said he'd pay if I wanted to go on, but what he really wanted was for me to take over the mercantile."

Tom scratched his temple under his hat and gave a hollow laugh. "I didn't want that. Now we got some female doctor out here and I'm covered in cow shit. Go figure." His eyes scanned the horizon. "I'm going to make us rich. I've got big plans. Whatever it takes, Grace. Whatever it takes to make the kind of money so that when Tom Robertson walks into a bank, the people stand and welcome him. That's what a man needs. Respect. When I walk into a room, I want people to *notice*."

Tom turned to Grace. "My mother had no respect. Not a shred. She used to warn me when she'd been nipping whiskey all day that I must never speak of what happened in our home. Never."

Grace wanted to ask him about those family secrets, but she held her tongue.

Tom dusted off his pants. "I'd best go check on the horses. With this drought, they may need water. You use care about how much water you waste on flowers."

Grace watched him walk to the corral, the upper half of his body tilted forward, head tilted to the side, as if he were always leaning into the wind. He dipped in through the gate and disappeared inside the barn. An uneasy feeling swept through her.

"Damn," Grace muttered as she stepped outside.

The wind had blown hot and dry for three weeks. *Too much wind. Not enough water.* Waves of scorching summer wind crashed into her. Stiff gusts ripped the rough-cut wooden door from her hand and slammed it against the inside wall. Chunks of hard dirt and grass skittered across the floor. Stories abounded about those unfortunates who built their doors to open outward, only to have a sod hut become a tomb when a heavy snowfall trapped them inside.

Despite the heat, Grace shivered as Tom slipped out of the soddy behind her.

"There's a piece of property over to the south that I'm going to go take a look at." Tom dipped his head to keep his hat from being torn off.

He'd promised that he'd make things good between them. She found herself gauging every word for some key to what had happened to him as a child. It wasn't what he said, but rather in what went unsaid that troubled her. She kept trying to calculate what brought on his sudden violent outbursts.

At one point he'd told her, "I can read your mind, Grace. I learned how to do that young. Had to. We kids had to read my parents and not do anything to upset them." Tom replaced a piece of sod torn off by the wind. "We never knew what would set them off, so we did our best to stay out of the way. Yelling. Fists flying. Mother screaming. I did my best to keep my younger brothers and sisters down low in a corner."

Grace imagined scared children huddled together. He'll learn, she'd told herself. *With time, he'll change. I know he will. He just hasn't had the chance yet. With time and love, he'll change.* But a heavy feeling settled deep in her stomach.

She pushed that memory away and touched his arm. "You go on now and check out that property, Tom. Supper will be ready for you when you get back."

She watched him ride south until he disappeared between the swells of the prairie. Balancing a metal tub full of laundry on her hip, she yanked the door shut and walked over buffalo grass the color of ripe wheat, inhaling the clean scents of the earth, drinking in the solitude. A haphazard V of geese sliced the sky and wisps of clouds edged the horizon. Mame whinnied from the corral and pawed the earth.

"I see you over there, Mame. How are you this morning?" Grace set the tub of laundry down and walked to the corral. Grace buried her nose in the horse's neck and breathed in her scent, running her fingers through the tangles in the mane.

"There you are now, girl. How's that feel?" Grace laughed as Mame pushed her head and body into hers. "I know. I know, feels good, doesn't it? Now, I've got to get to that laundry." Grace held her hands to her face and inhaled Mame's horse smell, as she walked back to her work.

Grace tucked her hair behind her ear and pulled Tom's wet shirt out of the water. She used the metal cask for weekly laundry and allowed herself a bath in three inches of tepid water on Saturday nights. She hauled water from the creek and boiled Tom's dirty clothes after she had rinsed out her underthings. She shook the wrinkles from the course material with a rough snap and hung it on the cedar fence of the corral to dry as she yearned for a clothesline and wooden pegs.

Something moved on the ground in the short distance beyond the fence and caught Grace's eye.

Rattlesnake? She froze. The tiny pattern of feathers formed the shape of a bird. Eggshell white embroidered with deep brown etchings. Pale yellow tinted the underbelly. The bird hopped away from the base of the soddy to stand on a small rise. The morning sun illumined a halo around her and emphasized the black V on her neck.

Grace inched forward, the laundry and worries about Tom forgotten. She sank to the ground, curling her legs beneath her. The bird looked at her, eyes shining, curious. Time stood still as the world was reduced to the two of them alone on the prairie. The bird sprang, searching for seeds or insects. Her movements created a single point of gentle focus for Grace, casting a spell.

A swift whooshing blur swept down and the meadowlark was gone. Grace shielded her eyes from the glare as she searched the sky and found the ascent of a hawk.

"No!" Grace leapt to her feet but could see the hawk carried nothing in its talons. Something fluttered in the dust. Grace picked up her skirts and ran. The meadowlark flapped against the dried grass.

"It must have missed you by a hair." Grace knelt to inspect for injuries and saw one wing beating against the ground while the other gave limp jerks.

"Oh, little one. A broken wing? Up you come now." She reached down as the bird doubled its efforts to escape. "There, there," she crooned and cupped her hands around the meadowlark's body. Its miniature heart pounded a tiny hailstorm against her palm.

Grace looked up to see the hawk circling, riding a thermal, before it soared upward and away.

"You're going to survive. You will."

"What do you have there?" A shadow slid across her hands and arms.

"Tom! You scared the daylights out of me. You barely left an hour ago."

"I forgot my canteen." Tom swung down off his horse. "What is it?" He came closer to see what she was holding.

MEADOWLARK

"A meadowlark. A hawk dove for it and somehow missed. Knocked it across the dirt and broke one of its wings."

Tom put out his large hands, tanned the color of saddle leather. He scooped up the bird and held it gently. "Poor little thing."

Could this be the same man who had handled her so roughly on her wedding day?

"It's a female," Grace said with certainty.

"How do you know that?"

"I don't know. I just do."

"Well, then, take *her* into the house," Tom said and smiled.

Grace reached out to take the bird and hold it close to her chest. "You go on and check on that ranch."

"All right, then." Tom went into the soddy and returned with the canteen swinging from his hand. He wrapped the strap tightly around the saddlehorn and mounted, laying the reins across the big bay's neck and wheeling him around. "And you, little bird," he called back over his shoulder, "You let Grace take care of you."

Grace walked into the dark of the soddy and wrapped the bird in a dishtowel to hold it still. She lined a large enamel bowl with another cloth and settled the meadowlark within its folds.

"If we keep that wing still, it might mend. You must be one tough little pipsqueak," The bird fixed its black eyes on her. "Pip. That's what I'll call you." Grace laid a finger on the top of Pip's head. "Shhh, now. Rest. I'll bring you some water."

Humming, she returned to the corral to hang up the rest of the clothes. All afternoon and evening Grace talked to the meadowlark as if it were a person who'd stopped by to visit. In her journal, she wrote of the meadowlark and the hawk. She sat studying the bird and carefully sketched Pip's likeness on the page. She took her journal outside, walked up the slope and sank down on the ground, pulled back the grass that hid the pink petals, and began to draw. When she was finished, Pip's image sat perched beside a prairie rose.

Grace waited up for Tom late that night, the oil lamp burning low on the table. Tom's dishtowel-covered supper grew cold. Long after she'd gone to bed and curled around herself, she heard a horse gallop up to the soddy, and someone stumbling when they hit the ground. Waves anxiety rolled through her body. Her breath came short and shallow. She tried to feign sleep when she heard muttering and grunting as someone crawled toward the door. She hoped it was Tom. At the same time, she hoped it wasn't.

"Goddammit…" a voice slurred as the door slammed open and Tom dragged himself in.

An acrid stench filled the room. *Whiskey*. Grace fought the urge to cover her nose with the blanket to escape the reek. Instead, she squeezed her eyes shut, every muscle tensed. The hairs on her arms pricked and stood taut against the sleeves of her nightgown.

Tom cursed again and began to retch. Please, God, let him pass out, Grace prayed. Her stomach lurched as he crawled toward the bed. The sour trail of alcohol and vomit pulsed in the air as he struggled to peel off his boots and pants.

Steeling herself, she held her breath as the weight of his body compressed the feather tick. Fall asleep, she prayed. *Please God make him fall asleep.* His hand found her hip, and jerked her closer. She sucked in a breath through her mouth to keep from gagging. She thought of running, but where could she go?

MEADOWLARK

3

Tom rose before dawn and leaned down to kiss her as if he had no memory of the night before.

He smiled and apologized for being late. "I ran into some old friends and they talked me into a few drinks."

Grace watched him as he dressed. When he slipped out to feed the horses, she got up and dressed, then lit the fire and put on the coffee before cleaning up the mess on the floor. She took Pip from her sanctuary and set the bird on the table while she made breakfast. Pip hopped about, exploring the cracks in the wood for crumbs.

"Let's go check on all of our flowers, Pip." Grace scooped the bird up to hold against her chest, walked outside and turned to the flower garden. Tiny green shoots poked through the surface, reminding her of the years she and her mother had celebrated such first signs of life together. Grace gently tipped the bucket, slowly darkening the soil around the plants. The feeling of the bird pressed to her chest calmed her as she watched her mother's flowers absorbing water.

Tom returned to the soddy and smiled when he saw Pip nestled in dishtowel on the table. He reached out his hand to scoop up the bird and Pip let loose a squirt of droppings. The inside air changed in an instant. A flame of anger ignited in Tom's eyes. He tensed and jerked back his arm.

"I'll get that cleaned up," Grace hurriedly picked up Pip as she walked past for a rag. When she returned, Tom held out his cupped hands, his eyes now soft. Grace hesitated then placed the bird again in his hands. She went back to slicing potatoes as Tom stroked Pip's head, that earlier flash of anger seemingly forgotten.

After they ate he left, saying he would be home before dark. The day passed without incident as Grace savored the silence and tended to her chores.

Late the next day, Tom rode up to the house and called out, "Grace, I brought you a cow!"

A young red cow, her large udder swinging, trailed Tom's horse, a rope around her neck. The afternoon sun turned her coat burnt sienna as she held her head high, eyes alert. She breathed hard and fast, her only movement a periodic snap of her tail.

"Hal Jenks was selling her. She's only been milked a few times," Tom said. "We might as well call her Red."

Grace wiped her hands on her apron. She had craved fresh milk, cream, and butter for her cooking. The coolness of the cellar would keep the milk, and any extra she could share with Mae.

"That's grand, Tom."

A sage grouse flew past and Red kicked and jerked back, pulling the rope from Tom's hand as she bolted in the direction they'd just traveled. Tom spurred his horse in a wide arc, hooves pounding out a staccato tempo on the hard prairie, and leaned forward to grab the rope bouncing beside the cow. He dallied tightly and brought the cow back around to stand in front of the house.

"She seems a little wild," Grace observed sardonically.

"She's young, is all," Tom replied. "She'll settle down. I'll push her into the corral." Tom moved his horse forward and said, "Hup!" to the cow. He hollered back at Grace, "I'm going to check those heifers to the south before supper."

Grace went back in the house, intent on Pip and fixing supper.

Hours later, Grace was covering a batch of rolls with a dishtowel as she set them to rise, when a low mournful sound came from the corral, followed by a nicker from her mare.

"Red! That's right. You need to be milked." Grace scanned the soddy and spied the metal bucket holding hay cats by the stove. Emptying them onto the table, she wiped out the bucket then scooped a handful of oatmeal out of the sack, and put it in her apron pocket.

Red greeted her approach by blowing snot through the fenceposts before pulling her head back and bolting to the far side of the enclosure. The geldings and Mame, in the pasture beyond the corral, bunched up at the fence to watch.

Grace opened the gate, stepped in quickly, and latched it behind her. She and Red eyed each other warily.

"The only cows I've ever milked have been stone gentle. They paid me no mind when I milked. You are not going to be so accommodating, are you, Red?"

The cow blew and shuffled her feet nervously.

"I know I can do this, and you'll feel so much better after. Look at your poor udder, it's bulging. I know that hurts. I'll help you if you let me."

Red snorted and pressed back against the fence. Grace blessed Tom for leaving the halter on the cow. With slow but determined strides she approached Red. When the cow turned to run, Grace stepped on the lead trailing the ground and bent quickly to grab and wrap the end of the rope around the closest post. Then, she braced herself. Red resisted, but only by raising and lowering her head several times.

Grace scooped out a hole in the dust near a post with her foot and filled it with the oatmeal. The scent of the grain was enough to bring Red closer. With each of Red's steps, Grace shortened the rope, until the cow stood next to the post.

When Red settled into chewing, Grace tied her off short and

went back to the gate for the bucket. When she squatted by Red's side, the cow raised her head sharply.

"There, now," Grace soothed. "There, there." Grace placed her cool palm on the hot bulge of Red's bag and the cow kicked. They repeated that sequence until Red tired and stood still. Grace squeezed one teat, then another. Exhausted from the day, she wished she could rest her head against the cow's side and relax into the rhythmic sound of the milk squirting into the bucket. Maybe with time that intimacy would come.

The bucket was nearly full when Grace heard the sound of a trotting horse and then Tom's voice saying, "Well, I see you two have made friends. First that doctor woman, then the bird, now the cow. You've even got your mare following you like a lost pup. Where does that leave me?"

Grace couldn't read the tone of his voice.

Tom had gone silent that evening and then turned his back to Grace that night in bed. It was a relief. But she wondered about what he's said at the corral. It was true that she turned to Mame for solace. Could he blame her? It was something he made no effort to provide and she found comfort in the feeling of being alone, loping Mame across the prairie, her body moving in rhythm with the horse's stride. She liked leaving her hair down, gathered at the nape of her neck so that it swayed along her back. If she could, she would ride on forever, the prairie grasses waving before her in the wind, the mountainous white clouds high above and the cleansing sun shining down to warm her chilled heart.

When Grace walked out to the corral early the next morning after Tom had gone, Mame greeted her by leaning her head over the top rail of the corral and reaching out to receive a caress to her muzzle. Mame's ears flicked forward to take in the soothing tones of the Grace's whispered words.

The trapped feelings that suffocated Grace in the sod house

fell away as she breathed deeply, filling her lungs with fresh air and Mame's scent. She exhaled and forced the uncertainty of Tom's confusing behavior out of her lungs, trying to rid herself of the effects of his dark moods.

Mame lifted her hooves high in the fresh air of the morning, prancing, and Grace laughed. "So you like to dance, too?"

Grace had attended dances ever since she was a baby wrapped in a shawl, curled up asleep in a corner. As a girl the lightness of her feet matched the joy in her heart when the fiddler played. Her skirts twirled wide around her as she spun, laughing and dancing, her blouse damp with sweat and the muscles of her legs aching. She'd dive back in amidst the dancers, grabbing the first available partner, and free herself to waltz or schottische with abandon.

"Let's dance, then," she said as she bridled Mame. Leaving the corral, she nudged the horse into a run. Mame gave a playful hop and set down low on her haunches as she dug in her hind hooves for a burst of speed, throwing clumps of prairie out behind her.

Grace yipped as the horse's muscles surged under her and the wind whipped through her hair. She leaned low over Mame's neck, her bent legs holding her body above the saddle, her skirts flying. Across the flatlands they raced, as Grace urged and Mame responded, stretching her muscles. Grace inhaled the fragrance of sun-warmed grass and earth, and she threaded her fingers through the course hair of Mame's mane.

They ran until tears streamed down Grace's face and were blown back to dampen her hair at the temples. Wispy clouds etched the sky as the rhythm of Mame's hooves thrummed in Grace's ear. Nearing a watering hole, Grace gathered the reins and slowed Mame to a gentle lope, and then a walk as they approached the muddy pool in a low-lying hollow that caught the spring snowmelt and summer rains. Bird tracks dotted the mud, stitched together with bug trails weaving between. The pungent scent of stagnant water prickled Grace's nose. Two cottonwoods edged the water, their leaves shivering slightly in the soft summer breeze.

Grace wiped the wetness from her eyes as she dismounted. Mame turned toward her, her sides heaving.

"That felt good, didn't it, girl?" Grace looked deep into the horse's liquid eyes. She reached out to pat the sweaty neck, her fingertips tracing the patterns formed in the damp hair. Grace buried her face in

Mame's mane and the horse laid her head on Grace's shoulder.

"Come on, girl. Let's cool you down."

She walked Mame toward the far end of the hollow. In the peace of that place she allowed herself to try to untie the Gordian knot of Tom's demons. She had so many questions and no answers to help her understand what prompted the sudden bursts of anger and cruelty. Something far beyond alcohol lay behind his erratic behavior and it was a subject she dare not attempt to discuss with him, a problem she must wrestle with on her own though she was at a loss to know how.

When Mame was cool enough for a drink Grace stood beside her and her thoughts took an unexpected jump to a boy who had been courting her, a boy with sky blue eyes.

"Dance with me, Grace."

Paul twirled her on the open prairie. She threw her head back and laughed as he looked at her with gentle, mischievous eyes. There was always laughter with Paul. He carried himself with ease, comfortable in the space he took up on this earth. Together, they had ridden the plains, always talking, their hands and arms gesturing as they rode.

Paul had comforted her when her mother died.

"Do you believe in angels, Paul?" she'd asked into his shoulder as he held her.

"Of course I do. Do you want to know how to find out their names? At night, right as you're about to fall asleep, ask them to tell you their names when you're sleeping. When you wake up the next day, just lay there with your eyes closed and listen."

One afternoon two months after her mother's funeral, Paul had come to her.

"I'm leaving, Grace. I've got to go. My folks need money bad, and I've heard there's good-paying work in Montana."

"But, what about hiring on as cowboy around here? Surely somebody needs help. You'll be near your family. And me."

"I've asked around. Been asking for months. People are just barely getting by. There's no money for more cowboys." Paul said. "Wait for me, Grace. Wait for me."

Grace thought of this, of how young she'd been, with no idea how rare that easiness was between a man and a woman, that it was something to be treasured and stoked. And then that good-looking

MEADOWLARK

Tom Robertson had asked her to dance and led her young heart away on a string.

"You've made your bed. Grace," she told herself as she mounted Mame. "You've no choice but to lie in it." She turned the mare toward home.

When Grace returned to the sod hut, the bowl on the bench under the window that had become Pip's nest was empty. Grace looked around the soddy for any signs of the bird. There were none to be found. She scanned the ground, then turned her eyes upward to the washed out blue sky.

"You did it, Pip. You escaped. Now you're free." She took the cloth and the bowl inside with a smile hovering around her dry lips.

Tom came in early that evening and settled at the table. "What's for supper?" Before Grace could reply, he added, "Where's the bird?"

Grace poured him a glass of milk from the pitcher. "She must have flown away. She was gone when I came back." The words slipped from her mouth before she could scoop them back up.

Tom looked out the window. He took a gulp of milk. "Came back from where?" he said frowning.

Grace set the food on the table and wiped her brow with the back of her hand. "I finished my chores so I...I took Mame out. It was a beautiful day. Didn't you think it was a beautiful day?"

Something in Tom's eyes shifted as she ladled beans onto his plate. The spoon suddenly flew across the room, when Tom knocked his fist up into her hand. "The beans are too done," Tom said. He gripped her arm. One fist connected with her face as he held her in place with the other. Again he struck her. Grace tucked her head and tried to curl her body.

"Please, Tom," she said. "Stop. Please stop. What's wrong?"

"You! That's what's wrong. I told you not to leave home, didn't I?"

Dinner forgotten, he bent her over the table and took her from behind, the swelling side of her face pressed into the spilled beans.

The weight of fear and despair kept her pinned down. She tried to pretend she was anywhere but there. In her mind, she picked chokecherries by the creek. She scrubbed the laundry. She swept the dirt floor. She floated over the corral to make certain that Red and Mame were safe.

When Tom finished, he shoved her to the floor, she stayed there until she heard him crawl into bed, then she rose to clean up the mess. When she went outside to dump the wash water over her sprouting zinnias, she vomited the bile sloshing in her empty stomach.

Grace didn't go to bed. She sat up all night in a chair staring out the window, praying that Pip was all right. She looked at Tom's rifle hanging above the door, and thought of her own, still in the trunk. What would happen to Mame and Red if she shot Tom and was sent to prison?

The next morning the side of her face felt like someone had laid a hot iron against it. She ignored Tom when he left the soddy. She didn't even have the strength to rise and light the fire. He returned a short while later and stood in the doorway.

"Grace, I…Well, I milked the cow for you this morning." He extended the bucket full of milk.

She looked at him through the eye that wasn't swollen shut. Reluctantly she rose. She stopped herself from wincing at the sore muscles in her shoulder where Tom had wrenched her arm.

"If you would like to ride today you can go with me to check the cows."

She nodded, knowing he wasn't offering her a choice. Choice was a thing of the past.

They ate cold cornbread for breakfast and washed it down with warm milk and silence.

Tom saddled Mame. Grace put her foot in the stirrup and swung up into the saddle. She could not bear to sit down fully, so she held her raw flesh up away from the hard leather with her feet pressed into the stirrups, her thighs on fire. She blessed Mame for having a gentle trot.

MEADOWLARK

She followed Tom into the day, but she took herself far away again, up to where clouds floated free in the sky.

In the late afternoon, when Tom had gone to check the cows down along the Cheyenne River, Grace heard a quiet knock.

"Hello?" she called out standing above the stove.

"Good day." A woman's voice slipped in, quiet and steady, from the other side of the door.

Grace's hand flew to swelling around her eye.

"A moment, please." Grace looked for something to cover her face, but found nothing.

"Hello?" the woman's voice said again.

"Yes," Grace said as she looked out the window. A sorrel horse was cropping the dry grass, the soft sound of tugs and rips drifting in the silence. Grace looked at the geldings and Mame walking lazily around the corral. She opened the door.

"I am Daisy Standing Horse."

The woman did not paste on a smile as a white woman would have done, Grace thought. She just stood there, an Indian woman, hair unbound. Beaded moccasins edged out under her long brown skirt. High cheekbones defined her face, almond-shaped eyes, the color of hazelnuts studied Grace.

"I'm Grace Robertson. Do you need help?"

"No." Daisy paused, taking in Grace's bruised face. "But it appears you do."

Grace kept her eyes on the wooden doorframe that separated the earth outside from the earth inside as her face flushed. "I ran into the cupboard. So careless," she said, bringing her hand to her swollen eye.

"You are not the one who has been careless."

Daisy's dark eyes held no judgment or threat and Grace let herself relax.

"May I come in?" Daisy crossed the threshold and said, "Thank you. Now you sit down." She reached into a pouch slung on her belt and withdrew a small bag held together at the top by a narrow leather tie. She removed a couple of pinches of crushed leaves, poured a bit of water from the dipper in the bucket on the table into the palm of her hand, and mixed them into a paste.

Grace watched wordlessly. She had never had an Indian in her house before. Her husband railed against them, yet she wasn't sure exactly *why* she wasn't supposed to like them.

Grace's nose twitched at the tangy smell of the herbs.

Daisy dipped her index and middle fingers into the paste and turned toward Grace. "Now, hold still, *Zintkala Opi*." Daisy applied the paste to Grace's swollen eye with sure strokes. "*Wasicu wagluhe* of a husband," Daisy whispered in disgust.

Grace didn't understand the words, but Daisy's tone made their meaning clear. She flinched at the sting of the ointment, but a moment later a welcome feeling of soothing numbness followed and she opened her eyes.

This was the first sense of maternal care Grace had received since her mother died. She closed her eyes, relishing the sensation of tender hands on her skin.

"Why do you call me *Zint...Zinta...*whatever it is?""

"*Zintkala Opi*. It means 'wounded bird' in Lakota."

"Oh," Grace breathed. "I had a little bird who rested here in a bowl until she could fly again. A meadowlark." Suddenly she realized that she had not offered her guest anything. "Would you like some coffee?"

"I would. And one day I will tell you the story of the meadowlark. Not today. Today I will tell you that I live with my family over by the Cheyenne River."

Graced poked up the fire and pulled the coffee pot to the front of the stove as Daisy continued.

"My father's name was Louis Bordeaux. He came from France and trapped for the American Fur Company. My mother is *Ptesanwin*, which means Gray Buffalo Woman. My husband, Jay Broken Leg, died last winter from what your people call consumption. In my alone times, I like to ride. One time I saw a woman walking, following a man driving a wagon."

Grace said nothing.

"I got off my horse and walked into a draw so I would not been seen," Daisy said. "I did not know what was happening, but I knew enough to know that it could be dangerous. I also knew that the Spirit Ones had shown me this so I would know to come over to watch sometimes in case you had need."

MEADOWLARK

Grace shuddered as she placed two cups on the table, but Daisy placed a reassuring hand on her arm.

"Your man doesn't know I come. I come to help and I will say nothing to anyone. This is often the way between men and women, though it is not good."

Daisy stopped speaking and just looked at Grace, almost as if judging what to say to ease her. "I have a baby. Her name is Ruth. She's with my mother now. It didn't feel safe to bring her here. Ruth came to me late in my life. When I first became pregnant with Ruth, I thought it was the change. What a surprise for one like me with gray coming in my hair. Then my husband died. I was so sad from losing him that when I felt the birthing pain and knew it was time, I couldn't put strength into helping her to be born. The doctor lady who lives over there," Daisy pointed in the direction of Mae's homestead, "she helped me. She helped me be strong. Usually, Lakota do not like white people anywhere near our homes. It is dangerous and never welcome. A white person anywhere near our homes brings fear to all. We take care of our own, but our woman who helps us have babies was already helping another woman. Someone brought Mae, even though I didn't want her. She helped me have my Ruth, my final gift from my husband."

A baby, thought Grace. *How would Tom treat a child?*

"You said Ruth was your final gift from your husband. You must have loved your husband very much."

"I did. I do still. He told me the story of Meadowlark. The time for that story is later. I will tell you a different story now," she said as Grace poured them both some coffee. "There are many ways to tell this story, but I will tell you as my grandmother told it to me.

"In the beginning, there was only *Iyan,* a rock in a great black space. Its spirit we call *Wakan Tanka*, the Great Mystery. *Iyan* became very lonely. He knew he could create something else only from himself, so he pierced himself and his blue blood flowed out and surrounded him to create a great round ball. It flowed and flowed until *Iyan* was shriveled and hard and cold."

Daisy was silent for some time, then continued. "All of his powers had flown out as his blue blood left him. This is how *Maka Ina*, what you call Mother Earth, came to be. The blue blood formed the oceans and the sky. All the power that *Iyan* contained is now the female Earth and the male Sky."

"I don't understand," Grace said.

"You will. You only know the creation story from your book. Our story tells us that Mother Earth and Father Sky must be equal in power. I will go now, *Zintkala Opi*, before your man returns. Look and listen for the meadowlark in the mornings. Meadowlarks are the messengers of good news. *Toksa.*"

Daisy fastened her pouch at her waist and slipped out, leaving the door open. She grabbed her horse's mane, jumped up and threw her leg over its broad back. Grace watched the pair until they were out of sight.

She did not fix supper for herself or for Tom. Instead, she wrote the story of *Maka Ina* in her journal, her brow furrowed as she guessed spelling of *Zintkala Opi* and the other Lakota words. She read the story aloud to herself, before tucking the journal back into the trunk.

When Tom came in, late, she stayed curled tight under the bedcovers, her face toward the wall.

Frantic whinnying and pounding hooves woke Grace as the gray light of dawn seeped in through the window. The sounds moved from the ephemeral into the real.

Crack!

Grace bolted upright. Beyond the window a cloud of dust roiled and rose above the round corral.

Crack!

The sound of a bullwhip shattered the air again. A horse screamed. *Mame!* Grace raced outside, her white nightgown tangling her legs and sharp stones stabbing into her bare feet. The horses churned inside the small enclosure, climbing over one another, crazed to escape. Tom stood in the center, snaking out a whip.

"No, Tom!" Dust bit her nose. Through the poles Grace saw the whites of the horses' eyes. Tom raised his arm as Mame sprang past. He missed, but another horse went down under the fusillade of hooves. Tom lashed out again. The downed horse struggled to his feet but the force of the tide knocked him to the ground again, rolling him onto his back. Grace heard the hard snap of bone and flinched.

She tripped and fell, scraping her knees on the rough ground.

MEADOWLARK

She climbed up the fence even as the weight of the horses crashed against it close by.

Tom glanced at her but his eyes returned to the rampaging horses. He sought out her mare.

"No!"

"That goddamned mare tried to bite me. I'll show her!"

He lashed the whip across the Mame's neck. Blood sprang red against her coat.

I've betrayed her trust. Grace cringed and shrank back into herself.

A piercing sting slashed across the back of Grace's hand as she held tight to the top of the fence. She grabbed the tip of the whip in her fist. She yanked back, ripping it from his hands and threw it to the ground.

"You'll pay for that," Tom said.

She spat in disgust. "I don't care!"

Tom stared at Grace. A predatory stillness emanated from his body. His eyes never wavered. Neither did Grace's.

Seconds, then minutes, passed. Eventually, one-by-one, the horses slowed, bumping and jostling into each other and shying away from Tom with startled leaps.

The heavy curtain of dust thinned and began to settle in a chalky film. Horses snorted, blowing blood-flecked foam into the dirt, their heads up, ears alert, their hides quivering over muscles that twitched beneath the skin.

Tom threw his hands high. "Get back!" The horses spooked away from the movement and Tom walked through the space created. His boots thudding the ground, he went out the gate and passed the barn in long strides.

Grace climbed over the poles and moved slowly to where the horses clustered, trying to hide behind each other. She spoke soothing words, her upturned hand in front of her, aware of skittish hooves so close to her bare feet. "Shhh…easy, now…there now."

Still nervous, the horses shifted, foam dripping from their muzzles.

Grace stood there, not moving, until the sun rose. One by one, the horses came close enough to stretch out their noses and sniff her hands.

Mame finally came forward, her head hung low, a scarlet strip peeled open along her neck, ribbons of sweat and blood curling down below her mane. She allowed Grace to stroke her nose and behind her ears. Grace breathed into the mare's nostrils, the stiff hair on Mame's muzzle against her own lips.

"I'm so sorry, my girl. I'm so very sorry. I know he singled you out because of everything you are to me."

Grace knew Tom was watching from some spot far off. She knew he resented the freedom she felt when she rode Mame. That small joy—one that excluded him—slipped through the hairline fractures in his arrogant armor. Tom sensed the pure spirit of deep love and wanted it for himself. Envy and jealousy worked through the fissures of Tom's control, penetrating the porous nature of the unstable wall he'd worked desperately to built around his wounded heart…if he still had a heart. Perhaps all that remained was an empty, cavernous space where his sense of wholeness should have been.

A low moan drew Grace's attention followed by a squeal as the fallen horse attempted to rise. Grace remembered the sound of bone breaking.

"No more suffering," she said and strode out of the corral and to the house. Minutes later, she stood above the horse's body, the sound of the shot still ringing in her ears and the barrel cooling in her hands as she looked at the small round hole in the indentation above the horse's eye. She bent to pull a single strand of sorrel-colored hair from the gelding's mane.

Later that afternoon, Grace placed that single strand of horse-hair between the pages of her journal.

That night she paid for defying Tom. A full moon hung low in the sky, swollen and ripe yellow over the horse's body she and Mame had drug far from the corrals and left to the prairie scavengers. Grace focused on the soft light weeping down on the landscape. It kept her from crying out. She couldn't stop him from hitting her, from abusing her, but she refused to give him the satisfaction of knowing he hurt her. Amidst the pain, she held strong to that moment of defiance.

MEADOWLARK

Paul came to her in a dream that night. They walked along the Cheyenne River. He pulled her to him and kneaded the small of her back. He kissed her, smiled at her. She felt soft in his arms, safe and protected. When she awoke, her hand flew to her mouth, fingers finding her own swollen lips. She blinked and the ceiling came into focus as she lay trembling, trying to recapture the lingering sweetness of that kiss.

4

Grace inhaled sharply, her mind instantly alert as the tangy film of smoke stung her nostrils and scraped away the haze of sleep.

"Tom! Wake up!" She ran to the window but saw nothing but clear air in the gray of dawn to the south.

She sniffed again. *Yes, smoke.*

"Tom! Wake *up*! There's a fire!"

Tom's eyes sprang open and he rose and stumbled outside, Grace right behind him. They rounded the corner of the sod house and gasped.

"Lord have mercy," Grace breathed. "That's over toward the Farthing place."

To the west, a thick plume smudged the horizon and rose in a great gray spine, connecting land to sky.

Back inside, Tom threw on his work clothes and Grace pulled

her dress on over her nightgown. No time for socks, she pulled boots onto bare feet.

"I'm going for the horses." Tom sprinted toward the corral.

Grace grabbed dishtowels and an old blanket, ran outside and drenched them in the stock tank. Tom came around the corner atop a black gelding, leading Mame as she balked and yanked her head.

"Check that cinch, Grace. She's skittish, wouldn't let me tighten it up." Grace threw the wet blanket up to Tom. He wheeled the gelding and spurred him toward the fire. The edge of panic wove its way up Grace's arms and crawled like tiny insects through her scalp. Her breath came fast and shallow. She rubbed Mame's neck.

"Whoa girl. It's okay." She tightened the cinch and threw herself into the saddle. Before she could get her feet in the stirrups Mame burst into a gallop after Tom's gelding.

Heaven help them. If the fire is big enough, it could burn to the river. With no grass the cows will starve.

A mass of dark bodies framed by a cloud of dust and smoke rushed toward her on the horizon. Grace squinted to see, her eyes widening when they registered what approached. A herd of bawling cattle—hundreds!—raced toward her. Her eyes searched for way to get out of their path. Dust flew up behind the herd of yellow, red, black, and white bodies surging in terror.

"Yah, Mame! Yah, girl!" Grace clutched the wet rags to her chest and leaned down across the saddlehorn and onto Mame's neck. The wave of animals was too wide to get around.

"Our only chance is to run with them, Mame, girl." She drew the reins down low and across the horse's neck and turned her back in the direction they'd come from. The sharp heels of the cattle thundered across the prairie. Closer, closer...

Sensing the danger, Mame squealed and ran faster. Grace heard the snorts and the pounding of hundreds of hooves behind them. She felt the jostle of the first steers pulling up next to her running horse.

Please, please don't trip, Mame. Grace tried to watch for prairie dog holes, but couldn't focus. She prayed Mame wouldn't go down as the lead cows rubbed against her boots and into Mame's shoulder. They tossed their heads and rammed into the horse. Grace edged Mame away, terrified a horn would catch the soft flesh of the horse's belly.

The ripe scent of singed hair and burning flesh swept upward from the fleeing cattle. Burn marks from white-hot ash stretched across their backs and faces. Grace clutched the reins, her legs aching from holding tight to Mame. There was no chance to slow down and let the herd pass, she and Mame would be crushed by cattle trying to climb over the top of them.

"Come on, girl," she urged. "You can outrun any cow. Come on!" Grace felt the burst of speed as Mame ran faster. The heads of the cattle dropped behind enough for her to begin to turn Mame, a hair's breadth in front of the herd. Mame raced on, Grace guiding her across the path of the herd, until at last they moved beyond the final cow and she reined the horse to a slow lope and finally stopped. She watched the mass stampede by, thinking of the tiny sod hut they raced toward.

"Can't think about that now, girl." Grace faced Mame toward the plume of smoke again and kneed her into a run. "Hah!"

"Grace! Grace!" a voice called from the distance.

Grace turned to see Mae in her buggy coming on fast.

"Have you heard anything, Grace?" Mae called above the pounding of the hooves.

"No." Grace yelled back. "You?"

"Not a thing. I was coming back from a call when the wind shifted and I smelled the smoke."

"Tom's gone ahead. Let's hurry." She kneed Mame into a lope.

"What in the world happened to your eye, Grace?" Mae called across the wind.

Grace's hand flew to her swollen face. "Oh, that new milk cow swung her head around and caught me." She forced a laugh and fought to maintain some lightness in her voice.

"You better let me look at it," Mae shouted as Grace outdistanced the buggy.

"Later!"

A high membrane of orange flames slid across the prairie as far as they could see, a tiny soddy directly in the fire's path. Behind the flames, the ground lay charred and black, smoke rising and spitting from pockets of hot cinders. Horses and wagons raced in from all directions as neighbors came to help extinguish the fire before it devoured miles of precious grass.

Grace could see Tom beating at the fire line with the wet

blanket. Other men and women were swinging burlap sacks.

A man call above the din, "What's next, Tom?"

"Over here!" He shouted and people gravitated toward him, assuming he would take charge.

Barrels full of water sat in the backs of wagons with men bracing their legs to keep them from tipping over as they bounced over the uneven ground. Lathered horses, crazed with fear, labored to pull as they shied away from the approaching wall of fire. Some reared and men jumped to grab bridles to urge them forward.

"Cover their eyes!" Tom yelled.

Women and children scraped dirt with shovels and threw it onto the fire, turning and running when the flames reared too high.

"There's Ike!" Mae called to Grace, relief sweeping over her features as she pointed to a cowboy who ran his horse over to one of the rearing geldings. He hit the ground and tucked a bandanna over the horse's eyes.

"Ike!" Mae hollered and he waved his hat high overhead, strain painted on his filthy face. "Take my horse and buggy."

"Take mine, too," Grace leapt to the ground, looped the reins over Mame's head, and smacked her on the rump.

"Mrs. Robertson, your eye!" Ike took Mame's reins and tied his horse and the mare to the back of the buggy.

"I'm fine! Get those horses to safety."

Mae leapt from her buggy to assist Grace, their faces, arms, and clothing quickly blackened with soot. Flames taller than a man sprang upward and spooked horses bolted past. Frantic shouts filled the air. "Over here! Quick! Here it comes!"

The fire exploded forward, popping and twisting under an inky veil of black smoke. Mae stumbled and fell headlong, the edge of her skirt flaring.

"Are you all right, Mae?" Grace ran to stomp the cloth and dragged her upright.

Mae frowned slightly then shook her head. "Yes."

Both women turned to beat the flames slithering toward them. Grace pulled the towels from her waistband and whirled them up and over her head, bringing them down again and again.

"Have you seen anyone here? The little ones?"

Mae shook her head as she continued the brutal struggle.

Ike returned, a yoke over his shoulders with two full

buckets. The women soaked their towels and turned to work the fire again. Ike rushed to the next person down the line, then the next.

"Dr. Thingvold! We need help!" rang through the popping of the flames. "Where's Dr. Thingvold? Mae!"

"Here! I'm here!" Mae looked in the direction of the voice and waved the towel above her head.

Ike ran back, his face pinched and white. "It's Jacob. His horse spooked and dumped him. He tried to outrun the flames, but they come right up over the top of him. He's burned bad. Tom got him into the back of a wagon." Ike's voice dropped a notch. "I couldn't reach him in time, Mae. I tried. I saw him fall. I saw him running to stay ahead of the flames. I pushed myself as fast as I could. I just couldn't get there in time."

"Take me to him, Ike. You did all you could do. Take me to him."

Ike grabbed Mae's hand and they ran together. Grace watched them disappear over a rise, Mae's underskirts white banners against the dark smoke.

Grace had taken her eyes off the flames and a sudden wall of heat pushed her back. She turned her head away and saw Samuel Farthing standing between the fire and his homestead.

"You're coming through me before you'll take all I've worked for!" he shouted at the flames. He turned around as his wife, Cassie, came outside. "Run, Cassie! Take them kids and get out of there! I'll hold it back."

Sweet Jesus, what in God's name was she still doing there? Grace ran toward her. "Cassie!" She bolted past Samuel, who looked at her with only vague recognition.

"Cassie!" Grace gasped, "Why are you still here?"

"The wind shifted, Grace. The fire was heading the other direction. We thought it was safe." Her eyes had the frantic look of a trapped animal.

"My babies, Grace!" She struggled under the weight of trying to carry all three of her children. Milt, the oldest, clung to her back as she held Cora and Elinore close to her body.

"Hang on to your mama's neck, Milt. Come here, girls. You're coming with me." They nodded mutely, as Grace settled one on each hip. Cassie hitched Milt up higher on her back, her arms under his legs.

MEADOWLARK

"This way. Run for the water!"

Cora and Elinore wailed on Grace's hips. They gagged as the smoke shrouding the earth filled their lungs. At the stock pond, Grace wallowed through the low water and mud to reach the middle. Cassie followed with Milt screaming on her back. Gasping, they stood with ankles sunk into slick gumbo as silty water swirled their skirts around their legs.

"Samuel! Leave the fire. Get away from there!" Cassie yelled. "Oh, Grace, he can't hear me!" She bent her head down and closed her eyes.

Behind them, Ike ran forward, leading a blindfolded horse pulling a water wagon. Men and women followed. Wet flour, sugar, and feed sacks flew, beating out a sharp, snappish rhythm on the prairie's drum, tamping out flames licking toward the soddy.

Grace's arms began to ache with the weight of the girls. She lowered them slowly to stand waist deep, clinging to her skirt to stay upright.

The blackened ravages of the fire stopped just feet in front of the soddy. People walked down the line of the fire, their arms still flailing away at hot spots, Samuel moving with them. Grace and Cassie waded out of the murky water. Grace's feet slipped on the mud that lined the insides of her boots. Her skirts hung charred and soaking wet down along her legs; her nightgown blackened and stained, dragged limply below the hem of her skirt.

She passed neighbors from near and far, all exhausted as they walked toward the water wagons. Grace hustled Cassie and her children along with them. Women linked arms and rested foreheads filthy with soot and smoke against one another. Men stood and shook their heads, wiping grimy hands across faces smeared pitchy black.

The fire, now a molten ring around a charred desert that reached to the horizon, left large spaces of smoky ash still sliding along the prairie. Only a few live patches remained.

"Grace." She turned to see Mae walking toward her.

"The man who fell?" Grace asked.

Mae shook her head. "Went into shock. Burned too badly. There was nothing I could do. They're taking him home now to bury him. He's leaving behind a wife and two children."

Ike drove up in Mae's buggy, Mame and his horse tied to the back. "It was my fault."

"It wasn't anybody's fault, Ike," Mae said.

He shook his head, unable to say more. After a couple of moments, he cleared his throat. "May I drive you home, Mae?"

"Yes. Thank you, Ike." He reached down and helped Mae up into the seat while Grace retrieved Mame.

"Do you need help, Mrs. Robertson?"

"No, thank you Ike. Mame and I will be fine. Thank you for taking care of Mae."

Ike turned the horse and buggy in the direction of Mae's shanty. Grace watched them go, Mae's hand looped easily through Ike's arm, the murmur of their conversation drifting back on the wind.

Grace didn't see Tom anywhere and she didn't have the strength or the heart to search for him. She climbed into her saddle and headed Mame home. Red would be waiting at the gate wanting to be fed and milked.

As the sun dropped the following afternoon, Grace rode over to take some canned food to the woman whose man had been lost to the fire. She found their soddy still standing but abandoned.

"Hello?" she called, but there was no response

Grace dismounted and looked inside. Empty, except for the stove. She walked around to the back and saw the blackened remains of the fire. All the grass had been cleared away and the prairie scraped clean, black and grey in the aftermath. Something in the ash at her feet caught her eye and she bent to retrieve what turned out to be a locket on a delicate chain. Intricate lace patterns carved into the gold rippled beneath her fingers as she turned it over in her hand, soot smudging her fingers. She opened it to reveal what was once a photo, now singed and unrecognizable. The family had abandoned not only the land, but its memories.

MEADOWLARK

5

In the heat of late June, Grace was thinking about all of the cooking she needed to do for tomorrow's branding while she hung clothes on the line Tom had built for her. They would soon smell of sun and fresh air. She looked over at the new chicken coop. Beef and potatoes had served as Tom's bachelor's fare, but when she told him how her mother had taught her to roast chicken, make chicken pies, and that with eggs she could bake cakes, the chicken coop, hens, and a rooster had appeared within a week.

As she pressed the wooden pin over the wet shirt, she noticed two male figures approaching on horseback. One was Tom.

The laws of common decency demanded she take down the shifts, their once white fabric now pale beige and she hurried to do it. With her delicates safely returned to the basket, she looked to see if the second rider was anyone she recognized. The man beside Tom seemed familiar, like a dream on the tip of consciousness the next morning. Grace walked around to get a better view.

He sat tall and thin in the saddle, the reins resting easy in his fingers. The two men talked—facing one another instead of her—and the dream came into sharper focus. Grace stepped up to meet the riders and her eyes locked on a pair of blue ones that widened in surprise. She felt her stomach spin.

"Grace?" Tom climbed down and looped the reins over his horse's head. "This is Paul Overland. He came looking for work so I told him I could sure use his help at the branding tomorrow. We need to bring the cattle up from the breaks along the river."

Tom rarely looked at Grace while speaking to her, his eyes always drifted to the horizon or the cattle. Now he patted his horse's neck and pulled at burrs caught in his mane. By the time Tom glanced her way, Grace had managed to regain her composure. She extended her hand and hoped Tom would attribute the slight trembling to the exertion of hanging out clothes.

"Hello, Mr. Overland. We've met before. Do you recall? Tom, I met Mr. Overland once when I lived over on the homestead near Plainview."

Paul took her hand with gentle firmness. "Yes, I do recall. We do know one another. Good to see you again, Gra...I mean, Mrs. Robertson. I hope you're well."

Paul had picked up on Grace's cue and his face appeared carefully blank and respectful.

"Grace, go make us some coffee. Paul, go ahead and hitch your gelding. I'll put my horse up and see about an extra saddle blanket for you. Yours looks worn thin." Tom turned toward the barn.

Grace walked to the house, pushing at the loose spiral of her hair. She couldn't stop the shaking of her hands, her whole body had turned into a web of sparking nerves and unsettling sensations. She dropped the coffee tin and it clattered against the shelf. Retrieving it, she set it on the table and rubbed her sweaty hands on her dress, as she forced herself to breathe deeply. Tom got testy when she was around other men. The price would be high if Tom guessed she had once been close to Paul.

"I had no idea who you'd married." Paul stood in the open doorway. "You wrote and told me you were marrying a rancher. You never gave me a name. Jesus, when I realized it was you standing there..." When she didn't respond, he asked, "How are you?"

"Oh, fine, fine." She looked up slowly. "And you?"

MEADOWLARK

"I deserved more, Grace. More than a bit of paper with a few scribbled words on it."

"You're right. I am sorry, Paul. Sorrier than you'll ever know."

The water in the coffee pot began to boil. Distracted by Paul's presence, she turned to pull it off the stove and grabbed the handle with her bare hand. The hot metal seared her palm. She shrieked and dropped the pot, water sloshing onto the dirt floor.

"Let me see." Without waiting for a reply, Paul took her arm and opened her hand to reveal the red welt. "You've been burned bad. It's going to blister. Where's the grease?" He began taking the lids off of canisters.

"I'm fine. Please." She pulled her arm away. "I'll take care of it. Please go and wait outside. Go on, now." Tears appeared before she could wipe them away. Paul looked hurt and questioning. Then his mood shifted.

"Yes ma'am, Mrs. Robertson, I understand. And Mrs. Robertson? You ever need me, you just let me know." Paul made his way to the door and walked outside.

"Go on, now. Go outside. I'll bring the coffee when it's ready." Grace dabbed bacon grease on the wound, then wrapped her hand in a towel. She whispered to the tension-laden air, "I will do no such thing. I got myself into this mess with Tom and I will stick with it. I won't mess up Paul's life. I will not!"

Paul had said, "You've been burned bad," without even knowing the hard truth of it all.

Tom walked in. "Bring the coffee and get some supper going. Paul brought his own gear and says he'll spend the night down by the creek."

After the men had eaten and talked of the weather, they left to gather cattle. Grace set about baking a cake and two pies for the branding. The beef she would cook over a fire tomorrow. In the morning she would boil and mash potatoes, make gravy and fix countless biscuits.

Her hand throbbed where she'd burned it and she dripped with sweat. The soddy had become the same temperature as the oven. Despite the discomfort she would never shame herself by serving a meager meal at a branding. Her mother used to tell her, "Oh, your father dreaded going to brandings over to the Hutchins place. Luke-warm coffee and a tiny roll in the morning and a thin piece of meat between bread for the midday meal."

It was understood that neighbors didn't pay one another to help at branding time. Instead, people were fed. It was unheard of for those giving of their time to bring food to the brandings. That chore was left to rancher whose cattle were being branded. Grace was determined that people would learn to look forward to the Robertson brandings for the fine meal they could expect. She decided to make a pan of cinnamon rolls to serve with mid-morning coffee.

While the piecrusts baked, she went outside to the pile of slough grass she'd gathered from the creek and twisted it into tight little bundles. There never seemed to be enough wood. She had used dried cow patties, but she far preferred the clean smelling smoke of these hay cats. She had soaked the grass overnight to soften it, but still her fingers bled and her burned palm ached.

It was dark when Grace gently wiped her tender hands on her apron and then laid the bundles outside the door for the night winds to dry. Her baking was done, all but tomorrow's biscuits. She surveyed the towel-covered food, the dishes washed, dried, and put away. Tom snored on the bed, deep in sleep. Paul was surely stretched out in his bedroll under the cooling sky near the creek. She wondered if he slept or lay awake, as she blew out the lamp to put on her nightgown.

She crawled into bed quietly, settling in slowly, trying not to wake Tom. She froze as his hand pulled at her nightdress, moved it up to her waist, up to her neck, and jerked it over her head. The rough hands on her breasts worked lower and she turned her head toward the sod wall and lay without response, tears making their way down her flushed cheeks. Tom took no notice.

When he finished he fell asleep on top of her, crushing her into the thin straw mattress. As his breathing took on the deep rhythm of sleep once more, Grace pushed him over and eased from the bed. She walked outside, welcoming the blistering winds.

She stood there letting the wind scald away Tom's touch and his scent, leaving her clean. She lifted her hair high and let it fall in a cascade down her back, then opened her arms wide and focused her eyes on the emptiness beyond. She envisioned every speck of Tom that she carried on her body being seared away to nothingness, until finally she felt herself again.

She gathered several dried bundles of grass, entered the house, and dressed quietly in the dark. She lit the lantern and sat in a chair and wrote, comforted by the soft scratching of the nib moving across the page.

Branding day promised no peace from the searing heat. Scorching winds raced up from the south, scratching the land as they slithered over the prairie and leeched precious moisture from everything they touched. Grace's skin stretched tight over her face and body, feeling ready to split wide open at a mere touch. Her hair crackled like rough-cut, sun-dried hay.

The glow of the oil lamp fell upon the table as she poured out the flour, salt, and yeast in the big white bowl. The soddy began to heat as the stove pumped and came to life. Rivulets of sweat dripped off her temples and fell into the dough. She mixed in the salty beads of moisture.

Tom shifted in bed before rising and pulling on his clothes. "Better go get the horses in."

He reached for the cup of coffee Grace handed him. "I'll eat breakfast with the fellows when they show up." He pulled on his boots, picked up his coffee, and walked out the door.

As Grace kneaded dough in the soft light she was startled to see her mother's hands extending from her wrists. Grace and her mother shared identical thin gold wedding bands adorning slender fingers and narrow palms. She held her hands in front of her and studied them, flexing and moving her fingers. The bones protruded slightly against the skin below the knuckles. Yes, definitely her mother's hands. She thought of the history in the blood running through the veins—connecting her, binding her to a legacy of feminine love, wisdom, and strength. Despite her absence, Grace remembered her mother's capable hands and smiled.

As she did every morning, Grace went out to water her flowers. This morning she expectantly peered down at the soil in the dark, taking enormous pleasure in the hope and anticipation. The week before, the first pale sprouts had shoved up against the soil.

The next day, a valiant few had emerged. And every morning since, a few more delicate shoots arched their way up to greet her.

The sun had barely peeked over the horizon and the prairie still lay in partial darkness as neighboring ranchers and cowboys filtered in off the plains. Grace produced pans of biscuits, potatoes, and eggs and provided a steady steam of fresh coffee for the men who slowly arrived at the front door. She built up the fire outside, where large cuts of beef would be set to roast for the noon meal.

"Mornin', Mrs. Robertson," she heard again and again.

"Good morning," she responded with a smile, "Let me get you some breakfast. I'm afraid you'll have to eat outside. There's just not enough room in here for everybody." Grace piled plates high. It would be a long morning of hard work before they would have a chance to eat again.

Tom's brother, Ed, recently elected sheriff, arrived. He tipped his hat toward Grace, but rode on to find Tom. Ed had little use for women. Tom told her his brother had followed him west because his tales of free land and good grass drew Ed like a magnet.

The air outside the soddy hummed with jovial conversation. Forks clinked as the men scraped every bit of food from tin plates. They exchanged the latest news regarding cattle prices, moisture, and the weather, whose cows looked good, what man had been in a horse wreck, when the cattle trains were due to arrive that would carry their stock east.

Tom returned from saddling his horse, trailed by Ed. The brothers greeted each cowboy with a handshake. Grace stood in the doorway, coffee pot in hand, nervous and fidgety, expecting each rider coming up from the creek to be Paul. She rubbed sweat from her brow with the back of her free hand.

Paul didn't come. Tom gestured for her to refill the men's cups with a wave of his hand. Grace walked among them, pouring into cups that looked tiny in hands enlarged by hard work and extreme weather.

"How are you, Ike?" she asked. "Good to see you again." Grace liked Ike. He had a polite nature and quick sense of humor. And, according to Tom, he was also a fine hand with livestock.

"Oh, I been good, Mrs. Robertson." Ike stretched out his long, lanky body, a twinkle in his eye. "I've been courting a new girl." A shy grin spread across his face.

"You have?" Grace's brow furrowed slightly, thinking of Mae. "Well, come on now, tell me about her."

"Oh, she's real pretty. Comes from a ranch out my way." He lowered his voice, in hopes others would not hear. "There is one thing, though."

"Oh?" Grace leaned in closer.

"I was over to see her the other night. Her family is real nice folks. After supper, she asked me to walk out beyond the barn to see the sunset. We walked up over a little rise and out before me, I see…" he lowered his voice still further and said with earnest desperation, "…sheep."

Grace choked down a laugh. "Sheep?"

"Hundreds of 'em. I said to her, 'Where's the *cattle*?'"

Grace put her hand over her mouth. "Oh, Ike, if word gets out to this bunch that you've thrown in with that girl's family, they will be ruthless."

A guffaw erupted. "Too late for that, Grace," Ed said. "Hey, boys! Ol' Ike here is sparkin' the daughter…of a sheep man!"

Ike's face turned crimson.

Shouts of "Baaaaaa-baaaaaa," floated above the dusty ground. Ike shook his head as Grace touched him on the arm with compassion.

As the cowboys dropped their plates, forks and cups into a washtub filled with hot, soapy water beside the door, Tom called them to gather near the corral. Men of all sizes and shapes mounted horses of every breed and color. Dusty, sweat-stained hats were set back on heads cocked to keep the rising sun out of their eyes as dust swirled and sharp whinnies skimmed the stillness.

"Say, Ike," Ed called out, "you plan on riding that old nag under a tree down in the breaks along the river again? You damned near got scraped off last year."

Ike smiled as he tugged down his battered hat. "Well, I just don't know what this old nag might do, seeing as he's a real cow horse, and not some citified damn thing that don't know one end of a cow from the other like that one you're setting on. He only took me under that tree because he was after a cow. I forgot to duck, that's all."

Whoops of laughter accompanied hearty shouts of agreement among the circled men. They loved to see a big wheel like Ed get jabbed. Ike reached over to pat the neck of his big bay gelding.

The sun rose higher casting a warm glow over the men and
their horses. The air, already hot, encouraged dark stains of sweat
under the men's arms and down their backs. Horses snorted softly,
shifting their weight, moisture already glistening on the soft, short
hair of their flanks.

"Thanks for coming to help today. I know I'm branding late
this year because of the drought and that damned fire. I've got some
big calves to work, so take care." Tom punctuated what he said with
fast, sharp thrusts of his hands. Beads of sweat trickled from under his
hat and slipped down his jaws.

"You know I'm not one for fancy riding that gets the cows
riled up and on the fight. They're already edgy. Paul and I brought
them up yesterday." All hats turned toward the few hundred head of
cattle in the pasture. "Let's work 'em slow and easy. Ed, help me get
the get the irons in the fires. Ike start picking out calves. Choose a
heeler to help you."

Ike started issuing orders as men mounted and snaked out
their ropes.

Grace watched a lone rider come up from the creek. He raised
his arm in greeting as he came toward the soddy. With flutters in her
stomach, Grace returned Paul's wave. His body moved as one with the
chestnut gelding he rode.

She turned toward the pile of dirty dishes that awaited her and
rolled up her sleeves. She wanted to be out riding with the men not
stuck in a dark, airless soddy by herself scrubbing pots and pans and
starting the next meal.

"Halloooooooo!" Mae's voice bounced across the morning.

Grace turned to see a figure bobbing up and down, trotting on
horseback up over the ridge.

"Hallooooo!" Mae waved her hand wide above her head, her
skirts blowing in the wind. "Grace! Thought I'd come help!" Mae
shook off her bonnet and swirled it sweeping circles.

The cattle stirred and bawls pierced the air as they caught
sight of Mae's antics.

"Mae! Stop!" Grace held up her hands. "Don't wave! You'll
spook the cattle."

Mae bounded forward, bouncing all over the saddle and
barely staying atop her strawberry roan. "Whoops! I haven't truly
learned to ride yet. Thought I'd practice instead of bringing the

buggy!" she cried as the horse shied sideways. Her skirts flew high revealing white underskirts that shone brightly in the sun.

Mae struggled to pull the skirt down. Her arms flapped, causing her horse to start and spook.

"Whoa!" Mae's voice rang loudly.

Grace reached for the horse's trailing rein, but missed.

A skittish cow bolted away from the herd. Ed and Tom, busy talking and getting the fire started, looked up to see cows bawling and scrambling.

Grace saw the commotion on the rise. "Oh, my Lord," she breathed. "All hell's going to break loose."

Shock passed over Mae's features as she flopped off the horse and landed in a heap at Grace's feet. She looked up at Grace, eyes wide and mouth in the shape of a large 'O.'

A loose horse exploded into the herd startling the cows and causing some to bolt. Horses tied to the corral spooked, two leaned back on their haunches until the reins snapped and the animals tumbled to the ground before rising to sidestep away. Ground-tied mounts bolted. Men swore.

Grace stood with her hands clasped over her mouth, then quickly helped Mae to her feet. The two women stared at one another, eyes wide. Mae burst out laughing, and before Grace could help it she joined in.

"Oh, Mae," she murmured. "Don't let the men see us laugh. This is really, *really* bad. Turn around!" They turned toward the soddy, away from the men.

"Do you think anybody saw me?" Mae chortled.

Grace lay her head against Mae. "Only the whole herd and every man from here to the Black Hills!"

The sound of a loping horse turned Grace into ice as her stomach drew tight with fear. It had to be Tom. Slowly, she turned around and gave a silent prayer of thanks.

"Mornin', ladies," Paul said, tipping the rim of his hat over a broad smile. "Anyone hurt?"

"We're fine," Grace managed to say.

"And a good morning to you." Mae extended her hand toward Paul. "I'm Dr. Mae Thingvold. I've come to help."

"Paul Overland." He took her hand momentarily and then sat back in his saddle and surveyed the scene. "Well, ma'am, I'd say you sure enough have helped everyone wake up this morning."

"My pleasure." Mae giggled as she dusted off the skirts covering her broad rump.

"I'd best go help gather those cows." Paul nudged his horse with his heels. "Mrs. Robertson?"

"Yes?" Grace looked up, shielding her eyes from the sun.

"I hope you have a fine day, ma'am."

Grace nodded to him. She couldn't help smiling.

Paul touched the tip of his hat then rode away. His low chuckle floated back to the two women. As Tom and Ed approached the soddy, grim scowls on their faces, Paul paused to suggest that they help him retrieve the loose horses.

As the men moved away, Mae said, "Ike told me that your Tom is the best cowman in the country. That he's always fair to the men working for him."

Grace tied Mae's gelding to the hitch rack.

Mae said, "Ike also said that the men had best watch themselves around him, though."

"What did he mean by that?" Grace asked.

"Ike said he'd seen Tom in a fight before, and that he is one tough goddamned sonofabitch. I'm sorry, Grace, I shouldn't have said that. But the look on Tom's face as he came this way made me think of that. Ike said Tom may not be big, but that shouldn't fool anyone. He saw Tom knock a man twice his size out cold, and then keep beating on him just to teach him a lesson. Ike said he wouldn't want to be on the other side of Tom's fists."

Grace picked up the huge washtub of dishes and walked into the soddy. Mae followed her.

"Like I said, Ike insisted that Tom's a fair man to the men working for him, though. A real cowman. Once Ike was having a hard time getting some money owed to him out of another outfit up north. A big ranch. They owed him for riding their herd during calving but then they wouldn't pay him." Mae stood at the kitchen table. "So, Ike went to Tom and told him what was going on. Ike had heard that Tom stuck up for the men who worked for him and figured maybe this rancher who wouldn't pay him might pay some attention to Tom, since he's one of the bigger ranchers around. Ike was just some cowboy to that fellow. 'Just a cowboy'," she sniffed, hand on hip, "Imagine! Shows how much *they* know."

Grace started washing dishes and motioned Mae to the dishtowel drying from the stove's warming oven. A sudden gust of wind caught the soddy door and slammed it shut. Dirt rained down on the women's heads.

"That's why I always cover the pies with dish towels, Grace said, surveying the clumps of dirt shaken loose from between the boards. She walked over and braced the door back open hoping to bring some air into the dank interior.

"Go on, Mae. Tell me the rest."

"Anyway, Ike said Tom rode up and spoke directly with that rancher and came back with every cent owed." Mae wiped the plate clean and set it on the table, before retrieving another from the wet stack. "Ike didn't think he ever would have ever seen that money if it hadn't been for Tom. Ike respects him greatly He said Tom would give any man working for him the shirt off his back and never complain. And Tom pays the best wages in the territory for day work, too."

Grace tried to equate the man Mae was talking about to the husband she knew. Tom being fair. Tom standing up for what was just and right. Tom giving another man the shirt off his back. Tom paying the best wages.

"Mae, why are you telling me this?" Grace asked.

"Oh, I don't know. Just figuring out why that nice Paul Overland was here working today. Did I say something wrong?"

"No, not at all. Hand me a few of those hay cats. Let's build up the fire and bake more biscuits."

When Tom brought in the men for dinner at noon, he glared at Mae as she walked past dishing out beef and potatoes to those sitting on the ground eating from plates balanced on their knees.

Ike walked up to Grace carrying a deep cast iron skillet. He removed the heavy lid with a flourish. "The boys and I took advantage of that fire you have going outside and fried up some prairie oysters for the meal, Grace."

"Prairie oysters?" Mae asked, walking over to peer into the skillet at the mound of round pieces of meat. "Why, there's no ocean here, whatever on earth are prairie oysters?" she leaned in closer, closed her eyes and inhaled.

Grace and Ike looked at once another. "Go ahead, Ike," said Grace. "You do the honors."

Mae opened her eyes and looked at Ike expectantly.

"Well, ma'am," he started slowly. "These here are the difference between steers and bulls."

Mae's eyes dropped again to the contents of the skillet and widened. "Oh! Oh, my! Well, yes indeed, so they are." Mae straightened suddenly and looked around for something to do. "Jolly well sorry about this morning, Mr. Robertson!" Mae said, turning her attention to Tom, reaching for the platter of beef and laying a chunk on his plate. "Indeed, I am."

Grace watched Tom's response to Mae as she followed with a pan and dipper to offer each man gravy. Tom struggled to control his temper—but there was something else hovering in his eyes and the way his glance moved over Mae's ample body as she leaned toward him.

"Well, now, I suppose it could've happened to anybody, Miss Thingvold," Tom said with uncharacteristic awkwardness. His eyes shifted from Mae's chest to her face. He drummed his fingers against the edge of his plate and expelled a long breath.

How odd that Mae made Tom nervous, Grace observed. It slowly dawned on her that he must be attracted to her.

"So how did you happen to come to God's country, Miss Thingvold?" Tom dipped his fork into the potatoes on his plate.

"When I heard the government was opening up land along the reservation, I knew it was my destiny. I met all the requirements: a citizen of the United States, twenty-one years of age or older, head of household, and I do not own over 160 acres of land." She finished with an upward flourish of her hand and gravy flew from the spoon.

"Whoops!" she called out making everyone laugh. Mae stirred the contents of the bowl tucked into the circle of her arm. "More, Mr. Robertson?"

"Yes, ma'am." Tom handed Mae his plate. "Tell me the rest," Tom said with such enthusiasm that it made Grace cringe.

"On the first drawing," Mae continued, "a hundred and ten thousand people entered the lottery for twenty-four hundred claims. Of course, my number wasn't drawn. What a sight that was to behold. Thousands and thousands of envelopes scattered and piled on the floor. A blindfolded child picked the first envelope at random. That fortunate person was given the choice of all the claims. And so it went down the line until all the claims were drawn."

"But you didn't get a claim then?"

"No. However, I'm a woman of diligence and hard work. My future and fortune set to such a game of chance didn't suit me well at all. At that time, I had heard of the possibility of purchasing relinquishments. Before arriving, I purchased the relinquishment from Miss Betsy Hansen. That's how I got my place just to the south of here, over that rise and down along the creek."

"I know where you live," Tom said, his tone rich and suggestive.

"Is that how homesteads have always been allotted, Mae?" Grace interrupted to break the unspoken invitation Tom was not-so-subtly angling for.

"Actually, no. Years ago, applicants lined up on horseback at a designated hour. A gun was fired and they raced to their desired locations and pounded a stake in the ground." Mae stretched out her arm in front of her, fingers pointing toward some distant horizon. "As you might imagine, this led to more than one murder as people squabbled over the same piece of land. That's when the lottery system took its place. Of course, you must know this already, Mr. Robertson. Did you come by this claim by lottery?"

Tom toyed with his fork for several moments before answering. "Uh...no."

"How then?"

"Well, I....just took it."

A long pause followed and an uncomfortable tension rippled through the listeners.

"You just *took* it?" Mae's eyebrows arched high.

Grace thought of Daisy.

"Yep, that's the way of it." Tom lifted a piece of beef. "Wasn't anybody making any claim on it. It was here for the taking, and so that's what I did. Claimed it for my own." Tom looked hard at the group of men staring at him, the hint of a dare in his eyes.

Mae stared at Tom as Grace held her breath. Mae studied the contents of the bowl of gravy she was holding.

"Well, this certainly is quite the country here, isn't it?"

Grace had the distinct impression that Mae was biting her tongue, leaving many thoughts unsaid, and upon reaching some decision, raised her eyes to look first at Grace and then to Tom.

"I'm pleased to make your acquaintance, Mr. Robertson. I do hope we'll be good neighbors."

Tom nodded and said, "I suspect we will be."

"What? After that escapade this morning, Tom?" Ed clapped Tom on the back and broke the silence, "Hooooeee, yessirree! Put a woman in the mix and all hell breaks loose."

Mae took the ribbing good-naturedly. "Now, you boys know full well that I was in *complete* control of my animal the entire time."

"Um…ma'am…was that before or after you…um…pulled them skirts back where they ought to be?" Ike asked, dipping his head and peering out from under his hat.

"Oh! So, you did see me then, after all!" Mae said, completely unabashed. She propped the bowl on her hip and shook the spoon close to Ike's face. "And if I hear tell that this *ever* gets back to the Medical Board from *anybody*," she eyed each of the cowboys in turn, "you'll have me to answer to, do you hear me?"

"Nobody will hear it from Ike or from anybody else, Dr. Thingvold," Tom said.

"Call me Mae," she said.

"Yes, ma'am."

The sun sank below the shadowed horizon, the ranchers and cowboys had departed for their own spreads, as Grace dried the last plate, stacked it on the shelf and turned to Mae, who was drying the final fork and placing it in the drawer. "Thank you, Mae. I am so glad you came today."

"Oh! The pleasure is all mine, dear Grace. All mine. Thank you for allowing me to stay and ah…help." Mae raised her skirts a few inches with her hands and laughed. Then Mae's face turned serious. "And that husband of yours?"

"Yes?" Grace asked.

"Well, and pardon me if I'm forgetting my prairie manners again here, but he does have a sincerity about him."

"Why, yes, he does, Mae. He truly does. That was one of the first things I noticed about him. That's what I trusted about him. Well, that's one of the reasons I married him, really. He just seemed so sincere in all he said and did."

"It's there, Grace. It seems he genuinely wants to do the right thing." Mae paused for a moment. "My sense is, though, that he oftentimes just doesn't know what that is, and that…" she drew a deep breath, "… that people get hurt because of it."

Grace stared at Mae, not saying a word, thinking how she needed to think about this and write about it in her journal. Maybe then she could make some sense of this truth that felt so close to the bone.

"Oh, now I have gone and done it, haven't I?" Mae swished a fly away from her face. "Gone and spit in the face of the prairie manners I'm trying so desperately to learn. I am sorry if I have, Grace. That isn't my intention at all. And frankly, this is the way I am. I tend to speak my mind and I'm not about to change that now, no matter where I live."

Mae threw both hands up in the air. "Ah, well, thanks so much again for today. Just wait until I write my parents about this. They will scarcely believe that I have participated in my first branding. Father will probably have to go for Mother's smelling salts!"

Tom appeared at the door, with Paul and Ike standing behind him holding their horses and Mae's strawberry roan.

"More pie?" Grace asked.

"No, thank you, ma'am," Paul and Ike said in unison.

Tom stepped inside and sat to wrench off his boots.

"I thought I'd ride alongside Miss Mae and see her home," Ike said. "We'll just walk the horses."

"Well, isn't that lovely," Mae said as she tied on her bonnet. She added with a grin. "Off I am then, my Grace!"

Grace stepped out into the evening air and sighed as Ike and Paul assisted Mae onto her horse.

"Thank you, Mae. I so appreciate your help."

Paul called into the soddy. "Thanks for the work, Tom."

"Anytime. Come back, anytime," Tom replied.

Grace heard him settling onto the bed and she reached past Paul to close the soddy door.

She and Paul stood side by side to watch Mae and Ike ride away as dusk stole the last colors from the sunset.

"And thank you, Mrs. Robertson, for such a fine meal." Paul tipped his hat. "I best be moving along."

"Where will you go?" Grace choked on the question.

"I've heard there's good work down south. I aim to head down where the winters are warm for a while."

"Good luck—wherever you go." She wanted to tell him she would miss him.

Paul nodded and placed his hat back on his head. "Thank you, Grace. It's better this way—with me far away somewhere," he said softly, and then louder, "And good luck to you, too."

With that, he put his foot into the stirrup and swung onto his horse. He gigged the gelding into a slow lope and rode into the overheated encroaching darkness.

MEADOWLARK

6

By July, Grace realized she was pregnant.

She had longed to hold her own baby since childhood. When her mother's sister came to visit with her latest—trailed by a passel of stair-stepped siblings—Grace had begged to be allowed to hold the baby. She sat carefully on the wooden bench at the rough kitchen table, cradling the child and looking into her innocent face, a tiny bundle wrapped in an old worn quilt with wide eyes that peered at her from a face so soft and smooth that it didn't seem real. Grace knew then that she wanted just such an angel of her own. She'd tickled under the little girl's chin and elicited gurgles and bubbles of glee.

Aunt Violet came to depend on Grace's love of children, insisting as soon as she arrived, "Oh, thank the Lord above, Grace. Take this baby from my arms before I lose my ever-loving mind." Grace thought the other young ones looked like the orphan calves, all wanting to suck on a surrogate cow at the same time.

By the time she was in her early teens, Grace balanced babies on her slim hips as expertly as any mother. She dreamed of giving birth. In the black velvet of countless nights, she awoke disoriented to reach out for the infant she was sure must be there. Or her hand would move urgently to feel the great mound of a belly, only to discover the hollow, flat plane of her flesh.

The drought's ceaseless decimation of the land marched through the month of July. Sparse stubble covered the ground where Tom assured her the grasses normally waved high as a horse's belly in the wind. Water dams that should have been several feet deep dwindled to brackish pools, the surrounding mud becoming a death trap. Every day, cowboys rode to pull cattle both dead and alive from the muck. With no live feed growing, people made long journeys to buy hay and grain. Savings, if there were any, dwindled then disappeared. More and more ranchers relied on loans from the bank. Everyone looked toward the clear sky, searching for the appearance of a cloud that might mean salvation.

As summer heat baked the prairie inhabitants, Mae hosted an outdoor evening picnic at her claim shack to offer prayers for rain.

Grace and Tom jostled on the seat of their wagon, up over the knoll above Mae's shanty and looked down onto the gathering neighbors below. Wagons, buckboards, and riders on horseback clustered around Mae's modest home. Men helped women down from the wagons, as children chased each other around the building and across the open land beyond. Women spread quilts out over the dry ground, placing baskets of food and canteens of water on the corners, a challenge to the wind.

"Hello!" Mae greeted them, drying her hands on a yellow apron when she saw Tom and Grace. "Look at that beautiful pie. You have outdone yourself again."

Mae took the mincemeat pie from Grace and brought it to her nose, inhaling deeply. "Heavenly. Let's put it on the table."

Grace followed Mae inside.

Mae looked ready to burst. "Oh, thank goodness you're here, Grace. I am just beside myself. Why did I want to do this? How am I going to host all of our neighbors?"

MEADOWLARK

Mae took a deep breath and brought her hand to her throat. "I am just too *much* for most people. I'm too loud and, and entirely too opinionated—and apparently too educated!—for a woman in this part of the world. But I don't know any other way to be. What am I to do?" She swept a curl out of her eyes and barreled on. "I try my best to fit in. I really do. But it seems the harder I try, the more of a mess I make of things. The other day, after I had fixed Mrs. Olmstead's daughter's twisted ankle, I hugged her after she paid me with eggs and..."

"What?" Grace interrupted. "Did you just say you *hugged* Mrs. Olmstead?"

"Of course, but you'd have thought I was trying to examine her nether regions, the way she stiffened up and glared at me. Then she closed the door right in my face. Not in a mean way..." Mae blinked. "She just seemed to be shocked."

Grace laughed so hard her knees buckled and she had to grab hold of the table to stay upright.

"What?" Mae's voice rose. "What am I doing wrong?"

Grace raised her head and smoothed back her hair. "Oh, Mae—unless you're related by blood, you do *not* hug other people."

"No hugs?" Mae asked.

"Well, you can hug me." Grace paused. "But you've only been here a short time, and with these prairie folk you may have to wait ...oh, say, forty, maybe fifty years to gain their trust and friendship."

"Truly? I'll never wait that long, Grace. But I will try to use a bit more discretion in the future. I really will."

Grace and Mae watched others arrive, riding or driving wagons, all calling out shouts of hello. Women in freshly washed dresses greeted friends laden with baskets and tins covered with cheesecloth. Soon sparkles of laughter, the shouts of playing children, and men joking filled the heated air.

Fragrances of shaving cream, new leather, and churned sod mingled with the scent of pot roast dripping with juice, steaming mashed potatoes dotted with melting pats of butter, warm bread, chokecherries and pies.

Men talked of the weather, the year's non-existent hay crop, and speculated on fall calf prices, their freshly shaved lower faces gleaming palely under the sun-tanned upper halves. As the men removed their hats when they entered the shack, their foreheads shone as white as the hair on a baldy calf's head above a strip of sun-bronzed skin around their eyes, nose, and brow.

Women clustered together in gingham dresses. After months of isolated work on the homesteads, their eyes gained renewed life just from seeing other women.

Before they settled down to eat, the preacher, who had traveled eighty miles from Rapid City, asked those gathered to bow their heads in prayer.

"Heavenly Father, well, it's just awful damn dry here. We seek your mercy and generosity, Father. The wind blows all the time and our watering holes are dry or muddy. Our cattle are thirsty and hungry, Father, and the calves bawl for more of their mama's milk and there's none to be had. We ask that you remember us, your humble servants, Father, and send rain to nourish our land and our souls. It is in the name of your son, Jesus Christ, we pray. Amen."

This was followed by the soft echo of more "Amens."

Then everyone heard, "Well, hell, I say 'Amen' to that!" as Ike cried out and pushed back his sweat-stained hat, a large grin on his face. Relieved laughter swept through the crowd.

People sat in the backs of their wagons, on Mae's as yet unsplit logs as stools or on the quilts spread on the prairie, to eat in the early evening light. Children played tag and jumped rope. One little boy walked by a wagon with a cake sitting on the back. He stopped in his tracks and stood eye level with the delicacy, then he leaned forward to take a huge bite. His face covered in frosting, he scampered away.

Grace's hand moved to her belly. Her eyes searched for Tom and she found him sitting on the back of their wagon, surrounded by a group of men. She moved closer to hear the story he was telling.

"So I was riding this huge old gelding," Tom said. "That sumbitch was crazy. I mean *crazy*. I lost count of the times that horse nearly killed me. Boy, did he have some cow in him, though. Once he locked onto a cow or calf, he'd follow that thing damn near anywhere." Tom reached up and pushed his hat slightly up and away from his handsome face and mopped the sweat with his hand.

"I was riding him back to the ranch last year, pushing along some steers. One of them took off like the devil himself was after him. I had barely set back into the saddle and that horse was on that steer like flies on a cowpie. He got a good head of steam going and we flew right past that steer and headed straight for the barn."

Tom threw his hands up into the air. "I tried plow-reining him around. I cranked his neck clear back to my boots. That horse was going forward but looking straight behind."

Whoops of laughter filled the air.

"I figured if I was riding a runaway, I would rather be on one who could see where the hell he was going. I let him have his head and he kept going like a freight train toward the barn. I started yanking back hard, trying to slow him up some. I'm staring at that low, open door and thinking that this horse can't be crazy enough to try and peel me off his back, but that is exactly what that sumbitch did. Peeled me right off the top of him and dropped me flat on my back. Knocked me out. First thing I said when I came to was 'That damn horse is *crazy*.'" The corners of Tom's eyes crinkled into faint creases.

Men laughed with admiration and clapped him on the back. Tom loved being the center of attention. No matter where he went, his good looks and charm drew people in. Grace wished she could bottle times like these in a jar to save and hold close to her heart. She wished for a moment in which the past ceased to exist, where she could forget the other man, the cruel man, who also inhabited Tom's skin. And then she wondered what price the horse might have paid.

Grace turned to stroll back to Mae's shack. Exposed wood boards framed the building, the narrow strips running horizontally from the ground to the roof, with black tar paper stretched and nailed into place over them. The slim door cut a rectangular opening on the side of the building, with a single slender window offering light to the dark interior. Inside, blue building paper lined the walls, providing some insulation against the wind, heat, and cold. Mae told her she had paid an extra ten dollars for that blue liner. Grace was curious to know if it had been worth the expense.

What will our child will look like, Grace wondered. And how and when to tell Tom. *I need to choose the right moment.*

"Haloooo!" Mae's distinctive voice floated out above the many conversations. She hitched her skirts as she climbed up on a chair, intending to step up onto the back of the nearest wagon.

Cowboys strained to catch a glimpse of Mae's stockings that covered her pretty ankles and shapely calves. Ike shoved his way to the front of the crowd, leaving a few men trying to catch their breath after receiving his sharp elbow by way of encouragement to look elsewhere.

Ike offered his hand to Mae, saying, "Allow me."

"Stand back, boys!" One man gasped, rubbing his ribs. "Ike will just as soon run you clean over, trying to get to Dr. Mae here."

Ike turned. "Damn straight, I will. And don't any of you forget it." He returned his attention to Mae. "Ma'am?"

"Why, thank you, Ike. That's most kind." She found her footing on the wagon bed as she grasped his outstretched hand, its sun-browned color dark against the pearl white of her skin.

"I want to thank you all for coming. Let us hope our prayers bring rain!"

Her voice rang out clearly. "One thing many of you don't know is in my youth I entertained fancies of singing in the opera."

Grace raised her eyebrows.

Mae smiled back and nodded. "My passion for medicine eventually outshone my desire to be on the stage, but I still enjoy singing." She paused. "With the hope it will bring much-needed moisture, I offer this aria for us all."

Silence settled over the gathering. Mae closed her eyes. She opened her mouth and released a single note into the air, a sound so perfect, so singularly pure, that Grace held her breath. Tones rose and fell, Mae's eyebrows lifting and furrowing in rhythm. No one moved, not even the children. Notes became words in another language, perhaps Italian. It didn't matter, their essence shone through Mae's voice, face, and body. Grace didn't understand the lyrics, but their meaning was clear. Mae sang of love and heartbreak. High lengthy strains caused Mae to raise her face to the sky. She seemed far away, her very soul soaring with her voice on the night wind, leaving only her flesh and blood there with her listeners.

This transcendence mesmerized Grace. She longed to ride the prairie wind along with the notes, to float above the earthly reality. She imagined peering down on it all from a high, safe distance, the plains rolling out below, a vast expanse of swells and undulations.

The notes danced over the top of the dry sounds of wind brushing against the confines of Mae's shack. How could anything be so pure and beautiful? Grace breathed deeply as a soft smile played on her lips. This was the feeling of her child deep within her being. This was the sensation of mother love. As Mae's voice peaked, Grace felt some invisible inner core expand. She wanted to hold tight to the experience, longed to lie down, pull the music up and over her, and create a cocoon of sheer peace, like some great featherbed composed entirely of Mae's lush song.

When Mae's voice fell from its zenith and drew to a close with a final clear note, Grace's self-recognition wilted, the translucent petals that had bloomed within drooping, laying limply against the harsh truth of reality.

"If that doesn't bring rain, Mae, there's nothing in heaven or earth that can," Grace whispered.

Mae's eyes shone, her flushed skin glowing with perspiration and radiance. "Thank you," she said quietly.

Still hands, roughened by harsh ranch life, burst into applause.

"And thank you *all*!" Mae offered a deep curtsy.

Ike stood next to the wagon, his stance emphasizing how ill-advised it would be for any other man to approach. He reached up to help Mae down and, linking her arm in his, escorted her to receive the admiration from her friends. Grace found Tom checking on the team.

He saw her. "That woman can sure sing," he said.

"Yes, she can," Grace agreed. "Tom, we're going to have a baby."

He looked at Grace who, confirmed her news with a nod.

He shook his head and held her arm tightly as they searched for Mae to tell her goodnight.

"Thank you so much, Mae," Grace said when they found her standing with Ike beside his horse. "Those prayers and your song are sure to bring rain.

"Anything else I can help with, Mae?" Ike lingered, holding the reins loosely in his hand.

"No, thank you. I hope you'll come again."

"I surely will, then." Ike put his foot in the stirrup and swung his leg over his saddle. "How about I come by tomorrow?"

"That would be grand. Lord knows I've got plenty of this good beef left over."

Ike clicked his horse into a walk. "Til then," he shouted back as he moved the gelding into a slow lope toward the ranch where he cowboyed, some ten miles away.

"That man..." Mae said.

"Yes, I know," Grace replied as Mae walked with her and Tom back to their wagon.

"Thank you so much for coming, both of you." Mae held her hands out to them. Grace edged close for a quick hug before Tom helped her up onto the seat.

"Grace Robertson," Mae exclaimed. "You actually hugged me!"

"Thank you, Mae." Tom snapped the reins over the team's backs and the wagon gave a soft lurch forward. "Ike's a good man."

"Bye!" Grace called. "You have a good time tomorrow."

The sound of the horses' hooves and creaking of the wagon mingled with the sweeping sighs of evening wind. Tom's elbows rested on his knees, the lines laced between his fingers.

"I want the best for our son," Tom said into the night. "I know it's a boy."

Grace smoothed the fabric of her skirt with her palms, rubbing the folds between her thumbs and forefingers. A lone coyote yipped in the distance and was soon joined by a cacophony of high-pitched yelps.

"Go ahead and howl, ya bastards!" Tom shouted, as his anger flashed. "I'll get you in the daylight. Your hides'll be nailed to the side of my barn."

Tom slapped the lines and the horses moved into a fast trot as he spoke with grim determination. "I'll teach him how to hunt and fish, and how to read a cow. I'm going to raise him right so he'll do me proud."

Grace dared not dispute Tom's dedicated notions about *his* son. A boy to run *his* ranch.

The coyotes ceased their song. The wind slid through the dry grasses. Grace worried a loose thread on her skirt with her fingernails. When Tom pulled up in front of the soddy and helped Grace down, she hoped for the warmth of encircling arms, but he had none to give. Grace knew that his affection, whatever there was of it, would now be saved for his unborn child.

In late August Grace rode with Tom down to the canyon breaks that led to the Cheyenne River. The flat prairie split and poured into slopes and valleys that stretched to the horizon. Rich green cedar and juniper trees tangled within the folds and cast colors in dramatic contrast to the tawny flatlands. Ripple upon ripple of tree-studded ridges stretched as far as the eye could see. Blue-green sage peppered the grass covered swales.

"It's tough to tell now, in the summer, but these canyons are ideal for cattle in the winter," Tom told Grace. "That north wind can blow wicked enough to freeze a cow in her tracks, but in these sheltered ravines the stock can get in among the trees and brush and enjoy more protection than the inside of a barn."

Movement caught Grace's eye and she turned to see the stiff white tails of deer flagging as they bounded away. She pointed, "Look! How beautiful."

"Goddamned deer are eating what little feed is left." Tom looked away.

Grace remained silent. She must learn to keep her thoughts to herself. She turned her eyes to swaths of sunflowers that created narrow bands of yellow draping through the trees. Chokecherries edged each canyon, their tiny red berries ripe to bursting. Grace could taste the tanginess on her tongue. She reined Mame down the slope.

"Grace?" Tom called.

"I'm going to gather chokecherries for jam." She held her breath. Her stomach tightened. She tensed in the saddle, not breathing, focusing on moving with the gait of the horse.

"All right. I'll check the cows. Be back directly." He reined his horse away.

Graced breathed again, relieved that Tom had not erupted in anger.

She followed a deer trail, studying the gnarled, sturdy trees that lined the way. Most didn't reach the height of her head. She had heard of places where trees grew so tall they blocked the sky and sun, but she was a child of the prairie. She couldn't imagine such a thing. The trees of Grace's world were short strong cedars or the ribbon of cottonwoods along a stream. The forests of the Black Hills gave the mountains soft, dark contours from afar. Even standing in the wooded areas there, a person could still see the horizon. She loved the endless expanse of the prairie right here where she could see it, steady and sure—a dependable companion.

In the middle of a thicket of chokecherries, she saw the bones of a cow. She climbed down, ground tied Mame and walked over to the jumbled shapes. Ribs lay across one another, their narrow shafts forming a pile. Grace ran her fingers along the curves, the texture smooth and fine under her fingertips. She followed the scattered remnants to the edge of mass of chokecherries where she reached down to lift the single curl of a hoof and studied it in her palm, running her eyes along the porous ridges within the whorl.

Dark red berries, warmed by the sun, clung thickly to the dense web of branches that reached Grace's waist. She pulled her skirts up between her legs and tucked the hem into her waist and took the flour sack out of the saddlebag to use as a basket. Moving slowly, and listening for the buzz of a rattlesnake she worked her way through the bushes. Tiny thorns scratched the skin on her hands as she to plucked the scarlet fruit, doing her best to ignore the thought of chiggers that might find their way to her flesh and cause her to itch without mercy.

As minutes stacked up into an hour, she felt as hot as a freshly ironed shirt. Mame neighed and stamped in the shade of a nearby tree. Grace looked up.

Tom stared down at her from atop his horse. He didn't need to tell her it was time to go. Her reverie interrupted, Grace gathered the edges of the sack and climbed the slope to where Mame waited. She stowed the wrapped berries in her saddlebag, mounted, and gave Mame her head as the mare plunged up the ridge to join Tom's gelding.

The next day Grace and Mae combined the berries they had picked. Steam billowed from the pot and filled Mae's shack with moist, heavy heat. The women dripped with sweat as they stirred the scarlet sap.

Grace took a deep breath and rushed it out. "I'm going to have a baby."

"Well, you two certainly didn't let any grass grow under your feet, now did you? Or shall I make that under your bed." Mae's eyes narrowed a bit. The smile on her mouth looked hesitant.

Grace blushed. "You'll be there, won't you? Daisy said you were just wonderful with her." Grace had walked past houses in town where women giving birth had screamed—sounds more animal than human.

"Of course. I've delivered lots of babies. Don't you worry," a slight frown creased Mae's forehead as she looked Grace up and down. "You're still more girl than woman. You've barely got more curves than one of those cedar posts in the corrals. Sometimes girls having babies too young have a hard time of it, but we'll make certain everything goes right for you."

Grace panted from the effort of stirring the heavy liquid, her cheeks flushed and eyes blinking.

"Hyah! Hyah!" echoed from outside. Mae grabbed the hefty black cauldron and set it atop a pad on the wooden kitchen table. "That sounds bad, Grace." She wiped her hands on the apron cinched around her ample waist. Casting a glance at the steaming open jars of jam already poured, Grace followed Mae through the door.

One of the Farthing boys dashed up on a horse slick with sweat, its burr-tangled mane flapping in the wind. He jerked the animal to a stop so fast it sat back down on its haunches and sawed its head against the tight rein. It struggled for breath, blowing out foam-flecked air.

"What is it?" Mae asked as she took off her apron.

"Sister. Coyote. Come!" the boy stuttered, tears streaking down. He wheeled the huge bay and slammed his heels into the horse's sides. The gelding spit sod against the shack as he lurched forward into a run.

"Grace," Mae said, "Bring the buggy. I'll get what I need."

"I'll go with you," Grace sprinted to the corral and slipped through the gate. She tied Mame's ground-dragging reins to the top rail, then haltered Mae's horse. She'd just finished throwing on the harness and was backing the animal between the shafts when Mae came huffing toward her, doctor's bag in hand.

"Tie Mame behind and ride with me," Mae said when she pulled herself onto the seat. "What can it be? First the prairie fire, now this…"

When Grace joined her, Mae ordered, "Hang on," and moved the horse into a full run toward the Farthing homestead. Grace glanced down to keep the wind from tearing her eyes and saw that she still wore her red-splattered apron.

"Leave it on," Mae said. "You might need it."

They dropped down over the hill into the hollow cradling the Farthing home, the ground and grass still charred from the fire. Children clustered around Cassie Farthing where she sat on the bloodstained ground. Grace took the lines as Mae slipped from the buggy. The children parted and moved to the side. The woman was rocking a small figure in her lap. She didn't look up.

"It's too late." Cassie lifted her head. Tears smeared the blood stuck to her cheeks The girl in her lap had been shot in the abdomen with a shotgun. Her mother held her shining entrails in place while she cradled her daughter's head against her chest. Grace set the buggy brake and wrapped the lines. She stepped down and opened her arms to the other children, who came to grab hold of her skirts. The oldest boy stood holding his heaving horse.

"What happened?" Mae asked

Cassie said nothing. She focused on trying to push her daughter's intestines back into her body, as if re-stuffing a doll.

"We were playing coyote," a boy about five said. "When Papa sees a coyote, he gets the gun down from above the door and shoots it. It was my turn to be Papa. I didn't mean to pull the trigger." The little boy shuffled his feet. "She said she wanted to be the coyote."

Grace closed her eyes as her hands moved to the curve of her belly. That was ranchers' law on the prairie. If you saw a coyote, you shot it.

"I'll never forgive my husband," Cassie hissed. "He asked me to come and help him in the field. How could I say no? It's feed for the cattle this winter. I didn't want to leave the children. They're too young. He told me I worried too much, that they needed to learn to take care'a their ownselves. I'll never forgive him."

Mae put an arm around the woman's shoulders.

"I want Elinor to have a proper Christian burial, Dr. Thingvold. I'm not just laying her in the sod without a man of God reading from the Bible." Then a guttural cry spilled forth and her shoulders heaved.

The children near Grace looked on solemnly.

Mae drew in a long breath. "Come now. Let us help you. Look at me, Cassie."

When the woman raised her crumpled face, Mae gently slipped her hands between the woman's fingers and the girl's split-open body. "I will carry her to the house now. We'll pick out her favorite dress and doll. Now, you walk ahead of me and show me where to lay her down." The woman nodded obediently. She stood as Mae gathered the child in her arms and followed. The other children filed behind.

MEADOWLARK

"Grace, please bring my bag," Mae called softly. She lowered her voice. "I'll need to bind the wound."

Inside Mae issued orders with quiet authority. She told Cassie to tend to her other children. Since the Reverend wouldn't be back in the area until the end of the week they would wrap Elinor and place her in the cool root cellar and light a lamp for her there so she wouldn't be alone in the dark.

Mae whispered to the oldest boy, "Where is your father?"

"He took off after he and ma heard the shot and came back and found Elinor dead."

"All right, then. You ride on over to your aunt's place and get her to come stay with your mother. I don't want her to be alone. Can you do that?"

The boy nodded. He went to place his hand on his mother's shoulder then walked outside. Grace watched him ride away, this time at a plodding, exhausted walk, then she helped Mrs. Farthing wash the other children's faces and hands.

Mae finished her work with Elinor and asked for clean clothes. The child looked like a worn-out rag doll with her limp arms and legs as Grace helped Mae dress her. Grace remembered the child's weight on her hip during the fire.

After wrapping her in a quilt, Mae handed the girl to her mother and they walked out into the blinding sun and across the horse-trampled yard to the root cellar where they placed Elinor amid sprouting piles of potatoes and jars of canned beef. The Farthings had no kerosene for the lamps, but Grace found a few candle stubs to light.

When the oldest boy returned with his mother's sister riding double on the dragging horse, Mae said, "We'll go now. I'll make the report in town tomorrow and ask that the Reverend come out as soon as he arrives."

Cassie nodded as she clutched her sister's hand.

Once the homestead dissolved in the dust from the buggy, Mae muttered, "Damn," and shook her head. "Just damn. All those children love stories, but Elinor loved tales about queens and fairies. Of course, they can't afford books, but I used to ask them to come over and I would put the rocking chair out front where the breeze was cool. I would spread a quilt on the grass and those children would cluster around my feet like chicks to a hen to listen to me read aloud."

"You can still do that, can't you?"

"I don't know, Grace. I don't know what will happen to them after this."

Grace watched Mae's silhouette, her normally square shoulders stooped with weariness and pain as she nudged her horse into a trot.

MEADOWLARK

7

Every morning and evening that August, Grace poured attention on her flowers. She greeted each day by watering them in the light of dawn when Tom had gone out on horseback. She watched the first glimmer of pale yellow as the sun edged the horizon, before rising to shed shafts of golden light in a great arc across the prairie as the melodic trills of the killdeers floated over the stillness. This was her time to enjoy solitude and beauty. Each day ended with the sky spreading out in a rich cornflower blue above her that lightened as the day ended then edged into a deeper shade until the stars began to appear, most often another time of respite for her.

Grace drank in the peace and quiet of that dawn like the zinnias drew in the moisture. She knew the exact contour and characteristic of each of the fledgling plants. She took enormous pride in the most minute transformations, just as she did in the changing shape and size of the child within.

She discovered a tiny green nub perched like a beetle atop the slender stalk of one of the zinnias. Dutifully, she checked on its progress daily and studied the intricate lines that curled down around the bud that would one day become a blossom. More delicate petals, still green in their infancy, beaded their layers down and around, one upon the next. Grace loved to trace the dainty edges with the tip of her finger as each new curl filled her with awe, the buds growing plumper with each passing day.

One evening, coming from the barn with a full pail heavy against her leg so she would not spill the milk, she spotted a splash of orange that lit up the flowerbed like a miniature sun. She broke into a wide grin and hurried, suddenly not caring about the sloshing that dampened her skirts.

It was all Grace could do to stay upright and not to curl up right in the dirt as she and Mae admired the blooming flowerbed.

"I am so tired all the time, Mae," Grace said. "I can't ever seem to move. I put my head down on the table to eat breakfast!"

"Oh, that's all quite normal at this time, my dear Grace. Bodes well for the babe. Quite excellent, actually."

"But, how am I supposed to get anything *done*?" Eyeing the level surface of the shaded ground and longing for a nap, Grace shook her head to stay awake.

"I have some news for *you*, Mrs. Grace Robertson," Mae announced

"So? I don't think I've ever seen you blush like that."

Mae stood smiling with sudden shyness and nudged a dirt clod daintily with the toe of her boot.

"Does this news, by any chance, have anything to do with Ike Thompson?" Grace prompted.

"Tom told you!" Mae peered at Grace out of the corner of her eye, her lips pursed in an impish grin.

Grace shook her head. "Tom never tells me anything. I'm making a guess."

Like a down pillow burst apart, sending a shower of feathers into the air, Mae exploded with excitement. "He asked me to marry him. Yesterday evening. He came to supper. As soon as he finished the last bite of pie he said, fast as he could, 'Miss Mae Thingvold, I want to spend the rest of my life with you. Will you do me the honor of being my wife?' He said it so fast and gave me such a surprise, I dropped my fork onto my plate and splattered roast beef juice all over my good white blouse." Mae threw her hands open wide. "You know how that stains! He picked up my napkin, dipped it in water, and went to work on the juice!"

"He *didn't*!" Grace covered her mouth in surprise.

"He most certainly did. When he realized what he was doing, he blushed like a schoolboy, then started apologizing all over himself. Oh, he was a mess! I've never seen a man turn such a bright red. I started giggling couldn't stop. Then he let out a little chuckle and then we were both laughing so hard neither one of us could say a word." Mae was momentarily lost in the memory.

Grace stomped her foot impatiently, hands on her hips, and declared, "And? How did you answer his question?"

"I told him, 'Why Ike Thompson, considering that you've already touched the goods, I do believe it would be best if we were officially engaged!'

"He picked me up and twirled me around in a circle—and you know that's no easy feat. He said, 'Does that mean, yes? And I said, 'Absolutely!'"

Grace threw her arms around Mae in a tight hug. "I will do the cooking, of course, and…"

"Grace!" Mae interrupted.

"What?" Grace said surprised.

"Do you know what I really want from you?"

Grace shook her head.

"A proper bride's bouquet. Could you make one from some of your zinnias? Just a few."

Grace looked at the pageant of color weaving a ribbon at their feet. "Of course. We'll pick them that morning at their peak of fullness. When? When do you want your wedding?"

"Neither of us wants to wait. Sooner would be better than later. The Reverend comes through next Saturday. Ike is riding into town today to arrange that. Do you think it will be too difficult to put everything together so quickly?"

"Not in the least."

"Oh, good. But I need your help with something else in the meantime."

"What's that?"

"Grace, I can read books in four languages, but I don't know how to milk a cow or butcher a chicken. I don't know how to properly clean a floor, nor how to can beef and vegetables. I never cared about any of this before. But now that I'm going to get married—well, I can't bear for Ike to know what a poor housewife I'll be!" Mae stood with her hands on her head trying to gather the hair that had escaped from the haphazardly placed pins.

"Oh, don't be foolish! You're bold, smart, and brave. I can teach you the rest. There's no need for you to learn to milk right away. We have more than enough milk. Ask Ike to build you a coop and we'll get you some chickens."

"Wonderful! There is something else though."

"What?"

Mae hesitated. "Two nights ago I was sure somebody was trying to get inside my shack."

Grace turned from pulling a weed, an anxiety gnawing in the pit of her stomach. "What? What happened, Mae?"

"I woke up because somebody was rattling the latch. I've never been so scared in my whole life. I sat up in bed. I hollered, "I've got a shotgun aimed right at you. I'm a doctor and I assure you I know exactly where your heart is!"

"And?"

"The rattling ceased and moved around to right below the window. Grace, I was sure I was going to see someone come right through it. Then the noise moved back to the door again and I gathered all my courage, and crept out of bed. I was so scared my legs were shaking and I don't know how I managed to move. When I reached the window, I drew back the curtain and peeked out."

"Who was it, Mae? Who was there?"

"It was Tom, Grace. I thought at first he needed my help, but then I realized by his movements that he...well it was clear he'd had more than enough to drink. He barely made it back on his horse."

Grace shook her head. The circle of the sun spun before her eyes. Mae caught her as she fell.

MEADOWLARK

Grace winced as she returned to consciousness. The ground felt oddly cool beneath her but not soothing. Mae stood over her holding a wet cloth to her forehead.

"I'm sorry, Grace. I should have found another way to tell you."

"No, I'm the one who's sorry. Sorry that my husband would be the one to…to…"

"Don't even think that. He may have only wanted someone to talk to, some company."

"Mae, thank you for not shooting him."

"That's just it, Grace. I don't actually have a shotgun. I don't own a firearm of any kind. I don't know how to shoot. That's the other thing I want you to do. Can you teach me how? It's something I should have learned a long time ago, but I have never had the chance or the need until now."

Grace sat up. "Help me to my feet."

Once steady on her legs again, Grace said, "Stay right here."

She returned with her rifle into which she levered a shell. She pulled the stock into her shoulder and leaned her cheek inward to sight down the barrel. With the slow pull of her trigger finger, she squeezed off a shot that exploded a grass tassel fifty yards away. The horses in the corral leapt from snoozing to wary attention. Grace eased sideways, chose another target, and repeated the process.

"Okay, your turn now, Mae. Come here."

The horses eased and settled in a cluster as far back from the noise as they could get. Still, the firing went on, one bullet at a time, until Mae had captured the rudimentary skills of loading, aiming and shooting. Drenched in sweat, Mae followed Grace inside and watched her put the rifle back into the trunk at the foot of the bed.

"And now, I even hate to ask, but this is the most important question of all," Mae said. "What do I need to know?"

"About what?"

"About you and Tom. If you tell me, I'll keep it to myself. If you don't, all I will do is worry myself sick about you. I've asked Daisy, but she refuses to say a word."

"Well, I'm so new to this myself. I've only been married a few months. What I can tell you is, well, sometimes I feel like I'm married to two different men." Grace faltered. "And I don't know yet which of those men is really Tom." Grace shrugged her shoulders and gave a small smile. "I don't know if all men are like that. Mostly, Mae, there's just an awful lot about it all that I don't understand. That's what I know about my marriage right now."

"I'll keep that in mind, Grace." The unspoken questions hung in the air. As if sensing something very fragile between them might break if those words were spoken, Mae asked, "So, what else, Grace, will I need to know to be a true woman of the prairies?"

Grace breathed a sigh of relief to be back in safe territory. She bought out a large glass jug filled with liquid.

"If there is one thing that every prairie woman must have, Mae, it is Lewis lye soap. You take this and scrub your floor with it and it will shine with splendor. You'll never have to worry about having Ike's boot marks on the floor."

Grace looked at her floor and started to laugh. It was fitting. Her floor was dirt. Tom left a boot print wherever he went. He left his mark on everyone and everything. No doubt about it. People noticed when Tom showed up and they noticed when he left.

The rest of the week flew by as Mae, Grace, and women throughout the area baked, cooked, and readied for the wedding. At the week's end, Mae Thingvold and Ike Thompson became husband and wife in front of friends and neighbors.

The bride and groom wore chokecherry-stained shirts for the ceremony.

MEADOWLARK

8

Tom came in the next evening carrying his saddle and dropped it to the floor. His face was chiseled with worry and fatigue, the lines carved by squinting at the sun splayed out around his eyes and stroked downward alongside his mouth. He took off his hat, rubbed his forearm across his brow and smeared fine silt into a dark streak. The salt-edged stains of dried sweat stiffened his shirt against his ribs.

"There's no damn water for the herd. We're almost to the end of August and still no summer rain." He slumped into a chair. "If it doesn't rain I'm going to have to move these cows or sell them."

Grace almost pitied him, but pity was quickly replaced by dark memories. She cupped her belly protectively.

Two pieces of white cotton fabric with the outline of a tiny frock were spread across the kitchen table. She took the straight pins from between her teeth and dropped them into a saucer. The faint plinking sound pricked the stillness. Tom picked up a rumpled cloth slung over a rusting tin.

"I had an odd experience with the Azarov brothers." Tom rubbed the oily rag into the sun-baked leather of the saddle's skirt and fenders.

"Who?" Grace asked.

"You know…the Mennonites who moved here a few years ago. They study the stars for weather. Their people back in Russia did that—they think they can predict the weather. They're saying that the planets are nearing a certain Jupiter disorder."

Grace stopped her cutting the outlines of the garment. "A *what?*"

"That's exactly what I said. The Azarovs explained that Jupiter revolves around the sun only one time for every twelve times the Earth does. Their ancestors noticed that when Jupiter was between the sun and some star—whose name I can't even pronounce, much less remember—it was a year of good moisture. But, when the stars are as they are now, heat and dryness follow," Tom moved his working hand in cadence with his speech.

His arm stopped in mid-stroke and he looked up at Grace. She froze, fearing that she would say or do something wrong. But he stayed in the chair.

He said, "This heat and dryness is something I've never seen. I don't have a good feeling about this. Not at all. Ike said he rode over to Philip for supplies last week and there was a line of wagons a mile long of people leaving the country."

Tom stared at the darkening window. "Well, this drought will get rid of those damn homesteaders. This land can't be farmed. It's too hard, too lean for plowing. The sooner those fools figure that out, the better it'll be for the rest of us."

He stood so abruptly that his chair tipped over. He didn't bother to right it before he threw the rag on the floor, shoved his hat on his head, and stomped out. The suffocating wind blew in through the door he didn't bother to close.

The alignment of the stars spoke the truth to the Azarov brothers of South Dakota, just as they had on brutal steppes of Russia. The dried plains split open and deep cracks wrinkled the earth. The wind leached moisture from ground so desiccated it had nothing left to offer. The cattle lowed listlessly searching for feed and water. Tom constantly checked for cows caught in creek bed mud and pulled them out with a rope around their thin necks. Everyone wore strained expressions. They talked of nothing but the drought. Tempers ran as hot as the wind. Women snapped at children over nothing and men rubbed chapped hands over dirt-lined faces.

Grace opened an old coffee tin where she kept a little money hidden from Tom. She found only a few coins. What would her mother, who took such pride in setting a beautiful table, say if she knew of the families Mae tended, who were reduced to picking new-sprouted Russian thistles and steaming them for supper, eating what not even the cows wouldn't touch. They made a pudding by grinding rationed wheat and then cooked it with water, and had survived solely on mush and skinny rabbits.

Grace wandered the prairie under the beastly sun and searched for anything she could burn to heat the oven and stove. Cow patties were all that remained and the soddy reeked with the smell.

Her normal exuberance exhausted, Mae stopped by to see Grace on her way home from her rounds. She parked her buggy in the shade but didn't climb down.

"What's going to happen?" Mae asked, pushing sweaty hair back from her forehead. "I used to have forty-nine homesteads on my route. I passed all of them this week and only one still has anybody living there. The rest are abandoned, left to the elements and animals."

Grace offered her a dipper of water. Mae took a series of hasty gulps. "Thank you. Come on over tomorrow, won't you, Grace? Let's visit to brighten our spirits."

"I will," Grace said. "Tell Ike hello."

The two women sat in the shade of Mae's home, swatting flies with a folded newspaper Ike had brought back from town. In the early light, the cut flowers Grace had brought for Mae shone bright against the muted shades of the earth. They shimmered with life and color in the lustrous jar Mae used for a vase.

"So *then* Ike says," Mae continued, "'But darlin,' if we're gonna be all hot and sweaty, we might as well be *really* hot and sweaty.'"

Grace gasped and laughed. "He didn't!"

"The man is scandalous, I tell you." Mae fanned herself with the newspaper, swaying back and forth in her rocker with a contented smile teasing her lips. "Absolutely scandalous."

"I'm so happy for you. Really I am." Grace stared down at the slight mound under her skirt.

"Things any better between you and Tom?"

"About the same. I'm all right, Mae."

"I wish it were different for you. How's Tom, Jr. doing?"

Grace stroked her belly and said, "Fine. Only I refuse to let him be called Tom."

Grace hummed on her return ride. The time with Mae had eased her heart and given her a sense of peace.

Despite the drought, life went on. She and Tom would figure things out. Once the baby arrived, he would settle into being a good husband and a kind father. Grace pulled Mame up at the round corral, and dismounted to open the gate. She walked Mame through and tossed the reins over the hitching post near the barn.

Uncinching the saddle, Grace pulled it and the blanket off Mame's back, and with difficulty she carried them to a rack in the barn's darkness. Warm and moist with Mame's sweat, the blanket exuded a rich horse smell. Grace inhaled deeply.

Still humming, she brushed the mare, following the direction of her hair with the coarse bristles. Mame leaned into pressure, expelling great sighs that could only be moans of pleasure.

"You like that, don't you?" Grace chattered to Mame as she knew she would to her child: "What shall we have for supper? The last of the canned meat and half-spoiled potatoes? Wish I had something to make a pie for Tom. Wouldn't that be nice?"

Grace slipped the bridle off Mame's head and scratched the ribbon of sweaty hair where the throatlatch had rubbed. Mame shook her head and dropped down in the dirt. Grace laughed as she watched Mame's legs pump the air.

"Come on! You can do it, girl. There you go!" She cheered as Mame managed the complete roll then stood and shook herself with glee.

MEADOWLARK

Grace walked toward the soddy, rubbing the slight pull in her belly, wondering which zinnias she would clip for the supper table. Maybe the royal purple or the creamy white. She leaned into the slight incline, her eyes searching for the welcoming spots of color at the door. The humming died in her throat.

Trampled flowers littered the ground, their withered roots exposed. Numbness spread from her feet up to her knees. She sank down, taking in the crushed petals and broken stems.

Tom opened the door. He swayed above her, the rank smell of alcohol poisoning the evening.

"Goddamn it! We got cattle dying of thirst and you waste good water on them damn flowers." He swayed and fell heavily against the doorframe. He stared, his eyes unfocused and bloodshot, daring her to say something. She knew better. She kept her eyes on the earth.

Tom pushed himself upright, unsteady on his feet. "I'm hungry. You best get in here and fix something for me to eat." He lurched inside, leaving the door open.

Grace surveyed the destruction. There was nothing to save. All had been trampled, shredded, crumpled and left to shrivel in the sun.

"Grace!" Tom slurred sharply.

She forced herself to rise. Her tearing eyes caught the wilted form of a bloom she had let go to seed laying off by itself. She stopped mid-step to glance at the dark door and said, "I'm coming." The stem was broken, but the head full of seeds remained whole. With care she picked it up and slipped it into the pocket of her skirt.

When Tom left the following morning, Grace eased the swollen flower head onto the kitchen table. She tenderly extracted every seed, spread them out, and counted. Twenty-four. Grace found the tea tin on the shelf. She pried off the lid and reached two fingers down until she felt the precious pouch made from her mother's dress. She pulled open the ribbon and with infinite care deposited the new seeds in with the ten seeds she'd held back.

"Thirty-four," she whispered. With shaking fingers, she drew the ribbon tight again and tied a clumsy bow, holding the pouch in her hand a moment more, then returned it to its hiding place. Tom was miles away, riding the cows, but caution had become second nature.

Grace scooped the pile of dried petals off the table, went outside outside and threw them high, watching as the wind scattered them, shards of faded color across the yellow ochre of the prairie. Steeling herself against all feelings, she took up her broom and swept the jagged slivers of pink, orange, yellow, red, purple, and white in the ruined flowerbed into a neat pile. She grabbed handful after handful and carried them away and tossed them to the wind until the pile was gone and there was nothing left but broken earth swept clean.

Despondent, Grace went in search of the prairie roses she had seen at the beginning of the summer. Their pink petals stood out against the dry landscape. She marveled at their resilience, their ability to bloom amidst the harshest conditions. How might she protect them from Tom? If he saw these, would he want to destroy them, too? Was there anything safe from his need to hurt and wound because he couldn't heal himself of his own pain?

The wind rustled across the grass and kicked up puffs of dirt where the ground lay bare. The song of a meadowlark glided through the air, soothing Grace's wounded heart. The song held her motionless. She waited, listening again for the lilting melody. Again the trill came, twisting and turning as it skimmed the still air. Grace cocked her head, focusing on bird's call. She turned her head slowly, following the trail of notes skipping across the winds.

"Pip?"

There, poised on the tip of one of the branches of the roses, a meadowlark.

MEADOWLARK

9

Grace stood washing the supper dishes in the tin tub set on top of the stove, steam rising hazily from the water, catching the dusky light of early fall streaming in through the window. They ate late in the evening, taking full advantage of the light before the short days of winter arrived.

"There's no feed for the cattle," Tom said. "I'm going to have to move them until this drought lets up."

Grace straightened her back and stretched the stiffness from her spine. "But, there hasn't been rain anywhere. Where can you take them?"

"Old Irish Tommy said that there's feed yet down near the Badlands." Tom tapped tobacco into a carved wooden pipe. He struck the match on the table and the tobacco flamed and glowed as he puffed until satisfied it was well lit.

"I'll drive the herd there and hold them until we get some rain."

"The Badlands? Isn't that all rocks and cliffs."

"Plenty of that, but there's good grass, too. I'll hire some boys to help me drive the herd next week. Ike'll come. No time to waste. If I wait any longer they won't be strong enough to make the trip. I'll start losing them."

Grace looked into the soapy water. *I want to go. I want to see the Badlands, too.* She'd heard stories of the cliffs and spires that composed a surreal landscape. Desire and longing tightened her throat.

Tom would never let her go. Women never went along on cattle drives. Never. Women were meant to stay home to cook, clean, do laundry, and raise children.

"No mares and no women around the cattle." How many times had she heard that? When she'd asked why, the answer had been that women and mares were a distraction, that men and geldings don't pay attention to their work when females are around.

Grace's hands shook as she dried the plates and placed them back in the cupboard. She wanted to get out of that sod hut and off that ranch. She wanted to see something she'd never seen before.

In the short time she'd been married, she discovered that Tom's reputation meant everything to him. When other people were around, Tom became the man he was before they married, the man she'd thought she *was* marrying. With others close by he was attentive and kind to her, impressing the ladies with his charming manner and the courteous way he coveted his wife.

Women whispered words laced with jealousy to her, "Oh, that Tom Robertson. How he loves you, Grace… My, what a lucky girl you are, Grace, to have such a fine man for a husband."

Grace did her best to offer a wooden smile, even as her stomach churned. She saw the desire in other women's eyes when they looked at Tom, how they watched him with hunger and admiration. If men were around, Tom boasted and bragged about Grace to the point of embarrassment. He wanted those men to envy him, to want what he had. When they were around others, Tom couldn't risk being rude to her, or lay a hand on her. She knew he wouldn't dare to damage his sterling reputation with bad behavior in front of other people.

"Tom, I want to come, too." She startled herself by speaking her thoughts aloud.

MEADOWLARK

"What? You can't be serious. Hell no! You're expecting a child, for God's sake. What are you thinking? That's idiot talk. Jesus Christ Almighty!" He shook his head in disgust.

"The baby's barely even showing yet. No one will know. I've only told Mae and Ike won't say anything if she asks him not to. I'll cook for the men. You know I can."

"Forget it. Dave Olsen would shoot me if I didn't ask him along. He's cooked for me every time I ever trailed cattle. Besides, the cowboys are used to him."

"I'll stay away from Dave and the men. I promise. Mame and I won't get in the way."

"No goddamned mare! Bring some bitch-horse in heat around all those geldings? Every man I lined up would turn his mount around and quit. Not a one would go."

"I won't ride Mame, then," Gracie said. "I'll take whatever gelding you give me. Please, Tom."

Something flickered in Tom's eyes. A flash of something that might have passed for sympathy, were it not coated in a frosty layer of calculation. She held her breath.

"Why is this so important to you?" he asked.

Grace screwed up her courage and lied. "I just want to be with you, that's all. Is that so unnatural?"

Tom set down his pipe and scratched the back of his head. "All right. You ride old Blue. I'll tell the boys you're coming along to keep an eye on me." He laughed and hitched up his pants. "They'll understand that!"

Grace exhaled, and for the first time in many days, smiled. She'd puffed up Tom's ego and it had worked.

As he tugged off his boots Tom said, "You better make sure Mae will take care of your mare, the chickens and that milk cow, while you're gone."

"Yes, Tom. I will."

"And hurry up with those dishes. It's time for bed."

Grace quietly went to work.

On the day of the drive, Tom rose at 3:30 a.m. to move the cows in the stillness of the morning. Grace tied her little bundle of

99

clothing behind her saddle. The yips and whistles of the cowboys glided through the darkness and the ghost-like forms of five hundred head of cattle surged. Blue's ears twitched forward, his eyes and stance alert. Grace held tight to the reins and murmured low, familiar sounds to soothe the gelding. The gentle thud of hooves punctuated occasional bawls mingled with the men's calls. Dave sat in the chuckwagon. Tom's horse snorted and gave a low whinny. Blue nickered his reply.

Mame raced around the circle of the corral, pawing at the fence poles as Grace rode past.

"Sorry I can't bring you, girl," she said. "Mae will be by to get you."

The sun cracked the horizon wide-open as they moved across the final plateau above the river. The flatland gave way to the yawning crevasse that cradled the mighty Cheyenne. Light filtered down on a ribbon of cottonwoods, their leaves edged with the gold of early fall, flushing out from the water's edge. The slope angled sharply down into a wide stream running the center of the dry bed, and ascended steeply up the other side. Small cedars dotted the ridges, pinpricks of ruddy green against the yellows and tans of the grasses.

"Here we go!" Tom called out, "Take it slow and easy. No need to get them worked up. The water's so low in this drought, we can cross. Looks like it may be deep through the middle, though. Ike, cross first and lead them. Grace bring up the drag."

Grace moved Blue aside as the cattle shoved past. Ike spurred out in front, his white shirt stark against the muddy brown water. He turned in the saddle to make sure the herd followed. Cottonwoods swayed in the breeze, the pale underbellies of their leaves catching the light. As Ike urged his horse into the current, his gelding's tail lifted and swirled out behind its back legs. The first cows balked at the edge of the water.

"Hup!" The flank riders called. Far to the rear, Grace waved her arm over her head. "Come on, now. Hup!"

Ike made it to mid-river, the water up over his thighs as his horse forded through. The first cow made a wild leap, landing with a splash, and swam, her head bobbing. The other cattle leapt after her. An orange and white sash of animals moved through the murky water, churning it to a froth. Ike's gelding hit solid ground and lurched up the other side.

MEADOWLARK

"Grace!" Tom called, "Push them on now!"

Blue shied, unsure and skittish, at the muddy bank.

"Come on. You can do it. Let's get it over with."

She gigged him with her heels and he leaned back on his haunches, gathered his strength and flew into the water. Grace barely had time to grab the horn as the current tried to wash her from the saddle. As water seeped into his flaring nostrils, Blue snorted repeatedly. Grace's heavy skirt swirled up on either side of him like little wings.

They rode through ground-hugging buffalo grass that twisted patterns beneath the trees and the yucca pointing needle-sharp stalks toward the sun. Mounded clouds piled together in the sky, the edges of their flat underbellies glowing, row after row, growing smaller and smaller until they faded into a hazy white gauze on the horizon. Grace stared at cliffs jutting out of the earth like sheaves. Odd shelved plateaus rose abruptly from the flatness, sharp as broken glass. Horizontal bands of white and red ringed the ragged bluffs. In places the exposed hardpan chipped beneath the pressure of heavy hooves.

From the tops of canyons, they dropped into the undergrowth of juniper with violet berries clustered in bunches on the branches. The cooling air brought relief from the glare. Fallen boulders pocked the ground where spry tufts of grass poked between rocks dotted with rust-colored lichen. Circular mounds of earth appeared like poured pancake batter, baked and hardened. At the base of a gnarled juniper, Grace spotted five deer bedded down, with a sixth browsing lazily before easing herself to the ground to join the rest. The white hair on her rump shone as bright as a flag of surrender.

That first night on the trail Grace learned there was an invisible circle fifty feet wide around the chuckwagon, and in that space Dave reigned as king. Tom had talked about cooks who raised holy terror if anybody entered their domain, capable not only of cussing out the cowboys, but the trail boss, as well. She could not imagine small, slight Dave doing such a thing. He seemed a gentle soul and the rough-bunch cowboys responded to him with respect.

Dave served beans, beef, and a round, thin flatbread called a *tortilla* that he'd learned to make on a cattle drive down to Mexico.

The men, not knowing what to do with the things, held them up with confused looks. Dave patiently showed them how to place the beans and beef inside, fold up the ends and then roll it.

"I got enough things to worry about trying to keep the herd together without having to figure out how in the hell to eat my goddamned..." Ike's eyes shifted to Grace, "Excuse me, ma'am, my gol-darned supper!"

Grace liked the lightness of the tortillas but she saw Tom fling his out onto the prairie.

Dave saw it, too, and he winked at her, eyes twinkling. "Don't worry, boys," he said, "I'll have biscuits for you come morning."

As the herd bedded down for the night, deep rolls of thunder bellowed up from the south. The cowboys murmured over their coffee. "God Almighty how I hate to be on top of a horse when there's a storm brewing," Ike said. "Nothing draws lightning like a hot, sweaty horse between your legs. Now there's a thought to make a man pucker."

Spidery webs of light crinkled across the deep purple sky, punctuated by a booming clap.

"Saddle up again, boys," Tom said still chewing the last of his beef. "Let's be ready. Ike, go tell those nightriders to keep them still."

The men moved toward the horses picketed on a line next to the cook wagon.

"You stay put," Tom said, walking past Grace. "Don't get in the way."

Dave looked away at the tone in Tom's voice and busied himself gathering the plates and cooking utensils for washing. Grace strolled over to where Blue stood, his mane lifted up at the roots, each hair electric. She watched Tom ride off.

The night came alive, veins of lightning bristling through the sky and thunder booming out its response. Wind whipped around Grace. In the darkness, she stared in wonder at the tips of Blue's ears, which glowed as if lit from within. She watched them dance in the dark, flitting nervously back and forth. Looking out over the herd, Grace could see those same glowing balls of light on the tips of their horns, hundreds of them, a festival of living light in the darkness.

The cattle shifted and started. The next flash of lightning illuminated their eyes, wide and glassy with fear, and outlined shapes of the cowboys surrounding the herd. The hair on her neck and arms stood stiff in air full of electricity.

MEADOWLARK

A strike of lightning lit up the sky followed by a crack of thunder that pulsated waves of needle pricks through Grace's body. Blue stood glued to the ground as Grace mounted and then busted loose. Blue reared, spun, and catapulted, ripping one rein from Grace's hands as he plunged, headlong, into the eerie night. Sights and sounds blurred together. Blue laid his ears flat against his head and stretched his neck low as he galloped. Grace scrambled to stay in the saddle and reached for the loose rein. God help her and the baby if Blue stepped in a prairie dog hole or hit a ravine. Clutching the saddlehorn, she stretched out and grabbed. Catching it, she pulled back slow and hard.

"Whoa! Whoa now!" Blue took the bit in his teeth and charged on.

Grace couldn't see. She couldn't hear. She leaned far forward in the saddle and grabbed the right rein at the bit and yanked back, pulling Blue's nose toward her knee. She prayed he would turn. Step by step he slowed. They ran in tighter and tighter circles until at last he stopped, his steaming body shaking.

Grace made her way back to the camp. She arrived at the same time that Ike limped in.

"Damned bronc threw me," he said to Dave.

"Need doctoring?" Dave asked.

"No, but I could use a gulp of that red-eye." Ike turned to see Grace sitting there on Blue. "Ma'am," he said, calm as a father with a boy, "you might want to get down from there before your husband gets back."

"Is everyone else all right?" Grace asked.

"The boys have kept the cattle calmed down. I hope to hell my horse stays with them."

Grace tethered and unsaddled Blue. She made her way to the bedroll Tom had laid out for her farthest from camp. She crawled inside and lay her hands across her abdomen.

"Thank you, God," she whispered to the storm-swirled stars. "Thank you for keeping my baby safe."

The next day when they stopped for their noon meal, Grace pulled the journal her mother had given her from her saddlebag and walked deep into the brush under a pale silver sky. She wanted to capture what had happened to her.

She closed her eyes and recalled the scent of wet ground, of horse sweat, the sound of nervous bawling cows and calves filling her ears. She saw the lightning and felt Blue's sides heaving between her legs. Recounting the incident led her deeper into herself as she wrote:

> How does one capture the sky above the plains, the feel of the air upon the skin, and play of light and dark upon the prairie? It feels impossible to capture the nuances, the subtleties, the violent colors.
>
> I see myself reflected as in a pane of glass, with a drape of darkness on the other side. A jumble of memories about Paul tumble within, fleeting images, each bumped by the next before it can settle—all with the rawness of the land as a central feature. The deep yellow moon that glows from a rich twilight sky, the indigo blue of lush morning glories. The sound of the meadowlarks piercing the still morning air with a tender sweetness. The muck and gumbo mud during the last rains. The snow driving sideways in the fury of the winter winds.
>
> The beauty. The bitterness. Not a land of mediocrity, but of stunning beauty and brute force. Any living thing that can't survive and appreciate both, will find little to love or live for on the plains.

MEADOWLARK

10

Tom sent Grace home with Ike after they found good fall pasture for the cows. Before they left, Tom shoved a roll of bills into her hands and said, "Here's money for supplies. Goddamn but life costs a lot. Don't buy anything we don't need." He shook his head, showing that he begrudged her the money, acting like he was indulging her, rather than seeing the funds as a necessary part of daily existence. She hated the feeling. She hated even more the look of concentrated neutrality on Ike's face when he helped her onto Blue. Pity skittered fleetingly across his brow.

Sensing the disapproval in the air, Tom said, "It's not that I don't want to come back with you. I can't. I've got to stay here with these cows. They are our livelihood. Our son's future. You know that, don't you?"

Grace nodded, but kept her thoughts to herself. She preferred to remain silent rather than give him the satisfaction of scolding her like a misbehaving child in need of condescending correction.

Ike kept a lively pace on their way home. Grace understood that he was anxious to get back to Mae and his own life. He did his best to make entertaining conversation to shorten the trip for them both. At night when they camped, Ike staked the horses and brought water while she cooked a spare supper. They slept on opposite sides of the small fire, which held the bite of cold fall nights at bay.

When they rode the final miles up to the soddy, he said, "Whoohee, I'll be glad to see my Mae." He waited until she dismounted by the corral, then he tipped his hat and said, "If you don't need anything, then I'll be going," and set off at a gallop.

"Say hello to Mae. Tell her I'll come for Mame and the cow tomorrow," she called after him.

The next morning, Ike was there with the animals. He turned them into the corral and came to the door with his hat in his hand. "Mae said to tell you hello and she'll come visit soon. She's been right busy with patients. She's working too hard for a woman in her condition..." Ike's voice trailed off.

"A woman in her condition, Ike?"

"Oh, don't tell her I told you," Ike stammered and blushed. "She made me promise not to, so she could tell you herself. I just plumb forgot in the moment."

"Well, that's wonderful news! Two new babies on the prairie! And don't worry, Ike, I'll be as surprised as ever when Mae tells me."

By mid-September, Grace's desire to hear another human voice became a constant ache, and her own was the only one there. In her loneliness she felt spirits visit her, voices that whispered the redemptive gifts of the written word. She turned to her journal for comfort, writing more and more through the long, dismal hours she spent holed up in the dark house after she'd fed the animals and milked the cow.

She longed for a trip to town, to see and hear other people. Instead, she wrote about the weather and the animals. She wrote about Mame and Blue's antics, or the milk cow's ailments. She wrote about Paul. She wrote about her fears and her dreams. Scribbling her thoughts kept her from going crazy because it reminded her that she was a thinking, breathing, living being.

MEADOWLARK

In the barn she found a rusted can thrown in the corner. Tom had probably saved it to use for storing nails or scooping grain. Though she was alone with no one to see, she clutched the tin close to her skirts like a schoolgirl hiding a stolen apple. The cold, acrid sweat of fear seeped under her arms and soaked her blouse.

Once inside, she blew out the dust and wiped a few dead spiders from the bottom. It was just big enough to hold her journal and small enough to hide with ease. With everything she'd written, she couldn't risk Tom finding it and discovering what was in her heart.

She sat at the table, savoring a few moments to read one of her mother's novels, a cup of coffee steaming before her. The bottom of the book rested on top of her belly. She felt a movement and the book bobbed up and down. Just once. One tiny arm or leg had stretched up just enough to let Grace know there was somebody there. She set her book aside and smiled. She wasn't as alone as she'd thought.

"Well, hello there little one." Grace placed her hand on the sensitive spot and the baby reached out once more to give her a gentle poke on her palm. Tenderness swept through her.

Every day proved a new exploration of the ever-changing landscape of her body. She was five months along in her pregnancy, and when she took off her nightgown in the morning, she spooned her hand over the roundness of her abdomen and gently rubbed the spot with the tips of her fingers and tried to discern what limb of her child's it might be, feeling for the bump of a miniature foot or hand. Her breasts grew tender. She marveled at the faint web of veins slowly becoming visible, little rivers that wound their way under her delicate, milky skin. Cupping them in her hands eased the soreness, leaving her in wonder at their increasing size and weight.

Grace knelt over the trunk at the foot of the bed. She set aside the rifle, lifted her neatly wrapped and folded wedding dress, and drew out a large envelope filled with letters from her mother and newspaper clippings. Just then, she heard a horse draw up outside the soddy, and she quickly she tossed the things back in the trunk and secured the lid.

She looked out the window, her heart thumping. Mottled snow flecked the bald winter landscape pressed by a leaden sky. A few bunches of dead grass poked up from the barren surface and jerked roughly in the wind. The cold bit through the frosted glass and chilled Grace's cheek when she pressed her face to it. Seeing nothing, she walked to the door to peek out. A slight figure dismounting. Not Tom. Daisy!

Relieved, Grace called over the cold November wind, "It's freezing. Come inside!"

Bundled in a heavy coat and clutching a trade blanket, Daisy stumbled through the door, a smile on her face, but her eyes solemn. She peeled off the blanket and opened her coat to reveal a baby tied to her chest. Black-brown eyes set in a round face gazed up at Grace from under a thatch of obsidian hair that stuck straight out like little thistles all over her head.

"Ruth," Daisy said simply. The baby's chubby arms escaped the cloth that held her to her mother. She waved them in greeting.

"I heard from Mae you were here alone again, *Zintkala Opi*. Look at what I'm making for your baby." Daisy drew a tiny pair of moccasins out of her worn pouch. Rows of beads sparkled across the tops of soft doeskin.

"How did you know?" Grace smoothed her blouse over her rounded belly. "I haven't seen you in months."

"I knew it wouldn't be long," Daisy said.

"Let me start the water. Sit down."

Grace filled the coffee pot and stoked the stove. Daisy set small bottles of glittering beads in a neat row along the table. She poured a set amount into a tiny lid, dipped in her needle and began to stitch as Ruth nestled on her lap.

"My grandmother told me the story of how she was to marry another man. His name was Black Thunder. He left to war against the *Wasicu* one time and came back injured. As he lay dying, he asked his friend, Lone Eagle, to marry my grandmother and take care of her. Lone Eagle agreed. Black Thunder died. My grandmother cut her hair." Daisy set down the needle to take a sip of the tea that Grace handed her.

Grace leaned over to tickle Ruth's belly. The girl giggled and turned her face away, into her mother's chest.

"Not long after that my grandmother was out gathering herbs and a Brulé man stole her and took her back to his own *tiospaye*. She had a child, a baby girl. Then that man died. The others allowed her to return to her own people. When she came home, Lone Eagle fulfilled his promise and married her. Their daughter was my mother."

The cedar popped and sizzled in the woodstove.

"You white women all live so far apart. You're so alone, like grass seed thrown up into the wind and scattered." Daisy rose to lay Ruth on a blanket on the bed.

Grace pulled her chair close to the stove and lifted a pale blue baby's sleeping gown from the basket. She began to stitch one of the sleeves as Daisy again took up her beading.

"My grandmother told me how in the days before the *Wasicu*, they moved to follow the buffalo between winter and summer camps. When the people moved, they stopped four times each day. The fourth stop was always the final stop. My grandmother called us the Female Buffalo People. We depended on the buffalo for everything.

"In April, which my grandmother called *pejitowi*, or 'Moon of the Tender Grass,' when the young buffalo calves are born, the circle of life on the plains began."

Daisy studied the pattern of her colors then chose a different shade of red. She looked up at Grace for approval and Grace nodded.

"In October, or 'Moon of the Falling Leaves,' the great hunts happened. The calves were mature and the people began to gather things for the winter. After a successful hunt, the men came home singing the Buffalo Song and the women joined in. The women claimed their husbands' kill, according to the arrows' shaft decorations. The skin belonged to the woman of the man who killed the animal, the tongue, kidney, and liver all belonged to her to serve raw as delicacies to her husband, and the brains she used to tan the hide. But the meat belonged to all the people.

"They moved in *thiyospaye*, in family groups. They moved together like the buffalo. People need an order, a structure to their lives. Without that, they are lost."

"Where did you learn to sew so fine, Daisy?"

Daisy gave a harsh laugh. "Flandreau Boarding School for Indians. Have you heard of it?"

"I've heard the name before."

Daisy forgot the beadwork in her hands. "It smelled like floor varnish. That's the first thing I remember. They took me away when I was thirteen years old, 'to learn a trade.' My father thought it would be good for me to learn the white man's world. I spoke Lakota with my mother and French with my father. I understood only a few words in English."

"That must have been hard for you."

"I didn't want to go. My mother didn't want me to go. She begged my father to let me stay home. She worried about me because I was a 'breed'—my mother Lakota and my father White. She knew I would not be treated fairly.

"My mother finally agreed. She told me to be brave. To do what I was told. To learn as much as I could.

"I learned, alright. I learned about the holes in the roof and walls that let the cold fall wind blow into the room, and the beds were lined up, one next to the other, so close they touched—like this," Daisy held up her hands and pressed them close together, her arms shaking with the pressure.

"The matron gave me a *Wasicu* dress to put on. I shook my head. She pushed the dress into my hands. I didn't understand the words that poured like hot oil from her mouth, sounds like hissing and crackling of fire burning wood." Daisy wrinkled her nose and mouth.

"I wore my finest dress that my mother had spent a whole winter beading as she told me the stories from my grandmother that I'm telling you now. With each bead there was a blessing. That school lady made me take it off. She held it away from her body with pinched fingers. She told me it smelled bad."

At the vehement tone in Daisy's voice, Ruth fussed and squirmed. Daisy picked her up and settled back into her chair and opened her blouse so Ruth could nurse.

"I put on the black dress that woman gave me. The dress felt so tight, like what the snake feels like when the skin becomes too tight and it needs to be shed. I couldn't run or move or even think.

"Another girl came into the room so I greeted her in Lakota. That woman slapped me. The sting was hot on my cheek. I stared at her. I had never been struck before. Her face twisted up like a mad dog and she showered me with those hot, spitting sounds. I understood just a few words. That night, after the lights were out, that girl told me that the white lady had called me a dirty heathen, that I was not allowed to use pagan talk, that I was there to be civilized, and she would beat the Indian out of me if she had to!"

Daisy lifted Ruth and moved her to nurse the other breast.

MEADOWLARK

"Two years of not enough food, and sickness everywhere. We worked from the moment we woke up, until we collapsed at night, growing skinnier and skinnier. Oozing eyes. Some died from it. Some they peeled back the eyelids on some of us to scrape the insides and then pour in boric acid to wash out the pus.

"Little girls and boys became ghosts after the first few days, with pinched faces and bony bodies. They cried all night. They learned not to cry during the day. Then came the tuberculosis. Every day I looked at the headstones in the graveyard there and wondered when my name would be etched onto one of them.

"I wanted to die. It would have been easier." The late afternoon light cast a glow over Daisy's face. "But I tried to make my parents proud of me. I learned English and I learned how to sew. We were never allowed to go home. I learned to be very, *very* quiet."

The north wind shrieked past the corners of the soddy, sliding in under the window, sending a cold chill throughout the room.

"They took away everything about me that was Indian, so I would become White. But, I could never *be* White." Daisy cupped the sleeping Ruth's head in her hand, picked her up and lay her back down on the blanket on the bed. She wiped away the trickle of milk that dribbled out of her mouth and down her chin, her dark lashes fanned out across the top of chubby cheeks. Daisy tucked the blanket around her daughter, watching it rise and fall with Ruth's even breathing.

"No matter how I dress, cut and comb my hair, or how I speak, to them I will always be a 'damned Indian.' So will my little girl."

The last of the sun's rays filtered through the window and the blue light of evening crept up the horizon. Grace lit a candle and it sputtered in the cold wind sneaking in under the windowpane. Shadows fluttered weakly across Daisy's face.

"Many hated the Whites for being White and they hated themselves for being Indian. I watched all of this. I watched the others who went along on the outside with what they needed to do in order to survive. I watched them lower their eyes in submission when Whites were around. But there was a difference in them that I could feel. At night, they prayed in Lakota or Ojibwe. They did what they needed to do, but they stayed proud and strong. I decided to be like them."

Daisy's drew back her shoulders and stretched. "As I scrubbed the floors, I spoke to myself in Lakota. I spoke to my mother and my grandmother. I made myself remember the names for everything. I remembered stories and told them to myself again and again, so that I would never forget. Because of the stories, I survived."

Night wrapped the outside of the soddy in soft folds. Inside the room pulsed with Ruth's soft breaths.

When Daisy quit speaking, Grace asked, "Why are you telling me all this?"

"Because the stories will help you survive, too. I know they will. I have a question I have wanted to ask my whole life. Maybe you can answer it for me."

"What is that, Daisy?"

"Why does the White man always have to win?"

Grace thought of Tom and stared in Daisy's wise eyes. "I don't know the answer to that. I wish I did."

A movement beyond the window stole Grace's attention. A shimmer of color peeked through the darkness.

"What in the world?" Grace stood.

Daisy set down her beading and moved to stand beside Grace. A panorama of unearthly lights shimmered and swayed through the sky, dancing flashes of blue, pink, green, and yellow shimmered through the heavens. Spanning behind the colors, infinite numbers of stars, glowing crystals that spattered across the black velvet in milky swirls and hazy spirals.

Daisy raised her hand to touch the pane, settling her palm against the cold glass. "*Woímnayankel.*"

"What does that mean?"

"That is a word that is difficult to explain in English. We say this when we experience something so big, so grand, that we are humbled and at the same time it makes us feel we are a part of the greatness."

The women stood close. Grace put her arm across Daisy's thin shoulders and said, "It makes me feel so very small. We're just specks really, compared to the heavens."

MEADOWLARK

11

Alone, Grace watched her belly grow through the winter and into spring from a small bump below her bellybutton into a full mound as she entered the beginning of her sixth month of pregnancy in December. She gave thanks for the heavy snows of winter, breaking the drought, at least for that year. Her breath now came in short gasps, as she worked around her distended abdomen to heave feed to the horses and Red. She tired easily and sat down frequently to rest. Once, exhausted, she plopped down in the snow and tried to catch her breath. Inside, the baby stretched and rolled. She tried to take a deep breath, but it felt like her lungs were squeezed into a small cramped space.

She looked back at the soddy. Wind blew the dried yellow tufts of grass sideways against the dirty snow. The sun set by 4:30 in the afternoon to create long, dark, lonely evenings.

Dusk had already settled onto the prairie and soon it would

turn inky black. Wrapping her hands around the pitchfork handle, she used it to heave herself up again. A slice of bread would serve for her supper. She had grown used to being alone and relying on herself for whatever needed to be done. Tom had become a distant memory. It occurred to her less and less that she shared her life with anyone but the animals.

When Tom returned in early March, he greeted Grace with bundles of fabric for new dresses and clothes for the baby, but she could only treat him as if he were a stranger. She remained polite but silent as he told story after story of his months away. He had gotten a decent price for the calves at the sale in Philip, and had brought home the healthiest, sturdiest cows. With a little luck, the recent snow would turn to rain and they would have grass again.

On his first day home, he rode down to the breaks to cut down a cedar tree. He trimmed off the branches with a handsaw, then put a rope around the trunk and hauled it back to the barn. There, he worked late into the night to cut boards and plane the wood. For almost a week he spent each evening working by candlelight to carve and fit the pieces together to make a cradle.

"And now for the finishing touch," he announced to Grace as he wiped the final bit of dust from the butter-smooth headboard. He brought in a branding iron from the tool shed and placed the TR into the live coals in the cookstove. When the metal glowed red-hot, Tom seared the Robertson brand onto the wood.

"There," he said. "*Now* that baby can be born."

Grace woke to a slow, soaking spring rain. Thunder cracked and lightning laced the sky. She lay in bed and studied the way her nightgown rose steeply over the mound of her belly. Mae had been by for a visit ten days ago and said the baby could come at any time. With another loud clap from the storm clouds, the baby within started and abruptly straightened its legs. Tiny feet kicked Grace right below the ribs. She smiled and rubbed where she felt the kick.

"It's all right," she whispered. "That's only thunder. Nothing to worry about."

Rain continued throughout the day as her abdomen tightened then relaxed, keeping pace with the thunderclaps. She tended to household chores feeling as if a vice had been clamped around her middle. When Tom came in at noon, Grace cradled the space under her belly as she set down the steaming plate of canned beef, green beans, mashed potatoes and gravy and fresh rolls in front of him.

"Something seems to be happening. I'm not sure if it's time or not." She breathed in sharply as another wave of pain clenched her muscles.

"Hmm," Tom picked up his fork. "I've got to ride the breaks this afternoon. That new bull looked lame yesterday." Tom ripped a bite off from a roll and used the rest to push beef onto his fork. "That's the most expensive bull I have." He chewed with haste, scooping potatoes into his still-full mouth.

Grace hadn't even sat down at the table when he wiped up the last of the gravy with his roll. He stood up and put his hat on before he had finished swallowing.

"Goddamn, if I'm out the money I put into that sumbitch bull..." He started to walk out the door but poked his head back inside, "I'll be back by supper."

Grace rubbed the small of her back and forced a smile. "I'll try to make this baby wait."

He walked out the door without looking back. Grace flinched with disappointment as the door slammed. Why did she let herself be hurt by his behavior? She should know better. She didn't bother to eat, but cleared the table and washed the dishes.

By mid-afternoon the pains around her belly had become strong and regular, leaving her clutching the table or the counter to keep from falling. A soft rain was still falling as she saddled Mame and pulled the mare close to the fence so she could mount. The tan prairie flushed green amid blotchy patches of melting snow under the dove gray sky. Mame's hooves made soft, slopping sounds on the wet earth. Rain beaded her mane in silver, and droplets trailed down Grace's cheeks.

She rolled forward in the saddle to clutch her belly and utter low moans. She couldn't think or focus her eyes on the trail, so she gave Mame her head, trusting her to find her way to Mae's.

She called out in a shaky voice as she drew near the shack.

Mae poked her head out. "What in the world? Oh!" Mae ran out and reached for Mame's bridle to hold the horse still.

"Is it time?" Grace asked, leaning down with her belly laying against Mame's neck. "Or should I go back home and finish my chores?"

"It's too late for chores. You're like a first-calf heifer not knowing what to do." Mae led Mame over to her corral, patting Grace's leg as she walked. Grace clutched the saddlehorn, her wet hands straining white against the leather.

Mae said, "When this one passes, we'll get you down. Whoa, Mame. Easy, girl."

When Grace was able to sit up straight again, Mae took her foot out of the stirrup and pushed Grace's leg over Mame's rump.

"Oh, where is Ike when I need him? Off checking to make sure no cows get bogged down around the dam. Here, my dear Grace, lean into me."

"No! Just look at yourself. Your belly's almost as big as mine!"

"One must do what one must, Grace. Now, just ease down the side here, and I can support you."

"Thanks, Mae," Grace panted.

"Why didn't Tom come get me?" Mae asked

"He's gone to doctor a bull."

"That figures."

As the two women walked like girls in a three-legged race to the shack, another pain dropped Grace to the ground on her hands and knees. She rocked back and forth, her head hanging low, a moan spilling out. She put her forehead on the wet earth.

"Don't touch me," Grace growled when Mae tried to rub her back. She bit her lip to keep from snarling more. She shoved her forehead harder into the cold ground. The pain subsided and Mae lifted her by the shoulders from the mud.

"Forgive me," Grace stuttered.

"No need for that. Holler out if you want," Mae chuckled. "I'm going to count and we're going to get you inside. Ready? One…two…three…and up! Pick up those feet, honey."

She leaned against Mae and they stumbled into the shack. Grace doubled over on the floor. Mae eased her out of her clothes and half carried her to the bed.

MEADOWLARK

The world became distant and hazy, she felt as if she were seeing it through gauze. Grace felt herself pulled further within, drawn into a place of nothing but pain and Mae's instructions to breathe. Had hours passed or days?

From a far-away muffled place she heard Mae say, "Your water won't break, it's slowing things down. I'm going to do it for you."

Mae's hands moved up along Grace's legs, Grace felt a tug and a flood of fluid soaked the bedding. A visceral urge to push alerted every muscle in her body. A wild, guttural sound ripped along with searing, unbearable pain. Through gritted teeth, she grunted and heaved as Mae coaxed her to keep pushing. An expelling with the temperature of fire felt as if everything inside was flowing from her. The searing waned. Mae set something warm and wet on her chest.

"Grace, you have a son."

With closed eyes, Grace laid her hands on the squirming figure. As her fingers slid over the baby's back, she felt the slender curve of thimble-sized shoulder blades. The boy jerked against her. She lifted him, so she could see his face. Eyes the color of the gray sky outside peered from a wizened, red face. She caressed the blood-flecked head.

"Hello, James. I'm your mama. Mae, I'm a mother!"

"Indeed you are." Mae leaned down to wipe the sweat from Grace's forehead. Mae tied a thread around the cord that still attached mother to son. She tied another above it and between the two, cut the cord.

Grace savored her son's fragile wrinkled skin against her soft, empty belly. Mae helped her to bring James's mouth to the nipple. Grace gasped in surprise at the force.

"Hard to believe such a tiny thing can suck so hard, isn't it?" Mae chuckled.

All Grace could do was nod and stare at James. His eyes were closed, and his lips engulfed her nipple, his mouth suckling as his bony fist kneaded her breast.

"This may hurt, Grace. You need to expel the placenta. I'll knead from the top to help work it out."

Mae pressed hard and steady right below Grace's ribs. She eased her hands over Grace's slack stomach. A mass of deep vermilion overlaid with a map of azure veins oozed onto the bed. Mae gathered it into a bucket.

"Mae, Daisy said to place the afterbirth up high in a tree, okay? If a coyote finds it on the ground and takes it, it will bring me disgrace. My boy will become lazy and bring shame to my family."

"Grace Robertson, you are the hardest working person I know."

"Please Mae. For me? For Daisy? Up high in a tree." Grace stroked the curve of her son's back.

Mae smiled. "Okay, dear one, for you both. If that's what you want. I'll walk with it down to the creek and stick it up in the branches of that lone cottonwood. That rain really is coming down, though."

The sound of a horse slapping through the gumbo came to a sudden halt outside. The door burst open and Tom rushed in, his slicker sloughing water all over the floor. He was out of breath.

"Is he here?" Tom eyes found the baby.

Grace trailed her finger around the curvature of the baby's ear. "Come meet James Theodore."

Tom nodded, but before he could move Mae said, "You best take off those muddy boots and filthy slicker. I don't want you tracking up my clean floors."

Tom obeyed. Mae shrugged into her coat and draped a scarf over her head. She picked up the bucket.

"I'll leave you two alone now." She closed the door with care.

Tom sank down on the bed beside Grace.

"Oh." Tom's eyes filled and tears slipped through the rough stubble on his cheeks.

"Want to hold him?" Grace lifted the baby toward Tom.

With calloused hands, Tom took his son. "Lookee, there."

He held the boy aloft and James, startled at being in mid-air, let out a wail. Grace pulled Tom's arms down close to his chest.

"Make a cocoon for him," Grace said. "So he'll feel safe."

"Hello there, son," Tom said as the baby gazed back.

"He looks like you," Grace said.

"Do you think so? I've got a lot of plans for him," Tom said. "Big plans."

"I think the two of you will do just fine," Grace said.

"I never did anything right." Tom kept his eyes on James, but Grace knew he was talking to her. "That's what I remember: feeling like no matter what I did, no matter how hard I tried, it wasn't good enough. I kept trying harder and harder."

MEADOWLARK

Tom smoothed his finger over the baby's arm. "Even though Mother told me I was special, that I was smarter and better than my brothers, than my dad. I was the one who was going to save her from herself."

Grace watched Tom swallow hard. "I know they loved me. So why'd they go and do what they did? How's a kid supposed to make sense of that kind of stuff?"

Tom drew James in closer, his arms tightening. "How's a man supposed to make any sense of what happened?"

James began to fuss.

"Tom," Grace whispered. "You're holding him too tight." The minute she said it, she regretted it. Tom would hear the words as criticism.

Tom loosened his hold and pushed the baby back at Grace.

He said, "I don't want my boy to ever feel what I felt. Never."

"I believe you," Grace said.

12

Grace slipped her journal from its protective hiding place later that week and sat at the small, rough table, her heart racing and hands trembling, listening for the sound of Tom rousing from sleep. She knew it was an insane thing to do, to put her thoughts to paper where they could be used as weapons against her, but the feeling that she would die, dry up and blow away without writing, overrode the terror. By the act of writing she was saying to the world, *I exist. I am.* Between that and the joy of watching James grow day by day, she knew she would survive. She scribbled quickly, the minutes rushing past like a flooding creek. When she heard Tom roll toward the edge of the bed, she closed her notebook and slipped it into her apron pocket.

She grabbed her coat and said, "The coffee's ready. Be right back." Once outside she let the late spring wind tear away her fear as she sought the solace of the outhouse. She cherished those few moments of reverie each morning before the busyness of the day overtook her.

"Shut up! Shut up! You'll wake the dead!" Grace heard the guttural yell from across the yard. She saw a silhouette in the window of Tom shaking two-month-old James at arm's length. The infant's head whipped back and forth.

"Stop!" Grace flew in the door and wrenched the baby out of her husband's arms.

"You. Get. Out. Of. Here!"

Tom stared down at her. James wailed against her neck.

"Now!"

Tom gathered his shirt and pants and boots and stomped out the door in his long johns.

"Shhhh, honey. Mama's here." She felt James' neck, relieved to see him raise his head to look up at her. Tears streamed from his bright blue eyes and streaked his smooth face.

"Oh, James. I'm so sorry. Mama's so sorry. Shhhhh...I'll never let him do that again. Never. Hush now."

Once she was certain Tom had gone, Grace fed the baby. She fastened his sunbonnet securely to protect his pale skin, then strapped him to her chest, as she'd seen Daisy do with Ruth, then went out to saddle Mame. She placed a cross-stitch that she'd made for Mae, along with the packet of beef sandwiches she had made for Tom to take for his lunch into her saddlebags.

There was no way she could stay in the soddy after what had happened. Her heart pounded as she mounted and turned the mare into a wind that was sweeping the exposed creek banks smooth as skulls.

"Grace!" Mae threw open the door and ran outside, wiping her hands on her apron. She helped Grace dismount, then pulled her close. She examined Grace's face and tucked a strand of hair behind her ear.

"Oh, it's been weeks, and Lord knows I've missed you."

Mae glanced down at the bundle squirming on Grace's chest and shifted her attention. "And, how is our fine fellow?"

Grace carefully eased the baby into her arms. Mae held

him aloft and smiled into his round face. "Oh my land sake's alive, he is just beautiful!"

"And look at you, Mae!" Grace laid her hand on the high belly under Mae's apron.

"Oh, yes, my own young one seems to be coming along just fine in there. Won't be long now."

"Where's Ike?" Grace asked.

"Off to help the Farthings."

"Where's Tom?"

Grace did not answer. Instead she said, "I brought sandwiches for our lunch."

Mae ushered her into the shack. "Sit down, Grace. It's been too long."

Grace settled into a chair with the baby on her lap. Mae hovered, studying James and touching his cheek, his hair.

Grace thought carefully before saying, "You know, Mae, there really is such a beauty in the land…"

"Beauty? Hah! Maybe a hint—when it's not trying to freeze us and our animals to death! Or dry us into shells. Or stick us in gumbo. Or starve out the cows."

"But still, there is that beauty, even amidst all the harshness, when we take the time to look. And the meadowlarks are back. I love the meadowlarks and their songs." Grace moved James from one arm to the other.

"What are you trying to say?"

"Speaking of songs," she said to shift Mae's attention away from a problem she was not willing to discuss, "do you remember the one about a mockingbird? Did you have that song in the East? I used to sing it as a little girl."

"Remember? Of course I remember. Come here. Let's teach this little boy how to sing and dance."

Grace and Mae twirled around the kitchen, the baby gurgling between them. Mae's brave operatic soprano blended beautifully with Grace's timid alto as they sang.

> *When the sun in the morning peeks over the hill*
> *And kisses the roses on Mockingbird Hill,*
> *Then my heart sings with gladness as I hear the trill*
> *Of the bird on the treetop on Mockingbird Hill.*

MEADOWLARK

Tra la la, tweedly dee dee, it gives me a thrill
To wake up in the morning on Mockingbird Hill."

Late in the afternoon, Grace rode home revived and comforted. She was surprised to see Daisy waiting outside the soddy with a basketful of food. Ruth, bound in a sling, straddled her hip.

Grace looked toward the corral, grateful to see Tom's horse wasn't there.

"He is not here. He is not coming for some time," Daisy said.

"How do you know?" Grace dismounted as Daisy took hold of Mame's bridle.

"I saw him going toward town. Did you put the afterbirth up in a tree as I told you?" Daisy walked with Grace toward the barn and shifted Ruth to her other hip.

"Yes. Well, I had to convince Mae to do it. I had the baby at her place."

"Good. That's very good. Now we won't have to worry about you or your boy getting lazy." Daisy broke into a grin.

"How did you know it was a boy?"

"Oh, I hear things. Can I see him now?"

Grace looped Mame's reins over the top pole of the corral and opened the buttons on her coat. Daisy tiptoed over and peered down at the baby cuddled against his mother's chest. In his sleep, James moved his jaw up and down and made small clicking noises with his tongue.

"He is handsome and strong. He's nursing in his sleep." Ruth started to squirm and wanted to be set down.

"Okay, okay, little girl," Daisy said. "Let me help unsaddle this horse and we'll go inside."

The women walked back to the soddy side by side. Grace lay James in his cradle. Daisy set Ruth down and straightened her dress. Grace pulled a quilt from the end of the bed and spread it on the floor for the girl. She gave her a basket of balled yarn to play with.

"Do you want a glass of water, Daisy? Soon we'll have another young one here."

"Another baby? Who else other than Mae?" Daisy accepted the glass and pulled out a chair.

"Just Red, the milk cow. She's ready to calve any day," Grace said. "I went over to see Mae this morning. She and I started singing a song called *Mockingbird Hill*. We hadn't sung that since we were girls." Grace said. "Only I was thinking that out on the prairies, we should sing *Meadowlark Hill*, instead."

Daisy looked out the window into the white-hot sunshine. "We believe Meadowlark teaches our people to never forget our dreams. 'Don't be afraid to dream,' she tells us. Meadowlark teaches us that we are brave. She teaches us to turn toward our fears, not away from them. She teaches us that it is in doing this that our dreams become possible."

"Turn *toward* fear, instead of away from it? I really don't like the sound of that."

Daisy laughed softly, "Nobody ever does. That's why Meadowlark reminds us with her song. Then it's our decision—whether or not we choose to listen."

"I'm not sure I have any dreams, anymore," Grace said. "Maybe I've let my fears get in the way."

"You stood up to your husband when he tried to hurt your son. That is turning toward your fear. And your dream is still there waiting to be remembered."

"Daisy, you unsettle me. How do you know these things?"

"Because I can hear and see many things. I see that you want to create a safe place for your son, so he will feel his roots sink deep into the ground, where they will hold him strong and firm. Whenever you hear Meadowlark now you will think of this and it will help you."

After Daisy was gone, Grace used some of the precious sugar to make a little cake. She wrote in her journal:

> *Today is my birthday. I am 18 years old. I baked myself a cake and ate it by myself, nursing the baby, looking out over the windswept waves of prairie. Tom never came home. I guess he stayed in town. I am so grateful for Mae, and for Daisy and Ruth. Without these women friends, where would I be?*

The milk cow lost her calf. When? Grace didn't know what happened. When she went out at dawn she saw the cow's dark shadow near the barn and heard the echo of her panicked call for her calf, ripe with longing. Long strings of frothy saliva dropped from her mouth onto the dusty ground, where they glistened in the pale light. Her udder hung hard and large, like a full wineskin stretched-to-cracking. She had searched, her hooves wearing a deep groove around the perimeter of the corral. Her dissonant bawl floated on the still air, hanging there even as the next hoarse bellow was released.

Grace tried to soothe her with soft words. She threw the cow some hay, but she walked over it without interest, the afterbirth hanging under her kinked tail like a bloody flag. It had to have been coyotes. The only thing she knew for certain is that Tom would be angry.

A prickly tingle swept through Grace's breasts and milk blossomed from her nipples to soak her torso. She walked back to the soddy to lean over the wooden cradle beside the bed. She lifted her sleeping son and carried him over to the chair placed under the window. She peeled the sodden blouse away from her skin and cradled James in her arms. His silken lips pursed and reached out. He burrowed his face into her breast. The tingling in Grace's body mounted and she felt the sweet release of pressure. A rivulet of milk slipped from the corner of the baby's mouth. Twin crescents of eyelashes the width of spider webs framed his eyes, casting a brush of shadow across his translucent skin.

When James had had his fill, Grace lifted him to her shoulder and gently patted his back, his bones feather-light and fragile under the steady movement of her hand. The baby's stomach tensed and a slight expulsion of air, laden with earthy scent of warm milk, escaped his mouth. Grace smiled and stroked the downy fuzz on his head. She placed him on her other breast.

Beyond the window, a silver slice of sun rose in the sky. Light drenched the land in water-stained cornflower blue and drew crisp edges of contour and depth, defining the curve of knolls and vales invisible to the eye in the full light of day. Her eyes moved from the mound of her breast out to the mounds and concave indentations of the prairie.

Grace saw in the prairie an evocation of the curves of a woman. She felt her body's link with the conformation and silhouette of the land. Peace settled around her like a fleecy cloud, despite the ceaseless plodding sound of the cow as she searched in vain for her calf. The low timbre of the wind rustled through the tufts of buffalo grass, and the soft pulsing cadence of her son's breath, echoed the steady soft murmur of each swallow.

The next day, under a snowy gray sky, Grace drowned in heat inside the soddy. It was washday. While she didn't enjoy the hard work of hauling water and scrubbing, she loved the crisp smell and freshness of clean clothes. She set the copper boiler on the woodstove, and added lye and soap as the water began to boil.

Snowflakes from the late spring storm added another layer onto the blanket outside, while inside the fire made the air shimmer, pricking and burning Grace's skin. She rolled up her sleeves and adjusted the hair piled in a sweaty knot on top of her head. Her shirt and shift clung to her perspiring body. She draped a pair of Tom's work pants over an enormous wooden spoon and dipped them into the water. The skin on her face blanched like a boiled new potato. Her monthly cycle had arrived and the soiled cloths she had used floated in a mixture of water and lye in another bucket.

A light knock on the door caused her to groan at the mess and her disheveled appearance. She glanced at James, asleep on the bed, and ran her fingers through her hair.

"Daisy? What brings you and Ruth out on this cold day?"

Flecks of snow clung momentarily to Daisy's hair, before melting into droplets in the heat of the soddy. Grace helped her peel off her heavy coat.

"I wanted a cup of your coffee."

"Let me move this washtub and put some water on, then. I'll make a fresh pot. Is Ruth sleeping? Just lay her on the bed next to James," Grace said in a shushed voice.

Daisy nodded and nestled the baby on top of the blanket next to James. The sight of the two infants side-by-side stopped both women long enough to take in James' milky skin and fair hair next to Ruth's shades of dark, rich earth and coal.

"The husband is gone again?" Daisy rubbed her hands over her arms to warm up.

"Yes. To see about some pasture to lease." Grace shoved the bucket of soiled cloths further in the corner.

"I didn't know you were coming or I wouldn't have left those out." Grace's face flushed bright red. "The curse. You know." She threw a dishtowel over the top of the bucket.

"What curse?"

Grace lowered her eyes. "You know, Daisy. The curse that visits women once a month. *That* curse." Grace had never discussed this before. She had never mentioned it, not even to her mother or to Mae.

"But curses are bad things, aren't they?"

"Well, yes. It's our shameful time, when we are dirty. When men think we are contaminated."

Daisy squinted at Grace. "Dirty? Contaminated? Oh, you *Wasicu* have such odd ideas. It is forbidden for our men to be near us during this special time. But not because we're dirty, but because our feminine strength is so strong. The men fear being made...how do you call it? When it doesn't work anymore?" She waved her hand in a broad sweep below her waist. "That is why women don't touch weapons or pipes or anything that is sacred when it is our moon time. Women bring life into this world and men do not. This is the greatest of all the mysteries. The most powerful."

Grace glanced at her gun, now hanging on pegs above the front door, where Tom's hung when he was home. She had worried that Tom would take it from her, but he let her keep it to protect the livestock from coyotes.

Steam rushed from the pot and Grace pulled it aside and measured in coffee with a dash of salt. "I've never thought of it that way before."

"When the blood flows that is when we are at our most powerful, our most sacred. The man? His role is simple, right? Lakota men fear us at this time." Daisy clasped her hands in front of her on the table. "They respect a Lakota woman who understands how to use her own power. Women and men have very different powers. Opposite powers, meant to compliment the other. The man is not superior, as you *Wasicu* believe. This is why I came to have coffee with you today. You have so much to learn. If I don't tell you, who will?" Daisy laughed.

Grace poured two cups of coffee with care. She set one in front of Daisy and blew the heat from the top of hers before taking a sip.

"I'm grateful for the things you tell me. But what I really want to know is how to not have any more children. Can you tell me that?"

"Yes. I can bring you the herb to make the tea. Are you certain?"

"I think so. You know, Daisy...you've known from the beginning about my husband. At least if I don't get pregnant again, there will be one less person in the world for him to hurt. What else can I do?"

"You will wait. And when the time is right you will know."

"Know what?"

Hooves thrummed and up to the front door. Both women stood to look out the window as Ike slid his lathered horse to a stop.

"It's time, Grace!" he burst in the front door. "The baby's coming fast. Mae told me to come get you." He paused when he saw Daisy appear at the door behind Grace, "Oh, Daisy, you're here...thank goodness! Mae's asking for you both."

"We will both come," Daisy said. "You go home now."

They lifted the sleeping babies, bundled them in blankets to their chests, and set out horseback. They found Ike pacing outside the shack, calling out, "They're here! Grace and Daisy are here!"

"Jesus, Mary, and Joseph, Ike, is driving me crazy," Mae said when the women bustled inside. "Daisy. Good. You can tell Grace what to do if I get too far gone. This baby isn't quite right. I can feel it."

Ike rushed in. "What's not right? What's wrong?" His eyes widened and he stumbled against the bed.

"Ike, please help these women to put the babies on some blankets on the floor."

"Here," Daisy said, after she and Grace handed off the babies. "You hold her leg, right here." She showed Ike how to hold Mae's knee bent and up. Ike blanched.

"I'll just...hold her *hand*." He gave Daisy a wide berth and knelt down to face Mae. He smoothed back the sweat-drenched hair from her forehead.

Daisy murmured in Lakota as she raised Mae's gown above her widespread knees. "It comes ready to dance," she said.

"Oh Lord! Breech," Mae groaned.

"We will sing it into coming with ease so it will know we welcome it." Daisy placed her hands flat on Mae's huge abdomen and motioned for Grace to do the same thing. Ike had his eyes closed and his lips moved in silent prayer.

MEADOWLARK

"Now, that's something I can do," Mae said. She burst into an aria, the complicated notes sometimes breaking off with the surge of another contraction. When she grew too tired to utter a sound, Grace took over and sang *Mockingbird Hill*. Then Daisy offered a repeated chorus in Lakota, her palms patting out a soft drum rhythm on Mae's body. Then she stopped and raised her hands skyward.

"Be ready, Grace," she said. "It comes, now."

With a gigantic shudder Mae released an outrageous wail and the baby slid into Grace's waiting hands. Everyone held their breath until the child let out a gargled cry.

"It's a boy," Grace said, as she placed the baby in Mae's arms.

Ike beamed and stared, before leaning forward to rest his lips on the baby's wet head. "It's a miracle, Mae. Just look at him."

"He's our miracle, Mr. Thompson."

"Now, Lord, if I don't need some fresh air," Ike said. "I'll be right back." He kissed Mae's forehead and wobbled out the door.

"Ladies," Mae whispered, "I am a bit worried. After a couple of days, when their milk comes in, new mothers say their breasts double in size. Why even you, Grace. Remember?"

"Mae!" Grace laughed.

"Good God Almighty," Mae said as she took her son from Grace and guided him to nurse. "I'll need a corset made of steel after this."

The women cleaned up the bed as the boy nursed with gusto. They washed Mae's face and brushed her hair and gave her a fresh gown. "Do I have to put the afterbirth up in a tree?" Mae joked.

"I will do that for you when I leave," Daisy said. "Just as you did for Grace when James was born. That way we will all be connected. Our children will be connected."

"Someday your girl can marry one of our boys," Mae said, looking at the top of the baby's head.

Grace and Daisy looked at Mae in surprise and then met one another's eyes, before slowly lowering them.

"Of course. Whyever not?" Mae asked.

"We can hope that's true," Grace said softly. Daisy took the placenta from a bucket and wrapped it in a cloth, just as Ike walked back into the house. His eyes widened, he averted them, and went straight to his wife.

Mae held her son up and gave him over to Ike's waiting hands.

"What do you think?" she asked. "Shall we name him after my father or yours?"

"What about both," Ike said. "Hey, there. Look at you, Corwin Robert Thompson. Look at you! You got your mama's eyes."

James and Ruth began to squirm and fuss on the floor, little arms and legs pushing against the blanket covering them. Grace and Daisy each retrieved their child and came to sit by Mae. Ike handed Corwin to Mae and the three women looked at one another and at each of the infants, then just shook their heads and laughed.

MEADOWLARK

13

A spring blizzard descended in 1916. Grace looked out the impeccably clean window of the soddy to a glittering prairie transformed into a sea foamy with ice crystals that clung to the grasses and turned them into brittle white posies. Her gaze moved slowly to the not-so-small figure that slept under the quilt. James, now four and a half, filled the room with his soft, rhythmic breathing lending Grace a feeling of calm. She decided to escape for a moment before he woke and, as the sun peeked over the horizon, she walked quickly up to the top of the rise and out across the plains to check an eagle's nest high in an ash tree in a draw.

She looked back over her shoulder at the new house that Tom had spent the previous year building after successfully selling yearling colts and just-weaned calves. The modest two story home faced south toward the creek, with a porch on the southern end to catch the summer breezes. Soon Grace would have a real kitchen, with water hand-pumped in from the cistern. A pantry off the kitchen had a window facing north, where she would be able see anyone coming down the road as she made bread or washed dishes. The kitchen opened into a combination dining room and living room, with the their bedroom off the living room. A narrow staircase led to a trio of smaller bedrooms with dormer windows.

Tom kept insisting that they add more children to the family and Grace, quite wisely, kept the herb Daisy had given her to prevent pregnancy her own dark secret. She had told no one, not even Mae.

The house was in the process of being painted a crisp white with green trim when the change in weather shut down Tom's work crew. By summer, though, the soddy would become a storage building.

Grace walked, frozen grass crunching beneath her boots. The rising sun cast her shadow—that of a determined woman with a long stride, arms and skirts swinging, a broad round circle of hat on her head. Grace slowed as she approached the ash tree and spied the nest of sticks spanning the thick branches. The male bird stood on the side of the nest, his feathers ruffled by the wind. She watched his mate arrive, talons outstretched to meet her landing place. They seemed a loyal pair and Grace hoped they would return year after year to rear their young. She breathed in the quiet of the morning, inhaling the peace and stillness of the day.

Tom was often gone now. With James and the animals to tend to, Grace rarely made it off the ranch anymore. She and her son lived in an isolated world unto themselves, as if they, too, were encased in ice. Sometimes, she felt that her world had shrunk to the size of the head of a pin. This contrast often struck her—the open land that seemed to go on forever that surrounded her, while her own world had shrunk smaller and smaller until it seemed to hold almost no air at all.

The hoarfrost held fast to each blade of grass, despite the warming sun. Grace bent to run her fingers the length of a tall sprig, peeling off fragile crystals. She rubbed her hands together feeling a texture like rough salt as they melted, then turned for home where the cow would be waiting to be milked, the horses waiting to be fed, and James waiting to be held.

MEADOWLARK

By November, Grace saw lines of worry etched around Tom's eyes and mouth. The price of beef had dropped by half. He quoted lines of scripture when he lectured James about drought and famine. He went to bed at night and lay wide-awake worrying where the money for food and necessities would come from with cattle prices so low.

Mae and Ike were expecting another baby.

"Grace," Mae said one day as they joined forces to can beef, "with things so tough right now, I am worried how we'll manage. My patients can't pay their bills and I can't ask them to give something they don't have."

Grace retreated farther and farther inside herself, while on the outside she focused on keeping the appearance of her family as bright and shiny as a new penny. The one constant challenge of her days continued to be the gauging of Tom's moods when he was home, and how close the web of another hair-trigger explosion of violence lay to the surface. Her life was focused on protecting James from Tom's volatile temper.

Tom burst in the door that afternoon, walking with his bent-over fast stride, calling, "I'm home!"

James looked uncertainly at him then went back to playing with a stack of wooden blocks on the floor.

"How is everybody?" Tom asked.

"Your father's home," Grace said.

James walked hesitantly over to his father, holding himself at stiff attention as Tom leaned down to pat his shoulder.

Grace kept her eyes on James's back, instead of looking at Tom. She had grown thinner since James's birth. Drop-by-drop, inch-by-inch, she felt her spirit being leached out of her.

"I want a wife who is happy to see me when I come home," he said as he turned to Grace. "Look me in the eyes. It's as if you don't even want me here."

How could she even begin to explain it to him?

"What's wrong?" Tom shouted. "Don't I take care of you? You've got a brand new roof over your head and food on the table. All you have to do is take care of a child all day. What do you know about problems? You never have to think about how we're going to make our next dime!"

"What? What do you know about what I think or feel? You don't know anything about our life here. What do you care?

You don't!" Grace's rage and exhaustion were so great, they overrode her fear. "You don't have to be gone all the time. You *want* to be gone! And who's left to take care of the animals, the buildings, making sure there's enough feed? Who is left to break ice on the dams in the winter, worrying all the while about James alone in the house, because it's freezing outside? Where are you when James is sick? Where are you when there's not enough food, and we've no money left, because you squirrel it away and hide it from me. Well, good. Go ahead and go. Get out!"

Tom raised his hand above his head.

"Mama?" James called from where he had retreated by the bed. He looked back and forth between his parents. "What did I do wrong?"

Grace looked one last time at Tom and then hurried over to kneel beside James. "It's okay, honey. Nothing is wrong." She smoothed his hair back from his forehead. "Here, you can keep playing with your blocks. See how they stack on top of each other?" Grace settled James in with the toys, and then leaned shaking against the wall.

Tom scrubbed his hand over his face and walked out. After the door slammed, Grace studied the prairie encased in frost and ice and fought back the tears that sprang to her eyes. The loneliness and sadness that she'd tried to keep at bay with the constant busyness of James and the chores found an opening in the now calm evening. She wiped the tears from her cheeks with the back of her hand and shook her head to push unwanted thoughts away.

The next morning she came back from milking the cow to find Ike and Mae waiting outside, talking with Tom. Corwin and James rode the split rail fence that surrounded the house, pretending to be horseback

"What a surprise!" She quickened her step, the steam of her breath condensing in the air. "What in the world brings you over here this morning?" Grace came to stand beside Tom, but she set down the milk pail and wrapped her arms around her waist for warmth.

Ike rubbed his gloved hands together. "Mae needed an excuse to get out of the house, so we thought we'd just come over to see you and James today, see what we could do around here to help out."

"Thank you." Grace looked at the couple, their faces flushed pink in the cold air.

"Mighty surprised when Tom rode up," Ike said. "He was just saying he got back a few days ago."

"Oh my goodness, it's too cold to be out here like this," Grace said. "Let's get inside, shall we? I'll make us some cocoa."

"We came to help, not to have you wait on us," Mae said, pulling off her coat and gloves. "What would you like us to do?" She slapped the top of the table for emphasis.

"Yes, ma'am," Ike said. "Put us to work."

"You all don't need to do anything," Tom broke in. "Just sit back and drink some coffee. Ike, let me show you this bridle I brought back with me."

As the men huddled to talk about the fine detailed leather of the bridle, Mae whispered under her breath, "Grace, we're not leaving here until we've helped with something. Life isn't ever easy, but at least my man is home at night. And just because Tom doesn't seem to notice this," Mae looked down at the floor, "Ike and I do. We're not leaving until we do something to help you." She folded her arms across her chest.

Mae was always the last to pass judgment or say anything that didn't look at the bright side of things. Grace didn't know whether to feel embarrassed or grateful. She could never get caught up with what needed to be done before she fell exhausted and frustrated into bed every night.

"Okay, here's what we'll do," Grace announced. "Mae and I will wash the insides of these windows. There's such a film of dirt, we can barely see out of them."

Tom's head tilted back and his face wore a expression of fixed blankness ready to erupt into anger at her taking control.

"Tom, what do you think?" She fluttered her hands through the air, hoping to diffuse the building tension. "What would you like to get done around here that Ike could help you with today?"

Tom surveyed the room, as if making some kind of important decision. "Well," he said finally, "I suppose we could work on the harnesses. They could stand to be cleaned and oiled."

"Daddy? Mr. Ike?" James and Corwin appeared from where they had been hiding behind the table. "Can we help?"

"Sure thing." Ike held open his arm and James slipped close to his side. The men trailed out to the barn with the boys tagging behind.

Mae wiped the windowpanes, while the coffee pot boiled and Grace stirred a pan of cocoa. Tom came in through the door first, carrying a full set of harness. The barn was too cold with no stove there. Ike followed right behind him with another load.

"We best bring these in to warm up," Tom said as he held the door open for Ike. "Wait until I tell you what happened when we were driving those new horses…"

Tom glanced back and his sentence abruptly stopped. He threw everything down on the floor, pushed past Ike, and strode out to where James had dropped one of the bridles he carried. He tried to pick up the long pieces, but the more he tried, the more he seemed to tangle the reins.

Tom's stride ate the ground between them. "James!" he barked.

James stopped moving and cowered. Corwin froze behind.

"Look at me when I'm speaking to you!"

James raised his head but kept his eyes lowered.

"You dropped them? How could you do that? How *could* you?" Tom towered over the little boy. "I said look at me when I'm talking to you!"

Tom reached down, grabbed James's shoulders, lifted him off the ground and shook him. James's legs dangled and his head whipped back and forth.

"Look at me! What's *wrong* with you? I can't trust you to do anything right, can I? Nothing!"

Ike moved behind Tom and said, "Tom."

That was enough for Tom to give James a final shake and drop the boy into the dirt. James legs buckled and he fell on his back.

"Now you pick up those bridles and bring them in the house. Can't you do anything right?" Tom whirled away and then stopped to look back at the crying boy. "I am so disappointed in you, James. Jesus Christ."

Tom spun again, this time with his fists clenched. Ike raised his open hands in a gesture of calm. Grace and Mae stood locked in the doorway. It had all happened so fast. Grace had had no time to react. She had watched her son's spirit be crushed before her eyes. It wasn't the first time.

MEADOWLARK

Mae put her arm around Grace and said, "Perhaps we ought to go."

"No!" Tom bellowed. "You stay. I'll go." He walked back out to the barn. Ike picked up the bridles and helped James to his feet.

"It's okay, buddy," Ike said. "Your pa's just having a bad day. Let's go in and get some cocoa."

Later, after the silent rest of Mae and Ike's stay, Grace saddled Mame, bundled James in his coat and a blanket, and rode down to the river. The mare descended a slope cloaked in spade-shaped cottonwood leaves beneath tall trees now stark and naked. Stands of junipers, their branches heavy with ripe blue-purple berries, created protected open coves. Dry yellow grasses, bent over by the November wind, carpeted the riverbed's sun-dappled floor.

Grace wandered, still numb from the events of the day. She led Mame, James in the saddle, his little shoulders stooped like an old man's.

Grace stopped well away from the water. Thin panes of ice lined the banks, like windows into the underworld where the muddy current moved slowly. A protruding rock caught the moving ice, the sound a sharp crunching rasp that tore through the gentle gurgle of the river like the sound of a heart breaking. What was she going to do?

Grace wrote in her journal as a blizzard blew in.

It is winter. I am alone again. The days are short. The sun rises long after I do and sets when the clock shows 4:30 pm. Tom is gone. He's always gone. Whether it's checking cows or going with them by rail to be sold, he's always gone. He spends months playing cards in bars. He averts his eyes when I ask how the sale went and quickly changes the subject. He always comes back with a smile on his face and a spring in his step, but without fail those disappear. He always brings a gift for me and a trinket for

James. Doesn't he understand that a wife doesn't want those things? A woman's heart wants a safe home and a good father for her children.

MEADOWLARK

14

James's chest heaved with the effort of breathing. The episodes began happening in the fall and evolved into a monthly occurrence. First, a dry cough that seemed to come from nowhere and appeared so innocent that Grace didn't pay too much attention. Then it grew increasingly worse, accompanied by a deep lethargy. James, who was normally a bundle of energy, lay barely conscious on the bed, his skin a pale, translucent mask, a web of deep-blue veins mapping his face, his eyes sunken in their sockets, surrounded by purple stains. He struggled for air in a coma-like trance. Even Mae couldn't figure out what was wrong. Grace squeezed water out of a cloth into his mouth and coaxed the muscles of his throat to open by stroking them with her fingers. Sweat plastered his hair to his head. When Grace picked him up, his body was limp with the weight of the dead.

"Something's wrong, Tom. James can hardly breathe," Grace said over supper.

Tom spooned another chunk of stew meat from his bowl. "I'm sure he'll be fine," he said, chewing with his mouth open. He washed down the food with a draught of milk. He'd no more heard what she had just said than the man on the moon.

"But, this is bad. I'm scared to death for him." She searched Tom's eyes, seeking some kind of an understanding. "Nothing I do helps, even holding him over a steaming pot of water with a dishtowel over his head like a tent."

"He'll be fine." Tom he reached for a roll. "Old Dick Johnson got $235 dollars for that nice black three-year-old colt of his. Never heard of getting that much money for one horse. Goddamn." He shook his head in wonder, swallowed the rest of his roll, and pushed his chair back from the table.

"Well, I best get on with it." Tom reached for the hat hanging by the door and walked out.

Grace stared at the surface of the closed door and drew in a deep breath that disappeared into the emptiness she felt inside, a hollow space where there ought to be the flesh, sinew, and blood... and her heart. She turned to James where he laid spread-eagled on her bed, his skin clammy and cold. *Does Tom not care at all? Can he be that closed-off, that hard-hearted?*

He doesn't want to love us, Grace realized. *He only wants to control us.*

Two days later, late in the afternoon, Ike rode up, dismounted, and looped the reins around the hitching post in front of the soddy.

"Well, hello!" Grace met him at the door. "It warmed up a little today, didn't it?"

"Yes. Now, let's hope this snow melts into the grass roots. I'm ready for spring." Ike smiled broadly.

"How's Mae feeling?"

"Big as a house is what she'd say." Ike laughed. "That baby ought to be here. She's still going out on calls, though. Not slowing down a lick."

"Would she have time to come check on James?"

"What's wrong?"

"He gets these spells where he can't breathe."

Ike raised his hand in greeting as Tom rode down the slope from the west. Tom raised his in reply.

"How are your cows doing?" Tom asked when he reined up alongside.

"Got one with a bad bag, but I doctored her good."

"Hi, Ike," James stumbled out and smiled up at the cowboy on the horse.

"Well, hello there, little man. You being good to your mama?"

"Yes, sir," James said, a pinched look on his face. "I'm not feeling so good, though."

Tom swung his leg over his saddle and eased himself down off his horse, dropping the reins over the hitching post.

"Well, *there's* Daddy's pride and joy!" he boomed. "Come here, son!"

James stared at him in confusion, then cast a sideways look at Ike. Embarrassment flashed over Tom's face. He stepped forward and pulled the boy into an awkward embrace as James held his body rigid. Tom attempted to tousle his hair, but fell short when the boy flinched as his father's hand came toward him.

"James, go back inside, honey," Grace said. "You shouldn't be out in the wind."

Tom watched him drag away. "That boy is everything to me, Ike. Just everything"

Grace fought down the bile rising in her throat. She pasted a smile on her face.

"Well, I'd best get supper on the table. Ike, promise me you'll ask Mae to come see about James."

"I will, ma'am. I promise."

The next week, Grace worked in the kitchen while James played hide and seek with himself by wrapping himself in her skirts. More than once, his attempt entangled her and almost sent them both crashing to the floor.

"James," she said to the boy hanging on to her ankles, "if you make me fall, I won't be able to finish the pie for Christmas supper. Now, go play somewhere else!"

Mae had come as Ike promised, and brought medicine for

James. His cough disappeared quickly and his old vivacious energy had returned.

As she set the table, her mind raced with all she had to finish before Mae and Ike arrived to help them celebrate the holiday. She wanted everything to be perfect and beautiful. She closed her eyes and hoped it would go well with Tom. He'd been more attentive lately, even talking to James at supper about the things he'd done during the day. When Tom acted kind and gentle, her heart went out to the ashamed, scared little boy he had once been, and she felt a sense of duty to try and make up for everything he'd lacked in his own childhood. She wanted desperately for Tom's life to be better—for their life together to be better.

Grace arched her back to stretch muscles tight from bending over. She hung a big tin dishpan full of bread dough over the stove with clothesline rope tied to the handles and suspended from a hook in the ceiling because she had no room on the stove.

She had spared nothing this year in preparation for hosting 1916's Christmas dinner. The aroma of the roasting turkey, stuffed with breadcrumbs and sage, filled the house. A garland of boughs she and James had trimmed from trees in the breaks along the Cheyenne River decorated the windowsill. A very small cedar tree stood in the corner, decorated with paper snowflakes, draped with strands of strung popcorn and cedar berries.

The door slammed open and Mae stumbled into the house, clutching her huge pregnant belly. Her eyes ran with tears. She closed the door behind her, leaned back against it and slumped her head forward, holding Corwin's hand. Corwin stood trembling.

"What's happened?" Grace laid her hand on Mae's shoulder.

Mae shook her head and took a few steadying breaths. Panic etched her face.

"What is it? Tell me. Is it Ike?"

Mae hesitated. "It was just a long ride on the buckboard. That's all. Here help me unwrap my coat before I melt." Mae's fingers trembled as she worked at the buttons. The door bumped the women from behind as Tom and Ike stepped inside.

Ike's eyes sought Mae's and some understanding passed between them. Grace detected a deep sadness in that look. Then it was gone and Ike reached forward and gave her a great hug against his barrel chest.

"So good to see you. Mae's been talking of nothing else and all I can think about is some of your mincemeat pie. Now, where's James hiding? Corwin's anxious to see him."

At that invitation, James sprang up from under the bed and ran into Ike's arms. "Mr. Ike, did you bring me anything?"

"James," Grace said firmly. "Remember your manners."

"I'm sorry. Did you bring me anything, please?" James said.

Even Grace had to laugh and scolded Ike when he reached into his pocket and brought out a taffy for the boy.

"Thank you, Mr. Ike!"

"Okay, but *not* before supper," Grace said. "And I mean it. You boys can play until it's time to eat." The two boys ran noisily up the staircase.

Tom turned his back and then busied himself adjusting the woodpile by the stove. Then the busyness of getting the meal on the table and serving the food, sharing the local news, and opening a handful of presents occupied them all. It wasn't until after the dishes were done and put away, James in his bed and Corwin laying down in Grace's, and the men gone out to check on the horses in the barn, that Mae turned to Grace.

"I don't know how to tell you this. I don't want to tell you."

"What is it?"

Mae drew a deep breath. "We met Tom about halfway here. He was checking cows and just rode on along with us. We talked and laughed the whole time. When we arrived, Tom opened the gate to the corral so Ike could drive the team inside. That new dog of his was tied up in the barn. He had chewed the handle of a shovel to pieces. When Tom saw it, he went berserk. He took his fist and beat him. That poor pup had no way to get away. Then Tom kicked him again and again. Ike ordered me to come up here to the house. Grace...pups chew things. It was just the handle on a shovel."

Grace swallowed and stared at the empty teacup in her hand.

"Tom was in a good mood when we drove up. He was laughing. When he saw that dog, he became another man. I didn't want to tell you, but I think you deserve to know."

"I never wanted a dog here," Grace said. "It worried me because James was so young."

"If Tom blows up *in front* of people, Grace, what does he do when nobody's around?"

Grace looked up but said nothing else.

"Ike and I wanted you and Tom to be our baby's godparents, but, we can't trust Tom, can we? Tom must never be allowed to be alone with our child. We've seen how Tom treats James and now what we saw in the barn... We've never allowed him to be alone with Corwin. We'd hoped that maybe with time... I'm so sorry. I don't know how you do it. How do you stay?"

Grace looked at the little tree in the corner and the half-eaten apple pie covered with a cloth on the table. Her attempts at beauty and festivity mocked her.

"How can I not, Mae? Where would I go? What would I do?"

Mae rose to put on her coat and Grace followed her outside. They found the men talking near the barn. Ike helped Mae into the buggy and went into the house to bundle up Corwin. Grace waited until they were out of sight before she quietly asked Tom what had happened with the dog.

"Don't deny it. Mae told me," she said.

Tom tensed. He said, "That dog deserved to be taught a lesson and I gave him one with the same damn shovel he chewed."

"Where is he now?" Grace asked. "Did you feed him?"

"No. I buried him."

MEADOWLARK

15

Grace stood at the sink looking out the window, watching the wind skim across the snow, lifting the top layer into swirls sliding across the prairie. She dried the final glass and placed it in the cupboard when a horse whinnied, brash and loud. It had to be Tom's greenbroke gelding. The geldings were all pastured on the other side of the corral and Tom had pushed the trio of new broodmares to the south for better feed through the winter. Another whinny. A gate slammed against the fence.

She dropped the dishtowel on the table and hurried out the door. The wind threw the snow and dirt against her skirts and whipped them around her legs. She rounded the side of the barn to see the gate of the stud pen open.

Certain she had closed it that morning after feeding and milking, she ran forward. Her heart froze. There sat James on top of the raw-boned gelding, just three years old and barely broke. The horse's ears twitched nervously and he pawed the ground.

"Look, Mama!" James crowed.

Grace held her breath. She put her hand out in front of her and moved slowly toward them.

"James. Don't move."

The big horse shifted his weight and gave a low nicker. James played with the black streaked mane.

"Whoa, boy," Grace commanded in a low voice. "James, stay still. I'm going to help you down." Grace stepped closer and extended her hand, palm-first to the horse as a gesture of trust.

He tossed his head in sharp jerks, his ears alert.

"I ride like Dad!" James flailed his short legs.

The gelding tensed then erupted. James flew up but instinctively tightened his hold on the mane. The horse lunged toward the open gate, his body catching Grace in the shoulder. She spun to the ground. She rolled over the frozen manure and jumped to her feet.

Somehow James stuck on top of the broad back. Grace grabbed Mame's bridle off a peg and scrambled over the fence to catch her. Pulling up her skirts, she jumped from the top rail onto Mame's back, gripped with her thighs, and touched her boots to the mare's sides.

"Hold on, James!" Grace shouted as she leaned over Mame's neck, urging her to go faster.

"Mama, he won't stop!" a note of panic edged James's voice.

The distance shortened. Clods of snow and dirt flew from the horse's hooves to pelt Mame's chest and Grace's face.

"Mama!" James screamed. His body bounced like a rag doll above the horse's back. "I'm gonna fall!"

Mame's hooves drummed across the frozen ground until they were alongside the horse.

Grace's right leg was crushed between the racing animals. She reached out toward James. Tears streamed down his dirt-streaked face. Grace leaned and reached to grab James around his waist.

"James, let go!"

James shook his head no, his nose bleeding and knuckles white in the mane.

"I've got you. Let go, honey. Let *go*!"

James's fingers loosened. Grace tightened her grip and

yanked him against her torso. James clutched her around the neck.

"Whoa," Grace called to Mame, "Whoa!" The mare slowed to a lope and bounced to a trot, then stopped as the gelding kept on running, full bore, for the open prairie.

"Don't you ever climb on a horse again without telling me." Grace crushed her lips into his tousled hair. "You scared Mama to death." Tears leaked down her cheeks and wet his hair. She wrapped both arms around him to still the trembling.

"Don't you ever do that again. Promise me!"

"I wanted to make Dad proud."

"What?"

"Maybe if I ride good, Dad won't get mad at me." James looked up with pleading, scared eyes.

Grace focused her eyes on the horizon that divided the world into two halves; the upper composed of the mottled steel-gray sky, weak sunlight leaking through the clouds, and the bottom a rough, marbled white and brown.

"Honey, you could have been hurt. You don't have to prove anything to your father." She held James tighter, amazed that he was still alive. James looked up, a drying trickle of blood connecting his nose and his chin.

James and Grace sat outside peeling potatoes for breakfast. The summer sun blazed down on the prairie in the early morning. Winds whipped the dust and made the insides of her eyelids itch.

"Mama, do you love Corwin more than me?" James said suddenly, keeping his eyes intent on the potato he peeled. Speckled brown curls of skin with tiny specks of blown dirt clinging to its sticky surface flapped under his hand. James ducked his head so his reddish hair hung down in a curtain over his eyes. His hands shook.

"What? What makes you say that?" Grace's mind raced. What did her son need from her right now? "Of course I don't love him more than you. Both of you walk with my whole heart always with you. I love you because you are my son and I love him because he is Miss Mae and Mr. Ike's boy and they are our best friends. Why do you think I love him more, James?" She reached out and lifted James's bangs so she could see his eyes.

"Because you're always taking care of him. When he stays over, I hear you come into our room and check on him at night. You used to put your hand on my chest to make sure I was breathing, but you don't do that anymore. How come you don't check on me?"

"Oh, honey...come here." Grace dropped the peeling knife into the bowl and drew James into her arms, cradling him against her.

"I guess I don't do that anymore because I know you're fine. I watch you all the time. But when Corwin comes, he's a guest and I need to take extra care that he's all right. Love is infinite. It's not something that if you give some to one person, there's less for others. It's not like a pie that you cut up and the more one person receives, the smaller the pieces are left for everybody else. Do you know what 'infinite' means?"

James shrugged and shook his head.

"Infinite means forever and ever and ever. Always. Bigger than we can even begin to understand. That's what infinite means. And, that's how love is. Loving one person doesn't mean you love another any less. It's not like there's only so much love to go around and then there's no more. Actually, I think it works the other way, a lot of times. The more your life and soul fill with love, the more there is for others. Love begets love, James, it doesn't diminish it. Love is like the sky. Just look at it."

She pointed up at the dome of blue that cupped the endless expanse of prairie.

"See, on the horizon, how it looks like the sky ends right there?" Grace pointed west.

James nodded.

"Now, if we saddled up Mame and Blue and started riding in that direction and tried to find exactly where the sky ends, we would never find that, would we? We could keep going forever and never find the end of the sky. That's how love is. So, when you look at the sky, in the daytime or at night, honey, know that."

Grace thought a bit to herself, drew in a deep breath and decided to continue. "There are people who spend their lives so scared that there won't be enough love for them, that they fight for it and then try to hold on to it as tight as they can.

James's brow furrowed in puzzlement.

"Imagine a bunch of coyotes fighting over a rabbit they caught out on the prairie. They each want that bunny. They snarl and slash to keep others away and crush it in their teeth, trying to get it only for themselves. They clamp down so hard it crushes the life right out of it. Can you see that?"

James closed his eyes and nodded.

"Now imagine being that rabbit," Grace said.

"That's what it feels like to be loved by someone like that. If feels just like that." Grace waited for this to settle in. "How good do you think that feels?"

"Not very good, Mama. Not very good at all," James replied. "That's how Dad is, right?"

The remark stabbed Grace. "Well..." she said carefully. "Yes, your Dad feels that there's only so much love and when that happens to people, they usually end up driving away the very people they want to love them."

James's head bobbed. "That's so sad."

"I know. It's heartbreaking. On the other hand," Grace patted his leg, "every time you feel like there's not enough love, all you have to do is look into the sky to know how very, very much there is and that it goes on forever and ever. That's how I love you. And that's how I love Corwin. And that's how I love Miss Mae and Mr. Ike. All of you. That's how much I love you."

"How do you love Dad?"

"The best I can, young man, the best I can. And you need to do the same, okay?" Grace tickled her son's ribs, eliciting an infectious laugh.

16

"*Grace! Tom!* It 's Ike. Wake up!"

The edge of terror in the voice broke through the thin sheet of Grace's fitful sleep. She stumbled out of bed and pulled on a robe over her nightgown. A full moon shone in through the window in the living room and cast blocks of light on the floor, lifting the shade of darkness so Grace could make out the outlines of walls.

"I'm coming!" She opened the door to find Ike, his face glistening with sweat, hand raised to bang on the door again. He stumbled forward, pushing Corwin ahead of him.

"It's Mae," Ike said in gasps. "I got home late. Had to pull a cow out of the mud near the creek. The baby's trying to come, but something's wrong again. She's asking for you, Grace."

Tom walked up behind Grace and stood beside her.

"I'll be back in two minutes, Ike." Grace ran to the bedroom and yanked a dress over her nightgown. She dropped down on the bed and jerked on her stockings and boots. When she rounded the corner by the door, Ike turned on his heels and bolted for the buggy.

"I'll be back whenever I can, Tom." Grace clambered up for the seat as Ike reached out a hand. "Put Corwin to bed in James's room."

They arrived to find Mae weak and pale, the sheets stained with sweat and blood, where she had lain straining for hours.

Grace knelt beside the bed and reached out to take Mae's limp hand. Mae looked out from under heavy lids, her face waxen.

"Grace? I knew you'd come." She gave an exhausted cry as her body doubled-up in pain.

"Ike," Mae moaned, "I can't. I just can't anymore."

"Yes, you can, Mae darlin'," Ike said, sitting down beside her. "You damn sure can. We'll help you. Come on, now."

Mae clutched his hand, writhing, trying her best. "Something isn't right. I know it."

"I see the head, Mae. Keep pushing. It's almost here."

With a mighty heave, Mae wailed and fainted. Grace grasped the blue-faced boy and fought to free the umbilical cord from around his neck.

"Ike! Oh, God. Hurry!"

They worked in tandem, frantic, as Ike puffed air into his lifeless son's mouth and Grace tried to elevate Mae's heavy hips where a fountain of blood pooled on the bed. She stuffed a towel into Mae and watched it turn red. She moved against the wall and tried to make herself invisible, tried not to intrude on the intimate, sacred, and terrifying moment.

"Mae? Mae!" Ike screamed, setting aside the dead infant. "Come on, girl! Wake up!"

He slapped her face and Mae squirmed, her hands rooting for the tiny wet body on her chest. Ike crawled up beside his wife on the bed. He nestled her body into his own and brought the baby to her breast, cradling them both in his arms.

"I'm so sorry," he cried. "So sorry I didn't get here sooner."

Mae lay back against his shoulder and shuddered.

"Oh, my Mae..." Ike sobbed quietly into her neck, his tears mingling with the film of sweat dripping from her face. "Oh, our little boy."

151

Mae wanted the baby buried at their homestead, where he'd be close. After the funeral, Grace gazed out over the small grave and wondered what other stories the prairie would tell her. She would listen. It seemed little enough to do.

She couldn't quite believe that Mae had not spoken a word since her son died. Even though they often went months without seeing each other, Grace had always felt Mae's steady, sure, and talkative presence with her. It had helped her feel less terribly alone. Mae had always been there. And now she wasn't. A yawning chasm of loneliness opened around Grace and she feared she would fall into it and never be able to climb back out.

Far off, a meadowlark sang. Daisy had told her Meadowlark sang to remind her of her dreams, that she was meant to turn into her pain to get beyond it. Well, she wouldn't be able to turn toward this pain, and neither would Mae. It was too much and no dream could come from it. Nothing could bring Mae's baby back.

Grace studied the wheat-colored grasses swaying to their own music. What memories clung to their blades, singing out their songs among the swells? Lakota women had moved with the rhythm of their life-dances, living, loving, giving birth, and dying here. White women had brought their own rhythm to these prairies only recently, stumbling through their own difficult dances on this beautiful but brutal land. That night she wrote in her journal:

> *Women's tears brought more water to the parched earth than any of the summer thunderstorms or winter snows ever did. Women nourish these plains with tears and blood.*

Night enveloped the ranch in an obsidian shroud. No stars peeked through the thin cloud cover. No moon shone saffron orange. No night birds offered songs of encouragement. Stillness hung from every blade of grass.

Grace forged through the rote motions of work, pulled her

nightgown over her head with the dulled senses of one who has been awake and worked more hours than she can remember, and fell onto the bed. She curled onto her side, pulled a pillow close to her waist, curved around it, and edged into an exhausted sleep, welcoming the numbed absence of thought. She lay on the verge of unconsciousness when she felt the bed creak and shift under Tom's weight.

He shucked his clothes, his breath reeking of liquor. His hand sought her hip in the darkness and pushed her flat on her stomach to take her roughly. Tears inched down her face and onto the fabric of the pillow. As shame and revulsion flooded her, she fought to keep silent, her body automatically becoming still as a corpse.

Grace tried to send her mind and soul someplace far away, but this time she couldn't escape. She remained piercingly present and something deep inside her broke—finally and irreversibly. The weight of this often repeated callous act cracked some parchment-thin veneer and she spiraled into the dark depths of the unknown. Something essential changed within her and there would be no going back.

Tom finished and rolled over onto his back. In moments he was snoring. But Grace did not sleep. She studied the different woman she had become—a brittle husk with hollow space inside. If Tom ever touched her again she would disintegrate into dust.

The next morning she made every excuse she could to avoid him. She laid out his clean clothes, left his coffee on the stove and his breakfast on the table. When he called out that he was leaving, she simply ignored him as she wiped dust from the jars of canned food in the pantry. The minute he was gone, she woke James and told him to get dressed.

"We're going to go see Dr. Mae and Mr. Ike." Her heart pounded as she packed her mother's coffee grinder, her journal, and a few clothes. She saddled Mame and Blue and hoisted James onto the gelding's back. She shoved her few possessions into the saddlebags and her rifle into the scabbard. She mounted, and gigged Mame into a fast trot, keeping Blue and James alongside. She swiped away the tears that stung her eyes because she did not want James to know how terrified she was. Broken dreams. Empty promises. Lost hopes. She shoved them all aside in favor of stone-cold reality.

She guided Mame over the mounds of prairie toward the safe bosom of her best friend. Thoughts of Mae were wrapped in memories, of late nights watching her talk and laugh, her face illuminated by the oil lamp between them as their fingers nimbly completed the task at hand—quilting, sewing, snapping beans, or any of the other endless chores. Grace had always listened to Mae with an inquisitive and attentive mind. Mae had helped her learn what it meant to be an independent woman and Grace had absorbed every drop of Mae's wisdom.

As the dark form of Ike and Mae's new ranch house rose above the flat prairie, Grace's heart leapt. She would be safe now. She and James could live in the old claim shack. Mae could instruct her in all the things a nurse needed to know and she could go with her on her doctor rounds. James and Corwin could be brothers to one another. Sharp tears of gratitude stung her eyes. She slowed Mame to a walk and Blue's staccato trot stuttered to a stop.

"Hello!" she called out.

Grace got down and wrapped her arms tight around Mame's neck. "Thank you, Mame. Everything will be all right for us now. You'll see."

The horse rubbed her head against Grace's shoulder.

James leapt to the ground and sprinted toward the house yelling, "Corrie! Corrie!" Grace looped the lead ropes over the corral fence. As she walked toward the boys wrestling playfully in the dark yard, her heart eased and she finally felt like she could breathe.

Mae took one look into Grace's swollen eyes and said, "Okay, you boys go on in. Ike take them inside and get them something to drink. There's fresh bread and honey on the table."

Ike put his hand lightly on Grace's back before following Mae's orders.

"Grace, what is it?"

"I left him." Grace tried to steady her shaking voice.

Mae looked hard at Grace. "Come with me." She took Grace by the hand and pulled her toward the corral.

"Where are we going?" Grace said to Mae's stiff back.

At the gate, Mae stopped and swung around to face Grace. "You get back on that horse and go home, Grace."

"What? No!" Grace stammered.

"Tom must've known he would drive you to this point some day. He told Ike if you ever tried to leave him, he would go to the sheriff and take James away from you and never let any of us see him again." Mae's voice rose almost to screaming. "Do you hear me? He'll take James away from you and never let you see him again! You get back up on that horse and go back to him. You can't stay here."

Grace stared in disbelief. Where was the wise, wonderful, warm woman she'd adored all these years? Who was this hard soul screeching at her now?

"No, I won't! I told you. He's broken inside, Mae. And that makes him mean. And his meanness is destroying me and James."

"I don't care. I lost my boy and I absolutely refuse to let you lose yours!"

"Please, Mae. What about love? I have no love. Not a shred."

"Love? Love?" Mae gave a dry laugh, "Love is only a dream. Like how I loved my baby. You're never going to have love, just like I'm never going to have my baby back. A dream is all that's ever going to be. You made your choice. You're his wife. You can't stay here with us. Not now. Not ever. He'll take James from you and *that* will kill you! Do you hear me?"

Mae jerked the ropes off the corral fence and called out, "James! Time to head on back home now." She handed Mame's reins to Grace, turned and walked back into the house without a single backward glance.

Grace stood rooted to the spot. Icy numbness started in her toes and crept up her feet and legs and torso until it lodged in her skull. She tried to make sense of what had just happened. An odd pricking feeling began in her fingertips and worked its way up her arms until her entire heart filled with needles piercing her from within, stabbing into the raw underbelly of her soul.

Breath wouldn't come. She gasped, her lungs grabbing for shallow intakes of air. She heard the wind whistling over the grass. Where could she run? Where could she hide? Where could she and James go where Tom wouldn't find them? Mae was right: nobody could protect her or her son from Tom. Like a cornered animal, she felt visceral terror. A moan escaped from her throat.

The boys dashed out of the front door, wiping their mouths.

James waved goodbye, calling out, "Thanks!"

Ike stood in the doorway shielding his eyes from the sun with a raised hand and a look of apology.

Grace and James rode back over the same prairie trail they had just traversed.

James said "Mama?" once, but seeing the look on his mother's face he stayed silent.

Grace sealed her throat by clenching her jaws. The entire way to the ranch, not one sound escaped. The rhythmic sway of the mare moved beneath her, carrying her back to a place she no longer wanted to be. Nor did she utter any word when she took James into the house and up the stairs to his room. She pointed at his bed and he understood that she wanted him to lie down and take a nap. She tucked the quilt around him, avoiding his sad, questioning eyes. Then she walked back outside to unsaddle the horses.

In the private darkness of the barn she allowed retching sobs to work their way from the ground into her toes, through her legs and hips, until they gathered force in the depths of her belly. She leaned forward and heaved them out into the cooling air. Great wracking cries erupted from her as she vomited. The freed horses skittered to the far side of the corral and stood with ears high, watching her.

If only she could disgorge her belly, her lungs, her heart, then maybe the pain would ease. But the only thing she choked up was rancid, bitter bile. Her keening hung in the air, dry as dust. Grace collapsed into the dirt and lay limp as the afternoon shadows lengthened into evening.

She had to get up and see about James, see about supper, see what she was going to do with the rest of a life without hope. She could not afford the risk of Tom finding her there lying in the dirt.

In that very moment she decided to stop feeling sadness or pain. She saw her heart as a small and sturdy wooden chest. Tiny chambers with exquisitely carved doors lined the front in neat rows. One by one, Grace closed each door and locked it securely with a little golden key. *Love:* Closed and locked. *Vulnerability*: Closed and locked. *Open Heart:* Closed and locked. On and on Grace went down the rows. *Sadness. Heartache. Pain.* Locked. Locked. All locked.

When all were secure and safely shut, she took a final look at the golden key that fit the locks on the hidden, sacred chambers, then threw it far off where it was instantly swallowed by darkness.

She envisioned herself a piece of granite, impenetrable and strong. Tom's harsh words and emotional blows would run down her face like rain, unabsorbed, spilling off of her as she felt nothing. She would be slick and smooth. She commanded herself to never feel anything again. *Never again.*

MEADOWLARK

She shoved herself to her feet. Eyes forward and back erect, Grace returned to the house. The world had become a distant, hazy place. She now inhabited some abstract dream in which nothing was real, where everything felt foreign and disjointed. She was no longer a part of this life, but rather she observed it from some remote faraway place where she would remain forever.

When Tom noted her swollen eyes that evening, Grace rubbed them in an off-handed way and turned back to the stove.

"Oh, must be something in the air. James and I rode over to see Mae and Ike and Corwin this morning."

"Everything fine with them?" he asked as he sat down at the table.

"I suppose so."

James came running down the stairs, but when he saw his father sitting in the kitchen he bolted for the front porch.

"James!" Grace called out. "Don't slam the..."

"I'm going to bust that boy," Tom said.

"Don't. Here's your supper. Don't let it get cold. I'll get him."

Drawing a deep breath later that night, Grace moved her head back and forth in an effort to loosen the tight muscles of her neck and back. The supper dishes were done. James was fast asleep. Tom was sequestered in a chair in the living room, thumbing through the past week's newspaper. She sat at the table with her journal open. If he moved she would see him and put it away. She wrote with haste, the ink smearing under her sweaty hand.

> *He doesn't care if I hate him, as long as I'm his. What makes a man force a woman to stay with him by using his own children? What takes place in his heart that possession is mistaken for love? What must it feel like to force a wife to stay in a marriage based on her terror? Is that the excitement of it? Or is it forever trying to prove to himself that he is lovable, that she* must *love him. He will force her into loving him. She will one day, surely, if he just makes her stay.*

Can't he see that with each forced kiss or touch, I recoil from him more and more? I know he wants love, craves the love that will prove he's worthy. Yet, with every act of forcing me, he denies himself that which he most craves. What is so very sad is that I know, in his way, that he truly loved me once and I loved him. I was so ripe, so anxious and eager to give him every part of me to love with no limitations. By forcing me to stay here, by forcing me to love him, he pushes my love farther and farther out of reach.

Does he think he can force loyalty by driving a stake through my heart? That somehow that will engender love? Love doesn't take root and grow without attention, without air and light. Love is like the other living things of the prairie. Grass doesn't grow under the boulder pinning it to the earth.

Well, I accept that I am a prisoner. He has taken my body and soul and misused them. They're his now. No longer mine, at all. He claimed them as his own. I will give back my fake smile and veiled eyes. I cannot escape with my body and my heart, but I will go away in my mind. I will race Mame across the open miles, leaning low on her neck, clutching her mane, and watch the prairie pounding beneath her hooves. I will go far, far away, to a place where he can never touch me or hurt me again. In my mind's eye, I see Mame and me racing for a cliff as my spirit screams, "Jump!" And we do.

Grace quit eating and quit feeling. She prayed for death. Only her love for James kept her from taking her own life. Without him, she would have welcomed a rope with a noose thrown over a beam in the barn. One sharp drop and it would be over and done with. Grief wrapped itself around her like a coat she couldn't shrug off. She kept her eyes down whenever Tom was around. She refused to look her jailer in the eye. *Maybe if I make myself a smaller target it will be harder to hit me.*

Whenever the weight of her choices became too much to bear, she walked out onto the prairie and allowed the silence to consume her. Deadened and weak, she curled up in a ball in the tall grass and begged the earth to take her and let her sleep forever.

17

On a bitterly cold day Grace and Daisy pulled their chairs as close as possible around the glowing stove, beading and sewing together. The wind whipped snow into gliding furls under a leaden sky. Grace looked out the window from her rocking chair. A clouded world of white and gray blended together and disappeared into an opaque haze. The women had wrapped their feet and legs in quilts against chill. James and Ruth, five and six, bantered back and forth over their card game.

Grace was studying Daisy's beautiful hair as it flowed over her shoulders and fell in a dark, gleaming sheet to her waist.

"Your hair is so lovely, Daisy." Grace clipped the seam on the waist of one of her skirts to tighten it to fit her bone-thin waistline. "It just hangs so pretty."

Daisy knotted the sinew close to the moccasins she sewed and cut it with a little bone-handled knife, before running her fingers over the cluster of beads nestled across the top.

"Hair is very important for the Lakota. Each strand contains the essence of the soul. That is why we only cut our hair if we are in mourning, if someone we love has died."

Daisy reached into the leather pouch on the table and withdrew a long strip of sinew. Stripping a strand down the length, she licked the tip and slid it through the hole of the needle.

"I am sure they knew this when they cut our hair at the boarding school at Flandreau."

"Why would they do that?" Grace held up the skirt to measure it against her frame.

"The first thing when we arrived, they lined us up and chopped off our hair." Daisy's voice dropped to a whisper so the children would not hear. "Of course, we believed this meant our families had died. That we were truly alone."

Daisy leaned forward in her chair. "You must always be very careful with your hair, Grace. The hair that comes out in your brush or comb, you must always burn those in the fire. Never leave them on your dresser or anywhere where somebody could find them. It's too dangerous."

"What do you mean?"

"Think about those children watching their long hair fall to the floor—strands of heritage, of memories, of love, of life. When the Lakota children saw that, along with images of loved ones' faces piled on the floor, it destroyed them inside, especially to see their hair swept up and thrown into the trash. Your hair must be treated with respect so that your soul will know it is loved."

Conversations with Daisy connected Grace to life, albeit by the thinnest of threads. Without her though, Grace was adrift, with nothing grounding her, the earth beneath her feet felt ripped away. She did not dare give voice to her sadness, it would only provide Tom another weapon to use against her.

As they sewed Grace decided she would never cut her hair again. What would happen if Tom got a hold of a strand that contained her soul? She would clean her brush and comb every morning and every night. She would become as silent as the darkness that bound her.

After that day, on her walks across the prairie, she left her hair unbound. The shadow she cast showed long strands blowing and swirling aloft. Untamed, her hair came to represent an expression of the freedom and wildness within her, femininity combined with independence. What had started as a symbol of mute mourning slowly turned into one of fierce strength.

Grace found sanctuary in her lack of expectations—hopes that were not built up could not be knocked down. She persevered. Not for herself—the only person she felt she had failed—but for James. If there was one thing Grace Robertson was determined to do, it was to never fail to be there for her son.

After years of hardly noticing James, except in public displays, Tom suddenly insisted on taking him to the state capital of Pierre.

"You've never taken him anywhere. For years, you've barely paid attention to him. Why now?"

"A son needs to spend time with his father," Tom told her.

And suddenly, she knew exactly why. He knew her weakness. It had nothing to do with his wanting to be with James. It had everything to do with control and fear.

"Get in the wagon," Tom said to James, "Now."

James looked up at his mother, confused. Grace wrapped her thin arms around his back and held him close. Tom reached out to pry the boy away. He peeled her fingers back one by one.

"Mama?" James said.

"Tom, please. *Please.*"

"He's five years old! He needs to be with his father."

Tom ripped James from Grace's arms and shoved him toward the wagon. James's eyes cried "Mama, help me!" but he knew better than to speak the words. Tom pointed to the seat and James shinnied onto the wheel and sat down while his father gathered the lines.

"He's just a little boy, Tom. You're doing this because you know it is the best way to hurt me, and you'll even use your own son to do it. Whatever it takes to hurt me and for you to win. Whoever it hurts, as long as you succeed in destroying me."

"This is your fault. You've set the child against me. He has to learn." Tom reined his horse around and said, "I hope, for your own sake, that you get over this anger that you seem to have. I can't figure for the life of me where it comes from. If you don't watch yourself, people are going start to talking, say I married myself a woman who went *crazy* on me." There was a note of sly insulation in his voice. He followed it was a self-satisfied, "Come to think of it. I believe, they already are." He laughed.

Tom clucked the team into a trot and and James looked back at her. Though he remained silent, she seemed to hear his terrified shriek on the wind, "Mama!" Watching his eyes fill with terror, the firm piece of ground that held her gave way to an abyss to which she saw no bottom. She pitched through open space and fell as the wagon disappeared over the rise.

Grace rode Mame into Faith the next day to see if could find somebody to help her. There had to be one person in the world who could tell her how to protect James. Despite everything she'd suffered, she still believed in basic human goodness. She talked to the Reverend. She talked to the Judge. She talked to the Ladies' Aid Society. Every one of them, without fail, told her she needed to go to the sheriff.

She finally dragged into Ed Robertson's office, already knowing what would happen.

"I'm sure you believe you've told me the truth, Mrs. Robertson, but a father has a right to be with his son."

"Haven't you sworn an oath to protect others? I'm asking you to help me protect my son. Tom hasn't spent any time with James until now. He couldn't have cared less. Now he's taken him off to Pierre to God knows what kind of experience."

"All right then, when they return, bring James in to see me. I'll have a talk with him and see what he has to say."

"You can't ask James, Ed. You know that. He'll be terrified to say anything, not only because he knows how his father will react, but because you're his uncle. You know Tom. You've seen the kinds of things he does when he's been drinking. I know this isn't news to you!"

"Mrs. Robertson, if James truly wanted to have no part of his father, then all he would need to do is express that. Tom is a loving father and I know he has James's interest at heart. He wants that boy out in the world learning how to be a man, not coddled at home by the fire learning to do women's work."

"Women's work? Do you consider feeding cattle and horses women's work? Do you think cutting firewood and setting fence posts is women's work? That's what James does! He helps me on the ranch because Tom is never home!"

Ed shrugged. "As an official of the law, I would have to hear all sides of the story. So if you expect me to do something about what you say is going on, then I'll have to speak to Tom and I will have to speak to James without you present."

"Are you saying you don't believe me?"

"I'm saying I need to hear all sides of the story."

Grace's insides turned to liquid as she straightened her shoulders and left the office. She wanted to spit right in his face and slam the door. She attempted to still the trembling in her hands and weakness in her knees. When she rounded the corner of the building, her legs gave way and she sank to the ground. She turned her face into the rough planks and a sliver of wood dug into her cheek. She pressed the thin shaft deep into her flesh, welcoming the pain in her body, hoping it could overcome the pain in her heart. A rivulet of blood, followed the curve of her jaw, and fell on the top of her hand.

"Ma'am?" she heard someone say. "Are you all right?"

The voice sounded so kind, so familiar that she murmured, "Yes," and looked up, right into the eyes of Paul Overland.

"Did you fall?" he said as he reached out to help her to her feet. "My God! Grace, is it you? You're bleeding."

"Don't touch me," she whispered, turning her face to the wall. "Don't help me. Go away."

"How can I go away? You're hurt. Let me get someone. I'll…"

"No! Please, Paul. I can't…" She tried to hold back the tears slipping down her cheeks.

"What's wrong? More than this, surely? Is it Tom?"

"No! Why are you even here? I thought you'd gone south. I never expected to…" She couldn't go on. She had to get away before everything in her succumbed to his outstretched arms, his pleading eyes. He loved her. She'd always known it, and she knew it now in a way that tore her in two. If she went to him, if she told him, if she begged him to... How could she? She couldn't. She could never lose James. Not for anything. Not even to save herself.

"Please, Grace, you need the doctor."

"No! I need to get on my horse. If you'll just help me do that one thing..."

She wouldn't allow him to assist her in getting to her feet, nor would she let him hold her elbow as she stumbled toward Mame. She did let him help her get her foot in the stirrup and boost her into the saddle. She took the handkerchief he offered and pressed it to the dripping wound. She had to tear her eyes from his distraught face, but when she raised her head to rein Mame away, she caught the harsh stare of the sheriff who stood splay-legged in his office doorway with a smile on his face. He had the gall to tip his hat.

Alone in the house, Grace woke in the middle of the night to hear James calling for her outside.

"James? James! I'm coming, honey. Mama's coming!"

With a final thrust, Grace disengaged her legs and threw back the quilts, calling as she rolled, falling out of bed. She rose and stumbled through the darkness.

"I'm right here!" Grace reached the front door and threw it open, "James?"

There was nothing but the dark, empty prairie.

Grace rubbed her eyes with the back of her hands. She tiptoed down the porch steps to look around the side of the house. *I heard him. I know I heard him.* Grace dashed to the other side, her bare feet beating against the ground, calling, "James? Where are you?"

Nothing but moonlight and the vast, silent land. Grace turned circles, scanning the night, her heart pulsing in her ears, until at last she realized that James truly wasn't there.

Love doesn't matter. Trust no one. Focus on the work. The work is the salvation. Block out feelings. Block out thoughts. Block out all. Block out people. Block out any idea of Paul. Focus on the work. Focus on the dust on this floor. Focus on this dish. Focus on this hen that needs to be fed. When thoughts start to creep in, sweep them out as quickly as you sweep the manure from Tom's boots off the floor. That's all they are, these thoughts. Manure. Sweep them out. They'll go away. Focus on the work. All that matters is the work...and James.

Ed Robertson stopped by the following afternoon. She met him on the porch saying only one word: "Sheriff."

"Tom sent me a telegram. He asked me to come out and tell you that he's decided to go on to the sale barn in Quinn. He'll be gone a month."

Grace bit her tongue to keep from screaming. As he turned to leave, she ground out one sentence with cold, jerking words. "If anything happens to my son, I'm holding you accountable."

The sheriff shook his head and laughed softly as he mounted his horse.

When he was gone, Grace managed to get inside the house. Then she curled up in a tight little ball and begged for sleep. She wanted to move into the realm of nothingness. She didn't care if the world passed her by while she hibernated with her pain. If the milk cow's plaintive bawling hadn't woken her, she might never have moved.

She struggled to her feet and out the door chanting, "The work will save me. The work is all that matters. The work. The work. The work."

"You look like absolute hell, I have to say," Mae said when she stopped by the house on her way home from a call. She took Grace's hand to feel her pulse. "What's going on? I know there's something terribly wrong and I want to help. Tell me."

Grace wanted to scream, *"It's your fault. I came to you for help and you turned me away. You turned my son away and now he's gone!"* Instead she stared back with a clenched jaw. If she said one word about Tom or James the wall she was trying so hard to hold up would come crashing down around her and there would be no going back.

Grace shook her head, dug deep inside, and pulled up one of the mindless responses she had become so accustomed to repeating.

"Oh, I'm fine. Just tired. Tell me about Ike and Corwin. And Mrs. Farthing. Didn't you say you'd just been to see her?"

"You're not fooling me. Not one little bit. Every time I ask how you are, you never answer me. You always ask me a question in return. Do you think I don't notice? That may work with some people, but not me."

"Things are tough right now. Tom took James to the capital. I miss James more than I can say." She placed the smile back on her face. "Tell me about Corwin."

"Well, he is as jealous as he can be that James got to go to the capital and he had to stay home and help his father with cows. But we'll take him one day. He says he wants to be a doctor when he grows up. Now where do you think he got that harebrained idea? Wouldn't you think that seeing me gone at all hours of the day and night would teach him to choose something different—like maybe a bartender or a gambler."

There had been a time when Grace would have laughed. Now she just looked at Mae. *Mae with her own child at home.*

"Yes, well, I have chores to tend to, Mae. I'd best get to them." With that, she turned her back on the woman who had been her best friend.

A sheriff's deputy showed up on the porch the following week. When Grace answered the firm knock at the door, the man said, "Sheriff Robertson sent me." He took out a paper and read, "You are accused of child abuse, child neglect, and endangering children."

Grace left her body. She broke into floating pieces that could not hold together. *Somebody else holds your heart in their hands by having control over your children. Somebody else has control of your children. Can you imagine such a thing?*

She looked up into the sky—*yes, it's still blue. The sun still shines. Yes, the clouds are indeed still in the sky, white, with underbellies of the faintest gray. The brittle wheat-colored grass still blows in the wind.*

Grace didn't understand why everything looked the same. The whole world had just changed. Why hadn't the sun turned purple? And the sky a rich emerald green with black stripes? Where were the horses dancing in ball gowns? The coyotes waltzing with antelope?

She looked at the young man in her doorway. *So young. So very, very young.* The he'd spoken floated unintelligible on the wind. Her mouth moved. Sound came out. And Grace stared at him, brow furrowed, trying to get make sense of what he was saying.

"You are accused of child abuse, child neglect, and child endangerment…"

"What?"

"Do not interrupt me," he said, giving a practiced response and continued reading in a unsteady monotone.

Looking down at herself standing there listening Grace remembered every moment, every delicate feature of James's newborn body, so fragile she refused to set him down. Images flashed through her mind—of Tom drunk and yelling, of Tom shaking and hitting him, of the shaming, of his cruelty to the animals, his brutality with her—it all moved like a river through her mind.

"May I come in?" the deputy asked and broke Grace's trance.

Numb, Grace said, "Yes, please do. Excuse the mess. I was busy outside with the livestock this morning."

She watched the deputy take in the single dirty plate in the sink and the less than perfectly clean clothes hanging on the pegs. Grace tried to be polite and respond to the young man's questions, but manic laughter was welling up inside her, itching to be released.

She tried to keep a straight face, but the insanity of the accusations burbled up and finally spilled over. She clutched her stomach and doubled over, rocking back and forth. Some long imprisoned emotion stretched and broke.

The frayed thread that had held everything together for so long snapped and Grace unraveled. The pitch of her unrestrained laughter rose higher and higher, a maniacal release of years of holding back, of swallowing down, willing her mind to fly away—it all came tumbling out. She knew it to be the last nail in her coffin, but still she couldn't stop.

MEADOWLARK

The deputy stood up and backed away, shaking his head. Everything he had presumed about Mrs. Robertson's malevolent character had been confirmed. As he opened the door, he said by way of parting, "I'll have the sheriff send a doctor."

Grace slid from her chair and crumpled to the floor, where she lay pounding the planks until the laughter eased into weeping eddies. And there she stayed, unmoving, unseeing, barely breathing. She lay in the same position as the world continued around her in shades of gray and the hushed tones of water moving over stones. When she attempted to move her arm, her hand, her finger, nothing responded. She acquiesced and gave in to her state. Her body softened, her muscles turned to dough, bones into soft strands of jelly, molding to the floor beneath her. She felt the earth reach up, envelope her in eternal arms, and Grace closed her eyes.

She did not sleep. Instead, she entered a world threaded with past, present, and future. Time had no beginning and no end. She slid between the worlds of dreams and consciousness, unable to respond in either. For the first time in her life, Grace fully surrendered.

Visions slipped through her mind, fusions of memories floated through her consciousness. Vaguely aware, she experienced disparate scenes from a distant place of no feeling, no judgment, no pain, a place of being, of essence, a place of infinite space as dust settled in a powdery film on her skin and clothing.

Through this fog, she heard banging on the door. A needle prick of awareness punctured her mind and forced clarity into its hazy edges of her world.

She heard Mae's voice. "I know you're in there! Grace! The sheriff rode over and told me what happened. I'm coming in!" Mae opened the door and saw Grace's crumpled figure on the floor. "Grace? Grace!"

Mae lifted Grace's head from the floor and poured water into her mouth. Grace gagged and groaned as Mae dragged her leaden body into the kitchen to pump water for a bath.

"I spoke directly with the Sheriff about this—foul man, isn't he, though?" Mae said. "I used my medical credentials to vouch for you. The charges have been dropped. For now, at least, though I fear he's up to something and I don't know how much good I can do once the law is involved."

Grace kept asking for something, but Mae couldn't tell what

is was that she wanted. Finally, Grace managed to make her understand that she needed her journal. Mae agreed to get it from its hiding place if Grace would agree to drink some broth.

With her hair damp around her face, with Mae attempting to spoon soup into her mouth, she wrote:

> *I am truly alone in this world. There is no one to turn to anymore. It is something—this realization. One of Mother's books contains stories of Africa. One tells of the people's belief in the ability to put a curse on another person through a little doll. Often they use real strands of hair or bits of clothing belonging to the person they want to curse. These dolls are said to contain spirits and enable their holders to curse and hurt the person from afar. The Lakota believe that a person's hair contains the essence of that person, and the people are careful that whenever they brush their hair that any left in the comb or fallen to the floor is picked up and burned immediately.*
>
> *Was I careless with my hair when I brushed it? Did Tom make a miniature doll of me, so he could hurt me, even when he's far away? I can feel them jab—needles deep in me, knives flaying the protective skin from my back—and they leave me raw and vulnerable.*

To Grace's surprise, Mae took the journal and read she had written. Grace didn't have the will or the strength to stop her.

Mae glanced up once and ordered, "Eat!"

Grace tried, but set the spoon back on the table. Mae read and read. Finally, she set down the book. She gathered Grace into her arms.

"I'm so sorry. I'm so sorry, my dear Grace. Tomorrow you are going to take those dolls back. In your mind I want you to rip those dolls from those who hold them. We are going to clear away a circle of grass on the prairie and scrape the earth clean with a sharp rock. We are going to place those voodoo dolls inside that space and stuff paper all around them. You are going to strike a match and light those dolls on fire. And when that fire burns out, you will be free. Do you hear me? Grace, did you hear what I'm saying? You cannot allow yourself to die.

"You have to live, because without you what will I do?"

18

Mae stayed with Grace for a week, caring for her as both doctor and friend. Tired of dealing with James, Tom had returned him and left again, mumbling something about checking on some cows over near Philip. Grace's eyes constantly searched James out, fearful he would somehow be gone again, until at last she trusted that he was truly home. The next time Ike came by to check on Mae, he collected James to stay with him and Corwin.

"Just us fellas," he told James, as James looked back over his shoulder toward the house with concern. "Don't you worry none about your mama. Dr. Mae is going to tend her just fine. You want to worry about something, how about you worry about what you, me, and Corwin are going to eat," which drew a giggle from the boy.

MEADOWLARK

One morning, a few days later the women watched a lone cow headed with determination over the western curve of the horizon. The brisk stride and alert angle of her head gave every indication that the cow knew exactly where she was going and why. Light caramel colored, the cow didn't resemble the usual wild and rangy cattle of the ranch.

"That cow doesn't look like one of ours," she said to Mae.

"It belongs to Daisy," Mae said. "We've seen her wandering around our place, even as far away as the Farthings'."

"Tom told me once that Daisy was a witch and he ordered me to stay away from her. He said he heard that she casts spells on men and women, that she can turn herself into a creature. Do you believe that Mae? That Daisy's a witch?"

"Of course not. I do believe she knows a lot that we don't know. I've always been partial to her insights and grateful that she was there when Corwin was born."

"I don't let Tom's opinion about her color our friendship. She somehow knows when he's not around. That's when she comes to visit me, and James loves playing with Ruth, but he knows to never mention either of them to his father."

Grace watched the cow disappear over the rise. She wanted to follow her and go see where Daisy lived. "Have you ever been there?"

"Where?"

"To Daisy's?"

"Yes, of course. I was there for Ruth's birth. Haven't been back since, though.

"Let's go," Grace said getting her coat.

"Where?"

"Let's follow the cow to Daisy's. I would so love to see her."

"Well, this is the most animation I've seen in you in months. Okay, I'll go saddle the horses and you pack us a lunch."

In minutes they were trotting off, side-by-side and soon spotted the cow ambling over the dry grasses. They kept far enough behind so that the cow wouldn't feel as if she were being driven. They rode in silence, each with her own thoughts. Finally, Mae spotted Daisy's home, dug into the side of a low ridge. She pointed it out to Grace. The cow walked directly up to the door and pushed against it with her nose.

Seconds later, the door opened and Daisy emerged to rub the

cow's nose and behind her ears, and murmur soft words. The woman sensed their presence and looked up and around, her eyes settling on them on horseback not far away.

"Well, look what you brought home with you, Maude," Daisy said as she walked out to meet them. "Good morning. I'm glad you came. I've been worried about Grace and her walking in the world of the spirits." Daisy's eyes took in Grace's pallor and bony shoulders and arms.

"We couldn't resist following your cow. I've always been curious about where you lived...and how."

Grace reached down to touch Daisy's hand, embarrassed by her work-rough skin and short, blocky nails trimmed with a knife. Grace admired the steely resolve and strength that emanated from the small woman, including her firm handshake. She held herself with a confidence and poise that bespoke deep wells of inner strength.

"Well, Maude must've brought you here for a reason," Daisy said with a rare smile. "Why don't you come in for a cup of tea?"

"We'd love to," Grace and Mae said in unison.

They slid off their horses, looped the reins over the hitching post in front of the dugout, and followed Daisy into her home. The roughness of the outside of the house gave way to a single room, floor-to-ceiling shelves lined the walls, each filled with folded fabric and small jars filled with beads. Ruth smiled up at the women from where she sat with a book on the floor. Dried herbs hung in bundles around the kitchen. Daisy served them tea in delicate cups with pink roses.

"Daisy, I did hear someone say, well, they say you're a witch," Grace blurted out.

Daisy burst out in delighted laughter. "Well, of *course* they do! And who do you think planted that seed out there to grow?"

Mae laughed outright but Grace looked puzzled.

"Well, I did! It's the way we stay safe out here, just me and Ruth."

"You, Daisy? You *want* people to think you're a witch?"

Mae laughed again. "Do you know who the 'witches' really were? They were healers, Grace, *healers*. You've read about all the women burned at the stake in Europe in the medieval times, haven't you?"

Grace nodded and noticed how golden flecks in Daisy's eyes

caught the light that streamed in through the window, reminding her of mica sparkling in the sun on rocks in the creek.

"All supposedly for being 'witches,' for 'laying with Satan.' Nonsense!" Daisy threw her arms in the air. "Stories created by men who were threatened by those women's knowledge and power. They were the ones who brought babies into the world, who knew how to use herbs to heal. Did you know once they burned four hundred women in one day in Toulouse, France? Anybody could accuse a woman of anything. They murdered the wise and independent women, the ones who wouldn't 'behave.'" Mae reached for her cup of tea, her fingernail resting on the delicate, intertwining roses.

"Well then, I am a witch—a healer," Daisy said. "I love my life because it's hard won. It is sacred to me and I don't want anybody coming around. I love being alone with Ruth. I love the plants, love the animals, love my quilts and beading. Just look at the colors of the fabrics and glass, bone, and shell." She gestured with a wide arc of her hand toward the shelves.

"I love the way the beads catch the light, whether it's from kerosene light at night or the sun during the day. I love where my mind goes when I'm working with fabric and beads. I don't have much use for what most people spend their time talking about. I don't care what the neighbors are up to. I can't abide gossip, so a lot of the people around here don't have much use for me. I believe in letting people live their own lives. I don't want to spend my life whispering behind other people's backs about what's not my business to begin with."

Daisy leaned forward across the table, her eyes fierce. "I was married to a fine man. Since he died, I've no interest in any other. I savor living by myself now."

"I've wondered, myself, why people can't just live their own lives," Grace said. "Seems to me it's the people who don't want to look at their own lives, who pass the most judgment on others. Easier to put others down than look at themselves." Grace walked over and ran her fingers over the stacks of fabric.

"That's exactly right. I would rather listen to the song of the prairie and all of her animals, than the nonsense of people." Daisy stood and walked over to look at the window.

"The song?" Grace moved over to join Daisy, in case there was something she'd been missing. "I hear the wind blowing, sure enough."

"Remember Meadowlark? Every place, every creature, every

person has their own song. You just have to listen for them. You have your own song, Grace. Deep within you. Most people live their whole lives and never listen to the songs of life, not their own or any around them. Scares them too much. It's easier to go through life living the way everybody else expects you to. But when you're listening to your own song, Grace, you feel deep peace, right here." She reached out and placed the flat of her palm on the center of Grace's chest.

"Why?" Grace looked at Mae, but it was Daisy who answered her question.

"Fear, mostly. We get caught up in thinking we need to live life one particular way or we're wrong. People are scared. Scared of the world, of others, but mostly, scared of themselves. Most people do what's expected of them, bury whatever feelings don't fit deep inside themselves in tiny, cramped spaces. They try to forget. They don't even know what their own song is, anymore. But, to live life in song, Grace, that's what the Great Spirit intended. Think about something that makes you happy and peaceful. Go on," she urged. "Close your eyes. Now, let your mind go to that place."

Grace closed her eyes. Images of Tom and his ugliness filled her mind with sadness, loneliness, and the sound of the whip cracking across the backs of the horses, and Mame turning to her, panic in her eyes. The images shifted. Some were happy and peaceful. She held James and nursed him. She rode Mame across the prairie and felt the horse's hooves connecting with the earth. She felt the wind in her hair, the sun on her face. She smiled.

"There's your song, Grace. Whatever you are thinking about right now, that's your song. When you live in song, it becomes your shield."

"Your song becomes your shield? How?"

"When you listen to your own song, and live by the song you were born with, you're protected from the barbs of others, the expectations others put on you. The song becomes your shield, the greatest protection any of us have."

"I'm going to need some time to think about this," Grace said as she sat back down at the table.

Daisy reached out and took her hand. "I know, I know. You've lived your whole married life trying to be what Tom wanted of you. It'll take some time to sift through that. But, it's there, Grace. We all have it. We each have our own song, and oh, how beautiful life can be when we listen to it."

"You know your song, Mae, don't you?" Grace's eyes filled with tears and she swallowed hard.

"Yes. I lost it for a while after the baby died. You know that more than anyone." The words hung in the air. "But it came back to me in time. Mostly it is the Habanera aria from *Carmen*, but sometimes it is just the beating of my heart when Ike holds me or Corwin snuggles up to me."

"How can I find my song when it feels like the world is intent on beating it out of me? It isn't right, it isn't fair."

Daisy laughed aloud, "Right and fair don't have a thing to do with this, Grace." Her unbound black hair framed her face. "Or life, for that matter."

"She's right," Mae said becoming very serious, "You listen to me, Grace. Don't waste your time on what's fair or right. I'm going to tell you how it *is*. You will *not* win if you fight him, Grace. You won't. All Tom has to do is walk into court looking handsome and humble, and say a few things, shaking his head feigning compassion and apologizing for wasting their time with such ridiculous nonsense." She waved her hand in the air dismissively.

"He'll then explain how you tried to take his child away from him and how you poisoned James's mind against his father, all the while shaking his head in disbelief, glancing over at you and making sure they see a look of pity in his eyes. What a burden Tom carries, the men in the court will think to themselves, having to deal with such a woman. 'She's crazy,' they'll say, and shake their heads in sympathy, and reach out to grab his upper arm in a gesture of masculine commiseration.

"The harder you fight, the harder they'll make it on you. They'll punish you. They won't care what happens to James and they'll use him to make you pay for what you've done. They'll revel in their power to do so. They'll enjoy every moment of it. Listen to what I say to you, Grace. *Believe* me."

"There is wisdom in her words, Grace. You will do well to listen to her."

The bedroom door slammed open and Grace awoke with a jolt. Tom lit the lamp that stood on the chest of drawers. The clock struck 2:00 a.m. He'd only been back one day. Grace's stomach clenched and she held her breath.

"I been reading your little book." He shook the small journal at her.

The stench of whiskey hit Grace full in the face. She curled into herself, trying to become as small as possible.

"I see you been remembering the good times, with some boy named Paul. If that's the same sonofabitch who has helped me run cattle, I'm going to kill him."

Grace gagged back the nausea that threatened to spill out of her mouth. She pulled the quilt up around her neck.

"I should order you to get the hell out of my house," Tom spat down at her. "I've always suspected you're a whore and a cheat." He sat unsteadily in the chair in the corner of the room. He reached to pull off his boot, his hand missing his foot and grasping only air on his first try.

Grace shut her eyes halfway and clenched the quilt to her chest. Tom attempted to take off his boot again, his hand fell heavily on top and he moved it with a jerk around to the back heel. After a few tries he succeeded in wrenching it from his foot.

Grace sat paralyzed in bed.

"You ever try to leave me again and I'll take this to the sheriff to keep you away from James, forever. I'm sure he and the judge would really like to see what you wrote. Fine things for a mother to write. They'll take James away from you in a heartbeat if they see this. And I will show 'em, if you give me cause. Don't you ever doubt me. I am a man of my word!"

Grace forced herself to swallow the acid rising in her throat and winced as it stung. She shifted her gaze to Tom and saw the heavy-lidded wavering that often preceded him passing out. She didn't say a word. Tom lurched toward the bed and fell down. He pulled off his other boot and smacked her in the head with it before he threw it to the floor.

Grace stared into the glow of the lamp and listened to Tom's heavy breathing. She must never write again. She must never, ever write again. Not anything. She must never risk giving Tom the ammunition to take James away from her.

MEADOWLARK

When she was certain Tom was unconscious, Grace eased from bed and picked up the journal from the floor. After tucking it under her nightdress, she blew out the lamp and left their room, every nerve on edge. She slipped up the stairs and peeked into James' room. He was asleep on the bed, face down, and still dressed. She did not go in, though she yearned to put a quilt over him and gather him close to her and hold him there forever.

Wide-awake, she ghosted into the kitchen. She carved a narrow slit in the wall under the windowsill near the pantry with a butcher knife. The newspaper insulation crinkled and rustled when she pushed the journal through the opening and nestled it in the wall. She mixed some flour and water to make a paste and replaced the narrow strip of wood in its spot, invisible under the window's ledge.

She sat in her rocking chair, but did not rock. While she remained still, her mind raced. Out of habit, her thoughts turned to writing—instantly extinguished by the question, *How will he use this against me?*

In the pre-dawn light she slid her tight body out of the chair, hurriedly dressed, and began making coffee. Half an hour later, she heard Tom snort as he awoke and then heard the heavy thump of his feet hitting the floor.

Her hands shook as she cracked the eggs. She waited, tense and alert. He walked into the kitchen, his shoulders hunched over and his head hanging low.

"Grace. Perhaps I owe you an apology," he said.

It would be shame this time. It was always either shame or guilt that colored his thoughts after these episodes. Grace just never knew which until he spoke. She could never second-guess him. Her role was to make as little as possible of what he had done. to relieve his embarrassment. To hold him accountable would only make everything much worse.

"Oh, well," she said lightly. "Come have your breakfast."

She filled his cup and set a plate of bacon, eggs, in front of him. She sat down at her place, but pushed away the basket of biscuits he nudged her way. What little she was eating would go the way of her writing. She had no appetite, anyway. Maybe if she made herself very small he would not notice her at all.

James stumbled into the kitchen, rubbing his eyes just as Tom was grabbing his hat and gloves.

"James!" Grace said opening her arms to him and smiling. "Oh, I missed you."

James seemed hesitant, knowing he wasn't supposed to go to his mother. He held himself tense.

"Get your boots on," Tom said. "We've got cows to check."

"Tom, he hasn't eaten yet. Let him eat and I'll ride out with him in a bit. We'll find you."

"Get going, son. If you'd get out of bed when you're supposed to, you'd have time to eat."

James ducked his head in acknowledgement. He turned and ran to his mother and hugged her around the waist. She slipped a biscuit into his shirt pocket. Then they were both gone and she was alone again.

MEADOWLARK

19

By July, the beautiful spring had baked into a hard dry summer and Grace opened her eyes in the darkness. What had awakened her? The fog of slumber clouded her brain as her eyes searched the blackness of the bedroom. There it came again, an insistent blow that rattled the door. She rolled over and reached her hand on Tom's side of the bed. He wasn't there.

She rubbed her eyes and shook her head. She pulled her robe from its peg and stumbled through the living room. "Hello? Who is it?"

"Mrs. Robertson? It's the law, ma'am."

Grace opened the door to discover a bear-sized man in uniform. He stepped forward.

"Are you the wife of Tom Robertson?"

"Yes," she said slowly.

"Your husband has been hurt." He paused a moment, drawing in a deep breath. "Do you know where your son is?"

"What?" she stammered.

"Some things were found with your husband and we need to know if your son was with him. If we need to," he paused again, "look for him." In the dim light, Grace saw sympathy in his eyes.

"Wait!" Grace ran upstairs to James's room. He had to be in his bed…didn't he? He'd been out riding with Tom earlier that day. But he had been with her for supper, hadn't he? A vice clamped down across her chest and she couldn't breathe. The world went dark and constricted to encompass only the distance that separated her from James. Where was he? She stumbled into his room, catching her shoulder against the doorframe on her way through. She felt frantically over the bedcovers. Her hand fell on the warmth of his arm. Grace reached out her other hand to rest on James's head. *Oh, thank God!* Her legs gave way and she sank to the floor beside his bed and listened to her son's soft even breath.

Grace forced herself rise. Fear oozed drop-by-drop from her mind. By the time she was back at the front door she was imbued with a deep calm.

"My son is in his bed, sir." Grace held open the door and gestured that the man should come in. "What happened?"

"Your husband was in a fight. He insulted and pushed a woman."

"He was drunk, wasn't he?"

He looked at her in surprise, "Why, yes, ma'am, I'm sorry to say that he was."

Grace nodded. "Go on."

"The woman's husband beat him pretty bad," the lawman said. "The doctor's with him now. You'll need to come with me."

"I don't want my son to be alone," Grace said. "I'll take care of that and then come to town."

"Are you all right, ma'am?"

"Yes. Thank you. I appreciate you coming all the way out here to tell me." She opened the door once more and he stepped out into the night.

"Yes, ma'am. The sheriff thought you should know as soon as possible."

MEADOWLARK

Grace waited for James to waken. She fed him a good breakfast, then explained that she was going to ride with him over to Mr. Ike's and Dr. Mae's and leave him for a few days. His father had been hurt and she needed to go see him at the doctor's office. No, he could not come with her. She needed him to be somewhere safe so she wouldn't worry about him. Would his father be all right? She didn't know and couldn't say, but she would come back as soon as possible and he mustn't worry about anything. He was to help Mr. Ike and Corwin. Was that understood?

When he said yes with all the conviction of a young man, she gathered him close and held him until he said, "I will. I will."

She found Tom lying in a bed at the doctor's house in Faith. She pulled up a chair and sat by his side.

When he regained consciousness, he turned to her and said, "I'm sorry."

Grace felt nothing. His brother Ed came in his official sheriff capacity to arrest him—just a formality—and to tell him he'd later have to take him to jail.

After that, Tom never spoke a word to her nor did he even look her way. He spoke to the doctor. He spoke to his brother. But he ignored her as if she wasn't even there. She followed along to the sheriff's office and inquired about the process of posting bail. She asked about the charges against him and found that Ed had talked the other party into dropping them. She wanted to argue with Ed and insist that Tom did have a prior record and she had the bruises to prove it.

She waited with him, staying in a hotel room, for the few days it took him to regain enough strength to ride back to the ranch. Hearing about his predicament, men stopped by to see him. They clapped him on the back, told him how sorry they were that he'd had to go through such an ordeal. They knew, of course, that he'd done nothing wrong, that he was just standing up for himself. And she watched without comment as Tom thanked them and never uttered a word about what had actually happened.

The day they came home from town, Tom left immediately to check the cows. He didn't ask about James. He said little to her. He left his saddle on his horse, grabbed a drink of water, and rode away.

When he returned that evening he was feeling mean, and Grace knew what was coming, knew it before he scraped his boots on the porch. Knew it before the creak of the door. Knew it before she saw the look of lust and arrogance in his eyes. Knew it before she felt him come up behind her and grab at the buttons of her dress.

Grace knew Tom Robertson was like a small child, and like a child he had to lash out and hit and *hurt* when things didn't go his way. There was no thinking, no looking outside himself at the bigger influences, and no looking within. He lived in constant terror of having to face the unknown.

At last Grace truly understood that Tom would do anything, even sacrifice his wife and his son in order to avoid looking into that great empty space in his own heart. She remembered all of the nights she'd hoped and prayed that he would somehow become the man she thought he was when they married, that he would be strong and brave enough to face his demons and come out the other side—whole and complete.

Now she knew—finally, truly understood—that would never happen. She also realized that she would not sacrifice her son's life to Tom's wounds and insufferable pride any longer. She had protected him from himself, at the expense of her sanity and James's well being, and she was ashamed.

This was burned into her very soul as he pushed her across the kitchen table and forced himself into her from behind. Pain ripped through her. *Not there, not there!. It hurts so much there!*

The distant trill of the meadowlark found it's way through the pain. She remembered Daisy's words: "Meadowlark reminds us to turn toward our fear, to turn *into* our pain and not to deny its existence or run away from it."

Grace knew she would never again allow James to suffer another harsh word or horrific slap from Tom's cruel hands. A great calm settled over her as her husband shoved and grunted, slamming into her to remind her she was nothing. There was no longer any fear, the familiar horror was replaced with a blanket of peace. The terror that had encased her and defined her disappeared. Her deep-seated anger dissipated. Her heart slowed to the rhythmic beat of one who has found complete clarity.

She knew in that moment what she must do.

She knew it that night as she lay awake beside him, her backside burning.

She knew it as she dressed at dawn and fixed her hair.

She knew it as she poured a cup of coffee for him.

She knew it as she stirred that little something extra that Daisy had given her into the dark liquid.

She knew he would ride away once he had finished breakfast.

And she knew he knew he would not return.

That evening Grace watched the prairie catch the glow of the setting sun and become a plain of shadow and light. She covered Tom's dinner with a dishtowel and put James to bed. Later, after the chores were done, the kerosene lamps cast the darkness of the living room to the far corners where it settled comfortably along the base of the walls.

Grace stared at the door, her back pressed straight and rigid against the wooden rocking chair. She focused on the door handle, imagining a slight movement several times in the weak light. Each jiggling of the latch caused her stomach to clench, joined by the familiar sensation of thousands of needles pricking at her skin from the inside.

Grace sat there through the hours of darkness. She watched the promise of light wash the horizon into lighter and lighter shades of black, then gray, moving up through the color of purple asters, before bleeding into a weak yellow, brightening into ever-bolder strength, and easing the darkness from the room until she realized the lamps were no longer needed. She eased her stiff body from the chair and put on the kettle to boil.

She looked out the window and up the narrow dirt lane that wound its way down to the house. Empty. She scanned the breadth of the landscape, her eyes catching a flicker of movement. Tom's gelding walked up over the swell and trotted briskly toward the corrals, the stirrups swinging freely at his sides. One rein hung limply from the bridle, the horse popping his head up every time the rein caught under his hoof. The other rein, snapped in half, swayed with the horse's gait. The worn leather of the empty saddle seat caught the sun's light.

Grace's eyes moved back to the spot where the gelding had come over the ridge, holding her hand in front of her as she came around to approach the horse.

"Whoa there, boy," she said in a low voice, her hand clasping the smooth leather of the trailing rein.

Grace looked into those large brown eyes and stroked the horse's muzzle. Mame walked over, whickering a greeting and Grace stood there a long while, allowing herself the sheer comfort of their quiet presence.

A team of horses and a wagon crested the rise and dropped down along the lane, the rhythmic clop hooves interspersed with the jangle of the tug chains.

"Halloooo, Grace!" Mae called, her arm looped through the crook of Ike's as he slapped the reins softly across the horses' backs. Corwin and James waved from the back. A meadowlark's trill bounced through the fresh air as Ike called "whoa" and the team jarred to a halt beside Grace.

"So! You're back. That's good." Mae's crisp white blouse shone in the sunlight. A slight wind lifted her hair and swirled it around her smiling face.

"Mama!" James leapt from the back of the wagon and threw himself against her legs. She leaned down to kiss the top of his head.

"Tom around?" Ike asked, looking up toward the barn. "Looks like his horse reared back and snapped that rein."

"No, Tom's not here. He rode out to check on the herd yesterday and didn't come home last night. His horse just trotted in."

"His horse came back without him?" Ike pushed back the brim of his straw hat. He sat up straighter on the seat, lifting his eyes to scan the surrounding prairie.

"I was puzzling about what I should do. I haven't even milked or fed yet," Grace said.

"He musta got throwed. I'd best saddle up and see if I can find him." Ike climbed down from the wagon.

"Thank you, Ike. Take Tom's horse. He's already saddled. There's another bridle in the barn."

Mae stood in the wagon, shielding her eyes from the sun to

look over the ridge. "I'll just wait with you and the boys while Ike finds Tom."

Mae lifted her skirts slightly to climb down. "Good thing we're here. Tom may have broken something."

"No doubt I'll find Tom afoot and cussing up a storm. But if he's hurt bad, I'll come back for the wagon." Ike lifted himself into the saddle and swung the gelding north.

"Mama?"

"It's all right." She patted his shoulder. "We don't know anything yet."

"Can me and Corwin go play by the creek?" he asked.

Grace looked at Mae and the mothers said in unison, "Yes. Stay out of the mud."

As they watched the pair race away, Mae reached out to rest her hand on Grace's arm, "How are you?"

"I don't know, Mae. I just don't know."

Ike returned two hours later. Grace, whose eyes turned to the windows and horizon every few minutes, saw Ike leading Tom's horse. One hand held the reins, while the other steadied a man draped over the saddle.

"Ike's back," she said to Mae and both women stepped onto the front porch.

Ike rode toward them, calling out, "Better come out here."

"Shall I bring my bag?" Mae asked.

"No," Ike said over his shoulder. "You won't need it."

The women looked at each other and then went down the steps to meet him. He looked at Grace and shook his head.

"I don't know what happened, Grace," Ike said. "He's dead. He's got quite a lump on the back of his head."

Grace studied the scuffed bottoms of Tom's boots. She nodded.

The three of them carried Tom's body into the house and laid him on the table.

Mae examined Tom. "Nothing appears broken." She felt Tom's neck, his head and the lump on the back of his skull. She felt his abdomen and stopped, looking quickly up to Tom's face, remained motionless for a moment and then turned to look at Grace.

"A heart attack," Mae said abruptly. "His heart quit him."
Grace let go of the breath she had been holding.

MEADOWLARK

20

Mae talked to Corwin and James after Ike brought them back from the creek. Mae had Ike set some planks on some barrels in the living room and then bring Tom's body in. She sent him into town to notify the coroner and the sheriff, then set about preparing Tom for burial while Grace read a story to James and Corwin upstairs. Then Mae fixed supper for all of them. When Ike appeared with Ed Robertson and an inquisitive coroner, Mae answered every question with medical authority.

Two days later they held the funeral in Faith, as hot winds ripped across the landscape, flattening the grasses into rolling sheets. Grace stared at the hard chunks of gumbo clay piled in a fresh mound. She studied the fancy casket his brother had insisted on buying.

She listened to the Reverend drone on and on about Tom's sterling character and everything he had done for his family and for the community. Through it all, James stood stoic beside her, holding her hand. Mae and Ike and Corwin lined up behind them. When everything was said and done, Grace threw the first handful of dirt into the grave and walked away. In her mind she spoke to Tom as if he were standing right in front of her.

The love I held for you—the love you chipped away with every alcohol-sodden breath, every time you hit me, every time you broke James, made him feel small just to make yourself feel big, your every urge to control every single thing we did—the thing you wanted most is what you chose to destroy. If you had only listened to me.

When I tried to leave, if you had just heard me and talked to me about a possibility for change, I would have tried to love you again. But when you threatened to take James away from me, you lost me forever. I did love you once and I wanted to love you again. You never could see that Tom, could you? All either of us ever ever wanted was for you to be kind.

Mae and Ike went back to the house with her. The women put the exhausted and confused boys to bed while Ike tended to the chores. Anxiety tied Grace's stomach in knots and her hands shook as she pulled the quilt up to James's chin and tucked him in.

When James said, "He's never coming home again, is he, Mama?" she replied, "No, I'm afraid not."

"Don't be afraid," he said. "I'm not."

"I'm not either, James. Not anymore."

Grace and Mae sat up late, long after Ike had gone on home to tend to his own livestock. The women did not talk. They rocked and they looked at one another, and rocked some more.

Finally Grace had the courage to say, "Thank you, Mae. I know you know what happened."

"What's that?" Mae asked, holding her hand up to her ear. "The wind is so loud I can't hear you." But she smiled, and then she winked.

MEADOWLARK

That's when Grace broke down and cried. They were tears of relief, tears of joy at being free from her tormentor.

Ed came to the ranch the next morning, shortly after Ike had returned to get Mae and Corwin. Grace sent James up to his room before she opened the door.

The sheriff took off his hat and extended his hand, "Good morning, Grace. I'm sorry to bother you, but I thought you'd want to know that since Ike and Mae spoke up for you, the child abuse charges have been dropped."

Ed's charming smile put Grace on guard. The air around him crackled with the tension of something unspoken.

"I know this may be hard for you, but I thought the sooner I came to talk to you about the future, the better.

"The future of what? Won't you come in? I just baked a pie. May I get you some coffee?" As she sliced the mincemeat pie, Grace said. "Please, sit down.

Ed pulled out a chair and placed his hat underneath the seat. "How are you and James getting along?"

"Well," Grace pushed a lock of hair off her sweaty forehead. "It's tough right now, but we'll be fine."

"Tom recently bought a piece of property. Good, sound pasture."

"Yes, he told me about it and the note at the bank. I'll go into town soon and see about that."

"I worry about you and James out here by yourselves. It's hard work running a ranch. No work for a woman alone, surely, you must know that." Ed cut into the pie with a fork.

Grace sat up straighter.

"I want what's best for you and James. Tom asked me to look out for you if anything happened to him, so I made some arrangements for you and James to move into town."

Grace stared at him and set down her cup with a clink.

Ed shifted in his chair. "Ranching is man's work and Tom was my brother. By rights, this is my ranch. This is what Tom would have wanted. I'll be very generous and give you and James a good allowance."

"Man's work, is it? Who do you think took care of everything here when Tom was gone?" Grace walked over and opened the door. "I'll thank you to leave now."

"Let me talk to James." Ed did not move from the table.

"No. I prefer not to be rude, but I will be if you don't leave this minute."

"Or what? You going to call the sheriff?" Ed smiled. "You really don't have any choice in the matter, honey."

"Don't you 'honey' me!" Grace kept her hand on the open door, but the other was clenched at her side.

"Just give me the deed, and I'll leave this minute." Ed shoved back his chair and picked up his hat.

"It seems to me, Sheriff, that if my husband wanted you to have this ranch he would have told you where he kept the deed. Now get out!"

"Where is it?" Ed jammed his hat on his head and she recognized the look in his eyes.

Grace grabbed her rifle from its place behind the door and leveled it. "I took enough of meanness for a lifetime from your brother. I'll put a bullet in you before I let you lay a finger on me. Now, get out of my house and off of *my* ranch."

"All I have to do is prove that you can't run this place or take care of James and the judge will turn it over to me. We aren't finished. Not by a long shot."

Ed stomped out the door and Grace followed him outside. She kept the rifle aimed at him as he mounted and loped up the lane. When he was a hundred yards away, she fired a shot that kicked up rocks at his gelding's heels and the horse went to bucking.

"There's your long shot!" she shouted.

"You're going to pay for that," Ed yelled as he wrestled his horse to a stop. In reply, Grace slammed the door and locked it. Then she went around and closed all the windows and locked the other door.

When the sound of Ed's horse's hooves faded, she sank into a chair. She saw James at the top of the stairs.

"Are you all right, Mama?" he whispered.

"Yes. You can come down."

"Did you and Uncle Ed have a fight?"

"Not exactly. But there is something you need to know. There's a piece of paper that's very important to us, and we have to find it. You father must have hidden it to keep it safe. Can you help me look for it? Look everywhere. If you find anything, you call me."

"All right. You want me to look upstairs, too?"

"Yes."

"Are we going to have to move into town? I don't want to go to town. Then I'd never see Corwin anymore."

"We're not going anywhere."

Grace paced her room throughout the night, racking her brain. She and James searched every nook and cranny in all the buildings. She checked Tom's saddlebags, as well as drawers, bags, trunks, boxes, the pockets and linings of coats. She checked in the rafters of the barn. She lowered a lantern into the well. They even checked the old soddy and the collapsed outhouse. Her eyes moved across the wide expanse of prairie. What if Tom had hidden the deed somewhere out there? She took in the miles and miles of unbroken land and nearly cried. Then she caught sight of her reflection in the window the next morning and was shocked to see a tired worn old woman looking back at her.

She was twenty-two years old.

Glancing out the kitchen window, Grace spotted a slender shadow slipping across the prairie. Attached to the shadow were the narrow legs of Daisy's horse, slowing from a trot to a walk. Daisy slid like a stream of water off her horse's back and started up the steps.

"Oh, Daisy. How wonderful to see you."

Daisy entered the house with understated composure. "He is gone now so I can come visit whenever I want to, yes?"

"Yes, of course. You know you're always welcome here."

Daisy ran a calloused finger around the top of the glass of water Grace placed before her.

"I saw you and James out on the prairie yesterday. Are you looking for something?" Her eyes followed a droplet of water sliding down the inside of the glass.

Before Grace could answer, Daisy said, "I don't know what you were looking for," Daisy continued, "but one evening, years ago, I rode by your place. Just to see how things were. See how you were. It was late and dark already. I heard noise out by the barn, so I stilled my horse. We were tucked down along the bank of the creek bed in the shadows. I was surprised that somebody would be outside that late, so I waited. Pretty soon, Tom rode out of the barn and headed north.

I had a bad feeling about whatever it was he was doing. He kept turning around in the saddle, looking back behind him toward the house. So I followed him."

Grace felt her heartbeat pulsing in her ears.

"He rode north. I stayed far behind him, so he wouldn't hear my horse. It was so dark that night it was hard to see anything. Pretty soon I noticed we were close to his brother's place. But he didn't go to the house like I expected. He got off his horse and dropped the reins off a ways from the corral and then walked—real quiet, trying not to make any noise—toward the gate. I could barely see him, but he kept looking toward the house and he was holding something in his hand. He opened the gate and went into the corral. I couldn't see what he was doing, but I heard digging. In a little while, he slipped back out the gate and walked real quiet back to his horse. He got back on his horse and rode back to your place."

Daisy raised her eyes to look at Grace. "I thought about it when I saw you and James looking for something. I don't know what Tom did in the corral that night, but it sure seemed like he might have hidden something there. I never told you before Grace, because I didn't know if it would help or cause you pain."

"Thank you for telling me now, Daisy," Grace breathed. "I think you may have just really helped."

Daisy finished her glass of water and slipped away as quietly as she'd arrived.

Grace sat at the kitchen table, listening to the steady ticking of the clock. At midnight she checked on James, then quietly opened the back door and slipped out. The half moon that cast a blue glow across the ground was both a blessing and a curse. It would give her light by which to work, but if Ed had sent someone to keep an eye on her, it would mean trouble.

In the corral, she softly called to Mame. The horse came close and pressed her muzzle into Grace's hand.

MEADOWLARK

"We've been through a lot, haven't we, girl?" Grace murmured against the warm hair of her nose. Mame rubbed her head against Grace's cheek and nickered softly.

"Shhhh," Grace murmured. "We've got to be quiet."

Grace slipped the saddle onto the horse's back and cinched her up, then picked up the small shovel she'd left leaning against the fencepost when she fed.

With only the soft thuds of Mame's hooves to mark their passage, horse and rider came up over the rise above Ed's ranch and saw nothing but darkness below. No candlelight glowed in the windows, no lantern showed in the barn.

Grace breathed deeply and tried to calm her nerves. She dismounted and led Mame down the slope toward the corrals. The sound of the Mame's hooves and her own boots seemed to echo in inky silence. Grace expected to see a light come on in the house at any moment. Her breath came shallow and fast.

She ground-tied Mame behind a large cottonwood along the creek, untied the shovel from her saddle, and eased herself slowly toward the round corral, walking heel-first to muffle the sound of her steps, until she stood at the fence.

Grace bent down and crawled through the gap between the rails. *Now where?* She looked around the corral and tried to imagine where Tom would have buried something. She tripped on an uneven mound of dirt and fell, the head of the shovel crashing against the metal water tough. Her heart seemed to stop beating momentarily and then pounded in her chest. Afraid to look, she turned toward the house, expecting Ed to come bursting through the door, shotgun in hand.

Nothing. She exhaled softly in the darkness.

For two hours, Grace dug in the corral, first one place and then another, until holes pocked the ground. Grace began to doubt she could find it before sunrise. And there would be no other chance. Once Ed saw someone had been digging in his corral, he was sure to wonder and keep a much closer watch.

Mame neighed in the darkness.

Grace closed her eyes and willed the horse to hear her mental plea for silence.

Ed's horses whinnied in response.

Grace heard bumps inside the house and boots walking across

the floor. She dropped to the ground and crawled across the corral toward the shadows. She pressed her body flat to the dirt, eyes on the house, and waited.

The door of the house opened and Ed's balding head glowed in the moonlight as he walked out onto the porch, the dark silhouette of a shotgun in his right hand.

Please, Mame. Please, girl, don't whinny again. Please. Grace's breath blew bits of dry dust and manure up into her eyes, making them itch and water.

Ed looked out toward the barn where his horses stood against the fence. He walked slowly in that direction, his head cocked listening for noises on the wind. Grace felt the thumping of her heart go down through her chest and into the hard earth beneath her body.

Ed looked over toward the corral.

Grace lay staring back at him in the darkness, too terrified to even close her eyes or look away.

He looked out beyond the corral and turned a slow circle taking in the full range of the homestead.

His horse whinnied again, seeking a response from Mame.

This is it. It's all over. I'll lose everything now. She waited expectantly for Mame's response from the creek.

It never came.

Ed's body relaxed. He walked over and patted his horse's head roughly and turned back toward the house. He stopped suddenly, still as a stone, as if he'd heard something.

Grace held her breath. Watching. Waiting.

Finally, shaking his head, he walked back to the house, went in and closed the door. Grace heard the thump of boots being dropped to the floor and all was quiet. She lowered her head to the ground and breathed out.

Tom had been an orderly man, to the point of being obsessed. She reassessed the corral slowly. Where? Where would he have hidden it? An orderly man wouldn't bury anything out in the middle of the corral, where he'd have to dig several holes in order to find it again. An orderly man would bury the deed to his ranch, knowing exactly where he could find it. Her eyes settled upon the posts that held the wide-swinging gate.

Grace crawled over to one of the posts and examined it, running her hands over the wood. Some of the rough cedar had been torn away near the base from years of use and hooves chipping it away, piece by piece. She ran her hands up and down the outside, feeling for anything different. All she discovered were a few good splinters.

She crawled over to the other post and knelt close to the ground, using the moonlight to guide her toward anything unusual. Where her hands met at the back of the post, she felt a slight groove with her fingertips. She pressed harder and explored the indentation, too deep to be a torn piece of wood and too regular to have happened naturally. It felt chiseled and angular. Scuffling around to that side, she made out the a neatly carved line beginning about four inches off the ground and going all the way to where the base met the earth.

As she lifted the shovel and began to dig, the first tiny hint of pre-dawn gray edged the horizon. She scraped at the earth with the shovel. Down one inch. Two inches. Three. Four. A foot into the ground, she heard the faint clink of metal on glass. When most of the manure had been scooped away, she scratched at the dirt with her hands. Finally, she was able to pry the canning jar from its hiding place.

Clutching it with both hands, she shoved dirt back into the hole and smoothed it flat. She quickly moved around the corral, dragging dirt into the holes she'd made with her boot, and flattening it. Holding the jar to her chest, she grabbed the shovel, climbed through the fence, and ran quietly to where Mame stood hidden in the darkness. With one foot in the stirrup, she flung her body up and into the saddle. It took every ounce of willpower Grace possessed not to press Mame to a run.

It seemed to take years to walk up the low slope and out of the homestead but it gave her a chance to shove the jar into her shirt and button it there. As soon as they were over the hill, Grace dug her heels into Mame's sides and lay down flat against her neck.

"Come on, girl!" she urged in her ear.

Mame lunged to a run and they disappeared across the prairie.

Grace made it into the house just as James came stumbling down the stairs.

"Are you just coming in from milking the cow, Mama?" he asked sleepily.

"No, honey, I overslept this morning." Grace said. "I'm just going out. Do you want pancakes?"

"Yes, ma'am. I'll go get dressed."

Grace started for the barn, pulling the jar from her shirt as she walked. She tried to twist the top off, but years of rain, mud, and manure had worked under the lid and formed a hard seal. She held the glass close to her body, grasped the metal lid and turned harder. When at last it gave way, she sighed with relief and removed the curled papers, rolled them tighter and tucked them in her pocket unread.

She set to milking Red.

On the way back to the house, she started reading. The deed was there, looking precise and formal. There was a second page filled with Tom's precise script, a diatribe about every person who had ever done him wrong, cheated him on a deal, or offended him in any way, a long list of names, most of which Grace did not recognize. It ended by stating, *If I should die young, it won't be of natural causes. Tom Robertson.*

James was waiting in the kitchen. "Mama? Should I build the fire in the stove?"

"Good idea. Here," Grace crumpled Tom's page in her hand and held it out. "Use this."

She rerolled the deed and casually slipped it between two cans on the shelf. The gesture went unnoticed by James. She would take it to the bank later, where it would be safe.

MEADOWLARK

21

A weak web of sunlight threaded its way over the prairie. Yesterday, Grace had gone to town and left the deed at the bank, where Tom had his accounts. With the accounts only in her husband's name and no instructions to pass along his holdings to his wife, she had no access. Today dust swirled between tufts of grass in the early morning breeze that would inevitably build with the heat of the day. She looked at the thermometer. It was ninety degrees at 5:00 a.m. Another scorcher. Wind whistled across the top of the empty rain gauge, with a mournful low whistle.

In the kitchen Grace opened the tin where she kept her household money. She reached inside and hoped somehow it had filled overnight. Like the shoemaker's elves in the story she'd read to James, she wished there were magical beings that had made a donation. Her fingers felt only the familiar coolness of the empty space. She could ask for credit at the store for flour and sugar, but how in God's name was she going to make the payment for the new piece of property Tom bought just before he died? The money Tom had in the bank went to his brother. That bank note loomed like the weight of an ever-present brick wall blocking her passage into tomorrow.

The upstairs floor creaked as James got up and dressed. Grace put on a bright smile for her son as he came down the stairs.

"Good morning. Did you sleep last night?"

James nodded, but said nothing, an imprint of the pillowcase still creasing his cheek. He had yet to speak of his father's death or of the trip they'd taken together. Grace had watched him struggle with feelings he refused to talk about or even acknowledge. The complexities of anger, grief, mourning, guilt, and relief crossed his face every day and inhabited his body, yet it was all too confusing and too much for him to put into words.

James went past her and out the door. Well short of the outhouse, he stopped, braced his legs, and released a steady stream, instantly absorbed into the chalky ground. Grace was watching. She wasn't pleased and she let him know as soon as he came back in.

"James! When you did that when you were two it was one thing, but you're seven years old now. Use the outhouse—or at least go behind the barn."

"I know, Mama." He reached around her to grab a warm biscuit from the top of the stove.

"Wait for breakfast." Grace smiled and tapped the top of his hand lightly with the spatula. The spit of bacon frying split the dry air. Grace ran her hands over her hair to smooth it away from her face. It crackled under her fingers.

By mid-morning, the thermometer read 110 degrees in the shade. By noon it read 115. The sun seared the bare skin on Grace's arms as she hung out clothes that pulled taut against the clothespins and spun into fitful dances on the lines.

Despite the steady breeze, the windmill wasn't spinning. She squinted at the still blades. Cattle gathered at the stock tank, agitated with thirst, shoving and pushing. Calves panted with heat and were shoved underfoot as the cows head-butted each other in frustration.

She walked inside and dropped the clothesbasket on the floor, calling, "James, the windmill's not working. We've got to go fix it or we'll have cows dropping by evening."

MEADOWLARK

Grace grabbed wire, pliers, a hammer, a wrench, and a can of axle grease from the barn, put them in a pouch and tied it around her waist. She pulled on her gloves as she walked toward the windmill with James, the gusts throwing heat and dirt in their faces.

"It is so damn hot," James said as he screwed his hat down onto this head. "I mean darn hot. Sorry, Mama."

"There'er much worse things in life than cussing," Grace laughed. "And, it *is* damn hot! You wait on this side of the fence. No need for you to get in there with the cattle. They're so thirsty they would just as soon go over the top of us as move out of the way. You stay on this side, you hear?"

"Yes, ma'am."

Grace shouted "Hyah cows! Hyah!" and pushed through the herd, the wind stirring dirt and manure into her eyes. She reached the base of the windmill, grabbed the rungs of the ladder leading to the top, and hustled upward. As she climbed higher, the force of the wind increased and she felt the structure straining beneath her. She clung to the wood, the vibrations crawling through her body. She didn't dare look down, so she focused on the steadiness of the horizon in the distance.

The wind flapped at her skirts and she gripped the frame of the ladder and looked to the top, where the wheel quivered against the wind yet remained frozen in place. The remaining distance yawned before her and while it wasn't the first time she'd had to deal with it, it still unnerved her.

Her balance wobbled, but she made herself reach above her head, feeling for the next rung. She kept on until she reached the top and stood on the narrow platform.

Dirt skimmed across the ground far below. James stared upward, holding onto his hat. He waved with his free hand and she smiled down at him. She studied the blades and set the lock in place. The thought of the heavy blades suddenly breaking loose and knocking her from the platform made her knees rubbery.

Layer upon layer of dust had hardened around the gears. She took the heavy hammer from the pouch and began to slam it into the dirt, chipping it off bit by bit. Sweat dampened her hairline and ran down into her face. Her back and arm ached from clinging to the structure in the wind. Slowly, bit-by-bit, she loosened the mass until at last she sensed the blades trying to shift.

She slopped grease around the seam and watched the gear slide an inch. She looked up and received a face full of the remaining dirt as the blades began to strain forward, creaking and moaning as they sloughed through the rest of the blockage. Grace put the tools back into the pack and stepped down two rungs. She reached back up and released the lock and the blades gathered momentum in the fierce wind. Down below, a trickle of water spilled from the pipe and splashed into the empty tank, the sound delicious and sweet. The cows jammed tight around it and started to drink.

"You did it, Mama!" James shouted, clapping his hands above his head and jumping up and down. "Next time let me go up!"

Grace waved and began her cautious descent. She would. Next time her young man would fix the windmill.

Tentatively Grace approached the window in the pantry and reached her hand up under the sill to feel the slender piece of wood sealing the spot where her journal lay hidden. She eased it from the wall, releasing a dank, musty smell from the hole. She knocked on the wall a few times, "Move away snakes," she called and listened for any rattling, before reaching her hand inside.

The newsprint rustled as she withdrew the book, pulling a sheet of newspaper that had slipped under its cover with it. The paper fell to the shelf and Grace glanced down to see the date 1916. One year ago she'd sealed the wall and the journal had remained there untouched. She blew the thin layer of dust from the cover, then carefully wiped away the remaining film with her apron. She couldn't open it. Even holding it in her hands made her queasy. That was enough for one day, just taking it out of hiding.

Mae had told her that each step from now on would mean growth and strength. Well, that was enough growth for her right now and she left the book on the table where she could see it, where she would be reminded of every experience she had captured during those years of loneliness.

Slapping her hands together to stop their shaking, she began chopping the carrots to go into the pan with the roast. She tried not to think too much about love and everything that she had lost. She tried to focus instead on the look of the prairie when the sun broke in the morning. She wanted to hold these glimpses of beauty in her mind, and be aware of the songs that surrounded her. She wanted someone in her life, but she didn't want just any man. Grace wanted a man who could hold his own, but who would allow her to be in charge of herself and of what happened on the ranch.

After Tom's funeral Mae had taken her aside and said, "You'll get married again when you find a man with balls bigger than your own."

Grace had dropped her scarf into the dirt. "Mae Thingvold! You ought to be ashamed of yourself!"

"I'm not a Thingvold anymore, but tell me I'm wrong. Tell me that Tom had any balls at all."

"Well, he did give me James."

"Okay, you win that one, but you know I speak the truth. You need a man who will stand strong and steady in this constant godforsaken wind. Someone who's easy and sure of his place in the world."

"Someone like Ike?" Grace asked.

"Of course! But there's only one Ike and he's taken. Someone else will come along, Grace. You mark my words."

She had not only marked Mae's words, she had taken them into her heart and nurtured them with thoughts of Paul Overland. Those she cherished and kept close at hand.

"Oh, Grace! Thank God you're here!" Mae flew in the door, followed by hot summer wind, as Grace pulled biscuits out of the oven. "Mrs. Vanbeek is in a bad way and Ike and Corwin have gone to town. Can you go with me?"

"What's wrong with her?" Grace dampered the stove and washed her hands.

"She's been telling me for years that she doesn't want any more babies, but, well, you know... Her daughter said there's lots of blood. We have to hurry."

"James!" Grace yelled from the porch. When he appeared with a shovel in hand, she said, "Take care of the chores. I might be gone quite a while. After chores, you wait for me in the house. There are biscuits there on the table.

"Sure, Ma. Hello, Dr. Mae."

"Hello, young man. Come and hug me, then we have to go."

Mae urged the horse forward, shouting over the beating of the hooves. "Last month when I saw Mrs. Vanbeek she asked me if I had anything for the feminine problems she'd been experiencing the past month. I told her to drink plenty of water and get lots of rest, but now, I think I understand. With eight kids underfoot and no way to feed them all, she did not want this new baby."

They arrived at the lonely homestead as the sun sank below the horizon. Nothing moved except the grass, small stunted tufts waving in the wind, as Mae drove up to the house. The oldest boy came out to tie the horse. They walked into a room thick with the scent of sweat and blood. Mrs. Vanbeek lay pale and semi-conscious on the couch, a curtain of red fanned out on the towels between her legs. Children of all ages circled around, looking on helpless and too afraid to cry.

"Where's your father?" Mae asked.

The oldest girl said, "He took a bunch of cows over to Belle Fourche."

"Okay, tell your brother to hitch up your wagon and all of you go to my house. Ike will be there and he'll put supper on for you. Tell him everything is in the oven. Understand?" Mae said.

"Yes, ma'am." The girl rounded up the children and moved them out of the house.

"Grace, get some water boiling." Mae knelt between the woman's legs and shifted the towels soaked with blood. "I hope we're not too late."

A slender metal probe lay on the floor. Mae picked it up and shook her head with disgust. "Mail-order companies sell these damn things as 'relievers of female complaints' and allow women to butcher themselves. Come here, Grace, hold this cloth close to her nose. Not too close, now."

"What is it?"

"Chloroform. It should help ease her pain."

Mae washed her hands in carbolic acid, rinsed them and set to work while Grace talked to the woman and stroked her unwashed hair.

"The doctor's here now," Grace said. "Mae is here. She's going to fix you up and make you all right."

"Get a lantern. You'll have to hold it so I can see."

An hour later, Mae said, "Well, I've done all I can do." She stood and straightened her back.

Mrs. Vanbeeks's breath had taken on a depth and regularity that gave Grace hope.

She picked up the metal probe. "What is this, Mae?"

"It's something women use when they're pregnant and don't want to have the baby. They try to scrape themselves out inside, but half the time they kill themselves with puncture and infection."

"She stuck this up *inside* herself?" Grace looked at the narrow sharp point.

"You'd be amazed at what women will do not to have a baby. Young girls who aren't married will do so much damage that if they're lucky enough to live, they can't ever bear children. Women who are too tired, too poor, or both will do just about anything not to bring a child into a world of suffering. It's as old as history itself. Most doctors won't talk about it. Women with money can afford discretion for the right price. Poor women, though, are left to take matters into their own hands."

"Why don't they just drink Daisy's tea?" Grace regretted the statement as soon as she said it.

"What tea?" Mae asked.

When Grace moved away, saying "I'll make us some coffee" Mae followed her into the kitchen.

"Well, this is interesting," Mae said. "I always wondered why you never got pregnant again."

"Oh, Mae. This is no time for joking."

"Then tell me what it is. Do you know how many women we could help? This is the thing that makes me so mad about that ridiculous Comstock law that makes it legal to search through people's mail looking for 'obscenities,' and that includes any kind of contraception. That committee can open up anybody's mail and take out anything they think is obscene."

"Contra...what?"

"*Contra*-ception when you want to prevent *con*-ception. When you don't want to get pregnant, there are things you can use for contraception. And with access to those methods, there'd be a hell of a lot less desperate women dying. And Grace…you don't have to tell me if you don't want to."

"It isn't that I won't tell you Mae, but I don't know what it is. Daisy gives me the herbs. I'm not sure if that's what worked or my fervent prayers to God to never let me have another child that Tom could harm."

"Well, there's that, plus the fact that you're as thin as a starving cow."

Mae took her coffee back into the living room. "The bleeding has stopped, thank God. There's a good chance she'll make it now, but I'll need to stay for a couple days."

Mrs. Vanbeek's eyes fluttered open. She looked confused and it took a couple of moments for recognition and understanding to fill her eyes.

"We've no money," she whispered.

"Never mind about that," Mae said.

"Not even to feed the children we have."

"You go back to sleep now. And I don't want you to worry about having another baby, either. I'll teach you how to soak a sponge in vinegar, tie a thread around it for withdrawal, and insert it."

"But, Dr. Mae, I don't want to…" Mrs. Farthing flustered.

"Just be quiet and listen. You don't know what lies ahead for you. Plus you'll need to teach your daughters. A lot of doctors won't talk to women about this. They feel it's a sin, against God's will to protect against pregnancy. I've attended too many dying women to take that view. Now, I want you to sleep."

"Thank you, Dr. Mae. I didn't really want to…I mean, I just couldn't…"

"I understand. And while I can't say you look good, at least your eyes don't have that haunted look they had the last time we saw each other."

Grace woke from where she'd fallen asleep, head on her arms at the kitchen table. She sat up, heart pounding and looked around the house, blinking her eyes to gain her bearing. She'd dreamt of the ride home after the wedding, the buckboard, the walk. She shook her head and walked unsteadily out the front door, out past the corrals, up the slope outside the house and onto the flat plain of the prairie. Hot wind lifted her hair and swirled her dress around her. A thin sheen of sweat covered her face and beaded on her upper lip.

"I will never forget what you did to me," Grace spit into the air. "Not for one day of my life will I ever forget or cease to hold you responsible for your actions and all the pain you caused me and your son. Not for one second. You always had to win, Tom. No matter the cost. You had to win, James and me be damned. But there's one thing I won't let you win. You will not win by turning me into a bitter, angry woman. This is the one thing you will not win, though the temptation is strong. It ends here, Tom. No more. I wish I could forgive you. Jesus says we should forgive. But, I suppose I'm not quite as far along as Jesus, yet. Perhaps some day I'll be able to stand here and say, 'I forgive you.' But, not today."

She walked, rigid with resentment, legs, arms, and neck stiff. She closed her eyes and stopped, felt the wind and sun on her face, inhaled the scent of prairie grass.

"I need you to know something, Tom. I choose beauty over bitterness, love over anger, and gratitude over resentment. This is the one thing I will not bow down and let you win. You cannot take this away from me. I choose life. I choose beauty. I choose love. I choose laughter. I choose peace. These are the things I choose for myself and for James, with the hope that he won't grow up to live the tormented existence that has passed through the generations of your family. That he may grow to be whole, wise, loving, and generous of spirit. I will work hard to release the anger toward you that I've harbored in my heart. I will work even harder to release the sadness of all of those missed opportunities for love."

Grace looked up at the wide-open sky. "Maybe where you are now you'll find peace and feel whole. I hope so. I truly do."

22

"Mama!" James's voice hollered from outside. "Someone's here."

Grace gave a final pat to the bread dough and set it to rise in the stove's warming oven. She wiped her hands on the dishtowel and opened the front door to a chill autumn breeze and a pair of eyes she knew.

Paul.

She stared, not knowing what to say or do. So many times she had hoped, *prayed*, to see him again, and now here he was, casually holding his horse, chatting with her son. It didn't seem real—more like she was waking from a dream. She opened her mouth but no words came out.

Paul looked up at Grace with the tenderness she remembered. The unspoken understanding they had always shared was still there. Somehow, they had always known what the other needed, known what the other was thinking, known how the other would respond.

MEADOWLARK

Why in the world had she ever given him up and married Tom?

"Mama, he says he used to work for Dad. Is that true?"

"That is true, James. Why don't you go on out and finish your chores and…"

"Aw, Mama! Sorry…yes, ma'am." James turned and headed back out to the corral. Shoveling manure wasn't his favorite task and it showed in the way he kicked every dirt clod his foot could find.

"Mrs. Robertson," Paul said, taking off his hat. The band of skin above his forehead gleamed white as a hen's egg below his light brown hair.

The hint of a deeper question flared in Paul's soft eyes and then it was gone, carefully tucked away. A black and white cow dog settled down onto its haunches beside him, cocking its head and studying Grace with intelligent eyes.

"Paul? Is that really you? After so long?" A rare smile slowly spread across her lips. "Paul Overland?"

"Yes, ma'am, it's me." Paul laughed, the sound rich with respect. "Is your husband around? I rode up from Arizona and stopped by to see Ike and Mae. Ike said you might be needing some help around here."

She pulled her sweater tighter around her arms. "A lot has happened, Paul."

"Oh, well, you know, since I saw you in town that time when you hurt your face…"

"Paul, let me think," Grace closed her eyes, remembering that day she ground her cheek into the wooden plank and why, "James was four-years-old, so that was 1916. Has it really been three years? That seems a lifetime ago."

"If memory serves, you asked me to go away that day." Paul said. "So I did. Found a good position as a foreman on a big spread in Arizona, a mighty pretty place. It was good to me. I loved it. Most everything a man could want."

"But you left. You came back here." Grace held the corner of the dishtowel thrown over her shoulder and watched the way Paul turned his hat in his hands, straightening the brim.

"Well, I woke up one morning and knew that I needed to come back *here*. Never questioned it. I drew my wages, sold my extra horses and spent a month riding back north. But now that I'm here, I'm looking for a job. Is your husband around, Mrs. Robertson?"

"Oh, he's around all right. About five miles over to the west."

"Hayin' then, is he?"

"In a manner of speaking…Tom died over a year ago, Paul. He's buried in the cemetery in Faith. It's just James and me here, now."

"He's dead? Ike didn't tell me that." He looked toward the barn, "You been running this place alone?"

"James is seven now. It's both of us."

"I…well, I am sorry."

"And who is this?" Grace asked to change the subject. She pointed at the dog seated at Paul's heels.

"This is Kip. Smartest dog ever to grace the face of this earth."

"Hello, Kip." Grace walked down the steps and knelt down. "I'm pleased to meet you." Kip bared her teeth and uttered a soft growl.

"It's okay, Kip, Grace is fine." Paul rubbed the dog's ears. "She's pretty protective. It's been just me and her for a long time."

"Then I had better pay her the respect she deserves. We haven't had a dog on the place since… Oh, never mind about that." Grace said, "Why don't you tie your horse and come up on the porch out of the wind. We can talk. I'll bring us some coffee."

When she brought out the tray with steaming cups, a glass of milk, and oatmeal cookies, Paul was seated with his feet up on the railing looking very much at home. Grace called for James to come take a break. He grabbed his drink and a handful of cookies but he sat on the bottom step to make friends with Kip.

As Paul asked her questions about the ranch, Grace found herself answering with ease, outlining the work that needed to be done, the bills that had to be paid, the primacy of the weather. Paul listened to her, really listened, like he truly cared. He remained relaxed and still, sipping his coffee and brushing crumbs from his shirt. He looked absolutely serene in his own skin. He made her feel safe and warm.

James walked up, tilted his head and looked at Paul.

"James," Grace said, "This is Mr. Overland. He's an old friend of mine and has been gone these past years."

Paul extended his hand to James. "I'm pleased to know you, James. You can call me Paul."

James took his hand and looked to Grace, who smiled.

"This here's Kip," Paul gestured with his chin. "I'm sure she could use a drink. How about you take her over to that stock tank and let her have a drink. She'll come if you call her."

"Come here, girl. Come," James looked to Kip and walked toward the corral. With a glance back at Paul, Kip followed.

"What do you think, Mrs. Robertson? Would you like to have a hired man on the place?"

Grace tried to organize her thoughts but they had scattered in all directions. Even with more sales and meat going to the troops, she had little money to spare.

"I would be grateful for a job and for twenty dollars a month, plus room and board for me and my horse, I'll sign up right now."

"But I have no place to put you," Grace said.

"He could have one of the rooms upstairs," James called, trotting back to the porch, Kip at his heels.

Grace looked from James to Paul and back again. "Well," she said slowly. "I suppose that settles it then.

James whooped. "Hired help *and* a dog to boot," he said. "I'll unsaddle and water your horse, sir."

Untying the roan gelding, James called, "Come on, Kip!" But the dog stayed on the porch, her eyes fixed on her master until Paul said, "Go on, have some fun."

Paul and Grace watched the trio trot to the corral.

"You've just made my son a very happy boy," Grace said.

"That pleases me more than I can say." Paul kept his eyes on the boy, the dog, and the horse.

"I haven't fed yet. We'd best go toss some hay into the corrals for the animals," Grace said.

Paul walked ahead and held open the gate.

"Thanks for waiting for me," she murmured as she walked past.

The next morning the sun's rays peeked over the horizon and slit the darkness with shafts of pure, golden light. Grace found Paul tidying the stack of loose hay.

She had brought him a cup of coffee, "Taking advantage of the morning, Paul?"

"I am and I've been doing some thinking." Paul paused to take a long draught of his coffee.

"About what?" Grace asked.

"About how it's been for you, that things have been worse than hell for you and I'm sorry about that. Sorrier than I've ever been about anything. If I'd had a decent bone in my body I would have kidnapped you and taken you to Arizona with me."

"That wouldn't have worked."

"Probably not. Please just tell me that it wasn't all bad."

"It wasn't. I have James. And I learned a lot about being alone. But there's one thing I've always wanted to learn but never did. I'm wondering if you'd teach me."

Grace took a deep breath. And Paul waited.

"I don't know how to rope. I never learned. It was something that only the men did."

Paul chuckled, leaning against the shovel, eyeing Grace with that look he sometimes got when she said something that didn't fit and he was trying to see inside her mind.

"I was hoping we might start today," she continued as fast as she could, "I've been waiting a long time and I'm anxious to begin."

"Yes, ma'am. Seems you've been waiting we'd better just get started this very moment." He grinned and set the shovel up against the fence. "Let me get a couple of ropes out of the barn."

"Don't you want breakfast first?"

"Later."

Paul showed her how to rope, first just standing on the ground. The morning sun glowed, coating everything with a burnished sheen. Paul's body cast a long, narrow shadow on the ground, while hers showed slight curves and escaped hair blowing long spiderweb wisps.

"Hold it loose in your hand like this. Don't put a chokehold on it. A rope is a living thing and it can read your mind. It goes where you send it. See how I cup my hand to hold it nice and relaxed? Okay, try that."

She tried not to think about how his hand, roughened with weather and work, felt on the skin of her arm. She grasped the rope, spun it at her side to uncoil it, as he'd shown her, and then held it lightly in her hand.

"Okay, good. Loop it above your head, like so. Keep your wrist moving easy, nice and smooth."

Grace raised her arm and twirled it above her head. She had seen the men rope enough times to have a feel for it.

"Hey!" James and Kip raced from the house stirring up a rooster tail of dust. "I want to try."

"Don't you think you ought to get some boots on?" Paul asked.

James looked down at his feet. "How the hell—I mean, heck—did I forget them?"

Kip whined at the sight of the ropes, certain that some cow chasing was going to happen.

"I think we should all go in and have breakfast and then Paul can take us out horseback and teach us all his tricks."

They ate like the house was on fire. Even Kip bolted down the bacon grease and corn mush Paul mixed in her bowl.

"James, get your boots on," Grace said.

By the time they reached the barn, Paul had his horse saddled, along with Mame and Blue. They rode out, three abreast, to find the herd spread out along the autumn-low creek. Paul took them through their paces slowly so they wouldn't stir up the cows. James caught a calf on his ninth attempt, Grace on her seventh.

"I did it!" she called out, laughing.

Paul clapped and whooped, "You sure did!" He rode in close to the calf and dismounted to slip the rope off its neck. The mama cow lit after him with a fury, and he ran for a lone tree, turning to bat the beast on the head with his hat. He made it around the other side of the tree before she charged straight for him again. Around and around the tree they went, dodging one way and then the other. Kip charged, nipping at the cow's heels, making things worse instead of better.

James was laughing so hard he nearly fell off of Blue.

Grace forgot she was mounted until Paul yelled, "Are you going to chase this cow off of me or let us play ring-around-the-rosie all day?!"

"Oh! Yes!" Grace nudged Mame into the fray and turned the cow back toward her bawling calf.

Out of breath, Paul panted against the tree. "Whooeee, she was picking 'em up and putting 'em down!" Sweat dripped in his eyes. He wiped his brow on his sleeve and put his hat back on his head.

"You look beautiful," he said to her so softly she wasn't sure she heard him right.

Paul turned to James and said, "We've still got to get that rope off of that calf. Any ideas?"

"If you run off in that direction and lure the cow over there, Blue and I'll just walk on over easy as you please and slip the rope off that calf's head."

"Oh, you think so, do you? How about one that doesn't get me trampled? I think you need to come up with a better option." Paul's voice sounded playful, but Grace could tell he was giving her son a chance to be a man.

"What if I sicced Kip on the cow?"

"Might be all right if you were standing on the end of the rope so the calf couldn't follow her. Try again."

"Rope the cow and hold her so you or Ma can get the rope off the calf?"

"Great idea. Show us how it's done."

"Paul?" Grace's mother instinct flared.

"I can do it," James volunteered. He spoke to Kip, telling her to stay back as he uncoiled his rope. He urged Blue forward and trotted after the cow, who had taken her calf farther upstream, away from the herd. As he got closer he circled his horse wide, coming into the cow at an angle.

"Paul?"

"He's fine, Grace. Let him have a go. I won't let him get into trouble." Paul whistled and his horse trotted to him. He mounted and chirped Kip to his side. Suddenly, they weren't laughing anymore, but just quietly looking at each other and then at James.

"He's got to know he's good enough, otherwise he'll resent me being here. I don't want that. Do you?"

"No."

"There he goes! He got her!" Paul jabbed his horse into action, swinging his rope overhead. He dabbed a second loop over the cow's head and yelled at James, "Dally. Back on up. Now stretch her tight!"

As the horses worked, Kip grabbed the loose end of the rope over the calf's neck and tugged back. "Your turn, Grace," Paul shouted. "Get that rope off so we can turn mama loose."

Grace dismounted and took the rope from Kip, praising her and telling her to stay back. Though her hands shook, she remounted and eased Mame forward, snaking the rope to get it to loosen. When the loop grew big enough, the calf simply walked out of it and bellowed toward the cow.

"Now," Paul said, and he and James walked their horses ahead, and in near perfect syncopation shook their loops wide and tossed them away while the cow was focused on her calf.

"Nice work, James," Paul said as they recoiled their ropes. "Have we had enough for the day?"

"I have," Grace said, pulling in her rope. "I wonder if you have any idea what it's like for me to sit astride this horse and throw a rope. It sets me free. Free from all the times I had to stand on the corral fence and watch. Free from days in a dark house over a pot on the stove. Do you understand the depth of the gift you just gave me?"

"Guess I never thought about that," Paul said. "How about you, James?"

"Don't know. Guess all I know is that that was danged fun." He let out a whoop of sheer pleasure.

So Grace joined him, tilted back her head and whooped as loud as she could.

Paul laughed and said, "Well, I guess that's about as good a response as I ever got from anybody."

After they ate dinner, Grace said to James, "Haying crews come tomorrow. We'd better bring in food from the cellar tonight, while Paul pitches hay to the horses."

As James ran ahead toward the cellar and Paul started down the steps, Grace reached out quickly and touched his shoulder. He turned around to look at her.

"I just want to say…" she fumbled, "thank you."

"Teaching someone to rope isn't much."

"Not that, Paul. For what you did for James. You made him feel good about himself and that means the world to me."

He looked at her for a moment, before saying, "It's the least a man can do for a boy."

"Thank you."

Paul touched the edge of his hat and turned away. She knew he had seen the tears in her eyes. Could he also see the sliver of trust wending its way into her heart?

23

By lamplight the next morning, Grace pored over the columns of numbers that represented the ranch, as Paul and James slept. The sound of the pencil against the paper rose from the page and drifted into the corners of the room. She studied the rows of numbers, written and erased, then written and erased again. Lines marked out columns and arrows indicated where numbers might be moved. No matter how she added up the figures, the final number was a deficit. Grace forced away threatening tears. This was all this ranch was to the bank: Expenses and income—the quantities of the former far outnumbering those of the latter.

Nowhere was there space for the things that represented the ranch's true value. Headings such as Life, Hope, Dreams, and God-It's-All-We've-Got did not exist. Nor was there room for Memories, Legacy, and Blood-and-Sweat. No item reflected the scent of the prairie grass after a summer rain. No place for the times Grace had rocked James and prayed that the land would sustain him through his lifetime. The numbers—small squiggled figures stark on a lined page—had no answers, either.

Grace sighed. What could she do? Light the color of weak tea seeped into the night sky along the horizon. The air already crackled. Grace rubbed her eyes, pushed back her hair. At least there had been just enough rain to grow the grasses enough to make hay. The haying crew would be arriving soon to cut and bind the feed for winter. She watched the sun's light slowly fill the bowl of land surrounding the ranch house and corrals, just like water filling a dam. The image planted an idea of what she could do. It had to rain again sometime and when it did, they could have dams built to catch the water. But that would have to wait because it was time to start cooking.

She dressed quickly and poured water from the ceramic pitcher into the basin on top of the chest of drawers. She brushed her waist-length hair, wound it into a coil at the base of her neck, and fastened it with pins. Nothing fancy, but the workers wouldn't care as long as their plates were full.

The wood James had gathered throughout the week lay stacked neatly beside the stove. By 5:30, Grace had prepared fresh biscuits, fried ham and fried potatoes, and enough scrambled eggs for the twenty men expected that day. The mid-morning snack of cookies and coffee was ready. The noon dinner would be roast beef, mashed potatoes, gravy, canned vegetables, cabbage salad, and bread with fresh butter. Mincemeat, apple, and chokecherry pies made yesterday sat on the counter next to six loaves of bread, covered with dishtowels. She wouldn't worry about supper until she had the noon dishes done.

Overhead the floor creaked and she heard the deep timbre of his voice rousing James from sleep.

"Breakfast is ready," she called up the stairs, making an effort to keep her voice steady. "You better get some before the haying crews show up, or you may not get any at all."

"I'm coming, Mama! Save some for me!" Rapid thumps of running feet and paws thundered down the stairs. Grace filled James's plate as she heard Paul coming down the steps, his spurs clinking.

"Good morning, Paul," she said, "How'd you sleep?"

"Oh, just fine." Paul pulled the chair out from the table and jabbed James in the ribs.

"Hey!" James reached over and poked Paul back.

"Boys," Grace said, "Put your attention on eating, not on playing."

"Yes, ma'am," they said in unison, their eyes laughing.

"Paul, I have a question." Grace handed him the basket filled with warm biscuits. "James, please pass Paul the jam, honey."

Paul sat up straighter. "Maybe I have an answer."

"Have you ever dug a dam before? I was thinking," she stopped and looked at Paul and James as they both listened attentively. "Well, this morning I was thinking about the ranch what could we do make money. What if we took advantage of this dry spell to dig some dams, so that when the rain does come, we can catch and save it for the cattle?

Paul picked up his fork and held it over his plate. "A fine idea and I have some experience with dams. It takes stout teams to drag those blades. I'll ask around today during the haying." He sprinkled pepper on his potatoes and took a bite. "We'll need another man, too."

"I'm old enough to help." James looked at his mother.

She looked at Paul.

"You would be a great help, James, and you'd learn a lot, too. It takes some pretty tough hands and arms to handle driving six-up. I imagine all that shoveling you've been doing is going to pay off."

"We don't have money to buy teams or even rent them, but maybe someone will loan us the horses in exchange for hay."

"Another good idea, Grace. We'll get to it after this hay is in."

As soon as the haying crew arrived, the morning rushed by in a blur of men taking turns to come and eat on the porch. Grace was elbow deep in hot water washing the dirty dishes with sweat trickling down her ribcage through her damp shirt when she heard someone come up the steps.

Grace called over her shoulder, "Come on in! The door's open."

"Grace?" Daisy peeked into the kitchen.

"Oh! Imagine you showing up right when I need a woman to talk to." Grace deposited a scrubbed pan on the drainer. You want something to drink? And, there's plenty to eat."

MEADOWLARK

Surprised by Daisy's non-response, Grace shook the water from her hands and lowered herself into a chair. "What's wrong?"

Purple-tinged shadows under Daisy's eyes deepened the planes of her face. She had always been slight, but her dress hung on her thin frame, her collarbones jutting out above the neckline.

"They are making me send Ruth away." Daisy held on to the table but she did not sit down.

"What do you mean? Why? Is she ill?"

"No. She is fine. They say I have to send her to the Rapid City Indian School."

"She's only seven-years-old, Daisy! How could anyone possibly expect her to be away from her mother?"

Daisy looked at Grace. "You know why, Grace."

"Oh, no. Not that. I mean, why can't she... I don't know what to say." Grace put her head in her hands.

"They say I will go to jail if I don't send her. What good will that do? Then she would have no one." Daisy cried, her arms crossed in front of her chest. "Tuberculosis is bad there. And what if they cut her hair? They'll throw her soul away. The law doesn't care. There are already hundreds of children her age in these schools. There must be a solution, only I cannot find it."

"Where is Ruth right now?"

"I took her over to Mae's so they can't find her. That will work for a little while. Please, give me something to do. Let me help. If I'm busy I won't think so much."

Grace fell into bed at 11:00 that night and when she rose at 4:00 the next morning, Daisy had already come down and had the fire going in the cookstove. Fast and efficient, Daisy never complained, even when exhaustion traced red rings around her shadowed eyes. Grace took in her spare frame and the way she kept her eyes on the food as she worked.

"Take another piece of roast, Daisy. And there's some pie there that has your name on it."

"Thank you. I never learned to make pie. Maybe you will teach me," Daisy said.

"I can teach you pies if you'll teach me about the wild plants.

Have you thought about coming to work here for me, and bringing Ruth, too?

"Yes, I am thinking, but I am not sure I would like it here. Don't be hurt about that. It's just that you have too many people here and too much happening. It is so busy I cannot hear my own prayers."

"It won't be like that once the work crew is gone."

"And Paul, will he leave, too?" Daisy asked.

"I hope not, Daisy. I hope Paul is one who will stay."

"Your son likes him and that is a good thing. You like him, too. Am I right?" Daisy offered a rare grin.

"Yes, I do." Grace blushed and held a hand against the butterflies beating against the inside of her stomach. "I've known Paul many years, from before I was married."

"I can give you something for that." Daisy laughed and held her hands across her own midriff. "It has been a long time since I felt that, but I know what it is."

"What is it? What is it that keeps me awake at night and on edge all day long?"

"Love."

"Really? And what would you give me for that?"

"A blessing, of course, but also a tea that will soften the tough surface of your heart like rain softens the baked dryness of the land."

For two days, the haying crew camped north of the house, surrounded by their teams and stackers. When the crew pulled out, Paul rode out to check the cattle, leaving James and Kip to take care of daily chores. Daisy had gone as well, saying that she appreciated the time with Grace and would let her know what happened with Ruth. Try as she might, Grace could not get Daisy to agree to come and live with her.

As lengthening shadows colored the view out the window, Grace stirred a pot of beef stew, while the James set the table and bumped into it on purpose to excite the dog. Then he set his sights on shoving Kip with his foot to make her race away then rush back.

"Stop that roughhousing and be careful you don't knock into the table." She saw horse and rider coming up the lane. "Paul's in from checking cows. Finish setting the table and then you can come outside."

Paul had already dismounted, his hands deep into his saddlebag, searching for something.

"How are the cows doing?" she asked.

"Lookin' good, Grace," Paul said, intent on his task.

"We're going to add mares to our herd, Paul."

"Mares?" He tilted his head slightly, so his hat would shade his eyes from the evening sun and withdrew a red handkerchief.

"Yes, mares. They're selling low, and hopefully we can make a profit each year off the foals. We'll buy a stallion for breeding." Grace looked down at the red handkerchief. "What's in there?"

He held out his hand and she gently unfolded the worn cloth. Inside, lay a single purple iris.

"Where in the *world* did you find this?"

"Remember that old homestead up north? The one that got burned out in the wildfire? It's in a low spot, you can't see it unless you ride right up to it. There's an outline of an old soddy and a row of these irises growing. I remembered how you loved flowers as a girl. Don't know why you don't grow any here."

Emotion tight in her throat, Grace did not try to speak. She lifted the flower and held it up to the late light. The center of the petal was the pale yellow of fresh butter, ringed by a hazy band of smooth white. Light lavender bled into the white and deepened into a velvety bluish purple.

Grace looked up and cleared her throat. "It's so beautiful. Will you take me there sometime, to see the flowers? Perhaps I can get a few bulbs in the fall. What a legacy of the woman who lived there."

"Of course."

James and Kip burst through the door. "What's that, Mama?"

"An iris. I don't think you've ever seen one. Be careful. It's fragile."

As James chattered with Paul, Grace walked back inside to get a jam jar full of water for the wilting blossom.

After supper, when she had sent James to bed, Grace joined Paul on the porch to enjoy the quiet, cool evening.

Grace gazed at the iris in the jar, iridescent in the moonlight.

"Still love flowers?" Paul asked.

"There's something about them that makes me happy."

"Maybe James and I should build you a flower bed."

"No sense in that, there's no water." Grace told Paul about the zinnia seeds of her mother, of the precious few that remained. She told him of the prairie roses she'd so enjoyed and hidden, what all of those flowers meant to her. Paul remained quiet for a good long while, just staring out into the evening.

"A little patch of flowers won't take much water," he finally said. "You've got the rain barrels and we can double them up. Besides it'll make a world of difference for you. In fact, that's what James and I can do tomorrow."

"That would actually be grand, Paul. I do love flowers." Grace fanned her face with her apron. "It was a hot one today, wasn't it? Oh, I found a jug of some kind of liquor the haying crew must've left behind. Do you want it?" Grace moved to stand.

"No. I don't drink anymore. Nothing at all."

"Why not?"

Paul's voice softened. "After I left here for Arizona, I took to drinking too much. I didn't want to feel anything and that was the surest way I knew. I didn't much like the man I became when I drank, but that didn't stop me. I got mean."

"I can hardly believe that."

"Forgive me if I'm wrong, but isn't that the same thing people said about Tom?" Paul said quietly.

Grace drew in a sharp breath.

"Believe it. I turned into hell on horseback, cranky when I was sober and mean when I wasn't. I kept thinking how my mother would feel if she saw me that way. Do you remember my ma, Grace?"

Grace nodded. "I remember she always seemed to be smiling."

"She listened to me. She asked me questions all the time. Even when I didn't feel like answering, I liked that she asked. They were questions that let me know she really was interested in what I was doing, what I thought about things. She'd give me her thoughts on things, but she was just as interested in hearing mine."

"I recall that she always looked on the bright side of things."

"One time when I was a kid, I told her, 'Ma, if I broke my leg, I bet the first thing you'd say is, 'Well, aren't you glad you don't have to go to school?' That's just the way she was. And she was a strong woman, in a quiet way. You could see a look in her eye. She didn't put up with much. She wasn't loud about it, she'd just put her foot down, got that look in her eye, and who ever she was talking to knew. Then she'd go about her business, not make a fuss over it. Being around her felt like being around a tree that you knew might blow a little with the wind, but nothing was going to snap or break it. It was a safe feeling."

"I think…well, that's the same way I felt about my mother. I miss her more than I can say."

"We were the lucky ones to have mothers like that. Thinking about my mother seeing me the way I was when I was drinking made me feel terrible. Thank God she never did. I don't think I could bear the sadness I'd have seen in her eyes." Paul wiped his hands on his pants like he was swishing away bad memories. The low hoot of a barn owl slipped through the air.

"Alcohol, Grace…it's like when a tree gets a disease." Paul stood up to pace on the porch. "See, imagine that the trunk is a man and all of the branches are everybody who has anything to do with that person—family, friends, well, everybody. And when he's drinking, he thinks he's the only one downing that bottle. But that isn't true. Being drunk is like pouring booze down the throats of everybody who has anything to do with him, like a poison that starts in the trunk and works its way out into all of its branches. I realized that I was poisoning everybody. When I close my eyes, I can still see it."

"What did you do?"

"One day I took my last bottle and threw it. Watched it go sailing through the air and crash. That night I was glad I was too far from town to be able to get any more. It took several weeks for my head to clear so I could see that the world set straight again."

Stars slowly peeked out and a nighthawk flew by the front of the porch, the soft beat of its wings a whisper. Grace looked out into the night. *Quiet.*

"Sorry to burden you with all that, but I felt like I had to tell you."

"I'm glad you did. I've done a lot of things I'm not proud of, Paul. Not proud of at all."

"You're a fine woman to me."

"You might not say that if you knew the truth about me."

"I would be happy to hear it." Paul came and sat back down, this time setting his hand on her knee. She placed her hand on top of his and smiled.

"I think we all create the story of our life. I created my story in my marriage and then wanted so desperately to believe it. I thought that if I believed in it hard enough, long enough, it would come true. I lived for what was expected of me. From the outside, it looked like Tom and I had it all. I can't tell you how many times I heard that from people. And I kept trying to live for that, to make that enough. Except I knew what life was really like for James and me—alone, scared, and angry most of the time, because Tom drank and Tom was mean, more than mean—with the alcohol and without it."

She stopped speaking and returned to studying the stars. Paul settled back into his chair and held the silence.

"I've come to think," Grace continued, "that most people live their whole lives trying to make the story in their head come true."

"What story do you want to come true right now?" Paul asked.

When Grace didn't answer, he stood up and faced her.

"I need for you to know one more thing. I never took another drink and I never will."

The next evening as a soft wind blew the heat of the day off the shoulders of the prairie, Grace knelt beside a flowerbed, laid out where she could see it from the kitchen window. The sun's final rays streaked the sky and etched lengthening shadows across the land. She lifted the pouch of zinnia seeds, retrieved from their hiding place in the bottom of her trunk, and withdrew a single seed. She leaned forward, to poked a hole with her finger in the freshly tilled earth, just as a movement in the window above caught her eye. Grace looked up to see Paul watching her.

"Thank you," she mouthed.

They held the gaze, energy vibrating along the invisible threads connecting them. She smiled and gently dropped her mother's seed into the earth.

MEADOWLARK

24

"Those new mares have sure settled in well," Paul said to Grace in the darkness before dawn that September morning, as she slid the metal spatula under over-easy eggs, careful not to break the yolks, and served them.

"I noticed one of the foals limping with a bad cut last night. Too late to see or do anything about it, but we'd better check on it first thing this morning."

"Is it something we can tend to?"

"There's a big flap of skin hanging off her back leg," Paul said. "We ought to doctor that before the gash rips open even more. Let's bring 'er in and sew it up. We're going to have to be quick, get them mares into the corral and out fast, with that new stud in the far pen. We've got nowhere else to put him and that leg has to be tended. We'll be lucky if he doesn't come right through the fence. So, in and out, fast."

"We can saddle up right after breakfast," Grace said.

"I'm coming, too!" James flopped into a chair at the same moment his mother said, "Wash your hands, before you eat."

"Ah, Ma, they didn't get dirty when I was sleeping."

"You've been petting Kip, I bet."

Less than an hour later, the three figures rode across the prairie under a sky bleeding with the shades of sunrise. A veneer of salmon pink, swirled with light blue, stained the sky and infused cottony clouds with tender colors. Violet seeped up from the horizon. Birdsong suffused the cool morning air that harbored a hint of winter to come.

Grace scanned the dips and swells for any sign of the herd. A red-gold glint poked up amidst the flaxen grass. It flicked back and forth—the twitching of a horse's ear.

"There." Grace pointed.

The lead mare spotted the riders, lifted her head to catch their scent, and rang out a sharp whinny. The herd flexed as a single muscle across the spine of the skyline. Manes and tails streamed in the wind as the leader pulled the others in her wake. Foals scampered, trying to keep up. The injured foal trailed behind, limping, its dam beside it. Fresh blood glistened down its right rear leg.

"Why do horses always have to run? Why can't they just walk like cows?" Grace muttered in exasperation.

"Turn them and head toward home. Take it slow."

The horses snaked around through the natural dips of the range, slipping along the contours of the land. Grace worked her way in front, leading them in the direction of the corrals as they moved in a synchronized band that reminded her of a flock of birds. She looked back and saw James flanking the herd, and Paul loping up from behind.

She reined Mame and dropped down into the hollow with the ranch buildings in sight. Grace jabbed Mame into a run up to the gate, leapt off, and flung it open wide. She jammed her boot back into the stirrup and threw her leg up over the horse, wheeling the mare out of the path of the galloping herd.

At the sight of the mares, the bay stallion in the far pen let out a shrill whinny and paced the fence, pushing against it with his massive chest. Ears up, eyes intense, the stud pawed the ground, creating clouds of dust under his belly. He exhaled a series of sharp snorts and reared, trying to get to the band of mares.

Grace searched the horizon for James. At last, his straw hat bobbed up over the swell. The lead mare parted from the herd as they approached the gate.

Grace kneed Mame forward, right arm raised waving, "Hah!"

Mame raced alongside the mare up the steep embankment, Grace's thighs absorbing the horse's lurches up the steep incline. Mame's hooves slid and pawed up the bank. At the top Grace pulled her to a stop and turned to study the scene below where the mare with the lame foal brought up the rear. The mare was torn between her desire to run ahead or to stay behind with her foal. She circled between her foal and the band of horses, her ears moving back and forth.

Grace urged Mame down the ledge, leaning back into the saddle, almost laying against Mame's rump as they slid down the ridge. The mare pushed into the center of the herd, the lame foal trailing behind. Grace swung wide to push them through the gate.

When the last horse, including the lame foal, was inside, Grace urged Mame up to the gate to block any exit. James swung wide to keep his horse out of the fray. She blessed him for knowing what to do.

"Wait right there!" Grace swung the gate shut and bailed off Mame to fasten the latch. She threw the reins up to James, "Here, hold her while I open the gate into the holding pen, so we can separate the foal. Where's Paul?"

"I don't know."

Grace ran across the hoof-rutted dirt. The stallion bucked and kicked, racing back and forth, slamming into the fence as he slid to a stop on his haunches at each end. Mame tossed her head and reared, nearly yanking James out of his saddle.

"Let go if she does that again! Better that than her pulling you off your horse!" Grace threw the gate open and ran to cut out the mare and wounded foal. Hooves pounded as the horses circled the corral. Grace kept her eye on the pair as the rest of the herd moved past her in a blur.

"Come on," she said softly. The foal stayed close to his mother.

Grace moved into the river of horses, allowing the others to slide past her like water over smooth rocks. When the pair approached, she raised her arms above her head, making herself a bigger obstacle. "Hup, into the gate!"

She tossed up a prayer of thanks when the mare and foal eased through the opening. When the little fellow stumbled after his mother, Grace closed the gate.

"James, move away from that main gate so the horses will come on out. As soon as they do, get behind them and push them out into the pasture and away from the corrals. Let's get these mares out and up over the hill, before that stud comes through the fence!"

She darted across the corral, opened the main gate, and took Mame from James. Grace vaulted into the saddle. At the sight of the open gate, the mares lifted their heads and streamed out, up on the hill and the herd split, one band moving over the rise and the other circled back around the cottonwoods and to the corrals in answer to the stud's snorts and sharp whinnies. They thundered past James, despite his attempts to stop them. Grace held her breath and prayed he would stay in the saddle. She scanned the horizon looking for Paul.

"That's fine, James, you tried!" she called as she galloped past. "Stay here. When I get them going again, you follow in behind and push them over that ridge."

Again and again, the mares cut back to the corrals, and the stud. Creamy white froth laced Mame's coat around the cinch and breast collar. Sweat seeped out from under Grace's hat and into her eyes, her soaked hair clung to her temples.

Finally, exhausted, Grace moved the mares out toward the open prairie and pushed them hard to the north where there was good grass and a full dam. As she watched the horses disappear, a bittersweet ache settled in her chest. She hoped the foals would bring money to the ranch. Their future depended on it.

James and his mother walked their spent horses back toward the barn. Paul was still nowhere to be seen.

"Let's tie them and go in for a drink of water then we'll go see what happened to Paul," Grace said.

"Race you!" James said and took off running for the house.

Grace started after him, then her laughter died in her throat. Tom's brother, Ed stood at the front door.

Instinctively, Grace reached for James ahead of her and circled her arms around him.

She kept her voice steady. "Sheriff," she nodded toward him. "What brings you out this way?"

"Hi, Uncle Ed," James said.

"Son, how are you?"

"Fine, sir."

"What do you want, Ed?"

"I stopped by to see how things are going. Came to see how you and James are getting along."

"As James said, we're fine. I would invite you in but we need to go check on some stock."

"I heard from the bank president the other day." Ed took his hand off the pistol at his side and raised it to slowly wipe his bottom lip with this thumb. "He said you were delinquent on the loan on that property Tom bought. Said he thought we might want to know since it could affect your standing regarding possession of this ranch."

"He is incorrect. I am not delinquent on anything," Grace said. "James go on inside."

"No, ma'am," James said and stayed beside her.

Ed rested his hands on his hips, a slow smile staining his face. "Too bad the bank won't loan to a woman without a man's signature."

"I won't need a loan, Sheriff, and I do not need your assistance so…"

"Not so fast. I came out here to offer to help you out. I arranged with the bank to buy this place from you outright. I've got the paperwork right here." He tipped his chin toward his horse tied loosely to the hitching post.

"What does he mean?" James turned to look up at her. "I don't want to leave the ranch."

"We're not leaving. Please get some water for your uncle."

Hesitantly, James walked toward the house. When he passed his uncle, the sheriff reached out to shake his hand and James complied. Then he went in the front door.

"Take that paperwork, get on your horse, and leave," Grace said.

Ed grabbed her by the shoulders, his thick fingers digging into her neck. She bit her lip. He tightened his hold and shook her until her head flopped. Then he forced her to her knees.

"Dammit, woman! You will goddamned do what I say!"

A shot exploded through the air.

Ed released Grace, turned, and crouched with his pistol in hand. His horse spooked and yanked at its reins. A horse in a dead run broke through the stifling silence. Paul appeared out of the draw, rifle raised as he slid his horse to a stop.

"Grace?" he asked first, registering when she nodded back and keeping his eyes on Ed. "Drop it. I don't care if you are the sheriff."

Ed laid his pistol on the ground. Grace rose shakily, dusting off her dress and rubbing her neck.

"I don't know what's going on here, but I've got a pretty good idea. And the only reason I'm not climbing down off this horse to beat the living hell out of you right now is because there's a young man looking out the window who's watching all of this."

Grace turned and saw James's pale face behind the glass.

"So mount up and ride off and if I ever see you anywhere near here again, there won't be anyone to witness what I do to you." Paul kept his voice low.

Ed looked at his horse and held both hands out in front of him. He bent to retrieve his pistol.

"Don't even think about it," Paul said evenly. "I'll drop it off in town for you tomorrow."

Ed gave the briefest nod and walked over to his horse, mounted and, without another word spurred into a gallop.

Grace looked at Paul and then flew through the front door to where James stood frozen.

She gathered James in her arms. "Mama's fine. Your uncle and I just needed to come to an understanding. Paul helped out with that. There's nothing to be afraid of."

Stiffness trickled out of James's body until Grace felt the silent boy relax.

"I thought he was going to hit you. I thought he was going to kill you."

"I'm just fine," she whispered into his hair, "and he's never going to come back here again."

"I'm glad Paul's here." James burrowed his face into Grace's dress.

"Me, too." Grace pushed her hair back out of her face, and straightened her shoulders. "Go on and get us some water."

She walked back out to meet Paul. The sun threw its midday

light up over the horizon into shafts that lined the prairie.

"James alright?"

"He will be." Grace drew in her breath. "Thank you. I have had similar dealings with my brother-in-law before, but he caught me by surprise this time. Things could've gotten…ugly."

"Looked to me like they already had."

"He wants this ranch. He thinks he deserves it. And times have been tough. There isn't much money, Paul. I suppose you already know that. Apparently the banker offered to make him a deal since everyone assumes I'll go under. Had the papers drawn up and everything. When I said no, that's when…" Grace focused on the shifting light in the sky.

Paul straightened and stretched his back. "I'd best go unsaddle and I'll tend to your horses, too. We need to doctor that foal. We can talk about what to do with the ranch over supper."

"Paul?"

He stopped and turned back toward her.

"What happened to you earlier, on the ride? Where were you?"

"Horse dumped me. Kip stayed with me. I had a bit of a walk on my hands to catch him again, but looks like I got back right on time."

"Your horse dumped you?"

"Yes, ma'am. I've been bucked off more times than I care to remember."

He headed toward the barn, his body moving with the horse's rhythm, a soft whistle floating on the whispery evening breeze.

Giving a soft laugh and shaking her head, Grace turned back to the house.

Grace felt stirrings she had long tried to ignore. As the days passed, feelings deeply denied welled up, feelings she'd worked hard to hold at bay. Had the time come allow herself to feel again? She wavered between the two choices: either looking deep within herself or refusing to examine anything below the surface. Was she brave enough? She didn't think so.

One night, when she was alone and the house was quiet, she took a deep breath, pretended she felt courage once again and mentally began to hazard a look inside herself. When she met resistance and immediately wanted to give up, she told herself at least she had tried, and continued to focus on the surface of things again.

Sometimes, though, when all was very quiet, she would find herself drawn, as if in a trance, into her own depths. Down she traveled past the layers that composed her, through the skin of the surface crust, and the few inches of topsoil, down through the intermittent stratum of soft, pliant sand and hardpan dirt. The layers reflected the story of her life; some yielded softness, acceptance, movement, and others fostered the formation of an impenetrable protective shell. She traveled down into her earthen body and ran her fingers lightly over the layers of landscape formed by the winds and weather of her experiences.

The prairie was Grace and Grace was the prairie. The prairie was feminine, an old, wise woman who had seen it all, who took temporal cares and softened them with her infinite wisdom and patience. Took their sharp edges and smoothed them, dulled them with her strong, aged hands and molded into them grooves and ridges, shapes that fit together and formed an interconnected whole, like a stone wall with each rock fitted within the cradle of others, knitting together to form a strong whole.

In her life Grace had walked the wild, windswept land and tossed her cares to the wind. The prairie caught them, relieved her of their weight for a time, and Grace walked lighter for a while.

MEADOWLARK

25

Later that week Grace heard the sound of a horse slowing to a walk and knew she had company. Paul and James had set out early to harness the teams for the men who would be carving away layers of dirt to create a bowls to catch rainwater. They wouldn't be in until supper.

"I'm coming," Grace called, dusting her hands on her apron, and walked out to find Daisy tying her horse. She still appeared pale and thin, but her face beamed with the most radiant smile Grace had ever seen. Daisy reached into the pocket on her jacket and pulled out an envelope.

"A letter from the boarding school." Daisy waved it like a talisman. She opened the envelope with trembling fingers, withdrawing a folded sheet.

"Here." Daisy handed it to Grace. Grace's eyes darted quickly across the page. When she reached the end, she looked up.

"Did you read that, Grace? They made Ruth go to work in Rapid City."

"Work? Daisy, she's just a child!"

"But now they 'regret to inform me' that they're sending her home," Daisy read on, "for 'not knowing her place.' *That's* my girl. I don't know why, Grace. There are thousands of children never returned to their families. I don't understand. There's no explanation. I will believe it when I see her."

"Oh, Daisy. I am so very grateful. I don't understand why either—one of those mysteries of life. So let's just accept," Grace said. "Come in and visit a bit?"

"No, I'd best get the house ready for my girl who doesn't know her place. She should be home tomorrow."

"Once the two of you are settled back in, will you bring her to come see us? James misses her and Paul would love to meet her."

"We will do that." Daisy put the letter back in her pocket and checked the cinch on her saddle.

Her toothpick thin arm and the rasp of her voice caused Grace to ask, "Are you feeling all right, Daisy?"

"Fine. A little tired. But I will be fine now that Ruth is coming home."

"Good then. Take care."

As she dribbled kernels of yeast, hard and smooth in her fingers, into warm water Grace tried to figure out what to do with her feelings for Paul. Still terrified to let herself write, the ghost of Tom's threats ever-present, the tiny stones of yeast reminded her of how she'd hardened her heart. She felt them dissolve under her fingertips, turning the water tan and slick. Perhaps she, herself, was softening, too.

Her growing affection, the rekindling of that old flame, both delighted and terrified her. How did she know he wasn't just like

Tom? Tom had been sweet and nice and funny before they married. Perhaps, she didn't have good judgment when it came to men. She was a fine judge when it came to horses. Maybe she should stick to that and play it safe. She could read a horse in moments. She could tell its personality by a certain look in eye that could not be disguised. If a horse was lazy or sweet or had a bit of the devil, Grace spotted it right off and knew what she was working with. Men, though, knew how to disguise the look in their eyes if they wanted to. If she imagined Tom and Paul as horses, what kind of horses would they be?

Tom would be small and quick, ears back, teeth bared. The kind of horse who would let you walk behind him once without incident, and then kick you with all of his might the next time. That kind of horse would do it just to prove he could. He would be high-strung and nervous, prancing about to draw attention. He would be dark, with tight muscles and a tighter disposition, and hard eyes with a glint of cocky malevolence.

If Paul were a horse, he would be big-boned, lanky, easy in his gait and movement, with large, liquid eyes. He wouldn't need to strut and prance to prove his dominance, but would move with a comfortable self-assuredness. He would emanate a tender strength that comes from a big heart and a deep sense of confidence.

A smart girl like her should have seen Tom Robertson for who he was, but he'd fooled her, fast and true. How could she trust herself to know what Paul was truly like? It might be best not to let Paul any farther into her heart. She should keep her distance and stay out of harm's way.

"Whoee, it's a warm one out there today." Paul leaned against the counter and gulped down the tall glass of water Grace handed him. He set it down before taking a deep breath and turning toward Grace. He took off his hat and held it loose in his hands.

Her hands clenched tight at her sides. Before he could speak another word, she said, "Paul, I can't. It's not that I don't want to…it's not that…it's that I can't."

"Can't what?" he asked.

Sweat trickled down the sides of his face reminding her how hard he worked for her and for James. How could she tell him that she couldn't let a man into her heart, that she could never risk being shattered again?

She picked up a cloth and began scrubbing the table hard enough to take off the finish. "I can't. I can't. I can't."

"Sometimes you are so damned prickly I fear I'd cut my finger if I touched you." He studied her with a mixture of gentleness and challenge.

"Well, you just might if you tried to touch me right now, Paul Overland, so you'd better not," she bristled.

"You know me well enough by now to understand that I would never touch you without an invitation, no matter how much I want to take you in my arms and kiss you right this moment."

She threw the rag in the sink. "Don't say that! Don't tempt me."

"I'm only saying…" A smile as big as sunrise lit up his face.

Grace looked down at the floor that needed sweeping and then dared to look into his eyes.

"I think you forget that I can see clear through you, see all of those private thoughts and into the depths of your heart." His voice was soft. "You're like a colt who's been broke rough and rode hard and never been brushed or petted. And I understand that skittishness. You have a right to feel the way you do. What you need to know, though, is that you can trust me, Grace. I promise you, with God as my witness, that I will never hurt you."

"I just can't, Paul."

He raised his hand and rubbed it across his chin and then up and down the side of his cheek. "You're like an onion and we are only at that outer layer that has been drought-stricken, sunburnt, and dried in the wind. I imagine that if we take our time to peel back those layers, we'll find that inner core that is pure and sweet and unharmed. I'm willing to wait."

"I said I *can't!*"

"Then begging your pardon, ma'am, I've got a dam to dig." He put his hat back on his head, tipped it slightly and eased out of the room.

Grace watched him walk away. She couldn't move. Her body felt numb and floating. She wanted to run after him, to catch up his hand and tell him how much she thought about him, and how he made her feel, and how he made her laugh, and that she remembered how his lips felt against her own, and how he made her heart pound and her body go soft, and how she felt safe with him and that scared her, and how she watched for him riding back over the ridge every day, and how her heart swelled so much with tenderness when she talked with him that she was sure it would burst.

But she didn't.

She stopped herself. *It's better this way.*

The dams Paul, James, and the hired men dug baked empty in the sun. Grace rode to pick up the mail. Her heart dropped when she discovered a letter from the bank. She waited to open it until she was back at the house. Her hands shook as she slipped the folded paper out of the envelope.

Dear Mrs. Robertson,

> *It is with regret that I inform you this bank has reached the full extent of understanding about your difficulties in making the obligatory payments on your outstanding note. If you continue unable to make said payments, the bank will be forced to take possession of your property to sell at auction to the highest bidder. As I have informed you previously, your deceased husband's brother, Mr. Ed Robertson continues to express interest in purchasing your property. If you would like to pursue this avenue, please contact me at your earliest convenience.*
> *Thank you and good day.*

Grace ripped the letter to pieces and threw it into the stove.

Paul walked in through the back door, hung his hat on the hook, and held out the frothy full bucket of milk.

"Is there anything else I can help you with?" He smiled.

"I don't need you to milk for me, Paul Overland, or do anything else for me."

He set the bucket down and backed up in surprise.

"Don't milk for me. Don't do anything for me. I don't need your help and I don't want to be beholden to you. I can do fine by myself. I don't need you. I don't need anybody! Do you hear me?" She stood clutching the edge of the table, tears springing to her eyes before she could stop them.

Paul took his hat off the peg.

"I don't want you doing things for me!" She grabbed the bucket of milk with so much force, half of it slopped all over the floor.

"Damn it! See what happens? Look at the mess I have to clean up now!" Grace slammed the bucket into the sink, wrenched open a drawer and yanked out a dishtowel. Her arm caught the sharp corner of the drawer.

"Ouch!" Blood oozed toward her wrist.

Paul extended his hand, "Grace, let me—"

"I don't need you. I don't want you. Leave me alone! And stop looking at me that way."

"What way?"

"All soft and tender and tempting, making me vulnerable and weak, fooling me into thinking…Go! Just go!"

"You can lash out all you want, Grace, but it won't change the way I feel." He walked out the door and it closed behind him with care.

She grabbed the bucket and threw it on the floor, watching the milk splash all over the cabinets. Drops of milk rained down on the coffee cups she and Paul had used that morning. Grace snatched the cups from the dish drainer and threw them against the wall. Shards flew in all directions.

Her anger at the bank ebbed. Dark flecks of dirt from Paul's boots floated on the creamy whiteness of the milk. Grace fell back against the counter and sank slowly to the floor. The milk seeped through her dress. She drew her legs up to her chest and wrapped her arms around them. She lay her head on her knees, rocking back and forth, whispering, "I don't need anyone. I don't need anyone. I don't need…"

Grace heard Paul say from outside, "Don't go in there."

"Why not? I want a glass of milk," James said.

"Your ma needs to be alone right now."

"What does that mean? Is she all right? Mama?"

Grace could imagine Paul putting his arm on James's

shoulders and leading him away. She could see him exhibiting his usual calm and her son soaking up the tenderness that he'd never had from his own father. Why couldn't she do the same? Why couldn't she confide in Paul and let him love her?

That night Grace dreamed of Paul. She wished she could take him into her body. Run her fingers over the texture of his skin and the muscles beneath, and feel the tiny separation of skin from muscle along his forearm.

In her dream, she wanted to breathe him in, as desperate as a first gulp of air after being under water too long. To run her hands over his landscape. She longed to feel his hands on her own terrain, exploring, tasting, scenting, loving, as her body molded to his touch, to his body, as their landscapes came together. She wondered if she tasted like dirt, earthy and dry as a hot summer day, or moist and rich after a rain? How must she feel, must she taste? She thought she must embody both.

In her dream, Grace lay down upon the prairie and closed her eyes. She saw the veins extending from her body, out her fingertips, her toes, her thoughts, her shoulders; thin veins grew out into the earth. The earth drank; drank her joy, her tears, her sorrows, her laughter. The roots of the prairie grasses plumped, sucking her juices. Outward, over the plains, she spread her roots and runners, creating new life, new hope, new faith—outward they flowed around her small human body, carrying her strength, the perseverance within her veins, back to where it belonged. Within each drop of blood, Spirit lived.

She lay silent in her dream, arms and legs outstretched, eyes closed, hair a bird's nest around her head, feeding the earth, feeding the prairie, feeding her child. She felt herself drift away. She watched the prairie suck at her juices until there was no life left in her, no blood, no water, no moisture, until she was a dry leather pouch of nothing, light enough to blow away on the wind. She was the prairie, "Dust unto Dust."

26

The letter from the bank haunted her as she stood at the kitchen window. Waves of autumn wind moved above the ground and made the corrals appear to sway and bend. Paul's lean form rounded the corner of the barn and headed for the house.

No, Grace. You will not allow yourself to fall for this man. She sat down as he stomped his boots outside the door. Paul knocked once and walked in, heat emanating from his body and dirt lining the creases in his face and hands. He took off his hat and wiped the sweat off his forehead.

"It's like being in the middle of a dust devil out there." He reached for a glass, filled it from the hand-pump and took a drink.

"I don't trust anybody." Grace straightened her back.

Paul's hand stopped mid-air.

"Not a single soul."

MEADOWLARK

Paul emptied the glass and said, "Well, hell, Grace. I just came in for a drink of water."

Grace laughed before she could help herself. Paul reached out to set the glass on the counter. A bead of water coursed its way down the side.

"You can trust me, Grace."

"Words blow away in the wind, Paul. I learned that the hard way. I don't believe people's words, anymore. I watch if people live their words, walk their talk, and make them real…only then, *maybe*, do I believe. Otherwise people say what they know you want to hear. They remember a promise for a couple of days and then it disappears. It blows so far away people swear they never even made it." Grace stood and walked over to the sink. She rinsed the glass and set it in the drainer. She stood eye to eye with Paul and he did not look away.

"You'll see, Gracie. You don't scare me. Hell, I lived in Arizona, home of rattlesnakes, scorpions, black widows, and droughts way worse than this one. But it's also home to sunsets so pretty they make you draw the air deep into your lungs, just hoping to inhale a drop of that color washing the horizon. The smell of the desert after a monsoon rain, so full of the richness of the earth that you can taste it spicy sweet on your tongue and feel it in your skin. But, like here, it is a place where words sink and settle into the ground and send down deep roots if you give 'em a chance. Isn't that what this is all about? About you being afraid of giving us a chance?"

"I've got to pay the bank something. Soon. Or they're coming after me. I think I need to sell some steers before they lose their summer fat. I've got to. That won't buy me much time, but it'll be some and that's better than nothing."

"And here I thought I was just coming in for a drink of water. You didn't answer my question, but we can save that for later. For now I agree that you've got some nice big steers. We could take a dozen or so over to the sale barn in Phillip. I'll get James to help me bring in the herd this afternoon."

Late in the day, Grace waited near the corrals talking to Mame over the fence. When she saw the dust cloud lifted by the feet of

241

moving cattle, she opened the gate to the holding pasture and stepped out of the way. At least three hundred pair, she thought. If we can just hold on. She'd thought of selling that piece of land Tom had just bought, but balked at the idea. That was her son's inheritance.

The bawling mass spewed inside and milled in circles, stirring the dirt and hanging it in the air. Paul rode over to close the gate as Grace moved into the outer edge of the herd to look them over.

A big, bald-face steer saw daylight beyond the dust and dashed for the opening. Grace shouted, "Hah!" and raised her hands high, then saw his front legs and belly as he launched to jump over her. The steer caught her full in the chest, knocking her flat on her back. Grace watched the sky spin. She couldn't catch her breath. She grabbed for her throat, mouth opening and closing soundlessly.

James ran over. "Ma, are you all right? Ma!"

She shook her head back and forth.

"Paul!" James shouted as Kip dove at the cattle coming in too close to where she lay.

"She just got the wind knocked out of her, that's all." Paul helped Grace to sit up. "Relax now. Try to breathe real slow." He rubbed her back until she was able to draw a sip of air into her aching lungs.

Grace spat and she shook her head. Chunks of dry manure rained into her lap. She tried to stand, but her boot caught in the tear the steer had ripped in her dress.

"Now that makes me mad. I was down to two dresses, and now this one is ruined." Grace looked down at the torn fabric.

"James, brush off her back," Paul said, holding Grace by the shoulders to keep her upright. "One step at a time now. We'll get out of here until these steers calm down."

"Let's go up to the porch," Paul said, "That wind has really picked up in the last few minutes."

"But the steers?"

"Don't worry about them. James and I will sort them this afternoon. Maybe take them to the sale barn later this week." Paul stayed behind her with his hands on her shoulders and moved her toward the house. Her feet dragged and her head felt like cottonwood fluff.

"But I want to help. I want to…"

"It doesn't matter what you want. What you need to do right

now is get out of the sun and the wind and drink a glass of water." Paul said.

James took hold of his mother's hand and helped her up the porch steps.

That evening, as Grace pulled a meatloaf out of the oven and set it on the counter to cool, she looked out the window to see Paul walking toward the house from the corral, taking a drink from his canteen. As he passed the flowerbed, he stopped mid-stride. He squatted down and poured the remaining water around the plants. He rose and stepped back. It looked like he was praying. When he raised his head, a smile played at his lips. Though he didn't see her watching him, she returned his smile.

Cries of "No! No!" awakened Grace from a fitful sleep. "No!"

James! Grace ran up the stairs to discover the boy sound asleep, entangled in the sheets and quilts as if he'd been struggling. Grace carefully straightened the covers and tucked them in around his shoulders.

She closed the bedroom door quietly and heard Paul's voice from downstairs.

"Is he alright? I thought I heard something outside and went to check."

"He's asleep." Grace tiptoed down the stairs. "It happens sometimes." Moonlight streamed in from the window at the top of the landing and wrapped the room in soft blue light. "I wish I knew what troubled him so. I don't like to think that he suffers with these nightmares."

"Boys dream about all kinds of things, monsters and mayhem...even girls." Paul raised his arm and leaned against the doorframe.

Grace came to stand beside him. "He's too young for girls. He's only eight."

"I doubt that. He talks to me all the time about Ruth."

"Ruth? Really? Well, the three of them, James, Ruth, and Corwin, run in a pack every chance they get." Grace said, suddenly very aware that she was standing barefoot in her nightgown.

"I always worry that he's dreaming about Tom being cruel to him. I should have stopped that. I should have…"

"What? Killed him? That's the only way anyone is going to stop a cruel man from being cruel. You did the best you could, Grace. You and James managed to stay alive and mostly sane. I would say you did a danged good job, overall."

A cold sweat had sprung up under Grace's armpits. Did Paul know what she'd done? Was he trying to find out what had happened to Tom? Or was this only idle talk meant to soothe her?

"Good night, Paul." Grace laid her hand on his chest and pushed him toward the door.

He didn't move. *Why won't he go away?*

"Grace?" she heard through the darkness.

"Yes?"

"Goodnight." He closed the door quietly.

Grace crawled into bed and buried her face in her pillow so no one could hear her cry.

That next morning, Grace looked out to see James, eyes narrowed fiercely, throwing rocks, again and again, at the shale wall along the creek. Kip sat behind him, watching.

Grace started outside, but slowed when she saw Paul approaching him from the corrals. Grace moved close enough to hear them without being seen.

As Paul neared James, and said softly, "Hi, bud." The boy twisted toward him, a stone still clenched in his fist. He stared at Paul as if he didn't see him, then recognition melted down over his gaze.

"Hey, Paul," came the guarded response.

"What are you doing?"

Silence hung around the boy in impenetrable folds. He lowered his eyes.

"Just throwing some rocks?" Paul ventured.

An almost imperceptible nod followed.

"Feels good sometimes, don't it?"

MEADOWLARK

James raised his gaze to meet Paul's eyes.

"Mind if I join you? See if I can hit the target?" Paul asked.

"I like to throw rocks by myself." James looked down and kicked at the dirt.

"Well, okay then," Paul said. "I'll be around if you need me."

James's head moved slightly in assent. Paul walked back up the incline and entered the soddy. Grace heard the dull thumps of rocks as she moved back into the shadows, then into the house.

Anger spilled over her and flooded her body. In violent bursts, she chopped carrots and potatoes for a stew. Harder and harder the blade slammed down on the cutting board. The fury she still felt for what Tom had done to James consumed her. She needed to do something more than chop vegetables or she would explode.

She ran from the kitchen, knife in hand, and across the yard to the barn where she grabbed an empty grain sack and pulled it over a full one. She thrust the knife through the four layers of burlap and then laid it aside. Grabbing her rope from a peg on the wall, she threaded the end through the holes in the sacks and tied it off. The other end of the rope she over a beam and pulled with all her strength, heaving until the bag swung heavily. Then she wrapped the end of the rope around a post and secured it.

She turned and slammed her fist into the bag, feeling the shock move up her arms and into her shoulders and back. Punching, pounding, kicking, she clenched her fists tight and hit it again and again. The course burlap scraped the skin from her knuckles. The enclosed heat of the barn drenched her in sweat as tears she'd held back flowed down the dirty map of her face. Her hair turned into a wet, matted nest. Grunting, she pounded the bag until the muscles of her arms and legs throbbed.

"What in the hell did that feedbag ever do to you?" came a voice from the door.

Startled, Grace fell forward against the bag.

"Leave me be." She turned and threw another punch into its center, feeling pain shoot through her hand.

"Gracie," Paul said.

"I hate it! I hate what that sonofabitch did to my son! Eight years of this!" She threw her punches with renewed force. "And I hate that there's not a damned thing I can do about it. It breaks my heart over and over again."

"Stop now. Your knuckles are bleeding." Paul placed his hands on her shoulders. She dropped her arms and leaned forward, resting her head against the feedbag, inhaling the earthy scent of the grain and burlap. She felt him waiting.

He turned her toward him and she sank against his chest, felt his arms wrap around her, but her body remained rigid, every muscle taut.

"Listen to my heartbeat, Grace. Just listen," he said gently.

She had to slow her breathing to hear it. Her anger flowed into the ground. She began to talk. She spoke of her feelings of helplessness and sadness. She spoke to the steady beat of his heart. Paul didn't say a word, didn't shift a muscle. His only movement was the the rise and fall of his chest under Grace's cheek, the slight movement of his ribs against the length of her torso.

Words tumbled out of Grace and scattered across Paul's chest, until at long last the torrent became a stream, and then a trickle, and finally, nothing at all. Silence settled around them, dotted only by the sounds of wind, birdsong, and an occasional horse nicker.

Grace drew back and looked at the wet patch on his shirt, where her tears had soaked it. Her gaze trailed over the weathered skin of his neck, the stubbled jaw, his lips, nose, and finally rested on clear blue eyes. Sprays of lines framed his eyes, carved from years of squinting into the sun. Dust motes floated in sunbeams around them.

Grace wiped her face again. "I'm ready to go back to the house now," she said.

His arms didn't loosen. "Well, what is going to be better for James, Grace? For you to spend the rest of your life feeling bad, or for you to get out there and be happy and create a good life for yourself and him? Are you going to spend the rest of your life feeling sorry? Is that what you're going to do? Ah, hell, Grace. It's your *life*, dammit."

"It doesn't feel like my life. Tom stole my life from me."

"Listen. One time I was feeling sorry for myself and was bellyaching about it around the campfire and this old boy looked at me and said, 'Play the hand you're dealt.' When he told me that, everything changed for me. Well, nothing on the outside changed, but everything on the inside changed."

Grace saw nothing but love in Paul's eyes. No meanness or cruelty, nothing but strength and resolve. She waited for him to go on, bracing herself for what was coming.

"You need to think about the present and the future. Look at yourself right now. Would you want James to see you this way? Imagine him living with a mother in such a state. He needs you to see yourself as strong and capable, as being happy and bringing laughter and wisdom into his life. It's your job to show him that no matter what life hands a person, it is always up to that person how to handle it. Are you going to give James a mother beaten down by life? Or are you going to give him a mother whose roots run deep enough for him to know he will be safe in any storm, a mother who believes in him?

"Well, which is it going to be? Your son deserves the best you have to give and this crying, angry heap sure as hell isn't it. You can't change the past, but you can damn sure move heaven and earth to create the best future possible for him." Paul let go of her.

Grace wiped away the rest of the tears that streaked her face. Suddenly, a handkerchief appeared. She took it and blew her nose, then tucked it into her apron pocket.

She took a deep breath and looked at Paul. "I guess I have to play the hand I was dealt."

Paul nodded in response. "You already are, Grace. Selling those steers will make a payment for the bank. You made that happen. And if you simply go on making those good choices, the rest will take care of itself."

Grace straightened her shoulders, stepped back, and smoothed the front of her dress and apron.

"Do you remember how we used to ride down along the river with the neighbor kids, Gracie? We would race against each other. You were the most daring of us all. That's what I remember about you. There was *nothing* you wouldn't do." He laughed and pushed his hat higher on his forehead.

"What else did that girl do? I need to remember her."

"You won't find her by looking backward. The truth of you isn't what you were. It's who you are now. Your past lives in you. It's there if you look for it. It made you what you are. Accept yourself as you are and move forward." Paul pushed lightly on the grain bag. The rope creaked against the wood.

"Please?" Grace kept her voice even and looked out across the yard. "Right now I need to be reminded about who I was."

Paul gave a soft smile of resignation, "You had a granite core.

But I wondered how you really felt about things. You always held everyone at a distance. You were friendly with people so they thought you were open by nature. But I always knew that openness only went to a certain level and beyond that you kept to yourself.

"Do you know what I remember most about that girl?" Paul continued. "I remember her telling me how she would jump off of fence posts onto the horses that her uncle broke."

"I remember," Grace said softly. "I remember being twelve with long braids down my back and leaping onto those horses and never knowing if they were going to buck or run. I remember what it felt like to hang on as they raced across the prairie, and then jumping off and rolling before they hit the danger zone of the breaks."

"That girl is still there, Grace. She's like a fine braided *reata*, a thing of beauty but made to work and made to last. Made strong by all her past experiences. When you rope with a grass lariat, they're not really any good until the kinks have been stretched out of them. A good cowboy will stretch a rope between a couple of posts and then put pressure on it. It's that pressure that draws the fibers of the rope tight together and makes them hard—a hard twist. You understand what I'm saying...hard twist?"

Grace tilted her head.

"One thing I didn't show you when we were roping is the importance of giving the rope some slack sometimes," Paul continued. "If you look on the horn of some of the old saddles you'll see where the hard twist burned around the base of it when they were slipping the dallies, because if they didn't, the constant strain might break the rope. Those old hard twist ropes will last a lifetime, but you have to know how to take care of them. You have to know when to give them some slack." Paul paused, "So, give yourself some slack, Hard Twist."

Grace looked him square in the eye and briskly shook out her skirts. "What are you doing hanging around the barn in the middle of the day, Paul Overland? Can't you see we've got a ranch to run?"

"Yes, ma'am," Paul smiled. He reached up and pushed his hat down firmly. "I better work on some fence. I'll ask James to help me."

He picked up the fencing pliers from the shelf of the barn, glanced at Grace sideways and smiled. He moved toward the door, the shadow of his form silhouetted against the bright day.

"Paul?"

He stopped and turned.

MEADOWLARK

"Leave that feedbag hanging there for a while yet. I might need it."

"Well, it'll be here if you do."

Grace watched him walk over to where James sat by the creek. She saw her son turn toward Paul. Paul pointed over toward the fence, his hat bobbing slightly as he lifted his chin in that direction. James looked and nodded. He stood up and tossed a stone to the ground. As Paul and James walked toward the fence, Paul pointed at something along the fence line and James reached out rest his hand on Paul's arm.

Mame poked her head over the top of the corral and whinnied as Grace approached.

"Hey there, girl," Grace murmured as she rubbed the horse's face. "I have a stew to finish for supper, but I know what we both need right now. Let's go cut us some slack."

She bridled the mare and climbed on bareback. Mame's ears pricked forward and she moved into a slow lope out the gate and west across the prairie. As horse and rider crested the rolling hill, Grace leaned forward and wrapped her hands through the horse's thick mane. She clutched Mame's body with her legs and gave Mame her head. Feeling Grace's energy and intention through her body, the horse lunged forward, gaining more ground and speed with each stride.

Grace whooped out loud. Tears of joy streamed down her face. The hot scent of Mame's sweat and the prairie's dust filled her nostrils. Courage welled within the cramped spaces inside her and her soul unfurled.

"Let's go out and watch the sunset from the porch and do the dishes later," Grace said.

James stared at her in surprise then raced outside, calling Kip. "Don't slam the…!"

The front door whammed shut and Grace winced. She carried a tray with coffee and Paul held the door for her. They faced the porch chairs to the west and settled in. A September breeze played with the tips of the grasses, sending soft ripples through the willowy blond sprays. Layers of clouds hung suspended across the full expanse of sky, the sinking sun casting rays upward to create an array hues as the faintest blush of pinks played among oranges, yellows, and purples with tints of pale buttercups, and a rich peach cupping the outer edges.

"Don't you wish you could taste those colors on the tip of your tongue?" Grace asked. "Like the tartness of the tangy orange, the creamy richness of the lemon or what must be deep cool crispness of violet."

"Taste them?"

"You know what I mean. What would that deep plum on the upper edges of the clouds taste like? A spongy poundcake? That wild rose surely would be a sweetness that could not be chewed, but only licked. Lavender must have the texture of buttercream icing."

"Tasting clouds…I never thought about that before," Paul said.

"And where is the exact point where pink turns to the color of peaches?"

"That might be too deep for me to contemplate." Paul laughed and sipped his coffee. "When I see clouds, I think rain and grass."

They sat in companionable silence and watched the colors deepen and intensify as the sun sank into the horizon. James and Kip quit rough-housing and came to stretch and yawn on the steps.

"James?" Grace asked as she stood and picked up the cups.

"Hmmm?"

"I hereby release you from dish chores. Why don't you go on to bed now?"

"Thanks, Mama. Good-night, Paul."

"Good-night, James. Thanks for your help today."

Kip came to push his nose under Paul's hand for a tidbit of affection before following James inside and up the stairs. Grace lit the kerosene lantern on the kitchen table when they came in, and a downy glow ebbed through the room.

As Paul started to clear the table, Grace blurted out, "Do you still like to dance?"

The golden flame of the lantern reflected in Paul's eyes. "Well, you know, it's been years since I've danced. I might not remember how at all, but I just might be willing to try if you'll remind me."

"I realize we don't have any music, and I can't very well play my violin and dance at the same time, but perhaps…" she faltered.

"We've got music right here." Paul lifted her hand and placed it on his chest above his heart. "Right here."

MEADOWLARK

He raised her hand in his, placed his arm around her waist, and drew her close.

The ghosts of her past, of pain and terror, appeared unbidden to tap her on the shoulder. She tried to push them away, out of her mind. *Go away. I'm done with you. That's over. Go away.*

It could happen again, they coaxed. *You know it can. We can come into your life again and destroy it all. We've done it before and we can do it again.*

Grace shook her head, wanting to cast them out of her thoughts, out of this room, but the fear they might be right made her heart recoil and clench into a protective tight shell. Then, quite suddenly she made a choice.

And they danced. They moved across the wooden floor to the cadence of heartbeats. First slow, then fast, they slid, then twirled, carried away on the winds of pure emotion. Grace threw her head back and laughed, as Paul pulled her close and spun her, his boots gliding across the floor. She was lifted up, joyous and alive. Everything else ceased to exist. Her life was complete in the moment.

27

"Someone's coming," James said as he sat Blue near the corrals where Paul sorted steers according to Grace's directions.

"That's Mae," Grace said. "But she never drives that fast." The buggy flew down the lane, a ribbon of dust lifting behind the wheels. The conveyance slid to a stop in front of the house, and Mae emerged from the cloud, walking briskly toward the front door.

"Mae!" Grace called. "We're over here."

Mae turned toward the sound of Grace's voice and hurried toward the corrals.

"It's Daisy," Mae shouted, as she approached. "She's got tuberculosis and no hospital will take her. They've put her in jail to keep her away from people. I knew you'd want to know."

"Jail? Mae, it can't be TB, not after Ruth just came home."

"I went out to see her a week ago. She said she was tired and coughing a lot. Said she wasn't ever hungry. She collapsed on the reservation when she went to see a relative and they took her to the doctor. When the diagnosis came in, the authorities took her to jail in Rapid City. Didn't even give her the chance to call anyone. Ike found out because someone was talking about it at the feed store."

"Oh, my Lord. I knew Daisy hadn't been herself and the dark circles under her eyes worried me, but tuberculosis? Ruth?" Grace gasped, "Where's Ruth?"

"She'd been farmed out to a local family and was set to be sent back to the boarding school. Ike went to collect her. He assured me he won't come home without the child. She'll stay with us, of course. And, here's the part you're going to hate," Mae said. "The hospitals and sanatoriums won't treat Indians. Won't even allow them through the doors."

"Paul?" Grace called. "Can you and James finish up here? I need to talk to Mae."

When he held his hat up in a sign that he'd heard her, Grace took Mae's arm to walk back to the house.

"Where have you been?" Grace asked.

"We were in Rapid City the past few days. I had ordered new medical supplies and they hadn't arrived when we first got to town. When they finally came in, another doctor showed up and tried to take my order. I told him I'd arm wrestle him for them. I ran my arm along the counter and cleared everything off that was in our way with one swipe. I plopped my elbow up there and said, 'Well?'"

"You didn't!"

"Oh, I did. And I won, of course. Ike said he should have warned the poor bastard, but he was enjoying the show himself. Anyway, that doesn't matter now, we need to talk about Daisy."

"We need to go and see her as soon as possible, Mae," Grace said as she rebuilt the fire in the cook stove.

"Now, hold on," Mae rested her chin on her hand. "I don't know much about the legal system in this regard, but I know enough to know that they won't let us anywhere near her if we just barge into the jail. They said they were going to relocate her to Faith.

We're going to have to be smart about how we go about this.

"Now, what else is happening here?"

Grace filled her in on the ranch's financial status and her experience with Ed.

"And Paul?" Mae asked as she stirred sugar and cream into her coffee. "And why do you blush chokecherry red every time I mention his name." She set the spoon down in the saucer and raised her eyebrows.

James sprinted into the house. "Dr. Mae! I haven't seen you in forever! Is Corwin here?"

Mae tousled his hair and he allowed her to wrap him in a tight hug. Grace laughed as James's eyes grew large, his head buried in Mae's embrace.

"How about you come spend the night with your Uncle Ike and Corwin and me tonight? Uncle Ike will be back with Ruth soon," Mae asked. "They'd love to see you. You'll have to ask your mother if you can get out of your chores, though."

"Can I, can I?" he sang out.

"Yes, yes, that's fine. Paul and I will do your chores this evening. You go and get some nightclothes and be ready when Dr. Mae says it's time to go."

The stairs rocked as his boots pounded up.

"Now, about Paul…" leaning forward, Mae spoke in a low voice.

"What about me?" Paul came in the kitchen door and picked up a coffee cup.

"Nothing!" Mae and Grace said in unison.

"Really? You two looked as thick as thieves. I hope you weren't planning some mischief to get into."

Grace's flushed face felt on fire. She reached up to feel her cheek and said, "No, Paul, we were trying to figure out how to help Daisy. She has tuberculosis and they've put her in jail to quarantine her. We're not sure they'll let us see her."

"What do you need me to do?" Paul asked.

James bolted down the stairs and stood ready and waiting to go.

"Well, it looks like somebody important is ready, so that question will have to wait." Mae laughed.

James gave a hurried hug to his mother, before rushing out the door and clamoring into Mae's buggy. Kip barked and raced in circles. When Paul followed Grace and Mae out onto the porch Kip dashed up to Paul and then flew back down to yelp at James.

"She doesn't know whether to stay or go," James said. "Can she come?"

"If she wants to," Paul said.

"Come on up, girl," James called and slapped his hand against the buggy.

Kip looked back to Paul.

"Go on with him," Paul said, waving toward James. Kip hopped up into the buggy and settled herself on the seat beside James.

"Yes, I'll bring him back tomorrow on the way to town," Mae said as Paul assisted her into the buggy.

Mae gathered up the lines and said, "Grace, I'll be by as soon as morning chores are done. We can leave for town directly."

"Thank you. I can hardly bear the thought of her locked up in there all alone."

Mae handed the lines to James and he took them with ease. "You drive," she said, "I'll sing."

James pulled out the thin whip and snapped it lightly above the horse so that it stepped out at a brisk trot. The high fluting sound of Mae's voice floated back to Grace and Paul.

"Well, you take the high road and I'll take the low road, and I'll be in Scotland afore ye..."

An unbearable heat covered the prairie in the late July afternoon when Grace noticed a billowing charcoal cloud, fringed with rings of yellow and pink on the horizon. Speckled shafts of light shone down on the prairie and spats of lightning intertwined and made the bulbous mountain of clouds glow from within. Grace stopped on her way back from the corrals to admire the spectacle.

Lightning wrinkled the sky, its patterns of living lace bordering the blackness below. The clouds skimmed closer to the ranch and a slight breeze picked up, a refreshing change. Wind loosened strands of hair around Grace's face and swirled them upward. Grace wondered if James was watching this from Mae and Ike's place.

The wind moaned and sharp whooshes of air zipped about. Grace settled on the porch to drink in the colors and sounds. The clouds tumbled forward, darkening and gathering momentum as they neared and a sudden shift edged the air and snapped Grace alert. The cloud was directly overhead and the winds howled. The door to the house slammed shut.

Black clouds roiled above the plains, in an instant shifting from something beautiful and far away to something dangerous and close. The trees lining the creek swayed and groaned in the wind that pushed Grace back against a porch post. With difficulty, she turned and dashed into the house, struggling to push the door closed behind her. The curtains framing open windows strained against their hangers and slapped against walls. She ran upstairs to close the windows. The front door slammed open.

"Grace! Tornado!" Paul bellowed up the stairs, "We've got to get to the root cellar. Grace!"

Grace ran down the stairs. "I'm coming!"

The wind shrieked through the air turned black as night. Grace and Paul sprinted out into the darkness, fighting their way against the winds, across the yard and toward the cellar. Hail rained down, stinging and bruising their necks and arms.

"Cover your head with your arm," Paul yelled against the noise, grabbing her hand and holding tight. A huge hailstone caught Grace on the temple and the world blurred for a moment. A tree cracked and broke somewhere along the creek. The barn door flapped and slammed in the wind. A window broke in the house somewhere. Horses and cattle in the corrals raced around their enclosures, bawling and whinnying in terror. A great roar built and thundered. Grace kept her eyes on the black overhead, using the light cast by lightning to scan the horizon for funnel clouds.

"Run, Grace!" Paul's voice slipped past her on the wind. They struggled toward the mound of earth that meant safety. Reaching it, Paul heaved open the door to the cellar, holding it against his body to keep it from being wrenched away in the wind. Grace stumbled down the steps, into the stillness beneath the earth. Paul yelled something she didn't understand and the door to the cellar slammed shut above her, leaving her encased in the complete darkness and eerie silence of the underground chamber.

"Paul? Paul?!" The sound echoed in the earthy still air of the cellar. She turned back down the steps. "Any rattlesnakes here?" she said loudly, as she always did when she entered the cellar. Hearing no buzz of a rattle, she felt her hand cautiously along the rough earthen ledge, feeling for the smooth coffee tin where the matches were kept. She pried off the lid with a scrape and lit the lantern, illuminating the space and the jars filled with carrots, rhubarb, green beans, chokecherries, beef, pork, apples, raisins, and other vegetables neatly lined along the plank shelves. A year's hard work. Burlap sacks full of potatoes leaned against the wall in one corner. The dirt floor was tamped hard and smooth from Grace's endless trips to stack new jars on the shelves or retrieve others to warm and serve. She set the lantern on one of the barrels.

The bedding was rolled and tied and Grace set about shaking it out and spreading it over the planks on the narrow bed. When she was finished, she propped the pillows behind her back and sat, waiting, listening to the muffled sound of the storm overhead.

Rain and hail pelted the wooden door. She heard the roar of the wind increase and cracking wood and things crashing outside. Where was Paul?

Grace waited, listening to the sounds outside the door. Anxiety was growing in her belly. The roar built to the noise and force of a freight train rolling overhead, so loudly it drowned out the sounds of the hail pounding against the wood.

The door flew open and shrieking winds and hail poured in as Paul turned and fought to close it behind him. Hail struck the stairs, bouncing in all directions before coming to a stop on the dirt floor. With a final yank, Paul pulled the heavy door down over him. It closed with a smash against the frame and he tumbled down the steps. Mud smeared his soaking wet shirt, jeans, and boots.

"You!" Grace launched at him. "You!" She curled her hand in a fist and with each word, she pummeled his chest, shoulders, and arms.

"I…thought…you…were…dead…you…son…of…a…bitch!" The final blow landed in the softness of his belly and he expelled air in a great gush.

"Grace! I…." he held his arms and hands across his chest, protecting himself from the onslaught of blows. "I had to make sure the gate to the round pen was open, so the horses could get out."

Grace panted.

"Mame and the others need to be able to run, to get away, if a twister comes."

Her breath slowed.

Through the silence, they heard the roar of the wind and hail outside.

"Gracie?"

Tears sprang to her eyes. She wiped them away with the back of her hand. "Yes, I'm fine, Paul. I don't know what's going to be left of this ranch, though."

Wind and rain howled outside as it beat the land into submission. Grace and Paul stood looking at each other, the lantern's flame casting their shadows on the softly lit walls. The movement of the flame fluttered shadows across Paul's face. Grace reached out to trace them.

"Grace," he said, catching the palm of her hand to his mouth. She felt lips, then tongue, searching. Gently.

"Years, Grace…years I've waited," Paul breathed into her palm.

The sounds of the storm diminished and the sound of her own beating heart grew as Paul's lips tracked upward, the delicate nerves of her wrist exploding with sensations as he licked and kissed a trail up the inside of her arm.

"Paul…" she breathed

His fingers gently pulled aside the collar of her shirt, as his lips followed the arch of her collarbone to the hollow at the base of her throat, where he lingered, his tongue tracing delicate circles there. His mouth moved upward along the soft skin of her neck, along the edge of her face toward her lips, but stopped at the tender edge of the corner of her mouth.

She felt his warm breath on her face and opened her eyes.

The lamplight played across his face as he looked at her, an unspoken question in his eyes. He smelled of rain, wind, the earth. The warmth and moisture of his body leached through the thin fabric of her clothes as he held her tightly. The question in his eyes remained. Slowly, she nodded.

Paul leaned over and kissed her gently on the lips. Grace sighed as the dam so carefully built against her feelings collapsed, unleashing a flood of desire. Tongues met, tentatively at first, hesitant, unsure, then deeper, languorously, around, over, and under one another.

He paused and looked deeply into her eyes, the hint of a smile playing on his lips. Years of longing passed between them as he tenderly touched her face, fingers tracing the contours of cheek and jaw. They held each other's gaze, everything outside themselves suspended as they silently acknowledged the depths of their feelings before he took her mouth again.

Grace felt the movement of fabric against her skin as his

fingers arrived at the first button. She drew in a deep breath, shuddering as a wave of tingling sensation passed through her body as she watched him slowly undo the rest of the buttons. She felt the soft cotton fabric slide over her skin and looked up, questioning, expectant, barely daring to breath, afraid to shatter the moment.

He eased the shirt down from her shoulders and off her arms. She kept her eyes on his face as it dropped to the floor. She was hardly aware when her skirt followed, leaving her only her cotton shift. He ran his fingers over her smooth belly and cradled her hips in his hands, pulling her against him for a moment before he pushed her shift upward and with her help, slipped it over her head. It fell to the clothing pooled at her feet. She stepped out of her boots and stood before him wearing nothing but the soft glow of candlelight.

It was Grace's turn and she felt no hesitation as she unbuttoned his shirt and ran the palm of her hand over his chest, pushing the shirt back over his shoulders, even as she laid her cheek against his chest. She heard the strong steady beat of his heart and felt his warmth. He smelled of open skies, horse sweat, and cedar. She felt the muscles of his arms move under his skin as he removed the shirt. She kissed the hollow of his throat, tasting the salt of his body on the tip of her tongue.

Grace felt a flush of arousal from deep within. Paul sensed it and smiled, pulling her close and wrapping his arms tightly around her. She felt her nipples harden against the heat of his skin. From the bottom of her soul, she sighed.

"Milky. Your skin feels like sweet butter," he whispered, breathing into her hair. "And you smell of prairie grass. I'd forgotten."

Grace reached up and wrapped her arms around his neck, savoring the sensation his skin against her own. They stood back to look at each other, knowing they were about to jump into the soothing water they'd yearned for yet skirted for years.

He led her to the cot, removed his boots and his pants, then sat down. He reached for her and pulled her to him and kissed her belly, caressing the small of her back then cupping her buttocks. His mouth slid upward and she dropped to her knees to meet it with her own.

Grace knelt in front of him, cradled on either side by his legs. Paul kissed her gently on the lips and loosed the rest of her hair from the ribbon that bound it. They looked deep into each other's eyes as an unspoken question was finally answered. He pulled her onto the bed beside him.

Murmuring, touching, nipping, soft skin, rough skin. Sighs. Soft, moist rhythms. A kiss for every lonely, cold night. An embrace for every day feeling so alone she thought she'd die. A burning hunger. A sharp intake of breath. Skin murmuring against skin.

Night. Darkness. Wind. Storm. Breathing.

"Thanks for waiting for me," she whispered into his chest.

At dawn the next morning, Paul and Grace inspected the ranch and discovered to their relief it had escaped any serious harm. Grace returned from the barn mid-morning to discover a glass jam jar of prairie wildflowers—white daisies and black-eyed Susans—on the front step. Two single prairie roses that had survived the storm entwined in the center, their blooms resting against each other. Her blue hair ribbon from the night before encircled the top with a bow.

MEADOWLARK

28

"We must see Daisy Standing Horse at once." Mae entered the sheriff's office in Faith like she owned the place. Shorter and smaller, Grace stepped out from behind Mae in the doorway.

Ed Robertson did not stand up. He sat leaning back with one leg propped up on his desk.

"You can't." His eyes rested on Grace. "How's that ranch, Grace? You taking good care of it for me?"

Grace didn't trust herself to respond.

"My good sir," Mae interjected with emphasis, "this is a public area and we are citizens of these good United States. We have every right to see our friend."

The sheriff looked confused, "What in the hell are you talking about?"

"It is our right to see our friend. Show us where she is. We know she is quite ill and in need of medical attention. I don't need to remind you that I'm a doctor." Mae tugged on Grace's arm and moved forward.

Ed heaved himself up and moved to block the entrance to the back of the building.

"You're not going in there." He put his hands on his hips, settling one on the top of his holstered pistol. "We can't chance spreading the infection."

"And yet you are breathing the same air that Daisy is breathing. Doesn't that make you nervous?"

It was clear that the sheriff had not thought of that possibility, but he pulled his gun and he held his ground. "You are not seeing that Indian unless you get a court order."

"Ah, yes, I do see now." Mae cheeks flushed and Grace felt her fingers dig into her arm. Mae stepped forward. "And in that case, sir, may I suggest a place you might consider putting that pistol?" her eyes glancing downward.

"Time to go, Mae." Grace pulled Mae around and back out to the street, and pushed her friend in front of her until they rounded the corner of the building and found themselves in front of the general store.

"Mae! You can't tell him that. This is South Dakota, for God's sake. They'll shoot you here for that kind of thing."

"Shoot me?" Mae threw her hands up in the air. "First I learn that I hug entirely too much, and now I'm being threatened with being shot! Well, no need to worry about hugging him. Although, as I think about that, it might help our chances."

"Mae!" They walked down the dirt street. A light breeze sent wisps of clouds across the sky overhead. "Like you said, we've got to be smart about this. No matter what he says, we've got to get Daisy out of there. She isn't getting the care and medicine she needs."

"I've got it!" Grace said suddenly, as they walked with linked arms. "I know how we can get Daisy out of jail."

"What exactly do you have in mind since no judge is going to release her in her condition? They'd rather she rot and die in there."

"We're going to break her out of jail. It's the only way," Grace whispered.

Mae stared at her friend. Something had changed.

"All right Grace, what's happened? I could sense a change in your voice but now I can see it in your eyes."

Grace felt her cheeks color. She looked away.

The blush did it and Mae laughed. "Oh, I see! Well, it's about time! Can't imagine why you waited so long."

Grace was embarrassed but glad Mae could guess her secret.

"Hmmm." Mae rubbing her palms together. "We can discuss *that* development later. Now, on to our new life of crime. The more I think about it, the more I like it. Of course if we get caught, it will mean the loss of my license to practice."

"That's the key to this whole thing. Your doctor's bag," Grace said, recovering her train of thought. "We'll have to wait until the new deputy takes over when Ed goes to dinner. He doesn't know either of us."

Mae drove her buggy into the alley behind the general store and stopped at the rear entrance to the sheriff's office. Setting the brake and tying the lines, she stepped down, holding her black leather doctor's bag firmly under her arm. She drew herself up and straightened her shoulders. She looked at Grace. "Ready, Nurse?"

"Ready, Dr. Thingvold. Remember to use your maiden name."

"Right. Let's go get our patient."

Grace nodded and followed Mae's bustling figure into the sheriff's office.

"Good evening. I am Dr. Thingvold and this is my nurse assistant," Mae nodded toward Grace. "We're here to take Daisy Standing Horse to a treatment facility at the jail in Belle Fourche. Please bring her quickly."

Surprised by Mae's sudden arrival, the new officer on duty stood and moved around to the front of his desk.

"The sheriff didn't tell me about this, ma'am. You're going to need to wait until he comes back."

"Oh! I should have given you the paperwork right away. We were here to see the sheriff this morning. He gave his permission and we obtained the appropriate forms from the judge."

Grace handed the man an envelope. The back was stamped with an official-looking seal. The women hoping the unfamiliar medical board imprint would pass.

When the officer started to open it, Mae said, "You can see that that document is addressed to the sheriff. Just leave it for him. We're in a hurry. We have to deliver Mrs. Standing Horse as soon as possible. Please bring her out immediately."

When the officer hesitated, Grace said softly, "Have you ever seen anyone with the late symptoms of tuberculosis? The blood in the lungs? The pain in the chest? The germs of the disease are floating in the very air you're breathing right now. I would counsel very strongly against exposure."

The officer shifted uncomfortably from one foot to the other.

Mae said, "Go on, my good man, go get her. I doubt the judge would want to come all the way over here to explain all this when he's already sent the papers."

"All right, ma'am." The officer gave a resigned shrug.

"We'll come with you. Our buggy is in the alley."

He led them to Daisy's cell, the last one in the row. Daisy, her pale face the color of ash, looked up in surprise and struggled to her feet. Her clothes hung limply on her skeletal frame. Grace stifled her gasp and kept herself from rushing forward.

"Good God," Mae said. "She's not a criminal!" Mae said as the deputy unlocked to door to the cell.

"Mrs. Standing Horse," Grace cut in, her eyes cautioning Daisy with a nearly imperceptible shake of her head not to give them away. "I'm Dr. Thingvold's nurse. Please don't try to speak. We know how difficult that is to do when you're having trouble breathing." Daisy looked surprised, and remained quiet.

Grace stepped forward to take her by the arm. "We're taking you to a hospital where you can receive proper care."

Daisy's eyes seemed so large in her thin face, and they were bright with fever. She raised her hands to clutch her chest.

"Here we go then, Mrs. Standing Horse," Grace said. "Just a few steps outside." Both women took an elbow and supported Daisy.

Mae turned to the officer. "Thank you, sir. I'll tell the sheriff that you were most helpful."

As the door closed behind them, the women lifted Daisy up into the buggy and sat her on the floor in front of the seat. It was a tight squeeze but there seemed to be so little left of Daisy that she melted into the space. Grace pulled a blanket from under the seat.

MEADOWLARK

"Wrap this around you. Cover your head, too. We'll explain everything once we're out of here."

"My friends. You came for me. I knew you would." Daisy sounded very weak.

"Look." From the pockets of her dress Daisy pulled out scraps of paper in different sizes and colors, her precise script covered the sheets. The wind caught them and they fluttered out onto the street. "I remembered, Grace, how writing kept you from losing your mind. I wrote on any scrap of paper I could find. The words on paper saved me."

"You're safe now, Daisy. Let's go home."

Mae and Grace took their seats and Daisy disappeared from sight as their skirts flared out to cover her.

"I feel like a true adventurer now!" Mae said as drove the horses onto the street. "And, Daisy dear, you and Ruth shall stay with Ike, Corwin, and myself through the winter. I won't hear a word against it. I have the medicine and wouldn't sleep at night if I had to think of you out there alone. I'm hoping perhaps you might even teach me to sew, though I'm bound to be hopeless—although, I can make a fine stitch in a wound!"

"Stay on the back streets, Mae," Grace said. "We don't want to risk running into anyone we know, least of all the sheriff."

"I rather like this!" Maid said conspiratorially. "Perhaps I should leave doctoring behind and turn to a life of crime."

"Oh, Mae," Daisy giggled and coughed. "Please don't make me laugh."

That evening after delivering Daisy to Mae and Ike's, witnessing the reunion between mother and daughter and returning to the ranch, Grace filled Paul in on the day's events and watched the outline of his cowboy hat as he shook his head and chuckled in the twilight.

"You three do beat all."

After Paul and James were in bed and she had ground the coffee for the morning, Grace walked into the pantry. Through the window she could see faint stars glinting from a black sky as she pulled the step stool to the counter and lifted the oil lantern so she could see the shelf above her head.

She took a deep breath, and even as her brain told her again and again that this could not be used to take James away from her, her soul clenched in fear. Her fingers found the small notebook. She pulled it from the back of the shelf and carried it and the lantern over to the kitchen table, where she sat down and opened the journal.

The past years of no writing had been like putting a stopper on a bottle. Initially, Tom's threats and the fear of losing her child had been foremost in her mind. Even after he was gone, she feared his brother and the nebulous idea that someone—*something*—could snatch James from her arms. The thoughts weren't rational, but governed by primitive maternal urges.

The safest way to begin to write again seemed to be to slip in through the back door. She began with the only thing safe enough to commit to paper: lists of ideas of how to help Daisy.

In the days that followed, Grace made slow and erratic progress. The lists became what she needed to do that day, that month, that year on the ranch. She composed lists and lists, with only a few whole sentences about her thoughts thrown in among them. With each frustrated session trying to write something, her sense of resolve strengthened. Could she trust the page again?

Over the next week, the few sentences grew in number—more lists, more thoughts. She only wrote in the morning or late at night, when she knew Paul and James slept. She always returned the book to its place at the back of the shelf. With each tiny flash of written authenticity, of experienced truth, Grace found herself waiting for her world to explode. She'd walk on eggshells for the next several days. Waiting. She watched Paul's every expression and move, searching for the telltale signs of guilt in the shoulders or an ugly mask of arrogance.

Paul always gazed back, his face open and curious. "What?" he would ask, his eyebrows arched in a perplexed expression.

"Oh, nothing," Grace would answer, watching for any sign that she might be misplacing her trust.

"Well, all right, then," he'd say, turning back to whatever he'd been doing.

MEADOWLARK

One day she realized the tense lens through which she'd perceived the world—that of constant vigilance when Tom was around—had been replaced by an ease of living, of being. She wasn't always on guard anymore. She'd exchanged wariness for peace and laughter and comfort. Grace and James now moved freely around the house, though fear could reassert itself at unexpected moments—a noise too loud, something broken, an animal who didn't behave—brought it back to life in a heartbeat. From instinctive memory, they both tensed and waited for the blow, the shout, the arrogant shaming tirade that now longer followed. Their minds and bodies relaxed until air and light filled their home and their minds once again.

One morning Grace pulled the notebook from its place on the shelf and settled at the kitchen table with the lantern, a pen, and cup of hot coffee. She opened her journal. "We've got quite a lot to catch up on."

And she wrote.

29

Mae nursed Daisy through the dry and open early winter of 1918 in the new house Ike had built, complete with two stories and a parlor with a piano. Deciding to take advantage of her focus at home, she wove schooling Corwin, Ruth and James into the weeks. Under her firm tutelage, they were soon reading, studying maps, and working with numbers.

As Daisy gradually improved inside, outside the wind whipped up dust storms where snowstorms should've been. Cattle died when their bellies filled with dirt blown into the meager hay. April came, and the wind and dust continued to blow constantly. All over the prairie, gaunt cattle bellowed pitifully, their hides hanging loose on sharp ribs. Mounds of thistles provided the only thing to feed after the years of drought and grasshoppers. Cattle bawled, weak and staggering, eating whatever piles of manure they could find. Carcasses littered the plains.

MEADOWLARK

Grace and Paul lay in bed one night, grateful that Mae had taken James and given them the time together. Even exhausted by the day's work, the sleep would not come for Grace.

"Paul?" she said into the darkness

"Hmmm?"

She felt him shift and move his head around toward her. No moon lit the sky that night. The room remained cloaked in darkness.

"I can't see how the ranch is going to make it. Not with things the way they are. There's just no money left and it seems this drought will never end. I can't figure out how we're going to buy hay to get us through next winter."

Grace turned toward the window to see the stars splashed like sugar across black velvet outside. She pressed her back against Paul and felt his warmth as he pulled her closer. The windows rattled in their sills as a bitter wind blew down empty from the north.

"What if we lose the ranch?"

"You're not going to lose the ranch, Grace. We'll figure out something. You've put too much blood, sweat, and tears into this ground to lose it." Paul nuzzled her neck and kissed her lightly.

"Sometimes, to take my mind off the ranch, I thought of our time together when we were young," Grace said. "It's full of the feeling that all was right with the world, all was happening as it was supposed to. It was all just so *natural*. That's the best word I can come up with to describe it. When things were really tough and I felt I couldn't go on, I'd close my eyes and allow myself to go back and rest my head on the pillow of memories of you and me together. I'd close my eyes and be young again, happy, and still living a life that made sense to me." Grace stared out the window.

"Then came the years when it seemed no matter which way I looked at my life, I just couldn't make any *sense* of any of it. None at all. That was such a lonely, lost feeling. Those good times with us together—before everything went so topsy-turvy—they were my only tether, my only comfort."

Grace turned back to him, "I never thought I'd get a chance to thank you for that, to tell you what those memories meant to me. They kept me remembering to take the next breath when what I really wanted most was to stop breathing altogether."

Paul gently traced the arch of her eyebrow. Then put his mouth over hers. The kiss was deep and slow.

He held her tightly and whispered, "Breathe, Gracie. Just breathe with me."

And she felt his breath on her cheek and in the expansion of his chest as he pressed her close. She matched her own breath to his and felt herself relax.

In.

Out.

In.

Out.

"Grace, listen to me." Paul touched her, softly stroking the landscape of her body. "You won't lose this ranch, Grace. *You...*" he leaned over to kiss the tip of her nose... "*won't...*" he pulled loose the ribbon bow at the top of her nightdress and draped it open... "*lose...*" he traced the curves of her breasts with his tongue... "*this...*" he moved above her... "*ranch...*" and she moved with him.

"Paul, look," Grace said, pointing to the north, the next day. "Look at those clouds."

"I like what I'm looking at right here just fine, thank you." Paul smiled, keeping his eyes on Grace.

"No really," Grace said and jabbed her finger toward the sky. "Look at those clouds over there."

"There ain't no way it can compare with what I'm looking at right now, ma'am, but alright." Paul lifted his eyes to see the dark clouds hanging low on the horizon.

"Dare we even hope? Every other time we've seen clouds build, they always head east around us."

"Those do look like they might bring a little rain."

"God, if only it would rain. A good rain to fill the dams and get the grass growing to fatten up the cows. We wouldn't have to buy hay for the winter and could finally sell some calves that weighed something." Grace squinted against the sun and looked out at the parched grasslands.

"Ain't nothin' we can do about it but hope, Gracie."

Grace tore her eyes from the clouds. "I'll go crazy just sitting here hoping it'll rain."

"Well, in that case, why don't we bring in that bull that

jumped the corral fence sometime last night? Knocked the top board clean off." Paul reached out his hand to Grace. "I'll go ahead and saddle up the horses."

They rode out slowly through the heat, the horses' heads hanging easy and their tails swishing away flies. The grass had been eaten down to the roots and the horse's hooves kicked up spits of dust as they walked.

"Now this bull's got a nasty habit of heading for the closest dam when he sees a rider coming his way. Just goes out there and waits out the rider." Paul shifted in his saddle and turned his body toward Grace. "I'm pretty sure he'll be near our only dam that has any water in it."

Paul pointed to the bull in the distance, a black island in a sea of yellow. A high-headed black angus, he ran straight toward the dam when he saw Paul and Grace.

"Yup, there he is now. Let's see if we can head him off before he gets there," Paul said, reaching for the bullwhip tied to his saddle.

They spurred their horses and Mame surged forward beneath Grace. Head and tail held high, the bull ran across the grass toward the dam.

"Hyah, bull!" Paul snapped his bullwhip above his head with a sharp crack. "Keep him moving, Kip!" Paul called to the dog nipping at the bull's heels. The bull continued to run for the dam. Grace reined in closer and tried to push the bull back around. He put his huge, heavy head down and swiped its heft toward Mame, catching Grace's leg and breaking off a stirrup. Mame lurched and Grace grabbed for the saddlehorn, hanging on with both legs. Mame stumbled and Grace envisioned falling beneath the bull's sharp hooves before she felt the mare catch herself and regain her feet. With her leg, Grace gripped the stirrup-less fender of her saddle that flapped against Mame's side as she reined away from the bull and stopped. The bull splashed into the dam and waded in several feet.

Paul galloped up alongside Grace, his brow tight under the brim of his hat. "Are you all right?"

"I'm fine, just a little shaken. I thought Mame might go down in front of him." She slapped the empty fender. "Looks like I lost a stirrup back there somewhere, too.

He reached out to touch her hand. "You're sure, now?"

"I'm sure. I better go get that stirrup now, though, so I don't have to worry about it when we're bringing him in." Grace loped Mame back along the path and spotted the broken wooden stirrup lying in the dirt. She hopped off Mame and tucked it into her saddlebag, before coming back up to the dam where Paul tried to move the bull by circling the dam with his gelding and popping the bullwhip overhead.

Belly deep in the water, the bull stood looking at the two riders, strings of snot flying out of his nose as he snorted and jerked his head toward the sky.

"This is the last time you pull this, you sonofabitch!" Paul ran his horse toward the dam. His gelding balked and shied away from the water, skittering sideways.

"Get in there!" Paul spurred and the horse plunged into the murky water. His horse twisted and hopped when the water hit his belly.

"Com'on!" Paul yelled, pushing the reins up behind the horse's ears and spurring him on. In front of them, the bull swam out to middle of the dam. Paul pushed his horse farther into the water until he lost his footing and began to swim toward the bull. Paul held the reins above the waterline with one hand, while the other held the bullwhip.

The bull turned back and started coming toward him. Grace's heart skipped a beat as the massive black body swam toward Paul through the opaque brown water. Kip barked from the shore, running back and forth along the edge of the dam.

"Hyah, you bastard!" Paul snapped his whip. *Crack!* popped the whip, touching the tip of the bull's nose.

Paul slipped off his horse when he snapped his whip and went under. Only two heads were visible then, horse and bull skimming the surface. Grace held her breath, thinking of the tangle of hooves and legs churning beneath the water. One second. Two. Nothing. Grace's blood ran ice.

A hand. A single brown work-weathered hand thrust upward to seize the saddlehorn. A forearm followed. At last, a face. Spitting out water, Paul hauled himself back onto his saddle and retrieved his hat.

The bull turned the other direction, nose smarting from the whip. From atop his swimming horse, Paul pushed the bull across the width of the dam.

MEADOWLARK

"Hah, bull! Get on there, you sonofabitch! Hah!"

Finally, the dripping bull lumbered up out of the water, Paul and the gelding right behind. The horse lunged forward when he felt ground under his feet and Paul slipped his feet in the stirrups, all as the horse plowed up through the water and onto the bank.

"Grace! Push him hard! Don't give him a chance to turn back on us again!" Paul nosed his horse into the bull's hind end, pushing him forward. "Hah, bull! Hah! Run him hard to keep him moving!"

Grace wheeled Mame and ran her around the dam, then joined Paul pushing Mame's chest up against the bull as they pointed him back toward the ranch. They pushed the bull well away from the dam before they slowed their horses to a walk and watched the bull run on ahead.

Panting from the ride, Grace looked over at Paul and his horse. A mantle of mud encased them both.

"Well," he peered up from under his hat, "I suppose that broke in my new saddle." His eyes twinkled above a slow smile.

The bull stopped on the horizon, when Grace noticed the cinch on her saddle felt loose. As they approached, the bull snorted and ran straight south and away from the ranch. Paul nudged his horse into a lope to circle around the bull and bring him back north. There wasn't any time to tighten the cinch. Grace urged Mame into a run after the bull.

She saw Paul's horse trip and go down. It all seemed to happen so slowly. The bay went down, rolled to his side, nearly unseating Paul, then stumbled two more times as he tried to regain his feet, and Paul slipped from the saddle.

When the horse was finally on his feet, he stood motionless, legs sprayed and body shaking. Paul lay on the ground, one foot caught in the stirrup. Grace stopped, not daring to spook Paul's horse.

Paul murmured, "Whoa, now. Whoa. Stay back, Kip." Kip stopped her approach and stilled, every muscle tense.

And Grace breathed a sigh of relief, at the same time trying banish the image of him being dragged across the prairie.

Paul's voice floated across the prairie, soft and low. "Whoa, boy. Easy now." Paul lifted his head and crooned soothingly to the horse. Slowly, he moved his foot back and forth in the stirrup, until he at last slipped it free. When Paul's foot dropped, the horse bolted back toward the ranch, tail high and ears forward.

"Grace! Grace, bring Mame over," Paul called.

Grace galloped over to him and slipped from the saddle. As soon as she had both feet on the ground, Paul kicked his boot into the remaining stirrup and flung his leg over the saddle. "I'm going to get that bastard." He kicked Mame into a run.

As Grace started to walk back to the ranch house, she saw the silhouette of Paul, cracking his bullwhip and galloping over the next hill. She waited and watched. Nothing. No bull. No Paul. No Mame.

Grace came over the slope and saw Paul's horse drinking from a dam in the middle of the pasture. He had settled and Grace caught and mounted him. She turned south, in the direction Paul had headed, when Paul loped up over the hill toward her.

"He got away. Again."

Grace noticed that he was covered in dirt and bits of dried grass sticking to the mud.

"The saddle slipped to the side. Guess the cinch musta been loose." Paul raised his eyebrows. "I fell off on the side that my own horse didn't roll on." Paul tipped his hat back with his fingertips, smiling. "Yep, I do believe it's time for a second cup of coffee."

"Yes," Grace laughed. "I do believe it is."

As Grace and Paul brushed down their horses outside barn, she tried to put her thoughts into words. Flies buzzed around the horse's noses, eyes, and hooves and Mame and the gelding stamped impatiently.

"Look at how the light catches the hair as it floats. Sure is pretty," Paul said, as he brushed his horse. "Luck was with us today. Luck and grace."

Grace stopped brushing and laid her arms across Mame's back. "Luck and grace. I've given quite a bit of thought to both," Grace said, moving the brush along Mame's back. "Some say grace finds us. Sometimes it does, I think. But I've found that more often, it's something we make."

Paul looked over his horse, resting his forearms along the curve of his back. "What do you mean?"

"You make grace by making some tough decisions along the way. Decisions that make your heart bleed raw at the time. Decisions it would be easier not to make. But deep down inside you know you have to do it. The more I live, the more I've come to understand there come times in life we just can't wait any longer for grace to find us. We have to go out searching for it, or we'll spend our whole lives just waiting." Grace paused and leaned against Mame, following with her finger the swirls of hair on the horse's flank.

The trills of killdeer drifted through the air as a red hawk soared in upward spirals overhead. Suddenly the image of another hawk came back to Grace. Memories of searching its talons for the meadowlark she'd been sure it had in its grip, of pip nestled in her bed of dishcloth on the kitchen table, Daisy telling her about Meadowlark.

"It's kind of like when you're having a baby." Paul's eyebrows shot up in surprise.

"Yeah, I just thought of it, but that *is* what it's like."

Paul returned to brushing, "Go on."

"Well, when you're having a baby, the pains have been going on for a long time, hurting more and more."

Paul moved his hand in steady, sure strokes along the gelding's legs and back, listening.

"They start so quiet you don't even pay them much attention at first," Grace turned her face toward the creek, noticing how the cottonwood leaves shimmered in the breeze. "You just go about your business. Then they sneak up on you and have you on your knees before you even realize what hit you.

"Life is like that. Pains and hurts start so quiet that you brush them aside for the busyness of life until some of them get to be so big they drop you to your knees. And you're just along for the ride in labor at that point, Paul. There's no turning back. The pain gets worse and it hurts like holy hell when that baby's head pushes through. Hurts more than you ever dreamed possible. And through the pain, you know the worst is yet to come and still, you can't imagine it being any worse.

Grace leaned against Mame, resting her head against the horse's shoulder. "Your body is on fire with it and you know you have to push the shoulders out. And you know those damn shoulders are bigger than the head. You know you have to do it and every square inch of you is screaming, 'No!'

"Pain blocks out the world and blinds you, filling every tiny piece of you, and you keep on pushing through the pain," Grace said, her hands clenched in tight fists at her chin, "until that baby is out and you're laying shaky and weak on the bed.

"I think making grace involves a lot of those kinds of decisions—that kind of pain. I guess it's like what Daisy told me."

"What's that?"

"She said Meadowlark reminds us to turn toward our fear, to know the truth and make our dreams come true. And, oh, how it makes the peace gained that much sweeter when it comes. But first you've got to push out those shoulders."

Paul stopped brushing his horse and rested his hands on its back. He was quiet for a long while, looking out at the prairie.

"Grace, you realize you're giving birth to yourself, don't you?"

Grace stared at the weathered face of the cowboy in front of her.

"I never thought about it that way, but, yes, that's exactly what I'm doing, isn't it?"

By evening, the clouds had grown larger and darker. Oh, please, please, please let it rain, she thought. Rain with no hail. Rain to make the grass grow and fill the dams and get us through another year.

By nightfall, the rains did come. Grace heard the first tentative drops spatter across the window as she lay in bed. *Please, please, please.* She clenched her eyes tight and prayed. Soon it sounded like pennies being thrown against the window. Grace got out of bed and went to look. Streams of water ran down the pane.

She ran outside in her nightgown. Fat drops of rain poured down out of the sky and drenched her in seconds. *Please, please, please, don't stop. Please don't be a rain that comes and goes before we get hardly anything.* The sky was black, clouds blotting out the stars in every direction, as far as she could see. Small streams of water ran over the ground, curling over and around her bare feet. She jumped up and down, kicking and splashing in the mud.

When she heard the door open, she threw her hands up high. "Look at this rain, Paul! Look at this rain!"

Paul ran out, lifted her up, and twirled her around. They threw their heads back to feel the drops on their faces.

It rained and it rained and it rained. Grace stood by the

window and watched the water streak the panes, thinking that now the grass would grow. I won't have to buy hay to feed the cattle this summer, she thought. The grass would get them through to shipping time, when, if things went well, they'd drive the cattle to market and receive their check for the year. Without having to buy summer feed, it should be enough to see them through the winter and well into next summer. The bank wouldn't be taking the ranch this year.

In her journal that night, she wrote simply, *It rained,* before tucking it back on the shelf.

By morning, the creek below the house was running over the roots of the cottonwoods that lined it. Grace, Paul, and James walked out into fresh air laden with moisture, the rich earthy scents of the prairie after a rain, and the sounds of the overflowing creek. The sun peeked through the parting clouds, sending down shafts of light. The parched ground had absorbed as much as it could hold and the water ran in sheets through the dips and grooves of the prairie, and down into the dams ready and waiting for it.

"If we're real quiet now, we'll be able to hear the grass growing." Paul leaned against one of the porch posts. "You know what you were saying yesterday, Grace, about how making grace was like having a baby?"

Grace's eyes were closed as she inhaled deeply the fragrance of moist earth and listened to the sound of water dripping from the roof. She opened her eyes and nodded.

"Do you think there's a less painful way to do it?"

"Sure. Like right now, this very minute. You and I make grace every day. It's so easy, Paul. It scares me sometimes how easy it is. But I think the easy times, the times grace settles in around you, they happen as a consequence of, well, pushing out those shoulders. In birth, we get a baby as a reward, and in life, we get peace. We birth peace."

30

In May 1930, James and Ruth married, both of them just eighteen. A quiet wedding on the ranch, with only the three families attending as the prairie greened from spring rains.

How had Mae known all those years ago, Grace wondered. The three women had watched the love between James and Ruth grow over the years and when the two young people shyly announced their intention to marry, Mae spontaneously burst into an aria. Grace and Daisy's eyes quietly met, knowing the difficulties the couple would face on the path ahead.

Glancing at Mae and watching Ike and Paul pat James on the back and hug Ruth, Grace said, "It's going to take all of us."

In the months that followed the wedding, Grace reflected on the twisting path that had led to that moment. For twelve years, she,

MEADOWLARK

James, and Paul had lived and ranched together, through the seasons. Paul still slept upstairs and Grace remained in her bedroom downstairs, which suited them both. They chose not to marry for reasons they kept to themselves.

The years had passed with James, Corwin, and Ruth trailing Paul through the seasons, each kicking up small puffs of dust, leaving muddy tracks, or footprints in the snow. Their shadows had lengthened as they grew from children into tentative teenagers.

Paul had guided James into manhood, had walked with integrity, humor, and humble dignity, an example for James to emulate. As Grace watched, James's anger and fear had slowly disappeared over the years, a sense of confidence and self growing in their wake.

And Ruth—Grace thought of how she loved Paul, too. From the moment she'd been drawn in by the downy fluff of a new chick and gathered it up into her hands, only to be chased and pecked by the mother hen. It never occurred to her that the mother wanted her chick. Ruth clutched the wee thing tight to her chest and ran for the fence, where Paul and Grace had found her, terrified, atop the post, the mad hen still flying and trying to get at her chick. From the moment Paul had reached up to take the chick from Ruth's hand and put it on the ground for its mother, Paul could do no wrong in Ruth's eyes.

In town, away from the protection of the ranch, Mae, Ike, James, Paul, and Grace formed a circle around the couple against the judgmental stares James and Ruth received. Corwin, who had inherited his father's easy-going manner and good humor, remained their fiercest protector, his only fights sparked in James and Ruth's defense.

Daisy lived with James and Ruth in the house he, Paul, Ike, and Corwin had built for the young couple on the ranch, completed in time for the wedding. Daisy had her own large room, which soon became the women's favorite place to gather. Floor to ceiling shelves filled with bolts and squares of fabric of every color lined the walls. Beads twinkled in the light from row after row of glass jars, neatly lined up by color and shade. The three women spent hours there, sewing, beading, and talking. Mae was attempting her first quilt. Her medical stitching skills had never quite transferred to fabric, but Daisy assured her the uneven pieces and bunched seams were beautiful and perfect.

The next November, Paul high-centered his truck while out hunting. The wheels spun uselessly as the truck perched atop a high swell he'd misjudged. Paul added rock and dirt under the tires, but the spinning sprayed them across the ground. Sometime toward evening, a sudden blizzard moved in and darkness fell. Paul ran the truck for heat into the night—as long as the gas lasted.

Grace waited and waited by the window for that truck to come over the hill north of the house. She lit candles in all the windows upstairs that he'd be sure to see. She made fresh coffee to warm him when he returned home. She turned frantic when the snow continued to blow sideways against the windowpane, all beyond etched pitch black. This wasn't like Paul—he knew how she worried about him.

The next day the neighbors searched for him. Ike found his truck first. And found Paul, sitting on the ground, leaning back against the truck, a burned cigarette still held in his lifeless fingers. The world stopped for Grace the moment she saw the truck pull over the top of the hill, driving slow. They were never sure what happened that night, if Paul froze to death or had a heart attack.

Grace didn't care how it happened.

Paul was gone.

Throughout the funeral and burial, atop the knoll Grace could see out the kitchen window, Grace remained composed. She didn't cry. Not one tear leaked through. James, stood strong beside her, his arm looped through hers.

"I'm right here, Ma," he said gruffly through the tightness in his throat.

She watched as James tried to put on a brave face for her, though she knew his own heart was breaking.

Holding tight to Grace's other arm, Mae stood staunchly beside her friend. Her curly hair still escaped its pins, white strands now threading the dark chestnut, fine lines fanned out around her eyes from years of smiling and rides in the buggy to tend the sick. Few babies in the area had been born without Dr. Mae's assistance.

Grace smiled, remembering that as the years had passed,

people quit being shocked as Mae spontaneously drew them into vigorous hugs. Some—though they'd never admit it—even found themselves looking forward to those stout embraces.

Ike stood beside Mae, the skin of his neck deeply creased and lined by years in the weather. He pulled his hat down to his brows, his arm tight around Mae. He stared at the mound of earth under which Paul lay. Grace saw the stifled jerks of his chest and shoulders.

Corwin, as lanky as Ike had been when Grace first met him all those years ago, stood solidly by his father's side, biting his quivering bottom lip, just as James was doing.

Daisy stood across from Grace, her long hair still unbound and hanging to her waist, a tapestry of whites and grays, now. She stood looking outward across the prairie, her lips moving soundlessly in Lakota, blessing Paul on his journey.

Between Daisy and James stood Ruth, her head resting on James's shoulder, her belly high and round with their child. Tears streamed down Ruth's face. Her beautifully beaded wedding moccasins, bright splashes of reds, blues, yellows, and oranges bloomed in the snow. Out of James's pocket poked the miniature lariat Paul had begun to weave for the baby. "I'll teach her how to rope as soon as she can walk," he'd promised.

My family, however did I create this, after all those years I'd given up hope? Grace took in each cherished face.

She did not shed a tear. Not until after everyone had gone. Not until after she'd assured Mae that she was all right and just needed a few moments alone. She watched as Mae and Ike walked down the slope with James, Corwin, and Daisy, ushering Ruth inside the house and out of the cold.

Then Grace dropped to her knees and fell forward into the mound of prairie dirt covering Paul. She curled her body into the pile of earth, moving into the ground until it molded to her, as Paul's body had. She burrowed deeper, eyes closed, imagining Paul's breath on her neck, his arms banded tight with muscles cradling her to him and his chest against the length of her back, the hard muscles of his thighs against the back of her legs. There she lay, tears pouring into the dirt.

Later, Grace heard Mae's footsteps and walking the slope. "Grace? Gracie?" she said kneeling down beside her. "You're freezing. It's time to go now, honey."

"No. I won't leave him." Grace's response was muffled against the chunks of prairie.

"I know, honey. I know. We'll come back," Mae said, taking her hand. "But it's time to go now."

"Just a few minutes longer, Mae. Just a few minutes more."

"Grace, it's freezing out here. Come on now. It's too cold."

Play the hand you're dealt, Grace.

"What?" Grace said.

"I didn't say anything"

Play the hand you're dealt, Hard Twist. We'll dance again one day.

"Did you hear that?" Grace sat up suddenly, frozen dirt and ice falling from her jacket and hair.

"Grace, are you all right? You look strange. You've been in the cold too long. Come on now, here we go." Mae reached down and grasped Grace under her arms and helped her to her feet. With Mae's arm supporting her, Grace cocked her ear against the wind. Listening.

Play the hand you're dealt.

MEADOWLARK

1983

On Grace's eighty-eighth birthday she knew
that one day soon she would close her eyes to sleep and find herself
standing on the prairie, young and strong again, that she'd look up and
across the distance would be Paul, waiting there with that lanky easy
way about him.

*"Paul? Paul!" She started toward him, walking first and then
running, pumping her legs as fast as they'd carry her. She wore a soft
cotton dress with pearl buttons and tiny pink roses, her hair long and
brown again, tied back in that blue ribbon. She felt the hem dancing
across her calves.*

*He leaned back his head and laughed out loud, "Gracie!" He
started running toward her.*

*Closer they came until they were a mass of laughter and arms
and legs and kisses, rolling on the prairie.*

"Thanks for waiting for me," she whispered.

DAWN WINK

MEADOWLARK

A Special Thanks

My deepest gratitude to my companions in this journey, without whose presence, spirit, and love this book never would have seen the light of day.

To editor extraordinaire, Annette Chaudet, whose expertise in all things literary and western reached through time and space to bring *Meadowlark* to authentic life.

To my literary agent, Elizabeth Trupin-Pulli, whose belief in Grace's story, and me, strengthened us both beyond measure.

Laurie Wagner Buyer, whose exquisite editing eye lifted Grace's story and burnished it until it shone.

Jennifer Wolfe, who read the manuscript in its earliest draft and has walked each step with Grace.

To Stephanie Jones for ever-believing in Grace and nudging her ever-forward into her own.

Pamela Keyes, who first heard of Grace under a mesquite tree in Tucson, and has kindled the flame of her story ever since, including a last minute round of refined editing, time for those margaritas!

Glenda Hogan, for believing wholeheartedly in Grace.

LouAnne Johnson, for her companionship in all thing literary and her oh-so-wise suggestion regarding Grace's journal.

Rachel Gantt, whose love for Grace and her story became my North Star in the final leg of the journey.

Dawn Dobras, for her generosity of spirit and deep friendship.

Mary Ann Dobras, whose way of walking through the world inspires me every day.

Prairie Flowers Mary Jane Lunetta, Mary Main, Nancy Cuthbert, and Ann Smith, whose roots, heritage, and love swirl throughout these pages.

Sharman King, who brought the horses to the ranch in time.

Lynn Schimmel, for her wisdom and love.

A Doris Quintana Brandt *por ser mi comadre en la brujeria y la vida.*

A Alicia Perez *por cuidarnos a mi y mi familia con tanto corazón y detalle, no lo hubiera podido hacer sin Usted.*

Kurtis Gentry, Grace's grandson, who shared a wealth of treasures.

Tove Skutnabb-Kangas, whose work, bouquets, and friendship infuse my life with ideas and beauty.

J.A. Jance, whose life and literary journey shone light in darkness.

Tina Le Marque Denison, who shared her story and told me, "Don't worry about being strong. Just grow."

Victoria Lovett, who guided me to Song.

Opus House/Truchas Peaks Place for the generous week of solitude in crafting this story.

To all in our *Dewdrops* community for each voice, each heart, each story.

To my brother, and sister-in-law, Bo and Lisa Wink, for their love and companionship in all.

To Dad, Dean Wink, for his dignity, humor, and honor.

To Mom, Joan Wink, without whose memories, spirit, and love this book would never exist.

Thank you all for walking with me through the years of tough prairie.

To Wyatt, Luke, and Wynn, whose grace and strength never cease to amaze and inspire me. I am the proudest mom, forever and ever.

To my husband, Noé Villarreal, who breathes life into the ember of my soul.

MEADOWLARK

A Note from the Author

*You know how writers are...they create themselves
as they create their work. Or perhaps they create
their work in order to create themselves.*
                                        —Orson Scott Card

It all started with a question.

In 1911, my great-grandmother Grace came as a sixteen year
old bride to a sod hut on the prairie of western South Dakota where
my family still ranches. My mom spent summers on the ranch as a
child and I grew up hearing stories about great-grandma Grace, her
life, and Paul. My own memory of Grandma Grace is of the feel of the
paper-thin skin on her hands.

In Mom's stories, her grandmother, Grace, came alive as a
young woman—one who worked hard every day of her life, made sure
my mom got the first weekly bath in the tin tub with three inches of
water on Saturday nights, so they all would be clean for church on
Sunday. The line-up for water began with my mom, then Grandma
Grace, then my Uncle Jim, and finally, once the water was cold and
had seen three bodies already, Paul bathed.

There are not many stories of kindnesses that happened on the
ranch in my mother's childhood. Almost all center around Paul, the
ranch foreman. In the summers of my mother's youth on the ranch, it
was the four of them: Mom, Jim, Grace, and Paul.

Again and again I heard the stories—of what happened on
Grace's wedding day after she climbed into the buckboard with her
new husband, and of Paul galloping his horse over the rise and toward
the ranch house shouting something nobody could hear and all ran
outside as he raced toward them until they finally made out the words,
"Skunks! Skunks!" and saw his smile. Paul made Grandma Grace and

my mom and uncle smile and laugh in a world that held precious little of either.

One day, years after first hearing these stories, Mom and I stood folding the piles of clothes that came with my three young children, in the same ranch house where Grace and Paul had lived all those years when I had a sudden thought.

"Mom, what about Grace and Paul?"

"I don't know." A slow smile spread across her face. "But, I've always wondered."

I wrote this book to find out.

Photo courtesy of Kurt Gentry

MEADOWLARK

The stories I knew formed the cradle into which I started to put research and information gathered about the time and places in Grace's life. I drove to every historical museum and bookstore I knew of. Piles of original journals, books written by pioneer women, stories and experiences of Lakota women, and cowboy journals grew on the shelves of my house, each filled with sticky notes and my own markings. Slowly, the stories I'd heard all my life gained the context of history and place. I scribbled notes, stories, and observations about the landscape in notebooks. Through the seasons—the heat and storms of summer, cool bite of fall, the hoarfrost of winter, and capriciousness of spring on the plains—I walked the land and listened.

And then Grace's story was interrupted by my own. My marriage ended and the intensity of that chapter of my own life took over. The books about the prairie and notebooks remained shoved onto shelves and closed for the next number of years until one day, Grace whispered from the past that it was time to begin to write her story again.

I dusted off the notebooks and lifted the story threads once again. What I didn't realize at the time was how integral Grace would be in the navigation of the shattered constellation of my own life. In my new world that felt completely foreign, I opened the notebooks and separated stiff papers pressed tightly together. The soft crackle of the pages releasing each other loosened something deep within me. Grace's story became a bedrock island in my quicksand world. The more I delved into her life and experiences, the more the veil between our worlds thinned, until I learned to trust the unknown.

The thinning of this supposed separation continued. My family and I spent this past Christmas with my parents on the ranch in South Dakota where Grace lived. One week before we arrived, a mysterious package was delivered, sent by our cousin, Grace's grandson, Kurt. Mom opened it to find Grace's wedding dress and riding jacket, both in perfect condition. I describe Grace's wedding dress in the novel as moss green. My thirteen year old daughter, Wynn, tried on the dress and jacket. When she walked out, the air stilled.

We spent the next week in the house where Grace had lived, on the land she where walked and rode. Noé and I walked to the corrals and he stopped and looked around.

"I feel Grace here," he said.

I felt her everywhere—standing on the steps of the root cellar, looking out the window above the kitchen sink, and walking with long strides out to the corrals. I felt her most keenly in the moments when I was deep in thought about something else.

Her bedroom is now our dining room. As we sat to eat Christmas dinner, I glanced at her shallow closet, now holding stacks of ceramic dishes and linens, I thought I saw the faint outline of dresses hanging from pegs.

After we'd returned to Santa Fe, Mom called me.

"Honey, there was a journal of Grandma Grace's with the dress and jacket."

It was a journal neither one of us knew existed. The first page of the journal reads:

MEADOWLARK

Rapid City, January 2, 1907

> *My dear daughter, May your life be like footprints in the sand. Leave a mark, but not a stain. Your Mother.*

Here are two pieces, written years ago, lifted directly from Meadowlark:

> *Tucked in the trunk, under her clothes and along with her books, was the journal bound in chocolate-brown leather that her mother had given her shortly before her death. Inside on the first page, in her exquisitely neat handwriting, her mother had written, "To Grace, A place to wrest to paper the many exciting and happy times you're sure to have. I wish you a lifetime of love and joy.*
> *Your loving mother. July 30, 1910.*

> *Grace looked at the floor. It was fitting. Wherever Mae went, she left her mark. No doubt about it. People know she's been there. Me? I feel more like dust on the wind. I want to leave a mark that I have walked this earth, breathed this air, loved and cried here. I want to leave footprints.*

Author Julia Alvarez discovered historical facts confirming what she had described in detail in *In the Time of the Butterflies* (a novel based on the real lives of three sisters, Las Mariposas, who lived and died under dictatorship in the Dominican Republic) *after* the book had been published.

Meadowlark is work of fiction, founded on that lingering question about Grace and Paul. Grace, Tom, and Paul, are based on my great-grandmother, great-grandfather, and the ranch foreman. They all became as much a part of my life as the living, breathing people surrounding me. They've never left the ranch. There are countless stories of their presence in the house and around the ranch headquarters.

"I heard Paul walking in the bedroom above me again last night," my dad called to tell me. "He had his boots on this time."

Other people joined Grace as I wrote. One day I lifted my head to see Mae Thingvold, doctor and girl homesteader from the east coast, driving her buggy up over the horizon and chiming, "Grace! Grace, dear, fret not! I'm on my way!" Ike was not far behind and he never failed to make me laugh. Then, Daisy Standing Horse slipped in silent as a shadow, and soon she and Grace were intent on their beading and sewing in front of the fire as I wrote.

As I came to know these women, their strength, resiliency, humor, and friendship guided me through the new terrain of my life. When life felt too painful in my own turn of the century, I slid gratefully into Grace's world. I raced bareback across the prairie, the wind on my face, the surge of the horse's muscles beneath me, and hooves pounding against the earth. I laughed with Mae and savored the way beads twinkled in the candlelight with Daisy. When the time came, I returned to my own world strengthened.

And, always the land. As I walked the prairie through the seasons, the rhythms of the plants, animals, wind, and weather seeped into me. The sun broke through the lead gray sky of winter and set the crystal beads of hoarfrost on the tree limbs sparkling in a million prisms. I marveled at the land's ability to shift between darkness and light at a moment's notice.

In writing Grace's story, I gained faith in my own. The sixteen year old girl who lived a century ago continues to take me by the hand. I'll follow.

Thank you, Grace. For everything.

MEADOWLARK

About the Author

Dawn Wink is a writer whose work explores the beauty and tensions of language, culture, and place. Co-author with Joan Wink of *Teaching Passionately: What's Love Got To Do With It?*, Wink created a literary, educational blog community, *Dewdrops.* (DawnWink.wordpress.com)

Associate professor at Santa Fe Community College, Wink lives with her family in Santa Fe, New Mexico. www.DawnWink.com.

Discussion Questions

1. The author describes the landscape as a primary character in the novel. How did the land shape Grace's experiences and what roles did it play?

2. What surprised you about the story?

3. The women's friendships and their isolation weave throughout the story. How does each influence the lives of Grace, Mae, and Daisy? Though the story takes place at the turn of the century, what parallels do you see in contemporary women's lives?

4. Mae and Daisy are both women very different from Grace. How do these women, and their unique perspectives, play into Grace's life?

4. Daisy's experiences in the boarding school reflect the experience of Native American children of that time. What do you make of her telling Grace, "They took away everything about me that was Indian, so I would become white. But, I could never be white." What parallels do you see in society today?

5. Daisy tells Grace, "To live life in song, Grace, that's how the Great Spirit intended us to live." Daisy has Grace lose her eyes and ind a place that's happy and peaceful. When Grace smiles Daisy says, "There's your song, Grace. Whatever you are thinking about right now, that's your song. When you live in song, it becomes your shield."

What is your song? What does "Your song becomes your shield," mean?

6. Paul tells Grace, "When you rope with a grass lariat, they're not really any good until the kinks have been stretched out of them…It's only after that pressure that a rope becomes good and strong, resilient."

What does this bring to mind in your own life?

7. Why do you suppose Paul and Grace chose not to marry?

8. Paul and Tom were men of the same time period, had similar experiences in adulthood, and yet became very different men. Why? What choices did they make? How did each experience life?

9. How do the lives of the women and men in the book echo the lives of women and men today?

10. The author writes of the thinning of the veil between past and present as she wrote. Julia Alvarez writes of discovering her words matched historical facts *after* she'd written the book. Isabel Allende writes of her relief to hear the spirit of her daughter moving furniture in their new house. Have you experienced this thinning of the veil in your own life?

11. Much of the book is based in history, of the characters and the time period, and became integrally interwoven with the author's life. How does knowing this affect your reading of the book?

CPSIA information can be obtained at www.ICGtesting.com
Printed in the USA
LVOW12s0008241213

366661LV00014B/197/P

9 781932 636970